Strange Peaches

HARPER'S
MAGAZINE
PRESS

Other books by Edwin Shrake

Blessed McGill
But Not for Love

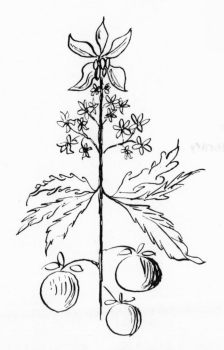

Strange Peaches

A NOVEL BY

Edwin Shrake

A HARPER'S MAGAZINE PRESS BOOK
Published in Association with Harper & Row
New York

"Harper's" is the registered trademark of Harper & Row, Publishers, Inc.

FIRST EDITION

STANDARD BOOK NUMBER: 06–127773–8

LIBRARY OF CONGRESS CATALOG CARD NUMBER: 79–181662

For Doatsy, Ben and Creagan—
Fellow Travelers

Book One

Book One

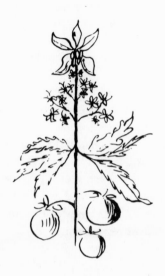

1

The door to the parlor of Francis Franklin's hotel suite was open a few inches, and we heard clucking noises inside. It was not uncommon for Franklin to have chickens in his suite. We heard a flopping sound, as though a great fish had been tossed onto the carpet, and Franklin's voice cried, "Oh, get down in it, baby!"

I held back from going in, but Gretchen Schindler pushed open the door. She laughed hoarsely and screamed, "What the fog are you doing, Francis?"

"God dawg, pussy has ruint his brain," Billy Bob Teagarden said, shoving past Gretchen and disappearing into the room.

Colonel Burnett looked quickly at me, wanting to share his anticipation. The Colonel was a tall man in his middle fifties with short white hair that lay close on his skull. He had purple pockets beneath each eye, so that he always appeared to be recuperating from a beating. Annoyed when I didn't grin or wink or slap him on the shoulder, he grabbed the arm of Jerre, a red-haired hooker, and dragged her inside with him.

I scratched the back of my head against the plaster in the hall. For the past week, traveling across the country on a promotional tour for the television series *Six Guns Across Texas*, in which I starred as a genuine, authentic, pistol-shooting, shit-kicking cowboy, I had been taking Bennies at the rate of about ten a day to keep my mouth and head working, and whenever I did try to lie down for a few hours I would get a rerun flash that would snatch me right back up again. In New York the night before, on the *Tonight* show, sitting there with all those cameras aimed at my face, an Italian starlet at one elbow and a blind man who whistled bird calls at the other, I had found myself saying that in fact I had a very low opinion of my TV series, and planned to quit it immediately and go home and make a movie about Texas in partnership with my good friend Buster E. Gregory, who knew how to take pictures, and we would tell what the place was really about as we lived it, not the crap people were supposed to believe if they watched *Six Guns Across Texas*. I hadn't intended to announce that just yet, but when you take a lot of Bennies you don't always know what you are about to say. Now, in this Washington hotel hallway, I could feel my heart plunging through my back against the wall. I'd probably had fifty martinis and Scotches since I'd last tried to eat anything but an Almond Joy, and I was entering that strange, illusory country where soon I might hop sideways to avoid a man in a black leather cape, or catch from the edge of my eye the flicker of a creature that had not been there an instant ago. All I really wanted at the moment was to keep from patting any invisible dogs and get back to Dallas.

On the wall outside Franklin's suite was a painting in an ivory-colored frame that had cherubs carved at each corner. The painting showed a shipwreck at sea in a storm, the ship rolling its masts down to the waves, and the lifeboats swamping, and men clutching at

4

broken timbers, and, far up in the right corner of the canvas, the sun faintly starting to cut through the clouds. My mother had a painting like that on the wall of her living room in Dallas beside "The Last Supper" and a picture of Jesus praying in the garden at Gethsemane.

"John Lee, come see what this big fool is up to!" Colonel Burnett called from the doorway with a glass of whiskey in his hand.

The Colonel and Billy Bob Teagarden were lobbyists who worked for Big Earl, the ninety-three-year-old Dallas billionaire, and his kind of simple-minded son Little Earl, and for Francis P. Franklin. Colonel Burnett represented the Republic of Haiti and Big Earl's family interests there in sugar, coffee and sisal, and had at one time influenced the prosperity of ranchers and sugar-cane growers in Cuba and the Dominican Republic. Billy Bob and the Colonel both put in a word in Congress now and then in behalf of oil producers, pipeline and heavy-construction companies and any other enterprises favored by Big Earl, Little Earl and Franklin.

"Better have a cocktail before you witness this scandal," Colonel Burnett said, giving me the glass. Gretchen's furry laugh came from behind him, and Billy Bob Teagarden was giggling through his nose. The clucking had ceased, replaced by a crackling sound, as though newspapers were being crumpled for the fireplace.

"John Lee, old cock! Hidy! Hidy!"

Hearing Franklin's voice, Colonel Burnett stepped aside. I saw Franklin lying on the floor with his feet together and his arms outstretched in a crucifixion posture. He wore only a pair of sagging Jockey shorts with orange stains on the pouch. At one time Franklin had been the tallest pilot in the United States Air Force. Laid out on the floor, his six-foot-eight-inch body covered nearly half the width of the room. His chest and stomach were stacked with paper money. Money had scattered all over the parlor. The carpet crunched with it. Money littered the coffee table, the couch, the bar and several chairs. Looking down at my shoes, I saw that all of the money was one-hundred-dollar bills.

"John Lee Wallace, old cock!" said Franklin.

Franklin's hands closed on two bunches of bills. Moaning and

5

clucking, he rubbed the money on his face, his chest and his stomach. He lifted the elastic band of his shorts and crammed money into the pouch.

"Gretchen, baby, come get your dinner," Franklin said.

"I'd like to get nailed on a bed of hunderd dollar bills," said Billy Bob Teagarden.

"I've did worse," Jerre the hooker said.

Jerre yanked off her high-heeled shoes and waded in money. She raised her skirt and the tail of her mink coat so she could kick money into the air. Gretchen dropped to her hands and knees and crawled through money, flinging batches of it over her head. Franklin sat up and pushed her and she rolled over on her back, wallowing in money, groaning and laughing. They were like children playing in a pile of leaves. Franklin hauled himself up to a cross-legged position. Hundred-dollar bills floated off him. Colonel Burnett filled glasses at the bar, pouring Scotch dark as Darjeeling tea. Winding up like a baseball pitcher, Billy Bob, in his green silk suit, wadded money balls and hurled them against the red velvet drapes, shouting "Low outside corner! Strike three! The mighty Koufax!" His expression was considerably happier than it had been an hour earlier when we had picked him up in Colonel Burnett's rented limousine outside a federal courts building.

I drank a couple of swallows of the Scotch Colonel Burnett had given me and, wincing at its iodine taste, looked over to see Franklin staring curiously at me. He still sat cross-legged in the heap of money, round-bellied and thin-chested, long arms reaching out to either side and fingers idly stirring money as though making rings in a pool.

"I read in the paper in New York that you were here for Billy Bob's trial, so I decided to come down to Washington and ride home with you," I said.

"Then you didn't know it's my birthday?"

"Not until I ran into the Colonel in the lobby of the Dupont Plaza this morning," I said.

I had remembered then that Franklin was a Virgo. He used to make fun of the signs. If someone mentioned astrology, Franklin would recite Virgoan traits—they are said to be neat, orderly, dependable, thrifty, painstaking, modest, hypercritical and so on—and would demand to know how any of these fit him.

"John Lee, goddamn, I was being flattered that a big star like you had come specially for my birthday," he said. "Anyhow, this'll make it a hell of a party. You can stay at my house."

"A girl's meeting me, Francis."

"Same old John Lee! You just coming down for a visit? It's been a long time since we've seen you and that maniac Buster Gregory running around naked in public and doing rain dances and causing floods. I can't say it's been dull, but we've missed your craziness."

"Buster and I are going to make a documentary movie about Texas, mostly about Dallas," I said. "We're going to tell the truth about it."

"That's a peculiar effort," said Franklin.

"Maybe you'd like to invest in our movie if you have any spare cash," I said, glancing at the carpet of hundred-dollar bills.

"John Lee, I don't ever use my own money for anything, you know that. Besides, what kind of truth are you talking about? Any kind of truth you and Buster try to tell is liable to make a movie that is way too far-fetched. Take my advice and get yourself a reasonable angle."

Franklin looked at me in a manner I took to be odd and maybe hostile, but I considered I might be misled by the Bennies and weariness. An oddly proportioned bug, a flying worm or tadpole, wiggled through the air in front of my face. I clutched at it. Franklin suddenly chuckled.

"Catch it, old cock, it might be real!" he shouted.

Franklin scrambled to his feet. He had aged very much for only a year to have passed. He was not more than fifty, but he had turned the corner. His hair was thinner and grayer, his flesh dry and loose under his chin where a year before it had been tight. His nose seemed sharper and had taken on a reddish hue. Broken veins spread across his cheeks. His stomach was rounder and more prominent, his liver swollen, but he still looked fierce as an ostrich.

"Girls, clean this stuff up," Franklin said. He tossed Gretchen a large airline flight bag. "Stick it in there."

7

Billy Bob lobbed a money ball into the flight bag.

"How much loot is this?" he asked.

"Two hundred thousand," said Franklin.

"Your birthday present?" the Colonel asked.

"Little Earl wants to give it to some A-rab," said Franklin.

I sat in an overstuffed chair and closed my eyes. Behind the flying worms were other strange-colored shapes. Colonel Burnett opened the drapes to let daylight in as Gretchen and Jerre scooped money into the flight bag. The Colonel looked down on Pennsylvania Avenue and jiggled the ice cubes in his drink.

"Hey, John Lee, here's your picture in the *Post*," Billy Bob said.

"Yours was in there once in handcuffs," said Gretchen.

"That wasn't damn handcuffs! I had my hands behind my back is all," Billy Bob said. He showed me the picture of myself on the television page. Since I had grown long hair and a mustache, whenever I saw my picture or a reflection it took a moment for me to recognize myself.

TV Cowboy
Quits Show

John Lee Wallace, one of the stars of the popular Western series *Six Guns Across Texas,* revealed on the *Tonight* show in New York that he will not return to California when the series resumes filming late this fall. The actor said he intends to shoot a film of his own in Texas, probably in his hometown of Dallas. Norman Feldman, producer of *Six Guns Across Texas,* told me today that Wallace's action is "preposterous nonsense. John Lee tends to be somewhat erratic, you might even say bizarre, in his behavior. This is merely an example of his whimsy. He will definitely be back on the show. . . ."

"Ain't it kind of stupid to quit?" said Billy Bob.

"I like to keep it moving," I said.

"Are you really a star?" asked Jerre.

"No," I said.

"Seems like I would of heard of you," she said.

"Here's his goddamn picture to prove it," said Billy Bob.

Jerre's round gray eyes studied the photograph, lashes popping like butterfly wings.

"I never saw that show," she said.

"It's about a old man and his crippled brother and his son and three orphan boys that live on a big ranch and shoot ever'body's ass off if they mess around," said Billy Bob.

"Are they queers?" Jerre asked.

"Queers! Shit-fire, this is a family Western show!" Billy Bob said.

"I hate violence," said Jerre.

"Hasn't the Colonel asked you to pound his bobo with a slipper?" Gretchen said.

"I don't do them things," said Jerre.

"Well, you should of seen John Lee when he played Tarzan," Billy Bob said.

Jerre looked at me skeptically.

"How long ago was that?" she said.

"Right after he left Dallas to go be a star," said Billy Bob. "He give up his TV show where he was doing real good on the news, and we thought he was crazy and ruint, and next thing I saw of him he was running through the woods with a towel around his waist."

"Maybe that explains his hair, but Tarzan never had no mustache," Jerre said.

"He only made one movie as Tarzan," Billy Bob said.

"Did they use a double for Tarzan?" Jerre asked me.

"For a lot of body shots and swinging in the branches and swimming underwater and for most of the animal rassling," I said.

"How come with so many real guys who could do it and would love to of got the chance they had to use a fake Tarzan?" she said.

"Tarzan was never real live in the first place," said Billy Bob.

"They wrote him up in a book, he was a English prince," Jerre said.

Franklin came out of the bedroom wearing a dark suit, white shirt and white tie. His cheeks were powdered, and the aroma of cologne floated around him. He hefted the flight bag and gave a hundred-dollar bill to each of the women.

"That A-rab can't count high enough to miss a couple of these," he said.

Franklin zipped the bag and hung it over his shoulder. Billy Bob phoned for a bellhop. In the lobby an assistant manager leaped around

9

his desk to beg Franklin's prompt return. Franklin got into the front seat of the limousine and told the driver to take us to a luncheon club for drinks. I sat in the jump seat with one knee mashed against the warmth of Jerre's thigh. The club was in a hotel. Billy Bob Teagarden pushed a button, and we heard a click. A carved wooden eye looked at us from a gilded triangle. We walked through a room that had a small bar of black tufted leather with a brass rail. Mounted fish gleamed against paneled walls. Billy Bob led us on into a room that had a player piano, stools with red leather tops, a sofa and two cocktail tables. The flight bag swung from his shoulder as Franklin sat down on a stool made from an elephant's foot. He left the bag on the floor and went to the bar, and we heard him muttering into the telephone. I peered into the third room at the dining table and paintings of pheasants. When Franklin returned, Billy Bob was telling Jerre about Franklin's appearance in court the day before, when Franklin had been called to recount what he knew about Billy Bob bribing a congressman to make sure a bill that raised the tax on earth-moving equipment never got out of committee.

"Two marshals had to go in the can and catch Francis by the feet and drag him out of a stall," Billy Bob said. Franklin stopped to light a cigar and summon a scant smile. Among Franklin's friends there was very little that might not be told about one another, except of course nobody told stories about Big Earl or Little Earl within their hearing. "Francis was shaking and sweating like he had malaria," said Billy Bob. "They put him on the stand and started asking if he was on the board of directors of this or that corporation—and he didn't know!"

"Nobody's perfect," Franklin said.

Being Big Earl's top executive and one of his few partners of consequence—Big Earl didn't have much use for partners—Franklin was involved with hundreds of corporations, many only as a name on a document.

"They got to naming off these corporations and asking if he was on the board, and old Francis got to guessing," said Billy Bob. "He'd say yes or no like calling heads or tails. He had a bad streak of guessing wrong. Finally they come to the Kum Klean Soap Company. You could see Francis looking at them gals on the jury like he knew ever' one of them used that soap."

"They all looked like my sister-in-law," said Franklin.

"The U.S. Attorney is a smart little Jew. He said 'all right, Mr. Franklin, are you on the board of the Kum Klean Soap Company?' Francis looked at them gals and pulled hisself up straight and said 'yes, sir, I sure am.' The Jew said 'no you ain't.' Francis said 'well, boy, I wish I was.' "

Jerre looked at Franklin as if he had confessed to being a vice-squad officer.

"I use that soap myself," she said.

"Billy Bob, you're so cautious with your mouth I can't imagine how you ever got in trouble," Franklin said.

"There ain't nothing to this little deal," said Billy Bob. "They'll drop it when the papers lose interest."

"On your damn head," Franklin said.

"They wouldn't let me go down on a thing as small as just trading some favors," said Billy Bob.

"Pretty popular with the Attorney General are you?" Franklin said.

Billy Bob fell to brooding. With money he had made from a company that sold spare parts for airplanes and helicopters, Billy Bob had put all eight of his children into private schools and had bought a big old house in Georgetown. What he seemed proudest of about the house was that when you opened a closet door a light automatically went on inside. At a cocktail party a year earlier he had taken me around the house opening closet doors and saying, "They'd jump through their butt if they saw this in Cotulla."

Between seizures of nausea and rushes of agitation, I ate half a bowl of cashew nuts and listened to Gretchen gossip about politicians. Gretchen had a German accent, a husband or ex-husband somewhere in the U.S. Air Force, and she was what we called an everywhere woman. Some said she was a spy for West Germany, and others said she was simply a prostitute. She was one of those people who is drawn toward power.

While Gretchen chatted on, and Billy Bob Teagarden struggled with his gloom, two young men in white linen uniforms and one in blue with a stethoscope around his neck entered the club. The two in white were wheeling a stretcher. The one in blue glanced at a piece of paper in his hand and then raised his head and looked around.

"Mr. Wallace!" he called.

"That's him!" yelled Franklin, pointing at me.

2

With the siren squawling and the red light whirling bars of light that banged back from store windows, the ambulance carried us through Washington traffic out to National Airport. Franklin insisted I stay on the stretcher because I appeared to be most in need of rest. A waiter from the club had stocked the ambulance with a bottle of Scotch, a bucket of ice and glasses. Feeling ridiculous, I had given in to Franklin's prank and allowed myself to be transported from the club on the stretcher with a sheet pulled up to my neck. "TV star. Collapsed. Just got weak in the knees, don't know why," Franklin told people in the lobby and on the sidewalk. Inside the ambulance we each had a draught of oxygen, and I was momentarily strong with blood. Franklin waved through the window to the crowd as the siren came on and the ambulance pulled away from the curb. "TV star succumbs," he said. He leaned forward and looked at Jerre and said, "I'd like to eat you bones and all."

The driver caught up to us as we entered the terminal. He handed Franklin the flight bag. "Found this in the ambulance," the driver said. Franklin took money out of the bag and paid off the crew.

Colonel Burnett arrived in the limousine with the luggage. While Billy Bob Teagarden arranged for tickets at the Braniff counter, Franklin bought another quart of Scotch. He unzipped the flight bag and forced the bottle inside, rezipping the bag so that only the neck of the bottle stuck out. Then he slung the bag over his shoulder and lurched on toward the plane.

We went to the first-class section in the rear of the Electra. With the bag in his lap, Franklin sat beside Gretchen. Billy Bob scurried into a seat beside Jerre across the aisle. That left the Colonel and me to take a double several rows farther back. I had hoped to read or sleep rather than be prisoner to a conversation, but we had scarcely cleared the river on the alarming takeoff from National when I understood that the Colonel definitely intended to talk to me. So I thought, well, Colonel, if you want blabber I'll have to give it to you, and I swallowed another Bennie with the first drink the stewardess brought.

"John Lee, I've never heard you mention politics," the Colonel said.

"I don't care about politics."

He seemed worried and thoughtful. "You're an actor," he said. "Those stories you do on TV are full of politics. The rancher wants to protect his cows and his land from the sheepherders, and so he gets the mayor and the sheriff on his side. That's politics. Suppose the rancher needs more land for raising beef cattle, and he asks his congressman to get the army to chase off the Indians. Politics. If the farmers get together and elect their own mayor and sheriff and run off the rancher and the sheepherders, too, that's politics, John Lee."

"You don't really need to relate everything to Western movie plots," I said. "Besides, in our show we don't fiddle around with politics, we shoot."

"Shooting can also be a political action. In this world you can't exist outside politics," the Colonel said. "You're a natural politician, John Lee. The way you get along with Francis and Little Earl and me one hour, and the next hour get along just as well with some of those left-wing friends of yours, or theatrical people, that's practical politics on a personal level."

13

"I try to have a good time. You take care of the politics, Colonel."

"I do my damndest," he said.

He looked as if he meant it. Among the things I had begun to understand was that many people mean the grotesque things they say, and think of them as important. Often I used this knowledge to my advantage, and in that respect I suppose I often played with people as a politician does. Of course, to accept their ravings as meaningful made my own life nonsense. It could be comforting at times to assure myself that everything I did was nonsense, but it was not satisfactory to dwell upon.

"Young men like you need to be involved," the Colonel said. "You know the saying—there's no such thing as an innocent bystander."

"I don't believe that's true, Colonel. I'll eat and drink and fool around, and not hurt anybody if I can help it, and when it's over I'll be as dead as you will be after you have connived for a lifetime in politics. It's all out of control, anyhow. Anything that's not a mystery is guesswork."

"If you'll pardon me for saying so, that's a whelp's philosophy. Irresponsible. Men are not angels. They're not very intelligent on the whole. They're not even decent in large numbers. Their thinking has got to be done for them. Their moral positions have to be set. Not to accept this responsibility is as great a crime against mankind as to be a Hitler."

We were finishing our second drinks. Both of us had refused lunch, a rare thing for me to do. I was on the aisle, and I watched the twitching rump of a stewardess going toward the galley. I was wondering how to reply to the Colonel with appropriate sincerity, and whether to ask for a third drink, when a face poked around the edge of the seat in front of me and looked back with a conspiratorial grin.

"Fellow up there said to pass this to you," the face said.

He handed me the flight bag with the bottle neck protruding from it. By the weight, I could tell the two hundred thousand dollars was still inside. With the Colonel holding both glasses, I tipped the bag and poured more drinks. The man in front looked around again.

"Want me to pass it back?" he asked.

14

"Take a drink yourself," I said.

"What is it?"

"Scotch."

"Never learned to like it."

He took the bag to relay it back to Franklin. I saw it pass above several rows of seats, being handed along in good humor by the passengers. Colonel Burnett allowed himself to smile before settling back with his drink and assuming a serious expression.

"John Lee, I'm terribly worried about Papa Doc," he said.

"Who?"

"I'm afraid they're going to kill him," said the Colonel.

"I didn't catch who you're talking about."

"Papa Doc. Duvalier. I know he's a bastard in the eyes of the world. Many of his own people don't exactly love him. But I don't want him killed. What would become of Haiti?"

"Who gives a damn?"

A small ghost passed across the Colonel's eyes.

"The Republic of Haiti has four million people," he said. "It may be true that under the rule of Dr. Duvalier they aren't allowed all the freedoms we spoiled whites are accustomed to. But the Haitians are smiling, gentle people. If our government murders Papa Doc, what will become of the Haitians? Chaos would overwhelm them. Did you realize most of America's baseballs are made in Haiti?"

"Come on, Colonel. I've heard about Haiti. They've cut down the trees and strip mined the hills. The country looks like a bulldozer park. A camera crew I worked with that had been to Port-au-Prince told me the room maids at the hotel dried them after showers and sucked their cocks for tips. How would anarchy hurt those girls?"

"Some people are the same regardless of the system," said the Colonel, smiling and sipping his drink. "If you would suck a person for money, it wouldn't matter to you what grander political schemes your betters might have in mind."

"That girl up there next to Billy Bob might argue about that," I said.

The Colonel looked out the window for a moment, the purple

15

ripples beneath his eyes shivering as if breathed upon. Besides the fact that he could drink a quart of Scotch and still say Washington, what I knew about the Colonel was that he had been born somewhere in New England, had gone to Dartmouth and had won a battlefield promotion to captain in World War II. During the Korean War he was recalled and given a big job in the Quartermaster in Tokyo. By figuring out the procurement of supplies, he wound up involved with sugar, meat, coffee and God-knows-what-else on an incredible scale, and he came to know a number of important people in those areas. Now he lived alone in an apartment building occupied mostly by upper-level civil servants. His ex-wife had married a college regent and lived in Denver, and his sixteen-year-old daughter was a heroin addict who lived in a beatnik house around North Beach in San Francisco, when she could escape from behind the walls where her father periodically locked her.

"That girl up there next to Billy Bob is not a political theorist," the Colonel said at last. "She is being paid two hundred dollars a day and expenses and is supposed to do what she's told. That doesn't require thinking."

"So who would kill Papa Doc?" I said.

"Bobby."

"Which Bobby is that?"

"That goddamn Bobby Kennedy."

"I guess he'll slip down there and put a golf tee in Papa Doc's taco."

"With your typical lack of understanding, you are making light of a very sinister man," the Colonel said.

"Well, he's your client."

"Not Dr. Duvalier. I mean Bobby Kennedy is a sinister man. He'll do anything to get what he wants. He has power, too, real power. I don't know how he can be stopped."

"Sounds like you're going to have one dead black rascal down there in Haiti," I said.

"You can hardly blame Papa Doc for what he recently did," said the Colonel. "He put a voodoo curse on the Kennedys. He swears Baron Samedi will call on them." The Colonel chuckled. "Imagine

16

believing magic will protect you from enemies.

"I've asked them not to kill him," said the Colonel. "I've asked Bobby personally, and I intend to ask Jack personally. I don't think you can trust either one of them, but I have to do what I can. I've told them if they won't kill Papa Doc, I'll promise to have him out of Haiti and into a Swiss villa by this time next year."

"Can you do that?"

"I think so. If I can talk Papa Doc into being scared enough. You know, besides his magic, he's surrounded all the time by mean niggers with guns, and he thinks nobody can get close to him. But they got Trujillo, didn't they?"

I nodded. The Colonel flipped the top of his gold lighter back and forth.

"Bobby can be a very vindictive person," he said. "He's persecuting poor Billy Bob Teagarden out of low-down spite. He wants to hurt Big Earl. Hell, Big Earl gave the Kennedys money! Big Earl likes Catholics! Now Bobby wants to kill Papa Doc, and he wants to kill old Diem over there in Vietnam."

"In Indochina?" I asked.

"That's what it used to be called. Little yellow bald-headed Buddhist sons of bitches, they kneel down out in public and burn theirselfs up with gasoline. What the hell kind of a way is that to act?"

"I worked in a film in Hong Kong, Singapore, Bangkok and Kuala Lumpur. Sure saw a lot of Americans over there."

"If Bobby wants to kill some repressive dictator prick, he ought to shoot Castro," said the Colonel. "That sorry Communist is executing thousands of good people on the Isle of Pines right this minute, and we don't do anything about it!"

"There was the Bay of Pigs," I said.

"Sabotaged from within! Castro is laughing at us. First thing you know, he'll have troops in Mexico."

"We can hold them at the border, Colonel. They'll never get past Laredo, if I know my Cubans."

"Goddamn Castro," the Colonel said bitterly. "Batista might have had failings as a person, but at least he was our friend."

17

"I guess you lost a few clients in Cuba."

"Good men, too. Damn good men. Big Earl, good Christ, what he lost! One of the finest ranches in this hemisphere! Swarming with Communists now! Come out of every damn thatch-roof shack and mud hut you ever saw, thicker than the cows used to be! Cigars! Good Christ, think of the cigars!" He was flicking the lighter lid madly. "Fine, dark Havana cigars—all gone."

"The Cubans can't smoke them all."

"You can't deal with a sonofabitching Communist." The Colonel had become agitated. He pinched the gold lighter between the thumb and forefinger of his left hand and spun it with his right. When the lighter stopped spinning, I saw that it was engraved "A Gift from Jimmy Hoffa."

"All over this world today they're pushing on us. Pushing, prodding, probing, testing. Indochina, Peru, Honduras. Open terrorism in Venezuela. Stirring up the niggers in Alabama. What's Jack Kennedy doing? Talking about selling wheat to Russia! I ask you, John Lee! His own wife out there in a bathing suit on that damn Greek's yacht, and Jack's coddling the Russians and wanting test-ban treaties. We need a man on horseback to lead this country. I fought and bled! I helped raise the flag. It's goddamn frustrating to see rich boys like the Kennedy brothers giving this country away to the devil. I know this much about Westerns like you're always showing up in, John Lee. If you don't have a tough, horny-looking stranger ride in to save the town from losing its balls, you got no goddamn Western anybody will care about!"

Uninterested in politics as I was, this kind of talk nevertheless made me begin to squirm. As opposed to other lobbyists I had encountered, the Colonel dressed with a diplomat's taste—dark blue Savile Row suit, gray silk necktie, an inch of white linen showing at the cuffs. Most lobbyists looked like college football coaches. Billy Bob Teagarden, in his green silk suit and green Argyle socks, with his reddened steam-room face and a manner that was obscene among his own kind and groveling in the presence of little girls and powerful old ladies, could easily have passed for the mayor of Cotulla, Texas, his hometown. Were it not for the odd purple marks beneath his eyes, Colonel Burnett would have looked quite dignified, until he began spinning his gold cigarette lighter and clicking his false teeth.

So I interrupted and asked about his daughter.

"Why do you want to know?" he said.

"I saw her once. She was a nice girl. I wondered if she'd got straight."

"I don't know how much you've heard about her," the Colonel said. "You couldn't really care. But I'll tell you this—she's back out in California with that beatnik trash, sleeping on a mattress on the floor, shooting dope in her arms, smoking marijuana. Probably getting screwed by a different bastard every night. She brought one of them to Washington with her last summer. Some peach! He had a beard and sandals and wore blue jeans and smelled like a wet horse. I said 'kid, let me remind you what happened to Jesus,' and I ran his butt off, I can tell you that. He couldn't leave fast enough. Then the girl lied to the doctors, lied even to me, sat around the house looking at television all the time, and finally she stole a couple hundred dollars from my billfold and took off again. I count myself lucky. This time I don't care if she ever comes back. I care about her about as much as you do."

"Hell of a waste," I said.

"Tragic."

"Think about all those dancing and piano lessons."

The Colonel looked at me as if he had never seen me before. He looked at me two or three times above his glass, all rather rapidly, and then he said, "John Lee, you're kind of a freak."

Franklin bent over and poked my shoulder for attention. His face seemed deathly in the strange light above the clouds, and he looked very tired but was somehow trembling with energy. Franklin had extraordinary energy. I don't know where he got it, I never knew him to take a pill, but he could fall down at dawn after drinking all night and two hours later he would be up, showered and dressed, demanding to know why nobody else was moving. He never had a hangover. Combined with his intelligence, that energy made Franklin a kind of natural aristocrat who would have risen to the top of any field he

19

chose. Before World War Two Franklin joined Big Earl's organization as a young lawyer and was sent to Austin to help pass or block action the Texas Legislature might take that concerned Big Earl. There was hardly a legislator who could drink with Franklin on anywhere near even terms, though most of them tried, and of course there wasn't a single one who could outwit him. I had heard that in three years—two sessions of the Legislature—Franklin's presence in Austin meant an extra twenty or thirty million dollars to Big Earl, who dearly liked that kind of presence.

When the War started, Franklin became a bomber pilot in England, the tallest man in the Eighth Air Force by two inches. First he had to argue with Big Earl and even with Franklin D. Roosevelt to be allowed to refuse a big civilian job in the oil industry, and then he had to get Roosevelt's signature on an order admitting him into the Air Force as a pilot despite his height. Franklin's wife Margaret stayed in Austin, and in 1943 their only child, a boy, drowned in the Colorado River where it turns through the middle of town. Franklin came back as a Lieutenant Colonel with a breastful of medals. He was elected to the state senate and served two terms while still working for Big Earl. There had been a strong movement for Franklin to run for governor. It was Franklin's man Wilburn who told me about it: "They had all kinds of meetings at this big white house we lived in, and they was plenty of high powered gentlemens come around with plenty of big money for Mist' Francis. But he never did like being in politics, and finally he got furious mad one night and throwed several gentlemens out of his house and phoned up Big Earl and said he wanted to move up to Dallas to work in the head office or he was going to quit. Big Earl couldn't never turn down Mist' Francis on hardly anything, so we moved up to Dallas, but sometimes I wish Mist' Francis had gone ahead and be governor. It would of been right nice for a while."

"First off the ship," Franklin said, looking down at us. "When we land, run to the front. I got a radio message through the captain."

"What're you up to?" the Colonel said, grinning.

"It ain't my trick this time," said Franklin.

The seat-belt sign came on. Franklin went back to his own row. I leaned past the Colonel and looked out the window as the stewardess began her landing announcement. Seeing the first of the gray lakes in the flat brown-and-green country, I was struck again, as always on returning, by inexplicable nostalgia for things that I had not even known I was fond of. The buildings of Dallas appeared below, like models, with sunlight striking off the shiny bank towers, and the dirty river bending through brown banks, smoke from factories rising into a sky of oddly blue Texas light that always seemed brighter than it should be. The plane slanted across town above low buildings flowing out from the swollen center, and we came up across North Dallas and turned back toward Love Field. Going home. Thousands of houses in twisty rows passed beneath us, then a highway crowded with small shops. A thin blue lake rose up. That moment of apprehension, wondering if we would clear the water. Now the bump of wheels and rush of engines.

The Colonel looked around at me and smiled.

"Dallas," he said. "My favorite city."

3

At the bottom of the ramp waited a black hearse with its rear doors open. On either side of the doors stood two young men wearing black suits, white gloves and white carnations in their lapels. A third young man, tall and grave and also dressed in black, looked up from the runway and gestured to Franklin with a bouquet of lilies. I saw a black limousine next to the terminal building, with a figure in a yellow jump suit sitting on a fender. Several people stood around him. They seemed to be laughing, and there was some sort of commotion on the other side of the limousine.

"Little Earl's done this," Franklin said happily.

Going down the ramp toward the inside of the hearse, where I could now make out stretchers along each wall and a kind of bier with a bucket on it filled with ice and the inevitable bottles, I kept looking toward the limousine, and at last I saw Dorothy. She was in the crowd around Little Earl. When I had phoned from New York, she had promised to be at the airport, and I did expect her, but it was a small shock to see her actually there, and I felt a seep of gladness at the sight of her. I never could tell what that girl was going to do, and when I thought I could I was farthest off.

She jumped up and down, extending one arm full into the air and waving with a motion of the wrist and hand, making a swan's head on the long neck of her arm. The show of emotion from Dorothy moved me more than it perhaps deserved, and at the same time made me strangely wary. I waved back, and started to break away from the group to go to her. But Franklin took my arm and urged me into the hearse. "She'll catch up to you in a minute," he said.

Inside, there was barely room for the six of us from the plane and for Wilburn, crouched in a white coat beside the bier pouring Scotch into glasses over ice. Once again I found myself mashed against Jerre, with the glass partition of the driver's compartment on my left. The two young men in black suits got into the front. The tall man closed the rear doors partway, then jerked them open and tossed in the bouquet of lilies. Right in behind the lilies bounded a lion.

With hot breath that smelled like egg farts, slinging slobber from a purple tongue, the lion scrabbled across our withdrawing limbs and crashed into the bier, knocking over the ice bucket and bottles of Scotch.

"Lemme out! I doan know bout no line!" shrieked Wilburn.

The hearse doors slammed, and the vehicle began moving across the runway. I could see astonished faces of people coming down the ramp from the plane, and then I threw up my arm as the lion's tail struck my cheek like a hairbrush.

22

There was general screaming, cursing and kicking. Heading toward daylight, the lion smashed his nose against the thick glass partition. His front paws batted Wilburn to the floor. Billy Bob's pants were raked and torn by the hind paws. I hammered on the glass. The young man on the right turned and grinned, and the driver nodded with satisfaction. The hearse speeded up. The lion was whining like a dog.

"That damn animal's gonna panic!" screamed Billy Bob.

"Stop this thing!" yelled Franklin.

Going faster, the hearse wheeled past the peculiar green-and-red terminal building and into the traffic. Water flew off the aura of lion hair. Jerre was crying and looking at a gashed knee. The lion began gnawing at the glass. The two young men in front refused to recognize that we were not crying with hilarity. Franklin yanked the handles, but the rear doors were locked. Wilburn picked up the bucket to use in defending his face.

With a great gasp and wrenching sigh, the lion loosed his bowels. Crap spilled out in yellow lumps the size of loaves of French bread, accompanied by a few gallons of lemonade. The odor flowed back in an immensely nasty wave. It was like plunging your head down a bunghouse hole in summer. I began to wretch. Hearing me about to vomit, Billy Bob grabbed for his handkerchief and coughed out strings of mucus.

The lion then sounded as if a bone were stuck in his throat. He gagged and growled and took heaving breaths, working himself up.

"Goddamn that Little Earl! He never did understand what's funny!" Franklin shouted.

Suddenly there were trees in the windows and no more buildings or cars. We all fell forward as the hearse stopped. The lion let out a heavy, coughing roar, and we scrambled back toward the rear, sliding and toppling over each other in lion shit. The doors of the hearse were jerked open. Smelling grass, dirt and air unspoiled by humans, the lion whirled and charged the opening, knocking us to various parts of the hearse. The lion hit the ground about eight feet past the two young men who once again stood rigidly beside each door. In two leaps the lion was gone. We rushed for the door and jumped out.

Colored bits of broken floral bouquets fluttered here and there in the cemetery, and oak leaves moved in the breeze. I looked down at the yellow muddy crud splashed over the pants of my conservative, dark gray, three-piece Brooks Brothers suit—which I had worn specifically to counteract the offense that my long hair would give to those citizens of Dallas who didn't recognize me as a cowboy actor, or as Tarzan—and I hooked my thumbs into my vest pockets and decided to do absolutely nothing but wait for the next event, which was bound to come soon.

Billy Bob Teagarden stomped his cordovan shoes, now yellow, into the earth, ripped pants legs flapping.

"Lion shit. Goddamn lion shit," he muttered.

Franklin walked over to an open grave near the hearse. He dropped the crushed lilies onto the headstone. The inscription read:

FRANCIS PAYNE FRANKLIN (1915–?)
He never believed in Jesus
And vice-versa

"Wilburn, where's that bottle?" Franklin said.

Wilburn emerged from the hearse with a bottle of Scotch. Franklin took it and sat down on a pile of dirt that had been shoveled out of the grave. Far off near the road on the other side of the hedge fence, we saw the black limousine.

"Wonder where I left that flight bag?" Franklin said.

The old blue Cadillac that belonged to Dorothy's mother pulled up behind the black limousine in the distance. Then we heard an engine, and a panel truck raised dust beside our hearse. A man in khaki, wearing leather gloves and carrying a chain leash, climbed out of the cab and approached. After one look at us, the hearse driver and his companion had gone around to the front of their vehicle and were keeping away from Franklin. The man in khaki looked at all of us, trying to guess who was in charge, and finally walked over to the Colonel, who seemed to have come through it better than the rest, although the gold lighter was spinning in his fingers.

"Where's my lion at?" the man asked.

24

"He's run off to the woods," said Franklin.

"You wasn't supposed to let him go," the man said.

"You know how lions are when they suspect they're about to get killed," said Franklin.

The man ran back to his truck and drove off across the cemetery with his head out the window, calling for his lion. The black limousine had been joined by two more, and the three cars were turning into the cemetery now, with Dorothy's blue Cadillac behind them.

"Here comes Little Earl. He likes his good times," Franklin said.

4

"John Lee, this is Dallas, not Hollywood. They'll kick you to death for having hair like that. You better wear a cowboy suit and claim you're Buffalo Bill. A mustache, too! I can't go anywhere with you."

Dorothy seemed nervous, somewhere between being glad to see me and yet afraid of me and angry that I had arrived.

I kissed her. Though she was a tall girl and big boned, and appeared to have put on weight in my absence, she still felt like a bag of feathers, and her lips were dry and rough. She pulled away as if embarrassed to be seen kissing me.

"Where's your suitcase?" she said.

My friend Buster came around from behind the blue Cadillac with a 16-millimeter Bolex on his shoulder.

"I got it all!" he said. "The lion leaping into the hearse at the airport and leaping out again at the cemetery, people falling and cussing, Little Earl laughing, the tender kiss at the reunion. Sets a classy tone for the movie, don't you think?"

I shook his hand, and after a tiny hesitation we hugged each other. Buster stepped back and grinned. He had dark skin that tanned very quickly, and very black, shiny hair. His face was round, faintly Asiatic. His grandmother was a Comanche, an orphan, raised by a farmer's family down in South Texas. The family used to tie her up and treat her like a slave. She finally ran off with Buster's grandfather when she was fourteen and he was close to fifty and passing through on a wagon with his tool-sharpening equipment. When Buster got angry, he was a madman. But when he grinned, it was wholeheartedly. Buster seldom bothered to conceal himself.

"Right after you called the other night I dug out the Bolex," said Buster. "I assume you've arrived with money to buy color film. I just about shot up my whole bank account on the arrival sequence."

"I've got a few thousand dollars," I said. "When that's gone, we'll find some more."

"We'll make a great movie," said Buster. "Our mamas and our ex-wives will be proud to have known us."

Buster and I had pulled off many stunts together and were notorious in Dallas outside our professional prominence. I mean things like our famous rain dance on the roof of a hotel in front of a considerable crowd. We had got drunk that day and gone out and bought Indian outfits, and an hour after our dance the drought broke and it rained for eight days and a friend of ours was washed off a bridge in his car and drowned. On another occasion Buster stole a waiter's costume at the Dallas Country Club and served the mayor a sorry old rotten carp for dinner. Franklin loved it when Buster strolled naked through various parties, and sometimes I did the same thing, and Franklin thoroughly admired it when Buster carried a piano player out of Little Earl's house one night and threw him in the lake for criticizing his body. Franklin and Little Earl and their friends had been attracted to us as much by our behavior as by seeing my face on the television news broadcasts or Buster's photos in the Dallas *Morning News* before he quit to become a free-lance photographer. Buster and I had gotten divorces in the same season and had shared an apartment for a while, and now I was going to move in with him again.

"I heard Little Earl tell the Braniff agent to take the bags to his house," Buster said. "We got to go there anyway, to Franklin's party."

26

"Let's go to your place first," I said.

"You look a little wore out," said Buster. "Need some heart medicine?"

"More of that's the last thing I need, but I never turn down a pill."

"Well, John Lee, I figured with your jungle experience, you'd of got a full nelson on that lion and taught him some manners," Little Earl said, walking over to us with his hands deep in the pockets of his yellow jump suit. "I swear, the very thought that a lion can shit on Tarzan's leg and not even be rebuked, why that starts to make me doubt ever'thing I was brought up to believe in."

Little Earl was tremendously pleased with himself. His grin was so large that his fat cheeks forced his eyes to squint. He was barefoot, his toes splayed out in the dirt road. He looked sort of like a frog that was digesting a moth.

"Damn it, Buster, quit taking my picture. I don't want to be in your movie," said Little Earl.

"Your subtle sense of humor will be an asset for us," I said.

"John Lee's cross," said Little Earl. That pleased him more. "Got a beautiful girl, got friends that admire him, got his picture on the television, got parties to attend, got his health, got money in his pocket. What does a man want?"

Buster drove the blue Cadillac. On the way to his apartment we talked about old times. Dorothy sat in the front seat, over against the door, looking out the window. I sprawled into the cracking leather upholstery and listened to Buster's voice, warming to the sound of it. When I sat up straight and warned against hitting a horse in the middle of the street, Dorothy looked around and frowned as if she thought I was being dramatic, but Buster smiled and drove on through the horse. I enjoyed several interesting brain shots like that, unalarmed, before we stopped at the apartment.

"You two go on in. I'm going to the liquor store," said Buster.

"I'll go with you," Dorothy said.

"I have to stop by the studio. You go on in," said Buster.

The apartment building was like hundreds built in Dallas during the previous ten years. It had a tropical name. Two floors of apartments opened onto a courtyard with a small swimming pool in the

27

center. A balcony fringed the upper floor. Most of the apartments had glass doors that slid open to the courtyard or the balcony. In front of the beige-brick building were a lawn and hedges, and you entered the courtyard on a stone-slab walk and turned immediately to the left to find the door to Buster's place.

Buster had a large apartment with two bedrooms, two baths, a den with brick walls, a big living room and a kitchen with a counter and bar stools, all for two hundred and ten dollars a month. Once inside, I slid the glass door shut and reached for Dorothy. She let me take her hand, and then she pushed me away.

"What's the matter?" I said.

"I don't want to screw right now," she said.

"Who said anything about screwing?"

"That's what you always want to do."

"I must be out of my head," I said.

Meeting Dorothy had been for me a relief and a blessing. After I broke up with my wife and was promoted from a reporter to an on-camera face, all in the same season, there were a multitude of girls and women of all kinds in and out with their dogs and their tales of this and that, and I began to get very tired and had the feeling I was being treated like cat food. After a year and a half of that, I moved to California, and things did not slow down a bit. In July of 1962 I had come back to Dallas for a visit, and Buster took me to a party at some strange old house near SMU. I was wandering around upstairs, and Dorothy came out of the bathroom in a yellow cotton robe and smiled at me. So I asked her to go to dinner, and we drank the first wine she'd ever tasted in a restaurant, and that night she slept with me at Buster's apartment. She stayed with me at Buster's for two weeks, until I returned to Los Angeles, and then I kept phoning her every other night. Six weeks later she said she was pregnant and asked for five hundred dollars to pay a nurse who did abortions out in Oak Cliff. Dorothy dropped out of college in September, and I sent her more money to come to Los Angeles. We lived in a pink stucco house I had rented on a hillside above Sunset Boulevard. She said that after the operation she was too sore to be touched and was plagued with

28

mysterious infections. But having her around helped to protect me from myself. It was enough of an excuse to pretend she kept an eye on me, and I even took to staying home some nights, and I began regathering the psychic and physical strength I had poured all over two states. Dorothy could be sullen and bitchy, and she had another onion at the core of her onion, but when she was in the mood to be good and beautiful she was so fine that it was a joy to look at her. I took her dancing at every place in town that had rock-and-roll music. The way men came after her, taking Dorothy dancing was like throwing raw meat into a kennel. In a very short while she heard the whole encyclopedia of Hollywood bullshit, was chased by surfers and stunt men and motorcycle riders and electricians who were just about to direct their first films, and she was offered dozens of modeling and acting jobs that somehow never quite came off. But Dorothy had grown up not trusting anybody anyhow, and she didn't fall for the bullshit, except once. It was in the early spring, after she had lived with me for nearly seven months. I had started working in *Six Guns Across Texas*. Being left alone all day, Dorothy would get up about noon and start roaming. She met a UCLA film student who was going to shoot one of those nice little boring sensitive films as his graduate thesis—a film full of long sequences of a girl walking on a beach at sunset with her hair blowing and gulls flying around, and in her eyes you could see how she yearned for a lover of the kind they just don't make—and the film student fell in love with Dorothy and said she was the girl for his movie. So for about a week I would come home at night and she would tell me about all the film they had shot at the beach that day. She was very excited about it and very sure it would be a beautiful movie and a winner at Cannes, and she even started talking Hollywood bullshit herself. Then one night I came home and she wasn't there. Three mornings later she walked into the house and said it was all over with the student, his movie stunk and he cared more about screwing than he did about art, and she was going back to Dallas, where her mother needed her. The peculiar thing was that by then I had decided I needed her—at the very least to keep me from trashing myself around every night, staying drunk and stoned—and

29

I knew that if she left, something bad was going to happen to me. But I was offended that she would choose an ignorant young film student over me, and I told her not to let the doorknob hit her in the ass on her way out. I drove her to the airport and was already missing her by the time I could see her face in the window of the plane. I watched the jet rise into the orange smog, understanding that, for a while, my life would be more difficult and certainly more dissolute. But you can't hold people back, and you can't force them to feel the way you think they ought to. I had not seen Dorothy now in more than six months.

Dorothy went into the den and pulled aside the drapes as if watching for Buster to return.

"What is the matter with you?" I said.

"Nothing. I feel funny."

"You're acting like I'm supposed to be mad at you."

"Is that all you can think of? That I'm guilty of something?"

She took off her shoes and sat on Buster's desk and started rubbing her feet. She had long toes that bent downward, and her feet were bony. They were low-rent feet that went with her lazy posture, which was slatternly, pelvis thrust forward, back swayed, shoulders slumped. Buster said she stood like the wife of an Oklahoma chicken thief. When she danced she usually stood erect, and she was remarkably beautiful then.

"Look," I said. "I'm tired and I'm going to lie down for an hour or two. Would you mind soaking the calves of my pants to try to get the lion shit out?"

"What will you wear to Franklin's birthday party?"

"The same pants. We can dry them with your hair dryer."

"My hair dryer's at my mother's. I haven't been living over here."

"We'll use the oven then."

"John Lee, there's something I got to tell you," she said.

I paused with one leg out of my pants and leaned against the doorframe. Dorothy sat on the desk with her back against the wall of exposed bricks. Above her was a huge blowup of a photo Buster had shot of her among the azaleas on Turtle Creek. She could have been a good model, but she would never stick at anything for very long.

30

"You're one of the worst bastards I ever knew," she said.

I removed my other leg from my trousers. Tiny bits of lion shit crumbled and fell off.

"I was looking through some of those cardboard boxes of stuff you left here with Buster, and I read a few of the letters your ex-wife wrote. She loves you."

"You've met her. You know better than that."

Tears appeared on Dorothy's cheeks. I watched them with fascination, unsure for a moment what I was seeing.

"Why should you be cruel?" she said. "You don't have to act tough and hard around here. It's not very becoming."

"Please, Dorothy, let's talk about this later," I said.

I took my pants into the kitchen and stood in front of the sink, wondering whether it would be hygienically superior to soak them in the kitchen or in the bathroom. I chose the spare bathroom, which was beside the den and opened into the living room. I ran a few inches of water into the tub, sprinkled in some detergent, got satisfactory bubbles, sank my pants up to the knees and draped the rest over the edge of the tub. This completed, I looked up and saw Dorothy's nightgown and douche bag hanging on a hook on the back of the bathroom door. She was standing in the doorway looking down at me with a thin frown.

"I sleep here some, when mother's being bad," she said.

"With Buster?"

"No. But he's so sad. He doesn't have a regular girl, and he misses his kids. I feel sorry for him. I'd sleep with him if he wanted me to."

"Are the beds made?"

"Your room is."

She followed me into the bedroom I was going to use. Low flower bushes pressed against the front windows, and above them I could see green lawn and then a telephone pole and the street, with trees on the other side. As Dorothy put my coat on a hanger, I noticed something on her hand, and reflected on it while she hung up my shirt and vest and tie.

"On your finger," I said. "Is that a pearl ring or a marble?"

31

5

There was an unfamiliar treble voice that rose to a screech. I heard it say, "Mothah!" The accent was pure New York. I swam up as if I had been three feet deep in the mattress. Aware that my mouth was open and that I had been drooling, I came on up into consciousness and felt my heart burst. I had no idea where I was. The ceiling was lime-green plaster, like the ceilings in dozens of motels I'd been in, and the voice threw me off. I heard Buster and Dorothy talking and I rolled over and looked at the clock. It said seven, but the light outside was peach and I couldn't tell whether it was morning or night.

In my shorts I walked through the living room, barely seeing the figures there, and went into the kitchen and opened the refrigerator door. The alien voice said: "Don't let him eat out of there, it's vile!" I squatted down and began rummaging through old packages of bologna, blocks of hard, stale cheese, a jar of mayonnaise, a knife with peanut butter on it, a carton of sour milk, a paper wrapper of spoiled hamburger, two or three eggs. The odor was wretched. A small hand with orange fingernails appeared before my eyes holding a thick cigarette. I accepted the cigarette and took a couple of drags without looking up. Now the kitchen smelled like a hayfield.

"You can taste the earth," said the unfamiliar voice. Then the hand reappeared and gave me a pear. "I just brought it. Buster's food is always ancient."

"There's a casserole in the oven," said Dorothy from the living room.

"It's tuna fish and Betty Crocker Noodles Romanoff," the voice said. "But it won't be ready for ten minutes."

Feeling suddenly heavily giddy, as though a chime had rung inside me, I looked up along a pair of black slacks to a curving butt to a white blouse to a smiling mouth with orange lipstick to eyes dark with mascara and penciled brows, on up to a tall twisting cone of lacquered orange hair.

"That's Jingo, the Tiger Lady," said Buster.

She offered me the joint again, and I shook my head. With some difficulty, I pushed myself up from the floor, grasped the drainboard and stood. Even though she was wearing sandals with three-inch heels, Jingo's face disappeared as I rose. The top of the orange cone of hair was almost level with my chin.

I ate the pear so fast I hardly knew I had done it. Buster kicked aside a heap of garbage and came into the kitchen.

"This here's my friend John Lee Wallace," he said.

"You ought to come see my act," said Jingo. "Buster's seen it."

"She fucks a tiger," Buster said.

"The tiger's a big stuffed doll. It looks real, but it's just a trick," she said.

Unable to get enough of my forces together to speak as yet, I went into the front bathroom. My trousers were hanging over the shower curtain. They were clean and only slightly damp.

"Jingo did that. She didn't mind sticking her hands in the lion-shit water," said Buster.

"Dealing with shit is one thing, but eating Buster's old food in that filthy kitchen is unhealthy," Jingo said.

"Thanks," I said.

"Well, I made the goddamn casserole," said Dorothy.

I went into the back bathroom and turned on the shower. The bathroom window was open at shoulder height. It was a warm evening that smelled like cut lawns and, somehow, honeysuckle, and two girls came along the sidewalk with rubber slippers flapping as I was looking out the window. I closed the shower curtain and sat in the tub with the water beating my head.

After washing my hair, shaving and taking two Bennies to get up for Franklin's party, I sipped a martini Buster had fixed. The martini had four olives in it and had been poured over ice in a highball glass, equivalent to at least a triple at 21 or The Polo Lounge. As I was coming out of the bathroom with the martini in my hand, the telephone rang on its stand in the short hallway.

"Put that damn Juliette on the phone," a man said.

"I don't know any Juliette," I said.

"Get her on the phone right now!"

"Who the hell is this?" I said.

"Jack Ruby. Who the hell is this?"

"John Lee Wallace."

"Hey, John Lee, I didn't know you were in town. I got this number from one of the girls down here." The voice abruptly softened. "Listen, man, you got to come see our new show. Juliette does a number with a stuffed tiger in a blue spot that's pure beauty. But maybe you seen it somewhere else. I didn't know you knew her."

"Just met her."

"I want you to bring your friends and be my guest. Now, could I talk to Juliette?"

She had heard me say her name and was waiting for the telephone. Immediately she and Ruby began arguing. I gathered it was an argument that had been going on for some time, and they were merely continuing after a break.

I ate a plate of tuna-noodle casserole and sat on the couch drinking the martini and reading the afternoon paper. An ad attracted me— a 7.65 Mauser with barleycorn front sight and leaf rear sight, hardwood stock clear to the end of the barrel, a five-round box magazine, on sale at a war-surplus store for $18.88 and available in a sporterized version, with the stock cut down and polished, for $24.97. Mausers had a beautiful bolt action. They were the basic model on which all great sporting rifles were built. For another few dollars you could get a five-power scope fitted on. I was pretty good with all infantry weapons when I was in the Army, except the .45 automatic and the grease gun. The grease gun looked to me as if it was on the verge of flying apart. With the .45 automatic, I would have been lucky to hit Jingo across the room as she shouted into the telephone at Jack Ruby. But I had shot Expert with the M-1 and the carbine. Years ago, before

I gave up hunting, I could knock a squirrel out of a tree at thirty yards with my .22 single-shot. Using my grandfather's old double-barreled 12-gauge, I had destroyed many a deer, duck, rabbit, snake, squirrel, possum, crow, blue jay, dove, quail and armadillo that ventured within my murdering range.

"You doublecrossin' mothah, you can't treat me that way, I'm a stah!" screeched Jingo.

"Freddy the Ad Man brought her over one Sunday afternoon for a swim," said Buster. "I took some pictures, and she's been coming back."

"Keeps you from getting lonely," I said, glancing at Dorothy, who was into a severe pout.

"I don't get lonely any more, John Lee. First thing I look at when I get up in the morning is the TV log. Some days I throw the rest of the paper away, don't even read the sports. If there's going to be some good stuff on TV that night, I'm happy all day about coming home and sitting down with my turkey pot pies, my jug of wine, my magazines and my TV. Never miss *Six Guns Across Texas*, of course. You ever seen that show high?"

"High as a man can get."

"Well. If I feel like talking I can always call up somebody on the phone who I know is stoned and watching TV. Or I go over to the End Zone and drink beer. Or people are always dropping in. I've got to where sometimes now I don't answer the door or the phone unless I'm pretty sure who it is."

"You got a good life," I said.

"A musician's wife brought over a paper bag of weed last week," he said. "Must be a pound or more. Jingo's got hers stashed in safety deposit boxes and packed in suitcases in Chicago. She doesn't believe in running out."

"Buster really hides his dope," Dorothy said. "The paper bag is on the closet floor in his room. He has a Prince Albert can full on the dresser with his pipe. There's a big matchbox full inside a sock in the dresser drawer. There's enough shreds and crumbs inside every one of his coat pockets to turn on the Marine Corps. The floor around his dresser looks like somebody's dried-up lawn. And of course nobody can overlook the Baby Giant."

"Why don't you bitch at me?" he said.

"I don't want you to get busted, is all," she said.

She went into the bathroom and slammed the door, and then we heard the shower running.

"That's some pearl ring," I said.

"She turned up here with it one day. Excited as a little kid. She kept parading around the room flashing the ring. Never saw her any happier." Buster looked at me for a moment. "You okay, John Lee?"

"I'm working it out," I said.

"You better meet the Baby Giant right away."

I followed him into his bedroom. Growing in a plastic wastebasket inside one of the closets under an infrared lamp was a bushy green plant about two-and-a-half feet high.

"Congratulations," I said.

"I can't tell you how satisfying it is for a man to grow his own crops with his own hands."

Jingo slammed down the phone. Her three-inch wooden heels shook the pictures on the walls. She lit a cigarette.

"That son of a bitch Ruby, I told him to get his goddamn dogs out of the kitchen!" she said. "The place smells like a kennel! Dog crap a foot deep all over the kitchen. Some damn fools eat the trash he serves out of there. The health inspector ought to lock him in jail. It smells so strong in my dressing room, I almost throw up. That's not bad enough, that damn fag has to keep peeking in at me. Christ, he sees me practically naked on the stage three times a night, but that won't do, he's got to peek in the door at me. For five hundred dollars a week, he thinks he gets to do this! Christ, he should pay me a thousand. For a thousand I'll show him how to really be queer! You get to be a stah in this business, you deal with some big-league perverts!"

"He called you Juliette," I said.

"I think it's my real name. Christ, I've had so many names I can't remember any more."

36

From her purse she produced a joint about the size of my thumb.

"I got to calm down," she said, lighting the joint with the other cigarette still in her mouth.

"Just take the edge off," said Buster.

To be mannerly, Buster and I helped her with it.

About seven-thirty, Jingo left to go to her room at the Holiday Inn, where she lived. She explained that it took an hour to put on her make-up, and she preferred to do it at the motel rather than in her gamy dressing room. Dorothy had driven over to her mother's apartment to fetch her hair dryer and a dress for the party. I stood in front of the telephone for a while, debating whether to call my little girl and talk to her, or my mother and father, none of them more than three miles away from me at that moment, and finally I decided to go see them later. I didn't know what to say to them on the telephone. Our conversations always sounded the same.

Dorothy looked spectacular when she returned. She had on a blue dress that came down an inch or two below her knees and had stripes going across her bosom. Her mood had improved, also. All the beautiful girls I ever knew, in Hollywood or anywhere else, were scared and vain. At age twenty, Dorothy was less scared and vain than, for example, my ex-wife, who was ten years older and did TV commercials, but even Dorothy worried about her appearance more than most men would have believed, considering her natural beauty. If she didn't feel right about the way she looked, you were in for a hard time when you took her out. On the other hand, if she knew things had clicked, she could become enormously cheerful. This is what had happened that night. When I mentioned the pearl ring, while Buster was in the shower, she smiled and held out her hand so that I could see it better.

"You'll find out anyway, and I don't care," she said. "I flew down to Mexico in Little Earl's plane. We went to his ranch. There were a whole bunch of us, nothing out of line. I was just one of several girls Little Earl asked along to serve drinks. The men went hunting in jeeps. It was fun. What's wrong with that?"

"Little Earl gave you this ring for payment?"

"Little Earl didn't give me anything. Some guy gave me this ring.

37

I don't know who he was. Just a guy. Some kind of prince, I think. He's married. Look at it. Isn't it pretty?"

I knew Dorothy would sleep with you for a set of tires if she needed them, or if she thought you really had to have her, or if she thought you were cute, so why should I think she wouldn't sleep with a prince for a pearl ring?

"It's fantastic," I said.

"I never had a ring this nice before."

Buster drove his Plymouth station wagon to the party, and I drove Dorothy in the old blue Cadillac. It was a good idea to have more than one car around if one of us elected to go elsewhere. Dorothy listened to rock-and-roll music on the radio and sang along in a childlike voice. Some of those songs I had heard dozens of times and had never been able to make out an entire line of the lyrics.

We cruised down a street of tall trees and passed the quiet clipped greenery of the Dallas Country Club, where thousands of blackbirds were sitting in trees and on telephone wires. I turned at Highland Park Village and went along Preston Road, a street that started at a fork where a white Spanish-style mansion sat in a green wedge of grass and hedges. Back down the street a ways from that mansion, though a few blocks over, in a lesser neighborhood, was the red-brick, two-story house where my mother and father lived. Driving through this area conjured up faces of aunts and cousins and street rats and old girl friends. There was a drugstore nearby where I had stolen hundreds of comic books in my time, usually by hiding them under my shirt, not to mention compacts, lipsticks, Esterbrook fountain pens, bottles of Quink, model airplanes and so forth. Nearly all the kids I knew were thieves at ten or twelve, and I was one of the wariest. I never came close to getting caught. For one thing, it was well known among adults that I was a nice boy who went to church at least twice a week. I was already adept at disguises. Some of my friends had pulled off what we regarded as major burglaries by the age of fourteen. I went along when we cracked the back door of a drugstore and stole all the magazines, ice cream, candy and money (about thirty dollars) that we could depart with in a hurry. But by then my interests were changing.

Several of my friends became burglars, stickup men and swindlers, but most drifted back to respectability or thereabouts, only occasionally relapsing into the criminal life with acts of random vandalism, drunkenness, reckless driving, street brutality, window-peeping, assault and other more or less condoned forms of crime. Others grew up into fields such as loan-sharking, auto and electrical repair, insurance, the construction business, politics and lawyering, and I am sure they felt no more moral sense against stealing than we had felt as children, with the advantage that now they no longer feared God.

"I'm sorry I was bitchy this afternoon. It felt funny seeing you again," Dorothy said.

"It hasn't been all that long," I said.

"It seems like a long time. So much has happened. I've had three different jobs since I came back, and they were all crappy. My daddy came back on leave from Germany and came to see me and Mama wouldn't let him in the house. So he took me out to dinner and got drunk and cried. You know he and my mama have been divorced for eleven years, and that was the first time I'd seen him since then? He's a master sergeant now with twenty-one years' duty. Think of that, twenty-one years in the goddamn Army."

"I thought your daddy was in the Navy," I said.

"That's my ex-stepdaddy that used to be in the Navy. He's the one who used to crawl in bed with me all the time and say he wanted to warm me up. He was always walking into the bathroom by mistake when I was in the tub or walking through the house naked and claiming he didn't know me and my girl friends were there. He'd talk real loud when he was making it with Mama. I could hear every word they said."

"What did your mama think about all that?"

"She kind of got a kick out of it," Dorothy said. "She's always told me I'm not sexy enough. Well, I can't help it, I've tried."

"You look sexy enough to me," I said.

"That's not what she means. Damn, if you could have heard the stuff she and my stepdaddy used to yell at each other in all those cheap enlisted men's quarters where we used to live with the cardboard walls."

"Tell me. Repeat it all."

"Oh John Lee, you fool," she smiled.

"Why haven't you been going to school?"

"I took Spanish the first summer term. Then I worked a while at a bank sticking paper in drawers until I nearly went crazy. I was going to enroll this fall, but I just never got around to it. I'll start again in the spring semester if things turn out all right."

"What things?"

"Things, you know. Like life itself."

I remembered one night when Dorothy and I were in the Polo Lounge, sitting around with six or eight guys in Beverly Hills cowboy outfits—silk shirts with pearl snaps, bandanas, pigskin pants, hand-made boots. Norman Feldman, the producer of *Six Guns Across Texas*, was insisting that he had been born in Amarillo and could recall snow on the mountains when he was a boy, and the others started thinking up hometowns for themselves, like Muleshoe, Uvalde, Pecos, Texarkana, and so forth, and later when Dorothy and I went back to the pink stucco house on the hill above Sunset she said, "John Lee, do you realize how weird those people think you are? I mean, you've actually been in those places they were talking about, and you really did work on a ranch in Pecos, and you never say a word about it, and they think you're very strange, and I'm starting to think so, too. I want to finish my education so I can meet a better class of people."

Come to think of it, she had met a prince with a pearl ring.

6

A Pinkerton stood beneath a carriage lamp at Little Earl's gate and looked suspiciously at the old blue Cadillac before checking my name on a list. We could see lights strung in the trees reflecting in the hood as we cruised along the road to the house, which loomed up like a mountain of white stone. A Negro boy in a white uniform ran out to park the car for me. We walked around a showering fountain, with purple and yellow lights wavering inside the geyser, and the lights in the trees and shrubs now shone on a small lake beside the house. From out of the darkness into a circle of light floated three swans, soundless among lily pads. A bubble appeared on the surface of the lake, and rings spread out as a fish or turtle rose for a bit of insect or air before diving away from the swans. We heard voices from the darkness beyond the lights on the water, and then the clatter and splash of oars. A gray-haired Negro in a tuxedo opened the front door and smiled. He greeted me by name in a soft British accent he had learned in Nassau.

"There is a great deal of gaiety going on, Mr. Wallace," he said.

Until a few years ago, Little Earl had lived in a three-bedroom, two-bath, ranch-style house in a middle-class neighborhood full of tricycles and shaggy grass. His wife Marianne had complained to me once that her dishwasher was broken and the transmission was expiring on her car, and because she had overspent her allowance she could not get them repaired. But Little Earl had been working secretly with an architect from San Antonio. One day, bulldozers arrived at a wooded pasture north of town and began smashing trees and rooting up earth for construction of what the closest neighbors, a quarter of a mile away, assumed to be a shopping center. High wooden fences

41

were erected to hide the construction. By the time it was finished, the prairie surrounding this mysterious forty acres was covered with houses, gasoline stations and shopping centers, and neighbors were speculating that behind the high fences that now were stone rather than wood, a new private college, probably Roman Catholic, was being built. Little Earl had lived in his new house for a couple of months before the neighbors realized it.

When the story got out, Little Earl would not permit newspapers or magazines to photograph his place or write features about it. Francis P. Franklin hinted to me that Little Earl had dared make the move only because Big Earl, who was then approaching ninety, was not quite as clearheaded as before, and that still Little Earl was wary that his father might decide against this extravagance. Franklin told me—and I never entirely disbelieved it—that Big Earl had visited the place and had taken it to be some sort of country club that his son belonged to.

As our footsteps clacked on the marble in the entrance hall, we could hear mariachis playing violins and guitars and singing in the main room ahead.

"John Lee, we got chicken enchiladas with mole sauce!" Little Earl said as we entered the room. He kissed Dorothy on the cheek. "Hi, dolly!" Although most of the men I could see were wearing dark suits or blazers, and the women had on cocktail dresses, Little Earl still wore his yellow jumpsuit. He gestured with a wine glass that had salt crusted on its rim. "How 'bout a margarita? You ever puke chicken enchiladas?"

I saw Buster standing with several people near the mariachis. He was wearing his more or less standard outfit of pipe-legged cotton khaki pants and brown corduroy coat, with a blue button-down shirt and black knit tie. Beside the mariachis, Buster could have been mistaken for a tourist who had gotten mixed up in a fiesta, but he still never did look quite like a gringo.

"Good music," I said. It was always startling to hear the mariachis' songs about death and violence at a party like this.

"How can you tell?" said Little Earl. "I think they sound fine myself, but all mariachis sound the same except the ones that are purely terrible."

"I don't see Franklin anywhere," I said.

"Francis isn't here yet. Margaret came while ago. I guess he's drunk someplace."

Little Earl's attention was caught by more arrivals. I picked a path for Dorothy and me across the huge room, moving around groups of people and clusters of furniture to a long bar that revealed itself when a wall panel—a mural of a hill-country stream, slopes of bluebonnets, a windmill and a post oak tree—was slid into the ceiling. Behind the bar in front of bottles, model airplanes and mirrors arranged to resemble the bar at the 21 Club in New York worked three bartenders in white linen coats.

With our drinks, we went over to join Buster. The mariachis had drifted away to another part of the room.

"Little Earl's still touchy about his house. He made me put up the movie camera," Buster said. "But that German woman followed me out to the car and split a smoke with me."

I heard Gretchen Schindler's hoarse laugh and saw her talking to Billy Bob Teagarden, who was wearing a red blazer that stuck up at one side of the neck as though still hung on a hook in the locker room. The sleeve covered the back of the thumb that was wrapped against a glass, and the red shone in his face. Colonel Burnett had placed his own drink on the mantel and was using both hands in conversation with one of Big Earl's executives. There were plenty of people present who had what I considered a lot of money, though few who were Franklin's equal and none as rich as Little Earl. Many of them had leaped from the farm or the service or the Depression shack into the country club and the opera league without a metamorphosis of feature; that coarse-faced lout in the corner might be a multimillionaire with a collection of Remingtons and French Impressionists. In truth, not many of them cared for the arts. But some could be talked into giving money to museums and theaters. Little Earl, who had gone to Yale, was one of the few at the party who'd had a good education, and he wouldn't have bothered to wipe his ass with Tchaikovski's original lead sheets, but without his wife Marianne there could scarcely have been a symphony orchestra in town—Marianne who had done two years at Stephens and could not have spelled Tchaikovski with a tutor.

"Hey, John Lee, from the back I couldn't tell if it was you or your sister, but your sister doesn't have a mustache," a voice said behind me.

My policy on remarks concerning my hair was to keep silent and look the speaker in the eye as if I hadn't quite heard him correctly. If the remark was repeated I would continue to gaze at the speaker with a vaguely perplexed look, and if he seemed about to persist, I would shake my head sadly and turn my back on him. But Charlie Withers in no way deserved this protocol.

"You wouldn't know a woman if you got your head caught in one," I said.

This was not the most tactful thing to say, because Charlie's wife Annabel had come up beside him and was smiling over what appeared to be a glass of water but which I knew to be vodka on the rocks. For an instant I hoped Charlie would say something else about my hair, and like a TV hero I would bash his dimpled chin. I felt a rush of strength and the hatred in my heart that Buster says is necessary for being invincible in a fight, and simultaneously I understood that the Benzedrine might be close to making me exceedingly cranky. Just as promptly, I knew Charlie would not continue speaking about my hair or my sister, and I would not bash him. These things seldom happened among adults except in beer joints or dance halls on the highway.

"Aw, come on, John Lee, I was only kidding, goddamn," said Charlie.

He was wearing a maroon blazer with a Texas A&M patch on the breast pocket—mostly, I suspect, to annoy Franklin on his birthday —and a Texas A&M senior class ring that he probably had not removed in twenty years.

"John Lee, our kids never miss your show," Annabel said.

Annabel was Little Earl's first cousin. Her father and Big Earl were brothers, but her father had become a veterinarian and obviously had

44

not made anywhere near as much money as Big Earl. Still, Big Earl looked after his own, as they always said, and Annabel's father was the richest horse and dog doctor in East Texas. Annabel's five brothers had all gone to work for Big Earl. Annabel herself was a director of a large bank. I had known Charlie Withers when he was a top-forty disc jockey and had a different wife and three children. He divorced her to marry Annabel, who already had four children by a golf pro, and they moved into a castle with turrets. But Annabel's brothers would not allow Charlie Withers to wriggle into the family funds. The house where Charlie and Annabel lived, and everything in it, right down to the carpets, were leased. So were all the cars and the airplane. There was no community property. Charlie was paid forty thousand dollars a year as vice president of a landscaping firm. It was his allowance. He never went to the office, and all he knew about landscaping was that the greens on some golf courses had bent grass while others had Bermuda. If Annabel got tired of him, he was another out-of-work disc jockey with child support to pay.

"Why don't you do a number for us?" Annabel said to me.

"Yeah, man, we can tape it on Little Earl's equipment," said Charlie.

"What kind of number?" I said.

"I don't care. Sing or recite. Surely you do some sort of monologue. All actors do monologues," said Annabel.

A crowd collected around us. Charlie began flipping switches on the wall. He produced a microphone. I heard someone across the room say John Lee was going to do a number.

"I don't have a number to do," I said.

"Sure you do," said Charlie.

"We've had some really big stars at our house, and they've sung or recited for us," Annabel said.

"Really big stars have got to learn numbers," said Buster.

"Yeah, I don't know any numbers. They won't let me learn any until I get big," I said.

"Let's see your fast draw!" someone said.

"Die for us!"

"John Lee, don't be so swell-headed," said Annabel. "You know damn well you can do some kind of number. It's for our collection. Say a poem."

"If you want something for your collection, you ought to tape this crap that's being said," I said.

"I am taping it," said Charlie.

"Should I tell you a few of the stars we've got on tape?" Annabel said. "Will that convince you that you're not too good for us now that you've moved to Hollywood and we're still poor backward hillbillies from Texas?"

"Annabel, I don't know any numbers," I said.

"You're embarrassing him," someone said.

"John Lee embarrassed? Boy, you don't know John Lee!"

"Charlie, make him do a number," said Annabel.

I looked at Charlie, and he looked back at his wife.

"I can't make him perform if he won't do it," Charlie said.

"John Lee, are you going to do a number for our collection or not?" said Annabel.

"I am not going to do a number," I said.

"Well then, if John Lee's not going to do a number," Buster said, stepping in front of me into the small open space around which the crowd had gathered, "maybe you'd like to see his prick."

Smoothly Buster pulled my zipper half down and was reaching into my fly before I pushed his hand away and broke through the faces that were peering into my trousers.

"So you won't be totally disappointed, have a look at my prick next," I heard Buster say.

There were gasps and laughter from the crowd, and one man pulled his wife away, demanding they go home. Zipping my trousers, I went to the bar. With the Bennies in me it was difficult to get euphorically drunk. Colonel Burnett was standing at the bar. He smelled like sweet pipe tobacco.

"I've got one thing to say to you, Colonel. Fuck the system," I said.

He smiled. "You are fucking the system," he said, "out of a very handsome living."

Dorothy came over to us wheezing. Sometimes she laughed so hard she looked frightened and confused, the skin drawn tight on her face as she brayed and dragged for breath with a look in her eyes as though drowning.

"Buster tied a ribbon around his deal," she said.

"That friend of yours is eccentric. I've heard people talking about him," said the Colonel.

I introduced Colonel Burnett to Dorothy. He held her fingers lightly and then bowed in a courtly way.

"You are a very beautiful girl," he said.

"Why didn't you sing for them?" Dorothy asked me. "I've heard you sing 'The Old Chisholm Trail' a hundred times. Or 'Blood on the Saddle.' You disappointed Annabel."

"Annabel's father lost a fine place in Cuba," said the Colonel.

"You mean Big Earl did," I said.

"Oh, Annabel's father, too. Big Earl lost a ranch, as I told you, and some other properties, and Annabel's father lost an excellent dairy farm. Annabel had some good riding stock there, too. Little Earl was buying a place right next to his uncle and cutting a landing strip so he could hop down there from his house in the Keys."

"Colonel, you make it sound like half of Cuba was owned by people in Dallas."

"It would be a tremendous exaggeration to say that," he said, taking me seriously.

"I'd like to eat you bones and all," Billy Bob Teagarden said.

With an arm around Gretchen's waist, he was leering at Dorothy. I had the impression that his arrival had made Dorothy fitful. She looked at him and then smiled, her wide mouth opening and closing again around the crooked upper teeth.

"Take me before Gretchen devours me. She can't get enough of my body," said Billy Bob.

Gretchen had put on dark glasses. While Billy Bob was talking, she picked up a gin bottle off the bar, filled her glass and dropped in one olive and one ice cube. She picked up the bottle of vermouth, studied it and put it back. Billy Bob hugged her.

"You want it all the time, don't you, baby?" he said.

"That is a ton of bool cheet," she said huskily. She staggered a bit and pointed at Dorothy. "You know it, honey. That's lies about the woman panting for more cock all the time. Only girls who do like that are crazy. Am I right?"

"I guess so," said Dorothy.

"Pardon me," the Colonel said, walking away.

Gretchen paused as if struggling to remember why.

"Yes," said Gretchen. "Girls fog for a lot of reasons. Money is a good one. To make a man like her is a good one. Sometimes a girl will fog for kicks or join in a threesome or a group. But the truth is, dolling, the best things for a girl are running water, a vibrator, other girls, dogs and then men, in that order."

Margaret Franklin was walking toward us. Little Earl's wife Marianne was coming with her.

"Women to each other in love are tender," Gretchen said. "Am I right?"

"I don't know," said Dorothy.

Billy Bob Teagarden looked back and forth at them with exceptional interest.

"You should find out! Don't go round fogging men without a damn good reason," Gretchen said. "It's a waste. Women are better for you, I am sure."

"Did you say dogs a minute ago?" asked Billy Bob.

"I did indeed," Gretchen said.

"Little Earl's got a dog," said Billy Bob. "Where is that little bastard? Melvin! Melvin! He's always here when you don't need him. Melvin!"

Whistling for Melvin, Billy Bob turned around and bumped into Margaret Franklin and Marianne.

"Melvin is in the garage," Marianne said. "Should I get him?"

"Not right now," said Billy Bob.

"Just a second ago you were practically screaming for him," she said.

"I changed my mind," said Billy Bob.

48

"Did you want Melvin?" Marianne said, looking at Gretchen.

"Who the fog is Melvin?"

"Our dog," said Marianne.

"What kind of dog is he?" Gretchen said.

"Alsatian."

"I'd rather have a spaniel," said Gretchen.

"Melvin is so cute," Marianne said, wrinkling her nose. "He's the sweetest thing."

I looked at the two wives standing together, Margaret with her young face and her Rugby-ball breasts, and Marianne bland and smiling, guiltless. Marianne seemed to have no sense of proportion; for her, one thing was as important as the next, so that there was no possibility for tragedy in her life, and no real joy, but everything was the same. Gretchen had begun scanning the room as if she had forgotten the two women were there. Dorothy moved backward a full three feet.

"Oh, here's the madam," said Marianne. "Isn't she pretty?"

Marianne and Margaret each rushed to take the elbow of a woman who had been pointed out to me as a retired Russian ballerina. She was not tall, but she held her head high on a long neck and turned slowly to look at each person who spoke. Her skin was powdered white as chalk, and her lips were scarlet, and her eyes were dark and quiet on either side of a sharp nose. It was impossible to guess her age, but her hair was gray with black streaks. Standing at either side of her, Margaret Franklin and Little Earl's wife seemed by comparison clumsy and top-heavy. The prima ballerina said she had wished to meet me because of my connection with the theatrical and because the length of my hair reminded her of Europe, where men of distinction, she said, were not afraid to let their hair grow. She pointed with her eyes toward a local impresario who was entertaining a semicircle of wives. He wore bangs and tiny daring commas behind the ears.

"Thees Dullus, eet squats on one," she said.

Just then the doors to the swimming pool patio crashed open and a large white turkey flew in with an angry squawk, flapped and bounced about ten feet, hit an elderly man between the shoulder blades and knocked him skidding on the polished floor. With a cry of triumph, the turkey shook himself and strutted with wings raised as if searching for another foe.

"Lyndon hits like a linebacker," Franklin said happily.

Franklin was pulling a large laundry basket on wheels behind him, the kind of basket used in hotels, with stiff canvas on a metal frame. A pair of feet stuck up from the laundry basket. Franklin was barefoot, lion-shit-crusted trousers rolled halfway up his thin white calves, but the pair of feet protruding from the basket wore black shoes sizes too big, and no socks. At once, you knew the shoes belonged to Franklin.

The entire room seemed paralyzed for a moment as Franklin and Lyndon both swept the place with a gaze. Since we happened to be standing closest, Franklin recognized us and called hoarsely: "Old cocks!" He lurched toward us dragging the laundry basket, with the feet bobbing slightly like fishing corks in the wake of a boat. Lyndon hissed a shot of steam, raised his wings and dashed toward the mariachis, slipping and scrambling in his eagerness to destroy them, and finally tumbling forward on his nostrils like a ground-looping airplane. It occurred to me that Lyndon was drunk.

"Hidy! Hidy!" Franklin said. His white shirt was torn, and he poked a finger at red spots on the front. "Blood," he said. "Freddy hit me in the mouth with a ashtray." He opened his mouth and showed us a pink gum. Then he noticed the prima ballerina. Franklin grasped his tie with both hands and slid the knot carefully upwards into place at his collar, which he then buttoned. He licked both his palms and smoothed his hair back. He winked at Margaret and jabbed her with an elbow.

"How'm I doin?" he said.

Margaret's mouth was agape in her elderly teen-ager's face, as though she were being strangled. Marianne's eyes flipped back and forth from Franklin to the ballerina to Lyndon, who had frightened the mariachis and several others into a huddle in the corner and was now attempting to strut but kept falling down.

Laughing, the prima ballerina applauded daintily, one small hand patting the other.

50

Franklin leaned forward and reached for her hand, as if to kiss it. But he had so far to lean that he lost his balance and fell to his knees before her. So he simply bent down and kissed her feet.

"Get up, you fool!" said Margaret, about to swoon with humiliation.

At this, the feet in the basket began to move, slowly and then vigorously, kicking against the frame, and the overlarge, untied shoes seemed ready to wobble off. In a moment the feet dropped down inside the basket, and the head of Freddy the Ad Man appeared over the rim. Freddy was an old drinking companion of Franklin's and was noted for never being entirely sober.

"Did someone call me?" Freddy said in his slap-bass voice.

Freddy felt his head. Satisfied that he was still wearing his brown felt hat, he looked at the prima ballerina and said, "Jesus, who's that?" Then he looked down at Franklin. "Frans, what doing? No time for that! Les get out here! Thought I heard my wife!"

"You thought right, you miserable bastard!" shouted a small blonde woman wearing a low-cut gown and a bracelet and necklace with several diamonds. Quivering, breasts throbbing, she charged out of a group.

Seeing her, Freddy stood up and clutched the sides of the basket as if it were a chariot and yelled, "Go! Go! Faster!" When the basket did not move, he tried to climb out of it. The basket fell over on its side with a flat whack. Freddy rolled onto the floor, wearing the shoes and hat and a red bathing suit. He got up, holding the hat on his head, and clomped out the patio door with his wife pursuing him.

We heard a splash from out back, and then we heard Freddy's wife shouting, "Go on and swim for it! You'll never get away!"

Francis had stood up and was shaking his head sadly above us.

"I worry 'bout Freddy," he said.

"Francis, you are not welcome in this house as long as that turkey is with you," Marianne said coldly.

"Lyndon's fulla fun," said Francis. "If Little Earl can put a lion in my hearse, I can bring my faithful white turkey to my own birthday party."

We looked at Lyndon. The turkey was up on the bar, hissing

viciously, crapping every few seconds and pecking at bowls of peanuts. For the first time I noticed Lyndon was wearing a rhinestone
collar.

"Eeet ees quite droll," said the ballerina, elegantly turning her head
toward Lyndon.

"Francis, catch that goddamn turkey and get out of here," Little
Earl said. He was very angry, his fat face twisted. "I'm not kidding
with you, fellow! Move!"

A frost of fear settled across Franklin's eyes for an instant. He
looked away from Little Earl. His eyes stopped first on Buster and
then on me. I could see straight into him. His wife was saying, "Oh,
I'm so sorry, Marianne, I wouldn't have had this happen . . ."

"I'll help you catch him, Francis," I said.

"We'll hem him in," said Buster.

"Lyndon don't hem," Franklin said.

"He shit all over my bar!" said Little Earl.

The three of us took off after the turkey. We ran across the room,
parting the crowd, some of them laughing and others trying to be as
outraged as their host. We began to exercise stealth and cunning as
we approached the bar, but Lyndon hissed and dived between us,
whipping my face with one wing, showering feathers. He plunged at
a fat lady who threshed back against a full-length portrait of Little
Earl. Running past, Buster knocked her back into the painting again,
and we heard Little Earl howl. Lyndon fled down a broad carpeted
corridor that led off into other vast areas of the palace. On the carpet
Lyndon could get good traction, and he fairly well moved out, hissing
and screeching and scattering servants and guests. At a bend in the
corridor, Lyndon was going too fast to turn. He collided with a statue
of a jaunty flapper that was a piece in the collection Little Earl was
buying on advice from a New York gallery. The flapper fell on her
face. "My God, he's broke my ort!" Little Earl screamed.

Lyndon spread his wings and bounded up a wide flight of stairs. He
ran along another hall and into a bedroom the size of half a tennis
court. There was an enormous fireplace in one wall, and a glass and
mahogany gun cabinet against another. Lyndon appeared to be head-

ing for some tall French doors, but instead he whirled and disappeared through another door.

"It's a bathroom! We've got him!" yelled Buster.

I ran through the bathroom door and bumped into Buster, who was gaping at the twin toilets that were divided by a partition of clouded glass.

"They're gold," Buster said.

Behind us came Franklin, followed by Little Earl, who had yanked a shotgun out of the cabinet and was stuffing 12-gauge shells into it.

"Little Earl, you can't shoot Lyndon, he's just a innocent turkey," Franklin said.

"Blow the sumbitch to bits," panted Little Earl.

"Are those toilets really gold?" Buster said.

"Where's 'at damn turkey?" said Little Earl, snapping shut the shotgun breech.

"He's trapped in here," I said.

"There's more than one door to a bathroom!" said Little Earl.

We ran into another room of the bathroom. This room had a huge sunken tub of black tile set in a platform up three white-carpeted steps from the llama-carpeted floor. Opposite was a large black tile shower cabinet with eight gold nozzles aiming at different parts of the body. I saw our group in several mirrors as we ran on through another door, into a dressing room with mirrors covering panel after panel of wardrobe closets. One closet was open, and I could see what I would estimate to be two hundred pairs of shoes in racks.

"In here!" Buster shouted.

Lyndon had preceded us into the other half of the tennis court. This was Marianne's bedroom, with a fireplace like her husband's but with a color TV beside the bed and a bookcase in place of the gun cabinet. The excited Lyndon had left a trail of droppings across Marianne's bed and for some reason had snatched up one of her brassieres, which had got tangled around his head and wattles, leaving one big baleful eye uncovered. With that eye, Lyndon glared back at us as he teetered on his perch on a wrought-iron railing of the balcony outside an open French door.

There was a BOOM and a crash of breaking glass, and Lyndon was gone.

We ran to the French door, leaving Little Earl peering at his smoking shotgun as if he hadn't believed it would actually shoot. In the light from the bedroom and from the windows below, we could see an unmoving white blob down on the grass.

Franklin moaned.

A crowd had gathered around Lyndon's corpse by the time we got downstairs. Franklin stood looking at the pile of white feathers bound up in the pink brassiere.

"Shot to death like a criminal," Franklin said.

"He's not shot," someone said. "He fell off that thing up there like a big rock and broke his neck."

"Poor Lyndon thought he could fly," said Franklin.

Franklin started dragging the dead turkey away across the grass. Buster and I followed him. We left the crowd behind. We went around a corner of the house into the darkness and continued our march across clipped grass until we came suddenly to a far end of the swimming pool. There was no sign of Freddy the Ad Man or his wife. Without a word, Franklin walked to the edge of the pool, still holding the dead turkey by a foot, and unzipped his pants and began to pee into the water. Buster and I did the same. It sounded like a bathtub being filled. Inside the lighted windows of the house we could see many people.

When he had finished, Franklin zipped his pants and said, "There's elements about this party I don't care for."

"Mist' Francis! Mist' Francis!" Wilburn said, coming out of the bushes.

"Wilburn, you better take Lyndon home and lay him to rest," Franklin said.

"Lyndon was nice for a turkey," said Wilburn.

"Best turkey we ever had," Franklin said.

He watched Wilburn dragging Lyndon across the grass into the darkness.

"I can remember when I wished a day would never end," said Franklin.

We walked around to the front of the house, where Dorothy was examining a gleaming blue Ferrari. It looked like a racing speedboat.

"I was coming to find you, but I found this first," she said.

"It's my birthday present," said Franklin. "We'll go for a ride."

"I'd rather go find that German woman," Buster said.

Franklin gestured for me to drive. I wasn't sure I knew how, but I got behind the wheel. Franklin urged Dorothy into the car, and she sat in his lap with her left arm around his neck. My hand hit her knee as I reached for the gears. The engine kicked off at once with a wet growl. I let out gently on the clutch, but the car shot forward, forcing a parking attendant to crash through a hedge.

"Make it scoot!" Franklin said.

We banged over the curb, drove through a flowerbed and around the corner of the house in a wild careen. The purple and yellow geyser of the fountain rose up in front of us, and in swerving to miss it, I came close to driving into the lake. I glanced at Franklin. He was grinning and clinging to Dorothy, who looked terrified and was trying to tell me to stop. We bounced over a curb again through an opening back onto the driveway and roared out the gate past the Pinkerton, missing a Cadillac that honked.

By now I had the car somewhat more under control and was feeling confident. If I had come through that maze around the house without cracking, it was likely I could drive anywhere in Dallas. I made a U-turn in the intersection and headed out toward the country. Lighted windows and dark lawns whirled past. The tires were going zingzingzingzing, and the engine was working deep in its throat. At the merest touch of my hands on the wheel or my feet on brake or accelerator, the car did precisely what I had ordered whether it was what I really wanted or not. In a few minutes we were on a lane lined on both sides with trees that moved past like a picket fence. I glanced at the speedometer and the needle was tipping between one hundred forty and one hundred fifty. I slowed for an instant but in the exhilaration knew I couldn't change pace. The car catapulted forward when I trod the pedal, with the feeling that all four wheels had left the ground. The top was off and Dorothy's hair tore out behind like a scarf and wind whipped her voice away. Clouds spun above. The stars

55

had tails. In a feat approaching the miraculous, I turned onto a freeway, twirled the car entirely around, wound up pointing in what I thought was the correct direction. Down the freeway at one hundred forty. Vapor lights ran above in an unbroken line. Instinctively I whipped off the freeway without being able to read the exit sign. All at once we went up the wrong side of a traffic island and back through Little Earl's front gate, leaped the curb and halted with water from the fountain pattering down on the hood like rain.

We sat there breathing for a minute.

"Did that happen?" I said.

"You dumb ass, you could have killed us!" Dorothy said.

She got out of the car and ran around the showering fountain toward the house. I watched Franklin watching her blue dress bob up the steps and through the door. I was still powered and in a supranatural state from whatever we had just done, and I saw right into his head again but disregarded what I observed as too bothersome to cope with at this moment.

As we sat in the car a black hearse pulled up in the driveway. Colonel Burnett came onto the porch and called, "Francis, you must come inside."

"If it's another lion I'll declare animal war on Little Earl," Franklin said.

Inside, there were a lot of grins, as if it was known what to expect and they could hardly wait to see how Franklin would react. Buster, Gretchen and Dorothy were in a corner beside a leaded window. Even though she had gained weight, Dorothy looked almost skinny next to Gretchen, who had a buxom torso and thin legs. A glass door slid open and six men, friends of Franklin, marched slowly in with a schoolboy attempt at solemnity. Between them they carried a coffin.

The crowd parted and the coffin was transported across the room and deposited at Franklin's feet. The pallbearers sang "Happy Birthday."

"Open it," one of the men said when the song was finished.

Cautiously Franklin reached down for the handle of the coffin lid. He lifted it an inch and listened for growls or rattles. Then he shrugged and opened the coffin.

A naked girl stood up from the purple plush lining with a birthday cake in her hands.

She stepped out of the coffin. She looked frightened and unsophisticated at this form of show business. Her thatch was like a sparrow's nest. She presented the cake to Franklin. With a cigarette lighter she had been holding beneath the platter, she tried to light the dozens of candles on the cake. But her hand was shaking and the lighter would not fire.

The Colonel leaped forward and wrapped his suit coat around the girl, who smiled gratefully at him.

"What the hell?" somebody said.

"Take that thing off!"

Instead, Colonel Burnett lit the candles with his gold lighter.

"Blow 'em out before the cake melts," said Billy Bob Teagarden.

Franklin inhaled and blew noisily and extinguished perhaps a fifth of the candles. He pushed the cake toward the girl. She blew out the rest and then ran out the back door with the Colonel's coat clutched around her.

As Franklin stood there holding the cake, uncertain what to do with it, the mariachis started playing twist music, and people began dancing, and Margaret Franklin began to cry. "Oh, Francis, there's so many candles," she said. He gave the cake to a waiter and put an arm around his wife. "Baby, there'll be more," he said. It was the first time I had ever seen him show tenderness toward her, and it was a nice thing to see—Franklin in his torn, bloody shirt with his long skinny calves and bare feet below rolled-up trousers, and Margaret in her white silk cocktail dress, hugging each other in front of all these people.

"Think what a good life it'd be if a man didn't have to drink all the time and buy clothes," said Billy Bob Teagarden.

I noticed Dorothy suddenly staring at something behind me. Two dark little men in shades and dark-blue suits had come in from the entrance hall and were looking around the room, holding themselves in an odd posture, as if gripping invisible submachine guns. In a moment a third man entered. He was somewhat taller and darker than the first two and wore a madras jacket.

"Where's Little Earl?" Billy Bob said.

"I haven't seen him in a while," I said.

"That's the guy Francis brought the bag to," said Billy Bob.

"Ah, the sheik," Gretchen said.

"Be right with you, Ah-med," said Franklin, still comforting his wife.

Paying scant attention to Franklin or to the others at the party, the sheik walked at once over to us. He bowed and kissed Dorothy's hand, and then Gretchen's. He did not even glance at Billy Bob or Buster, but he turned to me and said, "So strange looking to be Tarzan. Really, I would have expected you to have a much more athletic body. But perhaps you have not been exercising."

Smiling brightly, showing a platinum tooth, the sheik placed the fingers of his right hand at his throat, on his neckerchief, and awaited my answer. His face was pocked and greasy, and he could have done with a few push-ups himself.

"Sheik, I'm Billy Bob Teagarden," Billy Bob said, holding out his hand.

"Really?" said the sheik.

"I work for Big Earl and Little Earl."

"How splendid."

Billy Bob at last let his hand drop.

"It was most interesting watching you talk to that little ape," the sheik said to me. "Tell me, could the ape truly understand what you said?"

"You saw him do it," I said.

"But so much of the cinema is illusion."

"The ape did what I told him," I said.

"And what exact language was it that you used in communicating with the creature?"

"It was a sort of ape-think," I said. "When you get to know an ape pretty well, you start to chirp and gooble back at him, and all at once you realize you know what he's thinking about."

"I once bought myself a little ape, and the nasty beast bit me."

"It takes patience," I said.

58

"I suppose I did know what he was thinking about, though. That is probably why I killed him," said the sheik. "Tell me, does it bother you that the cinema in the United States is controlled by Jews?"

"Is it?" I said.

"Surely you must know that. It is quite smart of them to have gained control of such an important industry. It is impossible to overestimate the influence the American cinema has had on the thinking of the world. When I watched you swinging through the trees with your monkey friends, how I envied this state of frontier freedom you Americans believe is your right. Watching you slap those black niggers and throw their chief to the crocodiles was most pleasant. How thoroughly, completely American!"

"Tarzan was an Englishman," I said.

"Come now, that was years ago. In the fiction of Mr. Burroughs. The English would dearly love to behave that way, certainly, but their time has passed. Tarzan has been purely American since he was first put into the cinema. Mr. Crabbe, Mr. Weissmuller, Mr. Elmo Lincoln and the others, including yourself, did you detect an English accent anywhere among them? I have every Tarzan film in my library. I have seen them many, many times. I prefer them to Westerns."

"Your boys get a drink?" asked Franklin.

"My boys do not drink," the sheik said.

"I forgot," said Franklin.

"However, my golf professional is a Christian and he does drink. He is outside in one of my cars, if you wish to have a nigger take whiskey out to him."

"I'll just ask him in," Franklin said.

"He is not allowed in. What would my people think of me if a golf professional were allowed to attend the same parties as I?"

"I guess he needs a drink, all right," said Franklin.

"Say, sheik, you being a Moslem and all, you got any dope?" Buster asked.

"Mr. Wallace, I would like to know why you have not made another Tarzan film," said the sheik.

"Buster wants to know if you have any dope," I said.

"I fail to understand."

"Kief, hashish, Morocco dynamite, you know. Dope. Smokem up, hey buddy?" said Buster.

"Surely you are joking," the sheik said. He turned back to me. "I thought you had a promising career as Tarzan. I was quite disappointed when I discovered someone else has assumed the role in the next picture. You had a certain sort of style. It was still rough, not all could see it by any means, but it was there to be developed. I fear the cinema has lost a Tarzan with the potential of Mr. Crabbe himself. Why did you give it up?"

"They wouldn't use enough elephants," I said.

"Yes, yes, I quite sympathize. There were hardly any elephants at all in your film. Well, it is my misfortune to have lost a very promising Tarzan indeed. What is your next cinema venture?"

"To make a documentary film around Dallas," I said, half expecting the sheik to snap his fingers and have the airline flight bag full of money handed over to me.

"A dull subject. Texas is dull. Thinking about it makes me tired," he said. Buster and Gretchen had walked off, but Billy Bob Teagarden still hung in, and Dorothy was looking at the sheik in a kind of stricken way, and Franklin had come back from sending a bottle out to the sheik's golf pro. "I don't suppose you would consider doing your famous ape-man yell for me?"

"Those are recorded, sheik. We all use Weissmuller's."

"More illusion! The damnable cinema! Ah, but I had never met a genuine Tarzan before. This is a marvelous experience for me, Mr. Wallace. Might I have your autograph?"

He spoke in what I assumed was Arabic to one of the men in blue. The man handed me a leather-bound notepad and a gold Dunhill pen.

"Just write 'To my dear friend Ahmed, glorious defender of God, from Tarzan' and put the date and sign your name," the sheik said.

As I started to write, feeling perhaps more absurd than usual when asked for an autograph, the sheik spoke to Dorothy.

"My dear, the pearl looks superb on your slender hand. I shall send you a pendant to match, if you will leave your address with my man

60

here. It was an enchanting time we had, quite the most satisfactory of my entire stay."

I signed my name and gave the notebook to the sheik, but it was intercepted by the bodyguard without the sheik touching it.

"Sir," the sheik said to me, bowing slightly. "Dorothy," he said, pronouncing each syllable and bowing to her. He ignored Billy Bob and looked up at Franklin. "I shall see you tomorrow," the sheik said. One of his bodyguards went out ahead of him and the other behind.

"A A-rab is the next thing to dirt, in my opinion," said Billy Bob.

Franklin frowned. He looked at me and at Dorothy. "Can't win 'em all," he said.

Taking Billy Bob with him, Franklin went to the bar. About half the guests had gone by now. Dorothy had gotten tight-lipped again and was drawing herself up for an attack. Her eyes grew very round in her thin face.

"At least you got a big pearl," I said.

"You couldn't keep from saying something spiteful," she said. "Do you want to hear my side of it?"

"I can see your side of it on your finger."

"You really do think you're so damn smart and so damn good."

"That's not even close to what I think," I said. The Benzedrine was wearing off, and my psyche was falling down two or three steps at a time. When the Bennies cut out, they left you stranded. It could be a heavy feeling. The muscles in my face would go slack. I would be trying to demonstrate a response but would be aware that my mouth was sagging and my expression like that of a flounder on a bed of ice.

"I'm going home," Dorothy said.

"Go ahead."

"I mean to my mother's."

"Good night."

"John Lee, please, I didn't screw him."

"I'll get a ride with Buster."

She strode out angrily with tears that I felt too wrung out to react to. I plucked one last drink off a tray and went over to join Buster. He was talking to Laureen Cox, who rather defiantly and nervously was wearing a pillbox hat and a knee-length sheath dress—what was called the "Jackie Look." Laureen Cox had been a friend of Marianne's since grade school and was the close cousin of a senator, so her moderate political aberrations were moderately tolerated. Her husband Leroy was a consulting geologist, a nice fellow who, because of his wife's admiration for the Kennedys, was viewed with pity and suspicion by many of the clients his touch with Little Earl attracted.

Just as I said hello to Laureen, Charlie and Annabel Withers walked past on their way out.

"More's red than her head," Charlie said, pointing at Laureen's hair and then at the pillbox hat.

Buster started to scowl. "Laureen, dressing like Jackie must give you a thrill," said Annabel.

"Oh, I like it, I think it's real cute," Laureen said, smiling.

"When's Leroy going to let his hair grow and say Cube-er?" said Charlie.

"Leroy won't use that word these days no matter how it's pronounced," Laureen said.

"Laureen, you don't have to take any shit off people like this," said Buster.

"You've got to where you think you're pretty much big time all the sudden," Charlie said to Buster. "I've seen your damn pictures on the covers of those magazines, and they don't impress me."

"Charlie, I won't argue with you," said Buster.

"That's a good thing," Charlie said, relieved.

"Instead, I'll tear your head off in about one minute," said Buster.

"What're you going to say?" Annabel said to me.

"Charlie has that same effect on me, I can't help it," I said.

"There's ways to deal with people like you, Buster," said Charlie.

"You better think of one in a hurry," Buster said.

"Let's get away from here," said Annabel. She pushed Charlie away from Buster and kept pushing as Charlie played a mild charade of wishing to get around her and return. I was faintly surprised that Annabel hadn't allowed them to fight, or even pressed Charlie into it, but I supposed the embarrassment of seeing Charlie beaten up by a

62

photographer was stronger than any pleasure she might take in seeing Charlie bleed.

"Oh, Buster, you shouldn't have talked to them like that," Laureen said. "They've got a lot of friends, you know. They could do something terrible to you."

"Like what?" said Buster.

"I don't know. Anyway, there are people around here who give me a harder time than they do. One man phones in the middle of the night and calls me a Communist every time my cousin votes liberal on an issue. I get the feeling he would kill me."

"Who is he?" Buster asked.

"I won't tell you," she said, and then she named an oil man I didn't know. Dallas was full of oil men I'd never heard of, who were richer than I dreamed. I saw Laureen's husband Leroy talking to Charlie and Annabel Withers, laughing and slapping Charlie on the shoulder, and looking at us as all three of them laughed. Leroy had a facility for joking with people and improving their humors, which was quite a valuable talent for a consulting geologist.

Leroy came over to us.

"Charlie wants to destroy you, Buster. I suggested he just wait until you destroy yourself and then take credit for it. Couldn't be long," Leroy said. "John Lee, before you have time to beg, I'd like to inform you that, as program chairman for the month of November, I have booked you into a little talk before the Breakfast Brigade on November 22. Now don't bother to thank me. I know how grateful you must be. Actors love to make speeches, and how often does one have a chance to speak to the most powerful men in Dallas? You don't need to make a major address. Just a little talk will do. Don't mind people who shout from the crowd about your hair or your politics. They're a wonderful bunch of fellows, as I'm sure have learned by observing their decades of selfless public service."

"I don't have anything to say to the Breakfast Brigade," I said.

"You're too modest, John Lee," said Leroy. "The point is, you don't need to have anything to say. The Breakfast Brigade doesn't require it. In fact, the less you have to say the better they like it. Just get up and talk for a few minutes, and when they start coughing and shifting their chairs, sit down. And I've thought up a perfect topic for you to talk about without saying anything at all. You know our slogan at the Breakfast Brigade—'Selling Dallas to the World.' Well, you just take that as your theme, and talk about how much everybody in the world loves Dallas from an international TV and movie star's viewpoint. If you can't think of enough good things to say, I'll pass you some notes or ask questions. Now, please, John Lee, I've already told them you'd come."

"Why would they even want me? Most of those guys in the Breakfast Brigade detest me."

"No, no! That was before! Now you're the star of *Six Guns Across Texas!* They're giving you a chance, John Lee! Some of them love you. I love you myself. Laureen loves you. Buster we might ruin, true. But you we love. And you don't even have to be at the Breakfast Brigade until eight o'clock. That's eight in the morning, remember."

I had no idea what I might be doing in two months, or where in the world I might be, so I told Leroy I would speak to his club, and then I put it out of mind. But while I was talking to Leroy, Buster slipped out with Gretchen. I was left without a ride until a pro football player offered me a lift in his new Lincoln Continental. I said goodnight to Marianne, Margaret Franklin and the ballerina. "More interesting than one might have hoped," said the ballerina. Little Earl had not been seen for a while. Franklin walked out front with the pro football player and me. The lights of the house were on, and the fountain glowed. It was a warm night, dense with stars. As we stood talking and waiting for the car to be brought around, we heard sloshing in the lake and then oars rattling. Into the light, past the swans, floated a rowboat with red-haired Jerre the hooker pulling on the oars. Little Earl sat in the rear of the boat, holding up something we could not make out.

When the boat touched shore, Little Earl climbed out. He had with him a casting rod with a silver spoon for a lure, and he held up a glistening bass.

"Four pounds if it's a damn ounce," Little Earl grinned.

64

"Help me!" Jerre said.

The boat had drifted away from the bank. I caught the rope and pulled it to shore again, and Franklin grabbed Jerre's elbow as she jumped barefoot onto the grass.

"Honey, I'd like to eat you bones and all," Franklin said.

Jerre was clenching and unclenching her hands, sore and constricted from the oars.

"Don't anybody in Texas fuck any more?" she said.

7

The telephone woke me up. It was Dorothy saying I had to come over there quick, her mother was dead. I didn't know if I had really been asleep, because I was still dressed in my Brooks Brothers suit. My legs ached, and I seemed to be having a speed flash with sweating and palpitations. I said I would be there and hung up and tried to read my watch. It would not make sense. Washing my face I noticed that the top was off the Alka-Seltzer bottle. Every night before going to bed I took two Alka-Seltzers and three aspirins, and in the morning I took three aspirins, two Alka-Seltzers, two multivitamin capsules, a couple of vitamin E tablets, three or four vitamin C tablets. Depending on how I felt and what I had to do, I might also take a Dexamyl or Dexedrine spansule, 15 milligrams. But I made it a point of laying off the amphetamines for days or weeks at a time so my tolerance level wouldn't go out of sight.

However, I had swallowed so much Benzedrine in the past week that I knew I couldn't face Dorothy's dead mother without chemical assistance. So I mashed up a Dexamyl spansule to quicken the timed-release and took it with a cup of hot instant coffee to kick it off faster. Then I took another Dexamyl spansule that would come in later. I found myself idiotically whistling and looking at my teeth in the mirror. Again I remembered Dorothy and her dead mother. I had gotten involved with these medicinal rituals. I looked at my watch and saw that it was one A.M., earlier than I'd thought. I couldn't have been home for more than half an hour before Dorothy phoned me, but I could have believed any amount of time had passed.

I crept into Buster's room to get the keys to his station wagon off the bureau. Groping on the bureau in the dark, my fingers touched nothing. No keys. No billfold. No crumpled money. I turned on the light. Buster's room was in its usual condition. Sheets wadded up, mattress showing, piles of dirty clothes on the floor. It smelled like a locker room. At the foot of the bed lay the tennis shorts that he wore when he had no clean underwear. His jockstrap was hanging on a lamp. I opened the top bureau drawer, pushed aside a pair of pink silk panties and a brassiere, a pair of white athletic socks, a black sock that contained the matchbox of marijuana, a pair of pale blue panties and a pair of black silk panties. Buster was fond of panties.

Dorothy's dead mother. I kept looking in the bureau drawer for the keys to Buster's Morris Minor, but he had put them somewhere else or gotten rid of the car. I phoned a taxi. Thirty or forty minutes after Dorothy's call, I saw her sitting on the hood of her car under a streetlight on the corner by her mother's apartment building. I had expected that the police would be there, and the neighbors would be up, with the lights on. But it was dark and quiet.

"Where'd they take her?" I said.

"She's still inside," said Dorothy.

I looked at the dark brick building.

"Who'd you call?"

"Only you," she said.

"Well, my God, let's go call the police."

"I can't get in. I called you from the Waffle Shop."

"How do you know she's dead?" I said.

"The door is locked from the inside. She won't answer."

"Are you sure she hasn't got somebody in there with her?"

"This is my mother you're talking about," Dorothy said.

"All right. So what am I supposed to do?"

"Break in."

"I'll get shot for a burglar."

"Please, John Lee, just this once don't act like a butt."

The only tool I could find was a beer-can opener in the glove compartment of Dorothy's car. I tore a hole in the screen of a window in Dorothy's mother's bedroom. Threshing in the hedges and waiting for the people upstairs to shout at me or Dorothy's mother to blow my face off with a pistol, I unhooked the screen and took it off and heaved up the unlocked window. Then I got a knee up on the ledge and climbed inside. Crawling through the window, my hands immediately touched the mattress, and I was thinking how this was going to be a French farce with me coming in through the window and a lover hiding under the bed. Carefully I felt around on the bed and touched soft flesh. I shook the flesh gently, thinking to wake her, and realized that I had hold of Dorothy's mother by the breast and she had not moved.

Mumbling an apology, I crawled across her mother's body, got to my feet on the other side of the bed and switched on a lamp. In the pale light, her mother lay with her eyes shut and her mouth open, one shoulder strap of her nightgown pulled down and a breast revealed. She had a waxy look. I picked up an empty prescription bottle off the night table and opened the front door for Dorothy. She gasped when she saw her mother. "Goddamn you, Mother," she said. She went over and covered her mother's breast. I gave Dorothy the prescription bottle.

"This was for a hundred Seconals. It was nearly full," she said.

"I'll call the police," I said.

"Couldn't we just call a funeral home?"

Looking around for the telephone, I was struck by how drab and awful the bedroom was. Dorothy's mother looked like an older sister who'd had some tough times that showed in her face, but this was the room of a lonesome old woman. It had a pungent, sickly stench, as though the air had been all breathed up and only human exhausts were left. It was ridiculous for Dorothy to live in a place like this.

I saw the telephone on the floor by the bed. I put it on the night table and was starting to dial when it occurred to me to make sure her mother was dead. I couldn't feel a pulse, but I usually can't find my own. I bent down to her mouth and smelled vomit around her lips and discovered that she was breathing.

"Ina Mae," I said, shaking her. "Ina Mae, wake up."

"Are you crazy? Get your hands off her," said Dorothy.

Just then Ina Mae opened her eyes.

"Mother!" said Dorothy.

"We can take her to a hospital faster than we could wait for an ambulance," I said.

Dorothy wrapped her mother in a housecoat, and I dragged and carried Ina Mae out to the old blue Cadillac. She managed a kind of half-wit smile but could not talk. Dorothy sat in back with her and kept her awake by prodding and slapping and continually asking, "How many pills did you take, Mother? How long ago did you take them?" After several wrong turns, I drove to Parkland Hospital. It's the public hospital in Dallas, and it rises above the surrounding landscape off a broad road. I turned into the emergency entrance and parked about twenty yards from the emergency room. They were unloading somebody from an ambulance. Several police cars were parked in spaces allotted for them. Supporting Ina Mae between us, Dorothy and I walked her into the emergency room. By now it was nearly two-thirty. The bars had been closed for more than two hours, and the night's beer-joint casualties had passed through the emergency room into surgery or wards, or out again into jail or onto the street. The nurse at the desk had blood on the breast of her white uniform. We waited while she wrote down information given by a Negro boy who was holding a bloody rag to his forehead. She told him to sit on a bench where a dozen other people were waiting. The nurse looked at my hair and mustache for a long moment and then took in the vest and tie as well as Dorothy's clean young beauty.

"She swallowed a bunch of barbiturates," I said.

"Name?"

"Ina Mae Leclaire," said Dorothy.

"Age?"

"Thirty-eight."

"Address?"

Dorothy told her. I looked at Ina Mae, who was gazing at the nurse through half-shut eyes with a tiny smile, like an imbecile watching a kitten. I had spent years around emergency rooms with 16-millimeter movie equipment when I was a TV news reporter and cameraman, but I had never gotten accustomed to the way nurses persisted with their routine in the parade of agony.

"Are you responsible for her expenses?" the nurse asked me.

"She has Blue Cross," said Dorothy.

The nurse nodded. Another nurse appeared with a wheelchair. They put Ina Mae in it and pushed her off down a corridor. Dorothy tried to follow, but the desk nurse stopped her.

"Johnny, we got an attempted suicide here," the nurse said to a cop.

The cop looked at the form and began copying the information onto his clipboard. He was wearing a black leather jacket, and his cap was pushed to the back of his head, as if he were playing fighter pilot. A pistol and a flashlight hung off his belt, and the leather handle of a slapjack stuck out of a hip pocket. The cop peered curiously at me.

"You her husband?" he said.

"I'm her daughter," said Dorothy.

"How come'd she do this?"

"I don't know."

The outside doors swung open. An old man was carried on a stretcher into an examining room. His legs looked like sausages that had split open. He was sobbing, and his arms stuck straight up into the air, fingers curled, reaching for something. The desk nurse followed him into the examining room with her papers.

"Not even cold yet and he's caught his robe on fire at the bathroom stove. His plastic pajamas stuck to his legs," the cop said as the old man's ashy face went past. "Be a lot of burns soon as we get a norther."

The cop was making friendly conversation.

"You got something against barbers?" he asked me.

69

"I like barbers," I said.

"Oh. I thought he had something against barbers," the cop said, grinning at Dorothy.

A black man walked in through the swinging doors. His eyes were wild and yellow. Blood covered the front of his shirt and soaked his pants legs, and his shoes squished with it when he walked.

"They shot me," he said to the desk nurse. "I 'bout to die."

An intern urged the man to lie down on a wheeled bed. A nurse unbuttoned his shirt. I saw the look that passed between the nurse and the intern. The man had been hit by a shotgun. His stomach had exploded. A Negro orderly came out with a bucket and began mopping up blood.

"Who shot you, boy?" the cop said.

"Raymond."

"Raymond who?"

"Raymond over at the Polka Dot Club."

"What's your name?" said the desk nurse.

They had wheeled the man into the examining room beside the old man with the burned legs and were sticking tubes and needles into him. I moved over to where I could see in the door, but Dorothy turned away.

"Jesse Lee Jones," the black man said.

"Your address?" said the nurse.

"What you say?"

"Where do you stay at?" the cop said.

"I live with my auntie."

"How come'd Raymond shoot you?" the cop said.

"Doan know."

"You messing with Raymond's girl?"

"Nawsuh."

"Tell the truth, boy."

"I tell de troo."

"Where does your auntie stay?" said the nurse.

"On Evans Street."

"What number on Evans Street?" said the nurse.

70

"Raymond shot me."

"We'll take care of Raymond," said the cop. "What number on Evans Street do you stay at?"

"Doan know. By the bus stop."

Then he died. The nurses and the intern began unhooking their tubes. They pulled the sheet over the black man's face. The cop phoned headquarters downtown and said, "If you got a car handy go by the Polka Dot Club and see if they can find Raymond with a shotgun."

The cop came back over to us.

"Your mama's gonna be okay," he said to Dorothy.

The telephone rang and the desk nurse beckoned to the cop.

"It's that new kid from the *Herald* that stays up all night," the nurse said.

"Yeah, it's a gunshot," the cop said into the phone. "Deceased name is Jesse Lee Jones. Age unknown. Address unknown. Forget it, kid, it's a nigger deal." He hung up the receiver.

"If they put ever' nigger killing in the paper we wouldn't have room for the comics," the cop said to us.

A Negro woman was standing at the desk. She wore a uniform of some kind, hotel maid's perhaps.

"Talk louder," the desk nurse said.

" 'Quire 'bout Jesse Lee Jones," said the woman.

"You his girl friend?" the cop said.

"Yassuh. His wife."

"He's dead," said the cop.

The woman nodded and stared at the wall behind the nurse.

"You know Raymond at the Polka Dot Club?"

"Nawsuh."

"Wouldn't tell me if you did," the cop said.

The woman began to shake and emit squeaking noises. I remembered a night at the police station when Buster and I had walked into an interrogation room where two uniformed cops were whipping an old black man with their belts. He had dropped his pants and the belts would smack against his brown ass. After each blow the cops would ask which of them hit hardest. No matter what the old man answered, he was in for another belting. In high school our two football coaches used to do the same thing to us, except they used boards and did it in the Ping-Pong room and people went home from these sporting occasions with blood seeping down their legs.

"Miss Leclaire?"

A doctor in a white smock had come along the corridor and walked up to Dorothy.

"Your mother says she swallowed about eighty Seconals, but she threw up most of it. We pumped out her stomach, anyway. Now a staff psychiatrist has to talk to her. That's required. It'll be another half hour at the most."

Dorothy and I sat down on a bench. Five car wreck victims were carried in. Three were teen-agers, one a dying girl. A traffic cop who came in with them said they had been driving more than a hundred on the Central Expressway and had hit a truck. Dorothy glanced at me. A pregnant Mexican woman entered with her husband and five children, a number she was minutes away from increasing to six. A thin white woman, looking demented, came through the swinging doors with a little boy under her arm. The boy was about four, and his head dangled like that of a dead chicken.

"My boy's hurt," the woman said.

The desk nurse rushed around and laid the boy on a bed.

"His neck's broke," the cop said.

"He's hurt bad," agreed the woman.

"How'd this happen?" the cop said.

"He got his head caught in the chain on the porch swing. It was wropped all around his neck," said the woman.

The cop looked at his watch.

"What was he doing swinging on the porch in the middle of the night?" the cop said.

"He got hurt about supper time. I thought he'd be all right. But he never come to."

As a TV news cameraman I used to shoot film of the relatives of children who were very recently deceased, and sometimes ask for photographs, old snapshots or studio portraits of the kids smiling and dressed up in their birthday clothes. I competed with newspaper reporters for these photographs, and more than once I went into somebody's house and stole every photo of the dead child I could find to prevent other TV or newspapermen from getting them. This was what we called good journalism of the old Chicago school, and when that stolen photo would appear on the TV screen for a couple of seconds I was supposed to feel good about it, and sometimes I did. We were supposed to be proud of being professional, as much as the cop in the emergency room. One afternoon a little boy had been run over in front of his house. A reporter from the *Herald* walked through the little boy's blood without knowing it and tracked the blood onto the front porch, where he asked the mother: "How old was your son and how do you spell his name?" The mother collapsed. I told my ex-wife Geraldine about this later and laughed with the usual light-hearted cynicism I put on in the face of events that were incomprehensible. I remarked to Geraldine that the reporter was a real pro. "He's a monster," she said.

"I've got to go outside, Dorothy. I don't like it in here," I said.

"I'll wait here," she said.

I went into the emergency parking area and sat on the fender of Dorothy's car. Many windows of the hospital were lit up. Another ambulance stopped at the emergency room door, and a sheeted mound was carried in. I sensed a presence and looked to the right. Two Negro boys in their teens were standing between me and a pickup truck. I felt a prickling unease.

"You got a cigarette?" one said.

"I don't smoke," I said.

"No shit?"

"Quit a year ago."

"Hey man, isn't you on the TV?"

"Yeah."

"*Six Guns Across Texas.* You is a bad mothah!"

"That's on TV," I said.

"Nobody doan fuck with you or he ass has had it!"

73

"Where your gun at?" one asked.

"Don't need a gun," I said.

"Shoot! In Dallas? In Dallas you need a gun, man. They's lotsa bad mothahs here."

"They don't mess with me," I said.

"I guess they doan!"

"What you here for? You shoot somebody?" one asked.

"He say he doan have no gun!"

"Shoot! He could of thowed it away!"

"If he shoot somebody he wouldn't hang around the hospital where he at!"

"Finish him off, man!"

"This cat doan miss!"

One of them reached into the pocket of his shiny red windbreaker and handed me a switchblade knife.

"Lookit that baby," he said.

I touched the button and the blade sprang out.

"Nice," I said.

"Man, I seen you fight that big Indin that time when you both had your shirts off and they was just one knife throwed in the middle of the circle. He got you down and like to stobbed your throat and you kicked him off and he grabbed a spear and throwed it at you"—both boys had fixed me with a gape—"and you taken that knife and uh! uh! uh!"

I closed the blade and gave the knife back to him.

"Where your horse at?"

"Out in the country," I said.

"Do he buck?"

"If he's mad," I said.

"Do he thow you off?"

"Shoot, thow him off?"

"He never has thrown me off," I said.

"See!"

"You ever been in South Dallas?"

"I've been through there," I said.

74

"But you doan stay! Whooo, they's bad mothahs out there!"

"Is that where you live?" I said.

"That's where we stays at, man."

"You go to school?" I said.

"Sure! It cool!"

"Everything cool, baby!"

"On TV you the coolest of the cool."

"The baddest of the bad."

"The meanest of the mean."

"The coolest baby I ever seen."

"See you face on the TV screen."

"What you dream?"

"Meanest of the mean!"

They started laughing, and each of them slapped me on the palm. They walked off across the parking area in their blue jeans and tennis shoes. On the back of the red windbreaker it said TARANTULAS. They stopped and waved at me and then hurried on as a police car came up the driveway. I sat there for a while longer. Finally I went back to the emergency room. Ina Mae was sitting in a wheelchair looking embarrassed. The psychiatrist was stroking his mustache and talking to Dorothy.

"... emotional problems," I heard him say. "Not uncommon these days, I'm afraid. I gave her some tranquilizers and a prescription for some more. See that she takes them every day, and she'll be all right."

Ina Mae tried to stand up but was still too weak. I wheeled her out to the car.

"I didn't have time to put on make-up, John Lee," she said.

I lifted her into the back seat. Dorothy got in beside her. Driving home, Dorothy started crying.

"There, there, baby, don't cry," her mother said.

"Mama, you didn't have to take those pills. Why'd you do that?" said Dorothy.

"My stomach hurt so bad. I've got a rupture in my stomach. You don't know how bad the pain is."

"Mama, you scared me. Please don't do that any more."

"John Lee," said her mother, "if anything happens to me, you take good care of my little girl."

"Oh, goddamn it, shut up, Ina Mae," I said. "You've made trouble for Dorothy ever since I've known you. Why the hell don't you try to be a good mother for a change?"

"I'll get out of her life. I'll leave her alone," said Ina Mae.

Now they were both crying.

"Mama, don't say that," Dorothy said.

"John Lee's right. I've done nothing but make trouble for my little girl."

"John Lee doesn't know what he's talking about."

"John Lee's so good and decent," Ina Mae blubbered. "You be nice to him, baby. There's not many good men in this world. Oh, John Lee, take care of my baby."

I felt like a swine and a fool simultaneously.

Between us we walked Ina Mae up the sidewalk and into her apartment. I had left the lights on and the door open. We sat her on her bed. An ashtray had been knocked over and ashes and cigarette butts lay on the floor. She lit another cigarette and looked at me with a gentle smile as the heavy tranquilizer blew fog into her head.

"John Lee so good to my baby," she said.

Dorothy took off Ina Mae's housecoat. Ina Mae toppled back onto the bed with her legs spread. Dorothy removed the cigarette from her fingers.

"Mama, don't you smoke any more till I get back. I'm going to take John Lee home," said Dorothy.

"I'll call a taxi," I said.

"Take him home. I'll be all right," said Ina Mae.

"Stay with your mother," I said.

"I'll be back in twenty minutes," said Dorothy. "You stay right there, Mama, and don't smoke."

We listened to music on the radio and didn't say anything until Dorothy stopped the car in front of Buster's apartment. The sky was gray and pink. A newspaper boy rode past on a bicycle. Papers thumped against walls and bounced on lawns. Down the block an old lady was walking her poodle in the dew.

"Thanks," Dorothy said.

"Okay," I said and pushed on the handle.

"John Lee, I want to ask you something."

I looked around at her.

"Would you marry me?" she said.

Uncombed and weary in this early light, Dorothy seemed very fragile.

"I'll sign a paper," she said. "You write an agreement that I don't get any alimony or community property if we break up, and you don't have to ever be responsible for my mother or any of my debts. I'll sign it, and I promise I'll be good. I'll work hard and make you a good wife. I won't lie, I won't run around, I won't fuss. I'll cook. I'll get a job and make my own money."

Her eyelids were trembling. Tears formed and began to move slowly down her cheeks.

"I can't marry you, Dorothy," I said.

"Don't you love me?"

"I'm very strongly attracted to you, I know that. I can't seem to leave you alone. Most of the time I like being with you, and we've . . ."

"Don't make a damn speech," she said. "Talk real."

"I don't want to get married. Not right now."

"But I want to be married," Dorothy said in a kind of wail.

She put her head down on the wheel and opened up with a gusher of tears that lasted for perhaps a minute. Idiotically, I patted her head as if she were a sorrowing pup. I didn't know what to do and wanted for this to have been a fantasy.

Dorothy sat up and wiped her eyes with the backs of her fingers.

"Will you call me?" she said.

"Sure."

I watched the blue Cadillac turn the corner. As I opened the door of the apartment I heard someone clattering pans in the kitchen and figured Buster had just got in. Stepping inside, I smelled mud and sweet burning herbs, a very powerful odor.

"I'm using your oven to dry some grass," said Jingo.

She came out of the kitchen wiping her hands on an apron that she had put on over black slacks and high-heeled sandals.

"Where's Buster?"

"In his room with a German head. They are really stoned."

I listened at Buster's door but could hear nothing. His lights were out.

"Want a drink?" said Jingo.

"No, thanks."

"Smoke some dope?"

"No."

"You look tired. Let me put you to bed."

I shrugged and went into my room and sat on the bed. Someone had straightened it up and folded back the sheets. Humming merrily, Jingo undressed me while I receded into stupor. I tried to think about Dorothy's proposition, but it would not stay in my mind. Instead, I thought about the sheik. The amphetamine crashed against my plummeting spirit. Feeling as though my breath had enough weariness in it to poison a pigeon, I got between the sheets and lay in a coma, unable to speak or sleep. Sinking off at last I felt Jingo climb in beside me and begin rubbing my back.

Book Two

8

There is nothing like a divorce to put the spring back into a man's step. When I finally broke up with Geraldine after two long separations and passionate reunions, and a series of hysterical screaming lunatic bouts that left us both with trembling sickness, I found myself walking with a bounce and looking forward to things. There were strange sensations, unexpected pleasures. In the mornings in my own apartment I would turn on all the lights and play the radio loud and walk around talking to myself at the top of my voice, knowing there was no angry Geraldine to awake. It was like being released from a sentence. Once I got accustomed to the idea that I had a full pardon rather than a parole, I began a celebration.

But it took a while for the feeling of freedom not to be constantly interrupted by anxiety over having somehow failed our little girl Caroline as well as Geraldine and myself. I would have a period of exuberance and then suddenly be crushed by remorse. Buster was going through the same thing in the same way at the same time, and so were other people I knew. Nobody died from it.

Though three years had passed now, I still felt guilty and confused about Caroline. I wanted to see her, and I dreaded it. After sleeping until late in the afternoon, I dialed Geraldine's number, hoping she or her husband Herbert wouldn't answer.

"Hello," said Caroline.

"Hello, Caroline."

"Hi."

"This is daddy."

"Daddy who?" she said.

"Daddy Wallace, you silly kid."

"Grandaddy?"

"John Lee Wallace, your genuine father."

"Daddy!"

"May I come over and see you?"

"Are you in California?"

"I'm in Dallas."

"Oh yes, come on over. We're going out to dinner. I'll ask if you can go."

"I couldn't do that," I said.

"Oh."

"You know how it is."

"Hurry over, then."

She sounded so much older than I had expected. I carry pictures in my head of people as they were at a certain point during my experience of them, and a shock is required for the pictures to be brought up to date. Not having seen someone in a while and then seeing him drastically older, as had happened with Franklin, will change the picture. But my picture of Buster was still him in his middle twenties, and I thought of myself the same way. In my mind Geraldine was about twenty, and Caroline was about six. In fact,

Caroline was twelve and Geraldine was thirty. Geraldine had gradua-
ted from high school at fifteen and married me at eighteen.

Driving out to Geraldine's house in Buster's Morris Minor, I got
caught in the six o'clock traffic on the Central Expressway. For a
while before I went on camera as a face, which meant I had to be at
the studio for broadcasts at six and ten in the evening, I worked an
eight-to-five shift in the news department. Geraldine and I had moved
from our apartment, after another reunion, into a house we bought
in North Dallas on my GI Bill. The house was a pleasant little
eighteen-thousand-seven-hundred-and-fifty-dollar number, gray brick
with white trim, central heat and air, on an unsodded lot among
dozens of similar houses. I liked the house all right, but in periods of
little traffic it took me fifteen minutes to drive home from the station,
and in rush hour it took thirty minutes or more. Having lived in Los
Angeles, this now seemed laughably easy. But in that earlier time I
would drive about halfway home and break the journey at a place
called Gordo's, where I would always find Buster or someone I knew
drinking cold draught beer, and later there would be a call to Geraldine explaining that I was late to dinner again. Sometimes I didn't
call.

I almost turned off to Gordo's now, but instead kept the small black
car pointed into the exhaust smoke of thousands of cars edging along
the expressway. We crept past the Southern Methodist University exit
and the Dr. Pepper plant, and the traffic picked up a bit. I cut off the
expressway further on, taking a back road through a village and past
farms that had been surrounded but not yet destroyed by the city. At
the top of the hill on Geraldine's street, I stopped and watched the
sunset for a few minutes. Then I drove on to the house and parked
at the curb. Herbert's Volkswagen and Geraldine's Chevrolet convertible were in the driveway. Bad news. But I noted with some pleasure
that the lawn was thick and green, neatly mowed and trimmed, the
hedges clipped and the flowerbeds without weeds. Geraldine must
have kept Herbert working.

Caroline jumped into my arms on the front porch. I kissed her on
the mouth, on both cheeks and both eyes, and hugged her till she

grunted. I gave her a sweater I'd bought in a shop in Beverly Hills and a box of candy I'd grabbed in a drugstore near Buster's apartment.

"Your mustache feels so funny!" she said. "And your hair! Why is it so long?"

"This is the way I wear it on TV. Don't you watch my show?"

"Mother doesn't let me. It's too violent."

Caroline was growing into a tall girl with blue eyes, a few freckles and reddish-blonde hair. She was wearing Levi's, loafers and a boy's shirt. She led me into the den that I'd hired a carpenter to convert from a garage with the notion that I'd start a film studio in there. Before I could get around to it, Geraldine had packed me a bag and I was looking for another place to live.

Herbert arose slowly from my leather reclining chair and clomped across the linoleum floor with a good-natured grin to shake my hand.

"You turned into a beatnik," he said.

"California influence, Herbert. We get affected."

"I guess that's the truth," he said enthusiastically.

"Hello, John Lee. How have you been?" said Geraldine, being at her warmest. She was seated at her desk. She pushed her horn-rimmed glasses up onto her head and smiled at me.

"You're looking very handsome, Geraldine," I said.

"Thank you, John Lee. You're looking very hairy."

Geraldine had been doing pretty well making local TV commercials since before we were divorced. She had the kind of wholesome-young-mother appearance that sponsors thought sold bread and refrigerators, and there was a vibrating sensuality about her that attracted attention. When I met her she was a seventeen-year-old junior at the University of Texas and had a summer job as an actress in a repertory company in New York. She had several offers of screen tests, but she turned them down and got pregnant.

"Caroline, put that candy away. John Lee, you shouldn't give her candy," Geraldine said.

"There's just five pounds of it," I said.

"She's already needing two thousand dollars' worth of dental work," said Geraldine.

"Can I get you a drink?" Herbert asked.

"Sure can, Herbert. Scotch and water."

"We haven't touched a drop ourselves in over eight months, but we keep it for company," said Herbert.

"In over a year," Geraldine said.

"I thought it was eight months."

"It's a year," she said.

"I never have got around to quitting, myself," I said.

"I don't expect you ever will," she said.

"Daddy, thank you," said Caroline.

"For what, honey?" Herbert said from the kitchen.

"No, my other daddy. Thank you for the sweater."

I hugged her again, and she showed the sweater to Geraldine.

"Isn't it nice?" Geraldine said sweetly.

Herbert brought me the drink.

"That strong enough?" he said.

"No," I said.

"John Lee likes big drinks," said Geraldine.

"Don't see how you do it, John Lee." Herbert chuckled and sat down in my leather reclining chair. "Hey, honey, that's a cute sweater. Come let me see it."

Caroline crawled into his lap, and he made the chair recline to the three-quarter position.

"Are you still in that Western?" asked Geraldine.

"I guess not," I said.

"I hope they didn't fire you," she said.

"They haven't so far."

"What would you do? You're so restless. You're not really trained for anything useful."

Geraldine had a genius for making the worst of a bad situation. To a good situation she could bring such a withering lack of cheer that everyone around her began to feel mysteriously nervous and constipated. She was often in a mood to create problems where there had been none. If three couples were going to dinner and five people wanted Italian food, Geraldine required chile. The weather was always too cold or too hot. Being married to her had been somewhat like having a teen-age daughter forever demanding something she didn't want. More than a year after our divorce, while she was trying to decide whether to marry Herbert, she came to see me in California. She refused to stay in my pink stucco house. I had made my first film and hired her a bungalow at the Beverly Hills Hotel, which I thought was what a movie actor was supposed to do. All day while I was busy she locked herself in the bungalow. She would hardly go out at night or venture as far as the Polo Lounge. I doubt if she saw the swimming pool. I took her to a party where she got drunk and passed out in a bathroom and couldn't remember meeting Paul Newman. In less than a week she went home and married Herbert. Looking at her now, it was difficult to believe she and I had ever been married and yet almost impossible to believe we weren't still. I could recall her body very well, and the excitement she aroused in me when she wished. Looking at her now, she trapped me for an instant with her eyes and desire rushed back. But having lived apart from her long enough to get out of the habit, I could no more conceive of living with her than of never seeing her again.

"Sit down, sit down," Herbert said.

"I don't see a chair," I said.

"Sorry. I'll get you one from the kitchen," said Herbert.

I watched him struggling to climb out of my leather reclining chair.

"I'll get it," I said.

As I had found no place to put down my glass, I took it into the kitchen with me and spied the Scotch bottle on the drainboard. It was a cheap brand with a high content of fusel oil, but slightly better than nothing at all. I gave my glass some color. The kitchen was oddly bare. The round oak table that was used for dining had been taken apart and placed in a corner. The chairs were stacked beside it. I took a bar stool and returned to the den.

"Getting rid of the table?" I said.

"No, just packing up," said Herbert.

"We're moving to San Diego," Caroline said.

She seemed neither pleased nor saddened by this information, as though she had got used to it, but I was stunned.

86

"When?" I said.

"Tomorrow," said Caroline.

"Not tomorrow, really," Geraldine said. "Tomorrow we're going to Houston to see my mother. Herbert has vacation time coming."

"We'll go to Galveston," said Herbert. "You'll like Galveston, honey."

"I've been to Galveston," Caroline said.

"I took her to Galveston," I said.

"Actually, I took her. You just went along complaining all the way," said Geraldine.

"I drove, I took her swimming, I took her fishing, I paid the bills," I said.

"You haven't changed, John Lee. You always remember things backwards. I think the truth leaks out of holes in your head," said Geraldine.

The difference in our views of events used to alarm me. A man could fall down in the street before our eyes and break a sack of eggs, and Geraldine's vision of what had transpired would compare to mine as a giraffe to a zebra. Listening to her recount incidents so vastly removed from what I believed them to be, I used to think I was losing my mind. But I was working every day alongside reporters and photographers who saw most events approximately the way I did. If I hadn't had this confirmation, there was a time when Geraldine might have convinced me I was crazy. Perhaps her vision was true enough to suit her, but mine was the one that worked best. Buster called her The Hassler. He said she liked making trouble and had been furious since long before I met her. But after you had seen her eyes blur and heard her begin to shriek an argument over an unimportant matter, it became questionable how much enjoyment she was getting out of it.

"You both took me to Galveston. I remember it," Caroline said.

"You were only four," said Geraldine.

"She was six," I said. "It was the summer they threw us out of that apartment building where Buster and Alma lived across from us."

"It was at least two summers before that," said Geraldine.

87

"I'm sure getting hungry," Herbert said. "How about some fried chicken, honey?"

"I'm hungry, too," said Caroline.

"I'll get my coat," Geraldine said.

"It's warm out," I said.

"Then I'm sure I'll need a coat," said Geraldine.

Geraldine and I both started laughing. For a moment one of the forms of eros that had kept us together for nine years returned, and we laughed at ourselves.

"Bless you, John Lee, I hope you're all right," she said, touching my knee on her way out of the room. She looked at me as if she had just put laundry in the washing machine and roast in the oven and was ready to make love all afternoon on clean sheets in front of the mirror with the bedroom curtains blowing and the sound of neighbor ladies' voices coming from their own backyards.

"I'll need to put on my new sweater," said Caroline.

Herbert lowered the chair with a thunk. Caroline ran after her mother, and Herbert looked at me with an affable, puzzled grin, his usual expression. I crossed my legs and wished I had a cigarette to fiddle with.

"Why did you decide to move to San Diego all the sudden?" I said.

"You're wrong on two counts there, John Lee."

"Geraldine doesn't need a conversational replacement. Just answer the question."

"Two questions, actually," smiled Herbert. "One, I didn't decide. I'm being transferred. Two, it's not sudden. We've known for sixty days."

"Why didn't you tell me?"

"You hadn't called," Herbert said.

"You could have written," I said.

"So could you. Just sending the check every month, well, you know, we like to hear a little something too, some news. Caroline thinks the world of you. She's a wonderful girl. Don't you think Geraldine is doing a great job of bringing her up?"

"Seems to be," I said.

"Now we'll be closer to you, too. You can drive down from Los Angeles every few weeks to see Caroline. Take her to the zoo. Really be like a father. San Diego's a great town for a kid, with all that water. And you can be skiing in snow in an hour, I hear."

"What kind of work do you do, Herbert?"

"I thought you knew." He seemed mildly offended. "I'm an acoustical physicist. I work for the Navy in underwater research."

"I had the idea you were on the faculty or something at SMU."

"That's for appearances. We do work through the university, and I have an office over there, but our funds come from the Navy. I spend most of my time in one of the rivers around here or up at our little station on Lake Texhoma."

"Doing what?" I said.

"It's sort of secret stuff, actually," said Herbert. "But I can tell you we're working on underwater detection devices, new types of sonar for the most part, to use in Vietnam. Primarily in the Mekong River. Are you familiar with the Mekong?"

I shook my head.

"It's a very large river. Has a great deal of mud and silt in it, like Lake Texhoma. I thought you might have seen the Mekong. I remember you went to the Far East to make a movie. Did you see the river in Bangkok?" I nodded. "Well, it's like that, a very big river. I imagine I'll be going over to Vietnam to conduct some tests before too much longer."

"What the hell for?" I said.

"To see if our new devices work."

"That's not what I mean."

"Oh, why Vietnam? Mine not to reason why, John Lee. I'm not a politician or a soldier. It's none of my business why the Navy wants these things. My job is to do the best I can in my own field."

"You could get killed over there."

"You do like to dramatize things," he laughed.

Geraldine came back with a coat over her shoulders. She had put on lipstick and some pearls that I had given her.

"I'm sorry you can't go to dinner with us, John Lee," she said. "But we're going over to Aunt Ruth's. There'll be dozens of cousins and kinfolks. I remember how you hated them all."

"I didn't hate them," I said.

"I'm sure they'd be glad to hear that. They think you despise them."

"I was damn nice to those people. I didn't mind them a bit."

"Let's not argue," Geraldine said. "The fried chicken is waiting."

"I love fried chicken. Also black-eyed peas and cream gravy and hot biscuits," I said.

"Boy, me too, and banana-cream pie," said Herbert.

"John Lee, you are not going with us to Aunt Ruth's. You don't even really want to go with us," Geraldine said.

"When are you coming back from Houston?" I said.

"I don't know," she said, "At any rate we'll only be here one day while the movers load up. But when we get to San Diego, you can come down and see Caroline."

"I may not go back to Los Angeles," I said.

"What in God's name might you do?"

"I'm going to shoot my own documentary movie about Texas."

"But Texas is getting so urban," she said. "So much of it is highways and electric wires and little brick buildings, and the rest of it is just playlike Texas. What will you do when nobody wants to see this movie?"

"I might try to get a job down in Austin, teaching journalism or in the TV department at the university."

"John Lee, you are truly perverse," said Geraldine. "For years I tried to get you to go into teaching, and you wouldn't hear of it. You told me journalism and communications teachers were leeches. Then you insisted on moving to California even though your daughter was staying in Dallas. Now your daughter is moving to California, and you say you might move back to Texas and teach journalism. What kind of lunatic is in control of you?"

"You mean right now?"

"I suppose the craft of acting will recover from this loss. You never did work very hard on technique," she said.

"I thought you didn't watch me."

"I've seen you," said Geraldine.

"Daddy, look at my new sweater," Caroline said.

"Very pretty, honey," said Herbert.

"You look terrific," I said.

We both spoke at once.

"Do you still run around with your rich friends—Franklin and those people?" said Geraldine.

"Now and then."

"Those people don't like you, John Lee. They just use you as an object of fun," she said.

The only time Little Earl met Geraldine, he thought she was an airline stewardess and offered her a trip to his island.

"It doesn't matter to me what they think they're using me for," I said.

"Do I detect that you feel superior to the arrangement?" she said.

"There's no arrangement," I said.

"Certainly there is," said Geraldine. "Everything is an arrangement."

I excused myself and went to the bathroom. All but inundated by nostalgia, I turned left at the hallway without thinking and went into Geraldine's bath instead of into the guest bath next to Caroline's room. This bathroom had been the main reason I had bought the house. It was freakily large for a tract-house bathroom and had a big shower cabinet with a bench where I used to sit in the mornings, recovering from Gordo's or elsewhere while the shower hosed me down. Geraldine and I had made love in that shower cabinet many times, slippery soapy with her climbing up and clinging on me like a monkey to a palm tree. I saw her shower cap hanging over the towel rack. Surely she could not have had the same one for all these years, but it did look the same. I recognized one of the towels as the same, and the Kleenex holder was the same and the electric toothbrush that had briefly worked was still on the wall where I'd put it. There were the same scales on the floor. Geraldine still bought pink soap that smelled the way it used to. Then I looked in the mirror, and I wasn't the same person who used to live here. That person had been a little thinner, and saner looking and much younger.

I made a routine investigation of her medicine cabinet. No pills of interest. Geraldine opposed swallowing chemicals of any sort. Every bottle I noted in the cabinet had been prescribed for Caroline or Herbert. Coming out of the bathroom I stopped to look at the large bed with the hand-carved posts and the needlepoint spread that I remembered well. Through the window I could hear women talking in the dark alley by the gas meter. They were strangers. I thought of a quick search for the nude Polaroids of Geraldine, but they probably would have been destroyed by now, and I wouldn't have wanted her to catch me looking through her bureau drawers.

Caroline was waiting for me inside the front door.

"Mom and Dad are in the car. They want me to turn off the lights and lock the door after you come out," she said.

I bent down and kissed her.

"It was good to see you, Caroline. I love you very much," I said.

"When I was a little kid I used to think you didn't," she said.

She closed the door after me and pulled hard till it clicked.

"Bye, Daddy," she said. "I love you, too."

She ran to Herbert's Volkswagen. She was tall for her age and kind of awkward. Herbert began backing his car down the driveway as I walked across the lawn toward the curb. Geraldine and Caroline waved at me. I could see them in the porch light. Caroline's face pushed against the window, her lips mashed in a kiss. Halfway along the block, Herbert's taillights came on. Ten miles or so to the south I could see the lights of downtown Dallas. I stood at the curb for a while. It was a very quiet neighborhood. I thought a visit to Gordo's might be in order.

9

"**W**ell," said Jimmy Widgin, the columnist, "it used to be that when you came to town you'd call me up, and we'd have a drink, and we'd play like friends. And now I have to hear from other people that you're in town, planning to make a big secret feature film about Texas that you won't even tell me about. You know what I think the trouble is?"

"What?" I said into the phone.

"Dope. Ever since the night you and Buster tried to turn me on and I wouldn't do it, you haven't been the same toward me. Look, John Lee, I have a good time drinking Scotch. I don't need marijuana. Why should I expose myself to getting arrested or becoming an addict? Drinking Scotch is legal."

Jingo had opened the paper to Jimmy Widgin's column and was pointing out the item with an orange fingernail. *John Lee Wallace,* it said, *is hiding out in Dallas, working on the script for a big feature film about all us folks. It's such a hush-hush project that the TV star of "Six Guns Across Texas" won't even let his old hometown pals in on exactly what he's got planned. . . .*

"I think it's a damn sorry thing when dope can come between friends," Jimmy said over the phone. "You tell me that stuff is not addicting, but you're high all the time and you don't run around any more with people who don't smoke it."

"Where did you get that item about my movie?" I said.

"It's true, isn't it? Wasn't all that long ago I wouldn't have had to print an item about you that I hadn't checked. Because I'd have had the item out of your own mouth. To show you how things have deteriorated between us, now I have to get the item out of the trades."

"The what?"

"I saw it in *Variety*. Also Norman Feldman phoned and asked me about it. He said you talked about it on the *Tonight* show. Are you telling me it isn't true?"

"Not exactly," I said. "I just hadn't thought of it in the terms you used."

"So come to lunch today at the Kings Club and give me the inside."

"I can't do it."

"Look here, you prick, you know I won't print it if you don't want me to. But I don't want to read about it first in the other paper. I'll meet you at the Kings Club at one o'clock."

"I've already got a lunch date today," I said.

"Who with?"

"Big Earl," I said. "His secretary called before you did."

After a moment of silence, Jimmy said, "If you're not going to be friendly, at least I'd rather you didn't tell me lies."

I had no idea why I had been summoned, but it was true. I drove to Big Earl's house in Jingo's bronze Cadillac convertible with JINGO on the driver's door in gold letters an inch high. Big Earl lived in an unlikely location for one of the world's richest men. Rounding a curve in the midst of a worn-out neighborhood of small red-brick and white-frame houses with bicycles and junked red wagons lying among cedar trees in front, and two or three old cars parked in nearly every driveway, you suddenly came upon a big Tudor house on a hill surrounded by a high cyclone fence. Timbers crisscrossed through cream plaster and disappeared into brick walls. Above the bay windows and high gables, dozens of chimney pots of various sizes rose up like organ pipes. The flag of the United States and the Lone Star flag of Texas flew from twin poles in the yard, beside a brass cannon aiming out across the neighborhood. I stopped at the gate. From a speaker, a quavery voice said: "Who are you and what do you want?"

"John Lee Wallace. I want to see Big Earl."

"What for?"

"I don't know. He sent for me."

The wire gate unlatched itself and swung open. I drove slowly up the long semicircle of gravel, being careful not to collide with the deer, goats, peacocks and squirrels that roamed beneath oaks on acres of grass. An old Hudson, an old Buick and a shiny new black Chevrolet stood beside the house in the driveway and on the grass. As I got out of the car, Mr. Clwyd, Big Earl's secretary, came down from a side porch. He was tall and gray and wore a black suit and black tie.

"We're so pleased you could come," said Mr. Clwyd.

"I admit your call was a surprise," I said.

"He's waiting for you on the veranda, other side of the house," said Mr. Clwyd, glancing inside Jingo's car to be sure I had come alone.

I walked across in front of the house past the tall, scroll-carved double doors of the main entrance. On the west side of the house, a long veranda had been tucked in. The old man was sitting in a rocking chair looking out at his animals and at the rooftops among the trees below his hill. A tiny white poodle with a blue and pink collar started yapping. Big Earl paid no attention to the poodle or to me. He picked up a pair of binoculars and peered in the direction of the front gate. I could see a car down there. Then he lifted a hand mike from beside his chair and said, "Who are you and what do you want?"

"Who said that?" said a voice from a speaker in the wall.

"Who are you and what do you want?" Big Earl repeated.

"I come to see Big Earl."

"For what purpose?"

"It's about a fund for sending missionaries to Red China."

"Big Earl is out of the country," Big Earl said.

"I seen him this morning."

"He left since then. Go away."

"This is something Big Earl would like to help on," the voice said.

Big Earl turned a switch on the microphone and said, "Mr. Clood, there's a man down at the gate bothering me."

Big Earl put down the microphone and smiled gently.

"Hush, little Ginger Pops, this nice fellow won't hurt us," he said to the yapping poodle.

"Is that what you call him—Mr. Clood?" I said.

"That's his name," said Big Earl.

"Francis Franklin calls him Mr. Clyde."

"Now then, Francis Franklin is an excellent person, but he doesn't know everything in the world, does he?" said Big Earl. He smiled again, most gently, almost like a dear contented baby. His skin was pink and smooth as a baby's, and his hair was silvery white and so fine that it moved in a breeze I could scarcely feel. I found myself thinking that he looked like God.

"There's a wonderful view from up here. I watch the sunsets. All the colors laid out there along the roofs. It gives me the greatest pleasure in the world. Ginger Pops and I watch the sunsets together. Young man, why aren't you sitting?" He saw the reason and picked up the mike. "Mr. Clood, can't I have a chair out here for my guest?"

"Look at this," Big Earl said. He pointed to a large leather-bound book on the floor beside his chair. I lifted the book and saw written in gold *The Family Chronicle.* "It's a history of my family. There are nine volumes. I had a fellow do the research for me and write it up. This volume deals with the Spanish-American War. My youngest brother fought in the Philippines, you know. I'm sure you'll want to read these volumes."

A maid with hairy legs dragged a rocking chair onto the porch, and I sat with the book in my lap. Big Earl began rocking with his eyes shut. I opened the book and saw an old photograph of Big Earl's youngest brother in a campaign hat. The first sentence started: "In the glorious tradition passed down from their ancestral kings . . ."

"I was a very good poker player when I was a young man. You'll want to know about that," said Big Earl. "There were a lot of good gamblers in those days. We went all over East Texas and Arkansas and Louisiana playing poker and gambling with leases. I made a million dollars before I was twenty-five, was dead broke at twenty-six, a millionaire again at thirty and before I was thirty-two I had holes in my shoes and not a crumb of bread to eat. No matter what you might think, there is no security in this world. Everything can be gone in a wink. If they can't rob your money, they'll steal your life. I used to be afraid of them, but not any more. I went to a wonderful doctor in St. Louis, Missouri. He taught me how to crawl. Do you know how?"

"I suppose so," I said.

"You think you do, but I doubt if you really do," Big Earl smiled.

He deposited the poodle on the floor, where it began to prance in circles, yapping, like a toy. Then Big Earl himself slid forward out of his rocking chair, went to his knees on the porch and slowly crumpled onto his face. Thinking he'd had a heart attack, I jumped up.

"Sit down, sit down," he said. "Look here, now, I'm showing you how to crawl."

His face flat on the floor, his arms stretched out, Big Earl began to wriggle forward, with the poodle yapping at his ears.

"Most people think crawling is on your hands and knees. That's creeping! You must learn to crawl before you learn to creep. If you don't learn to crawl, you can never be healthy as God intended. Right from babyhood, your system will be all out of sequence."

Big Earl dragged himself to the wall and lay gasping. At last he rose to one knee, grabbed the door handle and trembling with a desperate effort pulled himself upright. He dusted his palms, straightened his bow tie and inspected the buttons on his double-breasted suit.

"How tall do you think I am?" he said.

"About five feet ten," I said.

His small mouth screwed up in displeasure, and his small blue eyes peeped suspiciously at me.

"I used to be six feet one, but now I'm only five-nine," he said. "Before she died at ninety-six, my grandmother had gotten so short she could walk under the dinner table." He placed one hand against the wall to prop himself up and looked down at a couple of deer that had come to the porch. "What do you think of chemistry? Do you think it can affect the mind?"

"I certainly do," I said.

This was the correct answer. Big Earl grinned. "I have a wonderful chemical that a doctor in Little Rock, Arkansas, gave me," he said. "When I used to be nervous and uneasy, I went to this man and he told me chemistry could bring marvelous cures. Have you ever heard of chlorpromazine?"

"How much of it do you take?" I said.

"Not so much now. But I used to take fifteen hundred milligrams a day. It made me feel pleasant."

"Good Lord! What did you do after you took it?" I asked.

"Oh, I sat in the yard with my animals, and sometimes the nurse would come and move my chair and remind me not to stare at the sun. Do you think psychiatrists are crazy?"

"I'd hate to say that. There's a lot of them I don't know."

"I think they're full of shit!" Big Earl said. He smiled and patted his lips. "I don't use that word ordinarily. But psychiatrists are the crazy people. They should be locked up and made to prove they can cure themselves before they are allowed to work on others. Ho Chi Minh says when the jail doors are opened, the real dragon will fly out. Have you heard of Ho Chi Minh? A little bit? Well, I prefer him to that Madame Nhu, to tell the truth. I don't like any of them in fact. Madame Nhu wants to come see me. When she speaks here in Texas next month. I won't let her in. She says they're going to kill her husband and her brother. Shoot them and beat them and stab them! Good riddance! Let the yellow people worry about the yellow people. I don't fear them half so much as I fear the worms in our own foundations. There's a Communist empire building up ninety miles from our shores. Kennedy thinks he can fool us by doing things the wrong way around. Did you know President Kennedy is coming to Dallas?"

"I read it in the paper," I said.

"Yes, Caesar is coming to the provinces to see how us Gauls govern ourselves," said Big Earl. "Caesar should stay in Rome where he belongs! Let's have our lunch. Don't forget to bring the book with you."

I picked up *The Family Chronicle* and followed Big Earl and Ginger Pops into a large parlor with a beamed ceiling. The furniture was fat with stuffing and looked comfortable, and there were colored photographs in gold or silver frames on the mantel and on several small tables. I saw a number of photos of Little Earl and his wife and family. Above the mantel was a portrait of a handsome woman with a regal pioneer strength in her face.

98

"My wife has been dead for seventeen years," Big Earl said, noticing me looking at the portrait. "It took me six years to pay off her inheritance tax."

"Why don't you have a portrait of yourself in here?" I said.

"I don't have so much vanity that I would wish to look at a portrait of myself when I can look at my loved ones instead," he said.

Scooping Ginger Pops into his arms, Big Earl tottered across a foyer and into a dining room where yellow sunlight shone on a long table that had been set for two. Big Earl took a chair at the end of the table. Beside his plate were a portable radio, a microphone, two telephones, a notebook and a fountain pen. Platters of nuts, radishes, celery, butter and brown bread had been placed around three pitchers containing different colored liquids.

Big Earl started munching nuts by the handful. There were half a dozen kinds. He offered me a silver dish of large rusty nuts I had never seen before.

"These are the hearts of apricot seeds," he said. "It is well known, even though the medical bureaucracy denies it, that apricot seeds cure and prevent cancer. Certain tribes who eat apricot seeds as a staple never had a case of cancer in their history. Years ago I had cancer, but now I am cured. I like you, young man. You pay attention to me. Eat apricot seeds, so you won't have to die so soon."

Big Earl flicked on the radio. The squawk of music brought the hairy-legged maid out of a swinging door. He turned off the radio, and she left, to reappear again with bowls of steaming soup. Meanwhile, Big Earl had poured each of us three different glasses of liquid.

"Fruit juices. I mix them myself. Haven't settled on the true elixir of perpetual health yet," he said, "but grapes are quite important. Whoever said wine is the water of life was on the right track. Do you believe in ESP?"

"Yes," I said.

"Do you have it?"

"I think with me it comes and goes."

"I have it more than anyone I have ever known. I know things there is no way I could know. I know where pools of oil are hiding under the ground. I know what people will do before they even think of doing it. I know everything that's going through your mind, and I'm impressed with you. I know that when I tell you there is a very real possibility that unscrupulous Communists have invaded John F. Kennedy's brain with radio waves and are influencing his decisions even though they don't yet control his mind, you will accept this as a legitimate possibility. Eat that soup. It's made out of uncracked wheat, like the bread. It's grown for me in Oklahoma in a little town that's never had a dentist or a cavity."

The yellow telephone rang. Big Earl held the earpiece to his ear for a full two minutes while I ate the soup. It tasted sort of like hot chicken feed, but not bad. Each glass of fruit juice tasted like a different punch, one with an orange flavor, one grape and one that could have been papaya. The hairy-legged maid took away the soup bowls—Big Earl's had hardly been touched—and laid out a platter of dry brown roast beef. Big Earl put down the phone.

"It wasn't for me," he said.

"Can you communicate with ESP?" I asked.

"With certain people I can. There is a lady whose name I won't mention. I talk back and forth with her from all over the world. Sometimes I see the future. I get flashes of it very clearly."

He snatched up the microphone and yelled: "Mr. Clood!"

Mr. Clwyd immediately stuck his head in through the swinging door.

"Did you get rid of that fellow?" said Big Earl.

"Yes sir," Mr. Clwyd said.

"He's still in the neighborhood someplace. Keep a watch for him," said Big Earl.

Without expression, Mr. Clwyd vanished. Big Earl turned to me. He was eating slices of roast beef like potato chips.

"I want to thank you for living the way you do," he said.

"The way I do?"

"Yes, young man, you are an embodiment of what all young Americans should be. I only wish Little Earl was a bit more like you. Strong as a good Christian soldier should be strong! Clean of mouth and mind. Fearless. It's a pleasure for me, an honor, to have you at my table."

He paused and looked at me with baby eyes slightly smeared with pink, his delicate lips puckering into that divinely wise and innocent smile, the fine silvery angel hair floating around his head.

"Last week I thought they had you for sure," he said. "It took a tremendous amount of courage and ability to get out of that one. Only a young man who could ride and shoot as superbly as you could have escaped and captured those thieves. It made me feel warm and proud. How you've grown up! I remember you as a short-haired boy, a lad, unformed. Most of the young men today just talk their dreams. But you've gotten strong enough to live yours! And your father, what a man! Reminds me of my own father. Brave and tough and kind. In the saddle all day, stand guard all night, at his age, and never falter. That's the spirit that took the Philippines. That's the spirit that beats in my own heart."

He reached out with his left hand and clasped my wrist as I was raising a piece of meat to my mouth.

"Would you like to be rich?" he said.

"Well, sure, I guess so."

"Get into natural gas," he said.

Then he began to look at his hand still holding my wrist. As he looked at it an expression of awe and wonder came over him.

"Do you know that I'm ninety-three years old?" he said. "And I don't have a wrinkle."

He got up and opened a cupboard and pawed a great many documents onto the floor.

Holding a bottle of thick green oil aloft, he returned to his chair. Big Earl removed his suit coat, hung it over the back of his chair and rolled his sleeves up to the elbows, turning the folds back neatly to reveal pink hairless arms.

"Ten years ago I had wrinkles," he said. "Not so much as the ordinary eighty-three-year-old man, but there were wrinkles on my face and the backs of my hands. In my Bible studies I read about a plant that was sacred to the Egyptians. It was called, in our language, the Growth of Permanent Beauty. So I had some of my people in the Middle East run down this plant for me. One of my laboratories made up a lotion. What does this look like to you?"

"Prell shampoo," I said.

He smiled and began rubbing the lotion into his left arm.

"I rubbed my face and body with lotion several times a day, and inside of a year my wrinkles had started to disappear," he said.

"Are you certain that's the right bottle?" I said.

"And after two years there were no more wrinkles at all," he said, massaging his arm with the lotion, which had started to bubble into a thick lather. "One of these days I'm going to put this on the market as a cosmetic. But as for now, we continue our experiments with it. I may begin taking it in pill form."

Big Earl glanced down at his thoroughly soapy arm. He unrolled his sleeves again, buttoned them over the foam, put his coat back on and sat down.

"Take that bottle to your father with my compliments," he said.

The maid served a diced fruit cocktail for dessert and brought me a cup of coffee. The red telephone rang. "I'll have nothing to do with it!" Big Earl said into the phone. "The man is my President. I knew his father. If you want to organize a demonstration against him, do it on your own. Leave me out of it. I can let him know how I feel without sending silly people to carry placards and chant slogans. It would just be a fiasco."

Big Earl hung up the phone. "Would you like to be president of a college?" he said. "I support several colleges that teach Americanism. You would be just the man. No? Some radio station, then. I have a radio network." Again the red phone rang. While Big Earl was talking, Mr. Clwyd came in and looked at me. Mr. Clwyd had told me earlier that I was to leave promptly at two o'clock; it was now nearly three. I finished my dessert.

"I have to be going," I said when Big Earl was off the phone.

"You're a fine young man. It makes my heart glad to talk to you. I wish Little Earl could have been more like you. I think I scared him when he was a little boy. I took him everywhere I went from the time he was three years old until we put him in that military academy. He toddled right with me into the oil fields. He'd say, 'Daddy, what dis? Daddy, what dat?' But he just didn't have the stuff in him. He can't read your mind. No psychic powers whatever. No instinct for gambling. Little Earl will make you a bet, but he won't bet you the whole pot. But he's a good boy. He threw a paper route, you know, and he worked one summer as a caddie. If he'd been a boy like you, with the advantages I could have given him, he'd be a rich man today."

He switched on the radio and listened to country music for a moment and tapped his fingers on the plastic case.

"I used to play the fiddle, you'll want to know that," he said. "Did you ever play an instrument?"

"I could play 'Billy Boy' on the trumpet when I was little."

"We'll play a duet sometime. If only I can find my fiddle!"

"That would be nice," I said. "But now I do have to go."

"But you haven't read the book," he said. He got up and opened *The Family Chronicle* in the middle, bending over the large volume, tracing a finger along the lines of print. "See here? My brother fought the Morros. I could have fought them, too. I could have done anything I wanted."

Mr. Clwyd came in again.

"Thanks for the lunch," I said.

Ginger Pops, who had been asleep, jumped up and started yapping as Mr. Clwyd led me to the door with Big Earl following. Mr. Clwyd opened the tall double doors in the foyer, and Big Earl pushed him aside and walked out with me. He plodded beside me, with Ginger Pops dashing between his feet, all the way to Jingo's car.

"Well, thanks again," I said at the car.

"Please stay. You haven't read the book," he said.

I saw Mr. Clwyd on the porch.

"I promised I wouldn't interfere with your nap," I said.

He squinted in the window at me, features bunching in the middle of his face into that petulant frown.

"You don't like me," he said.

"That's not true," I said.

103

"Telephone call, sir," yelled Mr. Clwyd.

"Do you have the bottle of Perpetual Beauty lotion?" Big Earl asked.

"It's right here on the seat."

With both hands gripping the door along the window slot, he leaned inside. His face very close to mine, I could smell a dry nasal breath, like mustard.

"This car is too flashy," he said.

"It belongs to a lady friend," I said.

"Much too flashy," he said.

His fingernails clamped onto a chrome strip so that white moons appeared above pink in the cuticles. Mr. Clwyd was gone from the front porch.

"I was twelve years old when the Civil War ended," Big Earl said. "We were on the move with my mama. I remember the Battle of Gatlinburg. We went by Mount Le Conte in the Great Smoky Mountains and saw the flames. When I was just a little boy I heard the cannons at Shiloh. We had been staying at Pittsburg Landing. My daddy was with Johnston and saw him killed. We went to Corinth, and, oh, there was so much blood and fire and noise! I heard the cannons all the time and saw men walking. It's all in Volume Three of *The Family Chronicle*. Which volume did you read?"

"The one about the Spanish-American War," I said.

"Yes, it wouldn't be in that one. My daddy was killed right at the end of the Civil War, did you know that? He was killed someplace in Mississippi by hoodlums that weren't even soldiers. They shot him down and stole his horse and his money. I've made my own way in this world since I was twelve years old. I picked cotton and worked on the railroad and clerked in a dry-goods store in Memphis. I didn't want to be a burden on anybody. By the time I was fifteen, I was the best checker player in Tennessee. I was the best at dominoes, too. Would you like to play some checkers?"

"I'm not very good at it," I said.

"I won't be easy on you. There's no room for sugar in a game of checkers."

104

Three deer, a few black-and-brown goats and two peacocks had come up around the old man as he stood talking. A goat was nuzzling his coat pocket.

"The whole story is in those books in my library," he said. "Did you ever hear that I won two hundred thousand dollars in one poker game in New Orleans in 1926? Well, it's true. It's the gospel. I can tell you the names of every fellow at the table that night. At one time I was a thirty thousand loser and was going to shoot my way out of the hotel if I didn't get back to even by daybreak. I won that much in one pot of stud poker with three nines. There's nothing for sure in this life except one thing—if you think you're going to lose, you're for sure going to lose. But if you're smart, and you believe you're going to win, sooner or later you'll win. Did you know that I've got more acres of land leased in the Middle East than there are men, women and children in the whole state of Texas? I could give one acre of the Middle East to every person in this state and I'd still have twice that much land left in the rest of the world."

"Why don't you do it?" I said.

"They'd just squabble over it," he said.

"How much money are you worth, Big Earl?"

"Sonny, if I knew how much I was worth, I wouldn't be very rich. But I can tell you this—the Lord Jesus Christ is up there in Heaven waiting on my restless soul, and there's no way out of the appointment. Best I can do is be late."

He began to sing:

> *Why should Jesus love me?*
> *What have I done for Him today?*
> *In my sinful simple features,*
> *Can He see a lonesome stray?*

"I wrote that hymn," he said.

"It's very nice," I said.

"I can play it on the organ. Come back inside and I'll play it on the organ and sing all of it. Maybe you can sing with me. Little Earl used to have such a sweet voice when he was a child."

"Mr. Clood is calling you again," I said.

Big Earl glanced around at Mr. Clwyd, who was on the side porch now, very close.

"I'm sorry, sir. It's time for your rest," said Mr. Clwyd.

"The devil with you! I won't do it!" Big Earl said.

"Please, sir, the doctor will be awfully cross."

"Will he?" Big Earl looked back and forth from Mr. Clwyd to me a couple of times. "I suppose that's true. Well, I'm sorry, young man. You'll just have to come back to see me another day. I must get my rest. I hope you understand."

"There's a car at the gate, sir. It looks like Colonel Burnett," said Mr. Clwyd.

"What does he want?" Big Earl said.

Mr. Clwyd pushed a button just inside the door, and the gate opened. Big Earl's fingers were still clamped to my window frame. Looking through the back window, I saw a rented Chevrolet coming up the drive with two men in it. In a grinding of gravel, the car stopped and two doors slammed. Reluctantly, Big Earl let go of my door and turned to face them. One was Colonel Burnett, who looked at me curiously from purple-socketed eyes and then smiled. The other man was a stranger with a crew cut, wearing a cheap tan suit. He had a sunburn.

"I have to take my nap," Big Earl said.

"Yes sir. We can wait," said Colonel Burnett. He looked at me. "Hey, John Lee. Seen the afternoon papers?"

"No," I said.

"Gretchen Schindler is dead. They found her this morning floating in the indoor pool at her apartment house with all her clothes on."

"Was it an accident?" I said.

"I believe they're saying so," said the Colonel.

"Gentlemen, please, we must move inside," Mr. Clwyd said.

"Business, John Lee, you know how it is," said Colonel Burnett, shrugging.

As I drove off, Colonel Burnett and the other man went into the house. Mr. Clwyd waited on the side porch, holding the door open for Big Earl. Rounding the drive, I looked around and saw Big Earl still standing outside in his blue bow tie and gray double-breasted suit, with his white angel hair blowing, and Ginger Pops yapping in his arms, and deer, goats and peacocks gathered around him. He was watching my car, and I waved, but he didn't wave back. Probably, he couldn't really see me. I wondered if he had ever told me why I had been invited for lunch.

10

Gretchen   Elizabet Schindler, age twenty-eight (I had thought her to be several years older), had been found about seven o'clock in the morning by a janitor. She was fully clothed and had a bruise on her forehead, probably the result of striking her head when she fell into the pool, the newspaper said. She was described as a "Washington mystery woman" and was called "beautiful" and "sexy." The wire-service stories mentioned that she was a frequent companion of Billy Bob Teagarden—"alleged influence peddler and friend to many in high places"—and spoke of a "powerful Southwestern set very much at home in the nation's capital." In a short recounting of Billy Bob Teagarden's continuing and often delayed trial, it was said that Big Earl—"a mysterious billionaire who lives in a fortresslike Dallas mansion guarded like a king behind high walls"—had been subpoenaed to testify but had been forbidden by his doctors because of his advanced age and weakened condition. None of the stories mentioned Little Earl, Franklin or Colonel Burnett. I supposed the Washington *Post* and maybe the *New York Times* and New York *Herald Tribune* would have carried much fuller accounts and used more names than either of the Dallas papers, but Buster and I decided it would be indecent to drive downtown to the newsstand just to read more gossip about poor Gretchen. In some ways, we already knew more than the newspapers had told.

Jingo recognized her from the photograph.

"That's the German broad that spent the night over here. Jesus, she must of sure missed the ocean."

I was thinking about the chlorine smell of that enclosed room, and the echoes of the water sloshing as they dragged Gretchen onto the tiles, and I wondered what she had gone to the pool for, but of course we would never know. Now she was dead, and her picture was in the paper. I turned a page and saw a photo of a young heir to a ranching fortune. He had died of pneumonia. He was born handsome and rich, which put him two-up on me before our feet ever hit the floor, but he was gone now, and I was still sitting here reading the paper.

When Franklin called to invite me to his hunt club, I had been telling Buster and Jingo about the lunch with Big Earl. Franklin said Wilburn would pick me up in the car. I assumed Franklin wanted to talk about Gretchen, since that was the freshest thought in my mind. I hadn't known Franklin belonged to a hunt club, in fact hadn't even considered that there was such a thing around Dallas. I got out the Bolex, loaded in some film and went into the living room where Buster had spread blown-up photographs of Jingo over the coffee cups and soft-boiled eggs.

"Time to capture another experience in this box," I said.

"What do you suppose they hunt?" said Buster.

"Whatever it is, it doesn't shoot back," I said.

Buster's bedroom door opened, and a tall girl in a bikini came out yawning. A German shepherd dog trotted out behind her.

"My dog made pooh-pooh all over your room. I'm going for a swim," she said.

"Christ, Buster, you ought to keep your girls out of the water," said Jingo.

As I left, the girl was floating in a steamy mist that rose from the heated water, and her dog lay drowsing in sunlight on the flagstones. I hadn't seen her come in the night before, but she looked like a girl who was trying to be a model and wanted Buster to shoot her a

108

portfolio. I shot a few feet of film of her, and she smiled for me. I wondered if she had seen the Baby Giant, or the airline bag, or the cookie tin or the seeds and roaches on the bureau and on the floor, and what she would think if she had. There were so many incriminating scraps lying around that we didn't dare hire a maid, but Jingo had promised to help us vacuum the place before we gave our big party around Thanksgiving.

In the car, Wilburn confessed that he hadn't cared much for Gretchen Schindler. He wouldn't say why, except that he didn't like the way she had treated what he called "working people." I gathered Wilburn didn't really approve of any of the women, other than wives, who moved in Franklin's crowd. Wilburn was partial to Margaret Franklin. He had worked for the Franklins for twenty-six years, and he loved Francis. "If Mist' Francis didn't have nothing left at all, if he couldn't pay me no salary whatever, I wouldn't leave that man," Wilburn said. "He has tooken me all over the globe and did so many nice things for me, money alone couldn't never get me away from him. He'd have to run me off with a stick, and then I'd sneak back. Mist' Francis tooken me to Argentina, Cuba, London, Mexico and Rome, Italy, and he tooken me to New York and Washington and Los Angeles so many times I couldn't count. He has introduced me to movie stars, generals, big-time politicians. He introduced me to President Eisenhower. Mist' Francis paid for my mother to be operated on in the hospital and bought her a little house to live the rest of her life in. Miz Margrit has give my wife all kinds of fur coats and fancy clothes. They put my son through college at Texas Southern University. Anybody that say anything bad about Mist' Francis or Miz Margrit has got me to battle with."

The hunt club turned out to be a red-brick ranch-style building on a private lake about an hour's drive east of Dallas. There was no sign on the brick columns at the gate. I could see members' cottages. I shot film out the window as we drove in.

"They shoots ever'thing here but moving pictures," Wilburn grinned. "Ducks, pheasants, deer, antelopes, you name it and they kills it. Couple of years ago they got some buffaloes down here and blowed them to pieces. One gentleman at this club, he got hisself a antitank gun that he keeps over yonder at his house. He can pop off any kind of a fierce squirrel or possum from three hundred yards away."

"Does Francis like to hunt?"

"I don't believe Mist' Francis has got exactly the same spirit about it as the other gentlemens," said Wilburn.

A portly old fellow wearing a red plaid jacket, white twill pants, laced-up boots and a red hunting cap strode out the front door of the club slapping his palms together. He stared at me and frowned at my movie camera, but he decided I must be all right because I did have a car and a driver. Behind him came a Negro boy carrying two shotguns, a bag of shells and a bird bag.

"Good weather for it today!" the old fellow said to me.

"Looks like rain," I said.

He looked at the clouds in the west.

"Nothing wrong with that," he said, beckoning to the boy with the shotguns.

Several more men in hunting costumes with gun bearers came out as I went inside to find Franklin. He was sitting in a leather chair, drinking vodka and apple juice and looking morosely at mounted heads screwed to the walls and stuffed bodies that stood here and there in the room as if holding poses in the midst of life. A peccary snarled beside his chair with an ashtray perched on its snout. Franklin was wearing a khaki jump suit, a pair of combat boots and a straw cowboy hat.

"Better hurry along, Francis. We'll be starting in a few minutes," said a man who was dressed as if his quarry that day would be the fox. The man looked at me with distaste. "I'll be shooting with the .410," he said to Franklin.

"That's a sport," said Franklin.

"I don't believe in overgunning," said the man.

"Best not to take chances, though," Franklin said.

"Mighty right," said the man.

When the man had gone, Franklin said, "Want a drink, John Lee?"

110

"Sure."

"There's no limit to what a man will do for money," Franklin said while we waited for the drinks. Other hunters trooped through and waved. "What kind of gun do you want?"

"I don't want a gun. Are you actually a member of this club?"

"Do a lot of business out here." He downed his drink and quickly ordered two more. He seemed a little drunk. "Plenty of real ty-coons in this place. That fellow that just left was telling me this morning that John Kennedy is a Communist and the CIA is a Communist outfit, and we should have invaded Hungary, and we ought to haul out our big sticks and head for Cuba right this minute. He wanted me to chip in money for a newspaper ad to tell Kennedy how us indignant citizens feel. Goddamn, I'm sick of hearing about Cuba. I wish it would sink."

"Do you own property in Cuba?" I asked.

"Not any more. The Cubans own it now. Like I told Little Earl, it's not worth getting blasted to ashes over. You can't win 'em all. When you lose at poker, they don't give your money back. Big Earl is a gambler, he knows. I may have said a lot of things that I was going to do about it. But anybody who does ever'thing he says he's going to do is short on imagination. I just can't stand these indignant citizens howling about Cuba and Hungary and Tito and nuclear bans and selling wheat to Russia, when what they really mean to say is they're scared some enemy is going to take away all this stuff that they know they got more of than they deserve, anyhow."

A bell rang.

"Starting time," said Franklin. "Let's go kill some damn birds."

Inside the door was a collection of walking sticks in a mahogany rack. Franklin picked up a stick as we went out. It was gray outside now and had begun to smell like rain; the temperature was probably in the seventies.

"You ever heard of The Great Runaway Scrape?" Franklin asked as we walked a mowed grass path behind the skeet and pigeon range, heading toward a thick stand of woods at the edge of a pasture. "It was when the word got out that Santa Anna's army was marching

111

through Texas to put the people back in line. So thousands of people who'd come here looking for an easy time of it, they packed up and ran as fast as their wagons would roll. They were going east, back to Tennessee and Georgia, and they ran into the Big Thicket. In those days the Big Thicket covered hundreds of miles from north to south and all the land from the Brazos River east to Louisiana, about two hundred miles, and you couldn't hardly get across it. They figured the Meskins had them trapped. The Alabama-Coushatta Indians that lived in the Thicket helped the people to hide and eat, saved them. Meanwhile a few people stayed and fought at the Alamo and some others went down and beat Santa Anna at San Jacinto, you know about that. Then these people who'd been caught at the Thicket turned right around and shot the Indians and then big companies come in and cut down the trees for timber and later drilled for oil. The Big Thicket is about gone now. They stomped it the hell out of the way in case they have to run again. The Great Runaway Scrape. If I was a moviemaker, I'd make a movie about that. But I wouldn't come back to Texas after I made it."

We began passing the hunters I had seen earlier. Each man stood at a cleared position in the trees at the edge of the field. Their gun bearers waited behind them. The hunters were fondling their shotguns. I was wondering where Franklin's shotgun was when I heard huffing and looked back and saw Wilburn coming along the path with a cardboard box. Franklin nodded and smiled and sometimes tipped his hat to the hunters as we went past them to his post. I was recording the scene with the Bolex. Franklin stepped into a circle of grass and reached out a hand to Wilburn, who put down the cardboard box and took a vodka and apple juice out of it. Wilburn put the drink into Franklin's left hand just as a voice over a loudspeaker said:

"Hunters ready!"

The men I could see up and down the line had tensed with their shotguns lifted to fire. As yet I could see no birds of any kind. Franklin swigged from his drink and gave the glass back to Wilburn, who had handed me a drink now. I put my drink on the grass and lifted the camera.

"Birds out!"

BLAM BLAM BLAM BLAM

It must have been like standing on the front row of the British Square when the Zulus charged. Smoke filled the woods, and the smell of gunpowder blew across us and feathers flew everyplace, and men were crying: "Good shot! Got that one!"

Franklin's long legs flailed a few steps forward out of the circle and he swung the walking stick. Something threshed in a bush at his feet. He whacked the bush several times with the stick, bent over and came back to the circle carrying a fat dead pheasant by the neck.

"Good hit, Mist' Francis," said Wilburn.

"Reload!" the loudspeaker said.

Wilburn laid the bird on the ground beside the box.

"Hunters ready! . . . Birds out!"

As the shotguns roared, I was watching closely through the viewfinder and saw a shape crash out of a wire tunnel, covered with brush and leaves, beside Franklin. For a moment the shape crouched on a spot of bare ground and turned its head. Franklin prodded it with a toe. The pheasant bounded two feet into the air, flapping useless wings. Franklin swung the walking stick and killed it. The pheasants had been raised in low pens and didn't understand that they could fly. Franklin posed with a foot on the pheasant's breast. Occasionally, as the hunting proceeded, a bird would boom out of a tunnel with its instinct intact and flap for the field, and two or three got away through the curtain of showering pellets. Franklin killed six birds with his stick and told Wilburn that was all he needed.

The shooting continued. Hunters looked around as we walked behind them along the path back to the clubhouse. Franklin had the walking stick over his shoulder with the birds tied to it by their feet. I ran ahead of him, shooting back with the Bolex.

Inside the clubhouse once again, Wilburn took the pheasants to the kitchen to be cleaned. Franklin and I returned to the leather chairs.

"Hunting is a thirsty game," he said, ordering more drinks.

"One of these days, somebody out here is going to shoot you, Francis."

113

"Not as long as Big Earl and Little Earl are on my side," he said. "Long as that's the case, I'm a good old gawky boy who acts a little strange. But that reminds me. I want to talk to you about something. You guess what?"

"Gretchen?" I said.

He seemed surprised. "It's a shame about Gretchen, but anybody who drinks a lot can drown any time. What I want to talk about is —Big Earl is going to finance your movie. He'll put two million dollars in it. What about that?"

"I'm astounded."

"Well, I don't know what you said to the old man out at his house, but he likes you. He wants you to make this movie about Texas. The real story, he told me, is what he read in the paper that you want to make. You write it, direct it, star in it, whatever you want. Big Earl trusts you, he says. There's just one catch. He's made me responsible for it. What that means on a real practical level is that I have to approve your script and every foot of film. If you write something about The Great Runaway Scrape, you're out of business. I ain't even just about to show Big Earl a two-million-dollar movie that he'll hate. That's the fact. You're totally free to do anything under the blessed sun you want to do in this movie, as long as I like it. Now, I don't want to cramp your artistic expression. I've seen some awful stupid bastards in Hollywood turn out some terrible movies because they sat down on people with talent. So I'll tell you right now, so there can be no misunderstanding about this deal, as a movie producer I am bound by only one rule. That rule is, whatever you do I will like it, or at least tolerate it, as long as I think Big Earl will like it. If I think he won't like it, it's out, no matter what. No arguments. No going over my head to Big Earl. I've worked for that man a lot longer than I've known you. Much as I might like you, John Lee, Big Earl is worth far more to me than you are. Years ago, I used to think I'd quit him. But he took care of me. When I'd get to the edge of quitting, he'd give me something I wanted. Somebody who does that, it's hard to leave him and it's hard not to like him. Whatever else he's done, he's been good to me. Better than he's been to Little Earl. And one of these days

114

he'll see to it that I've got a lot more than I have now."

"What do you want with more?" I said.

"Getting it is not all the fun, John Lee. Having it is fun, too. My daddy was a railroad brakeman. He never wanted anything for me except to grow up and be a good railroad brakeman, too. But I didn't want his kind of life. It was over years before he knew it. There's a fix in on just about everything in this world. The fix worked against my daddy, but it works in favor of me. I have goddamn well made it work in favor of me. Now, is it a deal? We can shake hands right now, and the budget commences flowing."

"But the movie I want to make is the real stuff, about what I see and do," I said.

"Be reasonable. Nobody is going to give you two million dollars to film your autobiography. Come up with something that's more than just a series of silly episodes."

"I want to think about it," I said.

"All right. Take your time. The truth is, I'm not busting my butt with eagerness to start into this thing."

The other hunters had begun coming back to the club, their faces red and happy, hauling in hundreds of pheasants, slapping and poking each other like comrades on a winning football team.

"You do know that Big Earl loves *Six Guns Across Texas*, don't you?" Franklin said.

Before I could answer, the man in the fox-hunting outfit stopped at our chairs. He held out his hand to me.

"John Lee, sorry I didn't speak to you while ago. I didn't know you with the hair and mustache, and that camera kind of put me off," he said. I recognized him as a clothing manufacturer, and shook his hand. "Don't let Francis ruin your liver. Hey, Francis, we sure got a kick out of the way you handled that stick. Boy, that was a laugh."

"Got to conserve our powder for the real thing," said Franklin.

"Some of us need the practice," the man said. "John Lee, why don't you come out next week for the rabbit shoot? It's really great sport."

"We let rabbits loose in that field and you try to hit them with a submachine gun. The winner is the guy who kills the most rabbits with one clip," said Franklin, grinning at me.

"Those little devils are hard to hit. You'd be surprised how many hunters never do hit one when the rabbits get to zigzagging around," the man said.

"We catch all the rabbits again in a net at the end of the field, but they're not good for more than three or four runs. Their hearts give out, or they get stupid and just sit there," said Franklin.

"Give my regards to your wife," the man said, shaking my hand again. "You know, Channel 8 has scheduled one of her ice-cream commercials right before your show every week, and her washing-machine commercial right after. You two must be pretty proud of each other."

"They brag on each other all the time," said Franklin.

"It's a real success story," the man said.

Franklin and I drank quietly for a minute.

"See, now, John Lee, you wouldn't want to put all this kind of stuff in your movie. Make up something believable," Franklin said.

"While we're haggling about the two million dollars, how about cracking Big Earl's vault for a few thousand for film and expenses?" I said.

"There's not going to be any haggling. Soon as you present me with an acceptable idea, you get the whole satchel of money. Until then, you don't get a penny."

"Why do you want to torment me, Francis?"

"It wasn't my idea to start with. But I admit to being interested in seeing how you act about this thing."

"Two million dollars would last a long time if I didn't get to hanging around restaurants," I said.

"One more thing I have to tell you if we're ever going to be podnuhs in the movie business," Franklin said. "That girl, Dorothy Leclaire? The one you used to live with and brought to my birthday party?"

"I know which Dorothy Leclaire you mean," I said.

"Well, I'm a little better acquainted with her than I might of let on. I don't know exactly what your feelings are about her, but Dorothy and I are pretty good friends. No big romance, or anything. But she's a pretty good kid."

116

"Have you been giving her money?" I said.

"A little bit, now and then, until she can get herself straightened out. Haven't you?"

11

After I pushed the button that rang the chimes four or five times, my mother opened the door.

"Oh, Johnny, it's so good to see you, honey. I was sleeping," she said.

I kissed her on the mouth and then hugged her for a moment. She felt very soft, ample in form but without enough stuffing, like a cloth figure that had been leaking, and the squeeze of my arms seemed to mash her slightly out of shape. As I touched her lips we both slid our heads to the side, away from this mysterious instant. Her hair smelled faintly like an old quilt and felt crushy as flowers against my face.

"Let me look at you, Johnny. Or should I call you Clive? How do you say that, anyway, is it Clive or Cleeve?" she said, stepping back and looking up at me, smiling, lipstick streaked past the corner of her mouth by our movement. On each cheek was a round red smear of rouge worked into the fine pink powder that covered her freckles and clung to the fuzz of hair along her jaw and chin.

"Any way you want, Mother," I said.

"Well, how do they say it on the show?"

"I guess most of them call me Cleeve," I said.

Clive Riordan was my name on *Six Guns Across Texas*. Thinking back, I couldn't remember that name having been spoken on the show since the first week or so. The other actors were reluctant to say it. But in every issue of *TV Guide* the cast listing was "Clive Riordan . . . John Lee Wallace."

"Like in Cleveland. That's easy to remember. Your daddy says it

117

Clive, to rhyme with hive. But he says Eye-talians, too. Honey, is that real hair you've got on?"

"Yes ma'am."

"Oh, I was hoping it was a wig and a stage mustache that you had to wear for your part. I was going to say you're home now, Johnny, you can take off your wig."

"It won't come off."

"Well, I guess you have to make some sacrifices. Nothing worthwhile is ever real easy. Do people stare at you on the street?"

"Some do," I said.

"My goodness, I just don't see how you can stand it. But I couldn't ever be an actor."

"I'll bet you could," I said. "Where's Dad?"

She looked around the living room in surprise.

"Why, I don't know where he is," she said. "Is his car out there?"

I looked through the muslin outer curtains behind the sofa. Mother's Oldsmobile was in the driveway, but my father's Chevrolet was missing.

"He could have gone to play golf, but I don't think so. He said his back was hurting," she said.

"Is he all right?"

"He's strong as he could be, for his age. He's been complaining about his back for twenty years, you know that."

"I mean is he drinking?"

"He hasn't had a drink for more than six months." She looked suddenly worried and occupied with the idea. "He didn't act like he was going to start drinking today. I came downstairs about five o'clock, and he was just finishing his breakfast. He was reading the paper and drinking coffee. We had seen an item that you were in town, so we kept thinking every day we might hear from you."

"I don't see why you get up so early when you don't have to," I said.

"Oh, I don't. I usually sleep until seven or eight o'clock. But your daddy's always up by four-thirty. The other morning he got up at three. He just can't sleep late. Some nights he goes to bed at seven, though, right after supper. Sit down, Johnny! Don't you want a piece of cake? Let me get some coffee."

While she was in the kitchen I stood in the middle of the living room, seeing myself in the long mirror above the fireplace, a freakish semistranger who looked like a daguerreotype, examining things in this house that had emerged as strange and complicated. The six thin windows on the landing of the stairs were red roses and bright green leaves of stained glass with four panels to each window; at noon, now, a pale light seeped around the roses to show in dusty columns on the landing. Across the lime ceiling several cracks set out like fault lines from the base of a chandelier of perhaps a thousand glass prisms tinkling in seven tiers. Through a broad doorway I could see the similar chandelier above the dining table. A color television sat on a table through another doorway that opened off the living room into a tiny room with two old couches, an air-conditioning unit and an electric heater. It cost so much to operate the furnace for the entire house of fifteen rooms and attic and basement that the folks had not lit it since my sister got married and left home fifteen years ago. On the glass coffee table lay a Bible that weighed as much as a medicine ball. It had a black leather cover, and inside was an attempt at a genealogy of my mother's and father's families. My mother's was Dutch and Cherokee Indian, although the Indian part was not mentioned; there was only my Cherokee great-grandmother's anglicized name, Carrie. I remembered going to see her when I was five or six. She lived in an old house on the plains far out in the Panhandle. I don't remember that she ever said a word to me. She rocked in a rocking chair with a blanket around her shoulders. My father's family was English and hillbilly and had come to Texas through Virginia and Tennessee. The last entry, under my name, was "Caroline."

Mother brought out the coffee on a little tray. We sat on the couch in front of the Bible. Two large wedges of chocolate cake lay on a crystal dish. Mother broke off a piece of cake and began eating.

"Honey, the most exciting thing happened the other night," she said. "I saw Jesus."

"That right?" I said.

"I knew I was dreaming but I knew it wasn't any dream. It was just so clear! I was in bed upstairs in my room, wondering when Jesus would come back. I was just lying there thinking about Jesus and knowing He is coming back to this earth one day and wishing I'd still be here to see it happen. Then I noticed there was some kind of light at the window. My room's too high off the ground for it to have been car lights or a street lamp. And the light got brighter. I thought to myself—that's Jesus! He's come! So I got out of bed and went to the window, and there He was so clear, up in the clouds, with His purple robes on and His little bare feet. I thought I ought to go wake up Fletcher—you know he told me one time he didn't hate Jesus but he didn't especially like Him either, he was just neutral where Jesus was concerned. But I couldn't leave that window! Jesus posed up there for I don't know how long. Then I heard Him say, 'Lois.' It was like the voice was right in the room with me, but I could still see Jesus in the clouds. The voice said, 'Lois Van Druten, thou art be-loved of God.' I can't tell you what it did to me to hear that!"

"Were you surprised?" I said.

"That Jesus would talk to me?"

"That Jesus picked you out as beloved of God," I said.

"Well, I was just stunned! I knew I didn't deserve it. Before when Jesus ever spoke to me, when I was praying or at other times, it was kind of like a feeling, like I heard an echo and knew what He meant, but never really heard His voice. This time there wasn't any mistake about it."

"Was it a deep voice?" I said.

"No, it wasn't really deep."

"Did you still know you were dreaming?"

"Yes, but I still knew it wasn't really a dream. I don't know what you'd call it, Johnny. It was just so strong and clear! Then Jesus started coming closer. I thought it was funny that people weren't running out to greet Him. I was expecting to hear car horns honking, and church bells ringing, like we had on V-J Day. But there wasn't anybody! They couldn't all have been asleep. So I thought—this must not be His coming back to earth, but it must be something special. Then He came right down to the window!"

"Was there any music?" I said.

"No music. Just the light. Well, up close, Jesus had such beautiful hair. It was brown like yours, and even longer than yours, and He had the softest blue eyes I ever saw. He was right outside the window for I don't know how long, a few minutes anyway, and I just stood there looking at Him. I didn't know whether to kneel down or what, I was so flustered! I could see the street corner all lit up, and the light shining on the cars in the driveway. Jesus wasn't as high off the ground as the top of that big oak tree by the porch, but He nearly was. He said, 'Lois, We are pleased with thee.' I said, 'Lord, all have sinned and fallen short of Thy glory.' And He said, 'Sister, thou hast done all right.' He didn't say anything more to me, but I could feel His love. The room was full of it, and I could feel it in my heart and my body so strong! I was so happy I thought I might die. I started crying, I was so happy."

I knew the feeling. As a little boy, I wept on Sunday mornings in terror and ecstasy, looking up at Jesus in the stained-glass window above the baptismal tank while the choir in white garments sang appeals to the sinners and the preacher urged us forward to dedicate or rededicate our lives. I was baptized at ten, grateful to be forgiven for my crimes and hoping Jesus wouldn't change His blessed mind. Thereafter I rededicated myself to Christ two or three times a year for the next three or four years. I used to go to church camps every summer. After prayer meetings and Bible studies and hiking and swimming, there were vespers in the evening by the lake, and every night an evangelical revival meeting in a gigantic tent. There was hardly a kid who wouldn't break down during revival meetings and begin to cry and stumble along the aisle to rededicate his life or offer himself for baptism. We would stand in a rank across the front of the tent, weeping for all the audience to see, fraught with Jesus. While the generators throbbed and moths struck the light bulbs, I stood there at least once a summer in the tent, singing and bawling, feeling every time that this time it would stick. We had gang fights and masturbation contests and patrols to creep through the night and spy on Monkey Island, the girls' dormitory, which resembled a large pen with wire walls. But in our moments of giving ourselves to Jesus, we felt we were overcoming all that sinning, were rising above ourselves to become sublime. We kept being reminded that heaven and hell were real and waiting, and we knew it was true even if our memories were short.

"Well, it sure was exciting, anyway," Mother said about seeing Jesus.

"Jesus had better hurry back while there's something left," I said.

"Honey, I know it! Ohhh, the world is in such bad shape. Every day you read the worst things in the papers. The President is being friendly with the Russians. I just don't see how the people can let him do that. Crime keeps going up. Why, we've started locking our house. You read about these nigras and beatniks roaming around. Johnny, wouldn't they let you get your hair cut and wear a wig?"

"No, they want me to keep it like this," I said.

"I guess you saw your show last night," she said, pouring more coffee.

"I missed it."

"It was sure a good one, honey. Your daddy and I are just so proud of you. This show is so much better than those awful movies you were in. I hope you don't have to do any more of those."

"I thought you liked a couple of them," I said.

"That first one you were in, that cowboy movie, it wasn't too bad, except it had a lot of cursing in it and too much drinking. I don't know who ever thought anybody would want to see a movie about rough, nasty drunkards. The second one, where you played that gangster and dope smuggler over in the Orient someplace, well, that one was terrible. The only good thing about it was you got killed off pretty early. And then—Johnny, honey, why'd you ever make that Tarzan movie?"

"It was clean," I said. "What was wrong with it?"

"It was so embarrassing. You in that little loin cloth. Honey, you just looked foolish."

"I didn't know you saw the second movie."

"I didn't see all of it. I walked out when you were dead and that man was in bed with that girl. I'd rather not even talk about that movie. It was disgraceful. I couldn't face any of my friends for months."

"You didn't like me as a dope-smuggling gunman?" I said.

"I didn't bring you up to be that way," she said. "I'd sure be a failure as a mother if I thought you were anything like the person in that movie. I may not have been the best mother in the world, but I tried to bring you and your sister up to love God and be good, decent people. I think I've done a pretty good job so far. I hope you still go to Sunday school and church."

I nodded.

I always lied to my parents to protect them. Even as a child, I felt life to be so full of crimes and perversions that to hear the truth would destroy my mother. I also lied to my sister, who was five years older, because I couldn't be certain whose side she was on. My sister and I were often called upon to choose between parents. We encouraged them to believe what pleased them, but we had no allegiance, although I didn't find that out about Brenda until we had missed our growing up together.

We heard a car door slam.

"That must be Fletcher. I'll start lunch," Mother said.

I met the old man at the door and shook his hand. As ever, he seemed sort of shy at the meeting, and after one fast blue-eyed look ducked his head away, saying, "Well, Johnny," and chuckling as if amused at a spot on the carpet.

"How you been?" I said.

"Better. I've got some new pills. My legs don't ache so much any more, but I still get down in the back."

He took off his windbreaker and brown snap-brim hat. As he walked across the room to hang them on a hall tree, I saw how bent he had become, not forward but sideways, his right shoulder slanting toward the ground, right arm dangling, feet far apart and shuffling.

"I've been in the park hitting some three-iron shots." He lit a cigarette and kept it between his lips, squinting at the smoke, while he took his stance. Now the exaggerated tilt of his left shoulder seemed almost corrected, and I wondered if he had been walking that

123

way to maintain his golf stance. "Johnny, I think I've finally got the secret. I've been playing the ball too far back, with the club-face too closed. That's why I've been hitting those low hooks."

"You've been hitting low hooks for forty years," I said.

"They get a lot of roll. How would you rather hit the ball?"

"Straight."

"Hogan says you should hit it with a slight fade. I was reading that Hogan book last night, and I saw exactly what he meant about prona- tion. Clear as could be! Let's see your stance. Play like you've got a three-iron in your hand. See, your stance is a lot more open than mine was. I had my right hand too far under the club, too. I moved it more on top. Every ball that didn't fade this morning, it went just clean straight."

"What was your score the last time you played eighteen holes?" I said.

"Eighty-one. Could have been a seventy-six so easy. I hit a ball out of bounds on number six and missed four putts under five feet."

"Well, if I was sixty-eight years old and could shoot an eighty-one, I wouldn't be worrying about low hooks and changing my stance."

He chuckled again. Mother brought him a cup of coffee.

"Think your maw's getting fat?" he said.

"She looks fine."

"My Lord, Johnny, she eats like a hog. Cake and ice cream all the time. If I ate as much sweet stuff as she eats, I'd weigh three hundred pounds and have the gout."

"You ate nearly a whole quart of homemade peach ice cream last night," Mother said.

"I got your letter from Kansas City. How is Brenda?" I said.

"Her children are so cute," said Mother.

"Brenda's all right," my father said. "She and her husband went out every night we were there. You know, she hasn't been here in two years. When we go up there, we get to babysit. It's a good thing they have the same television shows in Kansas City they have here."

"Those kids are darling. They're the sweetest things," said Mother, going back into the kitchen.

"Just between us, Johnny, I thought the way Brenda acted this last time was, well, it was uncalled for," my father said. Remembering it, the wrinkles in his face seemed to deepen, and he suddenly looked as if he might cry. I had seen him cry when I was a child and he would come into my room smelling of gin and ask me to love him and assure him he wasn't a bad father. I hoped he wouldn't cry now.

He put his coffee cup on a mahogany end table and lowered himself into an antique chair, blowing smoke out of his nose, cigarette ash hanging above his chin. "Brenda was downright spiteful to your mother. I don't mind the way Brenda treats me. Lord knows, I did everything I could for her, never so much as even spanked her, put her through seven years of college. I did a. lot of things wrong. But that's no excuse for her to treat your mother and me like niggers." He paused for a moment and his face brightened. "Johnny, you should have seen it at the golf course last Saturday. You wouldn't have believed how many niggers were out there, all dressed up in their loud-colored shirts, yelling at each other, running around. It was right comical." He started laughing. "There's more niggers playing golf every week. When I was your age, the idea of a nigger playing golf was just impossible. But they've really been coming out ever since Dallas got pro football. You know, pro football has made 'em open up the hotels to niggers. A fellow I play golf with told me a lot of nigger football stars wouldn't let their teams come to town unless all the players stayed in the same hotel. I think that's the way it ought to be. A good nigger is due respect. There was a nigger and his wife two rows in front of us at the Cotton Bowl last Sunday. They see those niggers on the football field and in the hotels and that gives other niggers the idea to go out to the golf course."

"Listen, Dad," I said, "after lunch, how would you feel about driving out to the farm with me?"

"The farm?"

"You still have the farm, don't you?"

"Yeah, but there's not much to see out there," he said. "The fields are leased to other farmers to make crops on, if they can. We were renting the house to a family that moved without paying the rent and left things kind of torn up."

"I'd like to go. I haven't seen the farm in five years."

"We'll go," he said.

Mother called us to lunch. Instead of eating in the kitchen or on TV trays in the tiny room in front of the color television, she had set the dining table with good china and silver, and linen napkins on a tablecloth trimmed with lace.

"I didn't know you were coming, so I didn't have time to make biscuits," she said.

"I wish you'd show up more often," said my father.

"Fletcher, you say grace," Mother said.

We bowed our heads.

"Father, we thank Thee for this day and this meal. Bless this food to our bodies for Jesus's sake, ah-men," said my father.

"Ah-men," my mother said, smiling and unfolding her napkin.

For lunch we had canned stringbeans, cold pot roast, lettuce-and-tomato salad with bottled French dressing, potatoes fried in the skillet, white bread, milk and canned fruit cocktail. My father smoked Camels all through the meal, but said he was thinking of cutting down from three packs a day to one. He continued to remark upon my mother's fondness for sweets and her plumpness—she looked no different than ever to me—and she referred to his oversmoking and his flirtations with a woman who lived down the block and walked past our house every afternoon on her way to the delicatessen on Cedar Springs Road. But my parents were talking to each other with a sort of affable camaraderie that I had never felt between them before. Once he spoke up with the opinion that when she'd dressed up to go to the theater she had looked very pretty. I had never known them to go to the theater.

We are elusive inside our skins and how different they were now than then, I thought, watching them at the lunch table. I wondered what memories Caroline might have of me, of details I never had recalled of nights I remembered scarcely if at all.

126

"Pretty good lunch, Maw," my father said.

"You must have been hungry," she said, pleased.

"Yeah, it was delicious," I said.

He offered me a Camel. I shook my head.

"Cancer is a germ, like a cold. Some people catch it, and some don't," he said. "If cigarettes caused health problems, I wouldn't be here today. I've been smoking for fifty-four years. I've outlived nearly everybody I used to know."

After lunch we each carried our own plates to the kitchen and put them on the drainboard. I asked Mother if she wanted to come to the farm with us.

"Honey, I just don't believe I will," she said. "You and Daddy go on. By the way, how long will you be in town?"

"I don't know exactly."

"Why don't you stay with us? Your old room's waiting for you upstairs. I sure wish you would."

"Well, I promised I'd stay with Buster," I said.

"Oh, yes," she said. Mother thought Buster's influence was somehow responsible for my divorce. It was a convenient thing for her to believe, as then the fault didn't have to fall entirely on me. "Have you seen Caroline yet?"

"They're in Houston."

"We went to see her on her birthday. She's getting so tall."

I got out the Bolex and shot a few minutes around the house.

"Oh, Johnny's putting us in the movies," said Mother.

"I told you we'd be famous someday," my dad said.

I trotted upstairs to Mother's bathroom. Standing at the toilet, I opened the medicine chest and looked at the bottles. From a bottle labeled ONE IN THE MORNING FOR WEIGHT LOSS I removed six green-and-white Dexamyl spansules and put them in my pocket. I wondered how Mother would react if I told her she took speed. She was at the bottom of the steps when I came down.

"Your daddy's waiting in the car," she said. "We'll visit some more when you get back."

"All right, but for only a few minutes. I have a date."

127

She gave me a look I had seen very often—a sudden wincing look of disappointment, mouth turning down, hands fluttering up as if to grab me. I kissed her on the rouged cheek and went out with the screen door banging and didn't look again until we were backing down the drive. She stood on the porch smiling and waving.

"You rent that car?" my dad said as we passed the Morris Minor at the curb.

"It's Buster's," I said.

"Buster, he's a rascal," my dad said, laughing.

12

The farm was about twenty miles northwest of Dallas. After we cleared the traffic circle at the edge of town, there were few cars on the road in the early afternoon. The weather was cool and dry. Water sparkled in ponds we had begun to pass, and cows looked back at us from behind barbed wire. The farm houses were white frame with sharply angled roofs, and they stood close to the road. The fields were yellow and brown, but the trees were still in full leaf, and long heavy tunnels of foliage ran along the creek beds. It had been a dry year, but you would hardly have noticed unless you were a farmer or tried to keep a green lawn in the city. Today the air smelled faintly like rain. There was a bruise-colored cloud against the horizon to the north, the tree line backlit with a silver aura. Light spilled over the cloud and darkened the shape of its shadow on the fields. I used to imagine that the clouds were mountain ranges.

"Hell, it won't rain. It's been looking like that ever' afternoon, and nothing happens except things feel kind of electric for a while," my father said.

For most of the drive we had been talking about football. My dad

128

drove with both hands on the wheel, looking straight ahead. He did nearly all the talking. Dallas had two pro football teams, owned by two young sons of two very rich old men who were contemporaries of Big Earl and had made their fortunes in much the same way. My father was of the opinion that Dallas would not support both pro football teams because there were not enough people who had money to spend on tickets when they could see the competing team on television for nothing. Also, the weather usually held good through Christmas, and you could play golf or go out in your boat on Sunday. However, my father didn't like to play golf on Sunday because the courses were too crowded. Since he'd retired three years ago as an accountant for a big insurance company, he preferred to play golf on weekdays. He was drawing four hundred sixty dollars a month in retirement, he said, and Mother would start getting her Social Security next year, and the house was paid for, and they got a little extra money from leasing out the farm, which was paid for, and he hoped they'd never be a burden on me or Brenda. But still if he took Mother to a pro football game, it was twelve dollars for the tickets, a dollar to park, four dollars for lunch at the Highland Park Cafeteria, two dollars for Cokes and peanuts at the game and look what you had: close to twenty dollars spent to see a game when you could have watched the other team on the road on TV. My father said he didn't see SMU play any more because they didn't win enough. But the University of Texas was undefeated, and a friend had gotten him two tickets for the Oklahoma game and he thought Darrell Royal might win the national championship.

As he was talking, we turned on to a county road that was black-topped now but had been dirt when I knew it best. For two years we had lived on the farm while my father tried to make the land pay off. I was ten and eleven in those years. My dad had either quit his job with an oil company or had got fired. He had bought this eighty-nine-acre farm a few years earlier, and when World War Two began he decided it would be a cinch to raise vital crops for the nation. The way he told it, I pictured long dusty columns of happy troops in khaki, with puttees and soup-bowl helmets, marching up to our gate to carry off baskets of corn, beans, peaches and watermelons, and metal cans of fresh whole milk, to the tune of "Smoke on the Water."

"There's a place I guess you've seen before," my father said.

Back off the blacktop, with a short red-dirt road leading to it, stood the schoolhouse I'd gone to for the fifth grade and part of the sixth. I aimed in on it with the Bolex. The schoolhouse did not seem to have been touched in twenty years except for a coat or two of paint on its pine walls. A dozen bicycles leaned against the building. A pair of seesaws made an upright X in the red-dirt schoolyard fringed with weeds. The old orange school bus with black stripes along the sides was parked near a basketball backboard beyond the seesaws. The bus had a melon body and the face of a pig. Behind it were wooden goal posts in a pasture used for a football field. When I was in school there, the bus was driven by Mr. Starnes, who also taught seventh through twelfth grades in one of the school's two classrooms, and coached the basketball and football teams, and taught shop. Down a slope behind the schoolhouse I saw a familiar wooden building about the length of a limousine with doors in each end and a partition cutting it in half across the middle. On one side it was a two-holer outhouse with a tin trough for the boys, and the other side was a three-holer for the girls. There were no covered stalls, and there had been so many peepholes drilled in that partition that if you'd flung a handful of grapes at it, at least one was bound to hit a girl squatting on the other side.

A smallish brown cow pony, the saddle girth loose, mouth rooting in the sparse grass, was tied to a post oak tree.

"Remind you of old Sam?" my father said.

I rode Sam to school when I missed the bus. Otherwise it was a seven-mile walk. Pedaling a bicycle for that distance on the dirt road was harder than walking. It was a terrible feeling to run to the gate and see the school bus bouncing in dust down the road past the Bramlett place and know I was a hard seven miles away from a peach-limb switching by Mr. Starnes, as well as whatever Edgar Bramlett might have thought up for me that day.

We turned off the blacktop, rattled across a cattleguard, and stopped at a gate that had once been painted red but was now almost the weathery color of the cedar posts of the fence. I pulled off the wire loop that fastened the gate to the gatepost. Kicking the gate loose from the sandy dirt, I walked it open and turned my face as the Chevrolet blew dust coming through. A hundred yards from the gate, across a field grown over with weeds, I saw the wooden farmhouse with the tall oak tree in front of it. Behind and to the left of the house were the barn, corral, loading pen, smokehouse, chicken house and yard, the milk house and my old pigeon coop. We drove on up to the house and parked behind it, near the barn. Several cats watched us from a sunny spot in front of the barn door. I heard a cowbell and saw six or eight milk cows grazing.

"Bramlett cows," my father said.

There was not enough air to turn the windmill blades, and the pump looked very rusty. My dad cursed. He'd had that well dug, and the good artesian water that came up from it was one of the few things he'd really liked about the farm. Watching him walk toward the windmill, bent again with his right shoulder dipping toward the earth and his feet scuttling out, I had a vision of him much taller, brown and sweating and angry, drinking gin in the barn and then coming up to the house for dinner and stepping in the middle of a line of baby ducks following their mother across the yard, and stomping on through, scuffing his dirty black street shoes against the earth as if he'd stepped in cow dung.

The house had a cyclone fence around it to keep the animals out. The fence had also been intended to keep our German shepherd dog in, to guard the house, but the dog had learned to jump the fence and kill chickens. We had tried tying a dead chicken around the dog's neck, but it didn't stop him. After the dog had killed a baby goat and maimed a calf, Edgar Bramlett's father came over with a .30-30 rifle and took the dog out behind the barn, and I heard three shots, and later I saw buzzards above the trees along the creek. The next spring, down the creek at the swimming hole that had sandy banks and large oak limbs with vines to swing from, I found bones and teeth and a piece of dry brown hide in the grass.

Inside the cyclone fence had been our version of a city lawn, with

131

an attempt at Bermuda grass and flowerbeds. I had a rope swing in the big oak tree. The house had a couple of broken windows now, and I could see a light fixture torn loose from the kitchen ceiling. Far out to the front a dust funnel passed along the road in the sun. Shooting with the Bolex, I left the house and walked down to the barn and opened the tack-room door. At the sound of the door latch, there was a vast soft scrabbling as rats scurried away from the light. Inside were several saddles and bridles, layered thick with dust and rat droppings, and blankets chewed with holes. It smelled wet and musty from the rats and the mildew, a rotting odor resembling in memory the smell of the flesh of one of our milk cows who'd ripped her leg on a barbed wire fence and who had to be tied down while we scraped the maggots out of the wound with a knife and a big kitchen spoon and finally had to be shot anyway.

I shut the tack-room door and walked along a path that led toward a strange oily-smelling bog that I remembered as being a mile or more behind the house, in a patch of woods, but now had crept up to within two hundred yards of the barn. I had come upon a mule sinking in that bog one summer afternoon. The mule was up to his neck when I saw him. His eyes seemed big as lemons and dark as Apache tears. I ran to the house, but nobody was there. With a rifle and a rope, I returned to the bog. But I couldn't pull the mule out, even hitching the frightened Sam to the rope and using a tree for leverage, and I wouldn't shoot him. So finally I sat on a rock and watched the mule sink out of sight. The mule had been letting out prolonged screeches when I first saw him. But in the last half-hour of his life the only sound around the bog was crickets. As the mule's nose went under, there was a little plop and a greasy bubble. I kept sitting on the rock for a while after the mule died. It was rumored that a Mexican gold train had buried its cargo under that rock before being massacred by Comanches.

Then I went on down to a water tank lined with corrugated iron where I'd put a dozen catfish I'd caught in the deep pond of the creek. On the day I saw the mule die, the catfish heads were floating in green scum on top of the water with white spines trailing and flesh eaten by turtles. I rode Sam back along the path to the house and sat in the saddle for a long time with the rifle across the pommel, feeling lonely and melancholy and alive to drama as the sun went down behind the barn and the milk cows came up from the fields for the evening milking. I did the milking in the evening and my father did it in the morning. The cats would gather around, and I would squirt hot milk from the teat at them, and the cows would kick the buckets over and make my feet and legs sticky with milk, and the flies always swarmed in warm weather, and my wrists and fingers never entirely ceased to ache from sitting every evening without fail on an upturned bucket pulling patiently at teats until I'd drained the bags of six cows. Then I'd pour the milk through cheesecloth and carry the cans into the cool concrete milkhouse and go from there to feed my pigeons and listen to them making their bubbling peaceful noises as they settled down for the night.

"Damn pump's broke," my dad said as I walked back to the windmill.

"What's wrong with it?"

"I don't know. It's broke is all." He took off his hat and wiped the sweatband with a handkerchief that was greasy from the pump. "Well, what do you think about the place?"

"It's kind of run-down, but it wouldn't take much to fix it up."

"I'm not sure what you'd have when you fixed it up," he said. "How come you wanted to come out here?"

"Just to see it."

"Maybe you think you like it now," he said, smiling. "But you sure complained enough about it when you had to live here."

"I don't remember complaining so much."

"You did, though. There was hardly a day you didn't complain about the chickens. I never heard of anybody who hated to rake a chicken yard and clean out a chicken house as bad as you did."

"I didn't have any use for chickens."

"You liked eggs well enough. Where did you think eggs came from?"

"I knew where eggs came from. Who had to stick his hand under

133

those hens every day and get pecked and crapped on?"

My father laughed. He put his hat back on and flipped the brim down at a stylish angle like a leading man of the 1930s, and he was at once transformed in my mind into a person I remembered with a strange yearning. His blue eyes moved slowly away from the windmill pump and swung toward me.

"I got to where I couldn't stand the sight of an egg while we lived out here," he said.

"Me, too. All I could think about was baby chickens inside."

"But I don't recall you ever turning down any fried chicken," he said.

"I like chickens all right if they're dead."

"Remember how I used to kill a couple of chickens every Sunday?" he said. "Started off, I'd wring their necks. But they'd flop all over the place. Then Bramlett taught me to put the blade of a rake across their necks and stand on the rake and pull on their feet and their heads would come right off. It was a lot easier. But damn, I hated doing it."

"I thought you liked it," I said.

"How could anybody like it?"

"I don't know."

"You did it," he said. "Did you like it?"

"I hated it."

"Well, we couldn't talk those chickens into committing suicide, though. Would of been kind of mean to fry 'em alive."

"I'd rake that chicken yard and rake the chicken house and shovel out all that crap and clean off the roosts and put clean straw in the nests and sprinkle lime to kill the vermin and put down clean bowls of water and spread the feed around, and the first thing the chickens would do is crap all over everything and then step in the water and turn it over."

"They're just chickens," he said.

"Another thing I couldn't stand was plucking. That hot water and those feathers and that rubbery chicken skin covered with goose pimples. I can still smell it."

"Personally, I thought horses were nearly as dumb as chickens.

But, horses could get away with a lot because they were good look-ing," he said.

"Sam was smart enough to eat by himself and run when you whipped him," I said.

We were walking toward the corral. I stopped and waited for my father to catch up.

"Your back really hurts," I said.

"Just some kind of a crick," he said.

At the corral we leaned on the fence and smelled fresh cow dung in the lot. The hayloft door was open. We could see a few bales of hay stored up there.

"Guess Bramlett's using the barn and the corral, too," my dad said. "Somebody might as well." He glanced at me. "Remember the day Sam threw you over the fence right about here and broke your arm? Your mother was afraid you'd never make a piano player."

I learned to ride when I was about five. We owned a big white quarterhorse that my father kept at a friend's farm. But I didn't learn anything about horses until I had to start taking care of Sam and two other horses on our own farm. I had thought of horses as devoted, intelligent creatures who would buck off the bad guy if you whistled and would save the Lone Ranger's life by stomping on a villain. But after I had been bitten and kicked and thrown over the fence and run away with I learned that a horse should never be overestimated. Summers in high school I worked on ranches in West Texas and central Texas and rode different horses. Mostly, though, my ranch work was digging post holes, mending fences, clearing brush, burning cactus and cedar and chopping weeds with a hoe. I'd done plenty of hoeing in our peach and pear and plum orchard at the farm, and in our Victory Garden in town, and regarded hoeing as worse drudgery than cleaning the chicken house or milking cows. Those few hours a week on the ranches when I was allowed to get on a horse and play cowboy became such joy in comparison with the routine work that I could have revived my romantic feeling for horses if they hadn't been what they continually turned out to be. I rode in a few small country rodeos in the bareback bronc event, with no distinction, and on a summer night when I was seventeen a horse hurled me for a midair somersault. I landed on my face in the arena, with the hooves knocking dirt clods into my ears and hair. Lying there feeling the ground shake as pickup riders shied the bronc away from me, I could think of no further reason why I should ever get on a horse again. I decided that night I wasn't meant to be a cowboy. It was time to change my direction. Until many years later when a movie producer I was interviewing on TV asked if I could ride a horse, I'd hardly had another thought for the cowboy life.

"Look who's here," my dad said.

An old red pickup with a shotgun in a rack in the rear window stopped by the corral and a man wearing coveralls, railroad shoes and a straw hat got out of the truck, grinned at my father and looked at me with his head cocked to one side as though striving to make out a dim street sign.

"Mr. Wallace, is that John Lee with you?" the man said.

"That's him, Edgar."

"Looks just like on TV," said Edgar Bramlett.

"Hidy, Edgar," I said.

"Shee-it, John Lee," he said.

Edgar gave my hand a crushing grip but without vicious intent. He had been milking cows for nearly twenty-five years, and his wrists were immensely strong. Edgar reached up with a freckled hand, whipped off his straw hat and stood grinning.

There was a lower tooth missing in front. His face was red and bony, and his eyes squinted out from deep wrinkles, but his forehead was so white that it looked like transplanted flesh.

"I come over to see about the cows but never dreamed I'd run into a real star," said Edgar.

"Still on the farm, huh?" I said.

"Not ever'body gets to leave and run all over," said Edgar. He grabbed a handful of his short, dun-colored hair and pulled it, nodding at me. "Whoo, you got more hair'n my mother and sister put together. How come the cowboys on TV has got long hair, and all the cowboys I ever seen hasn't hardly got no hair at all?"

"The TV show's supposed to take place a long time ago," I said.

"Whoo, I guess! A cowboy that looked like that nowdays'd get poled. I guess you know 'bout getting poled."

"That's not something I'd forget," I said.

Being poled was being grabbed by a bunch of boys, picked up, legs spread, and having your crotch rammed into a pole or tree. Edgar had instigated a great many polings using the goal posts at the school.

"No shit, John Lee, I seen you on TV just last night, and now here you are! Last night you was riding like a cyclone and shooting people dead with a Colt six-shooter till there couldn't of been a crook left in Texas. Say, Mr. Wallace, you got a key to your storm cellar?"

"Didn't know it was locked," my dad said.

"Them Okies that was here put a padlock on it. I was wanting to go down there and bring up some peach preserves and pickled cucumbers that of been down there since last fall unless them Okies stole 'em."

"Break it open," said my dad.

"Shee-it, yeah!"

Edgar got a crowbar out of the tool room in the barn, and we went to the storm cellar near the windmill. On top of the ground the cellar appeared as a mound of dirt, like a large grave, with a heavy wooden door lying almost flat in the earth. Whenever there was a tornado scare, we used to open the cellar door and be ready to descend. The cellar was about eight feet deep, ten feet long and six feet wide. We kept blankets down there, and a coal-oil lamp and a portable radio. Like the other farm women, my mother would can fruit and vegetables in Mason jars and put them on wooden shelves in the storm cellar. We only used the cellar twice to escape approaching tornados. One came so close we could hear the freight-train rumbling of it and feel electricity popping in our skin and see the black funnel poking down from the black cloud to throw debris where it touched the ground; but at the last min-

137

ute it jumped our farm and came down again two miles away to destroy a house and kill three people. It never did seem really credible to me that a tornado would hit us. We were more afraid of the snakes, scorpions and spiders down in the dark cellar than of the weather.

Edgar snapped off the padlock, fetched a flashlight from the glove compartment of his truck and went into the cellar. I remembered the day I saw him come up from that same cellar holding hands with Brenda and grinning. Although we were in the same class at school, Edgar was five years older than I, the same age as Brenda, who was in the seventh-through-twelfth-grade room. It was Edgar who gave me my first practical introduction to what he called farking. Edgar ordered me and three other fifth-graders, who were about ten or eleven years old, to meet him after school in a gully behind the outhouse. We assumed he was going to torture us in some way, but there was no choice about going. Edgar arrived with a little girl from our class named Molly. She had long brown hair that curled up at the bottom. On Edgar's command, Molly took off her dress and panties and hung them on a cedar tree. We were astounded. I had seen Brenda naked, of course, and had watched most of the girls at the school through the outhouse partition, but I couldn't imagine what Edgar had in mind for us. Then he demanded we remove our pants and shorts. "You go first," he said to me. "If I went first none of you kids could touch the sides." Molly scraped out a place for herself in the dirt and sat down and started playing with me. I didn't know what to do, but she showed me. "You little kids can tell when you're finished because you feel a tingle and blood comes out," Edgar said. For me the tingle came soon and I was glad to stop, but when I got up, there was no blood and I was afraid Edgar would make me continue. Instead, he motioned for the next boy, a little fat fellow who started crying and couldn't do it. Edgar sentenced him to a belt line the next day. The third boy performed immediately. The fourth boy was one of Edgar's younger brothers, who took his turn after various manipulations by Molly and threats by Edgar. Then Edgar pulled off his own overalls. We

138

were astounded again. It looked like a knockwurst, huge and thick and reddish-purple, close to a foot long. I looked at Molly, whose expression had remained one of mischievous amusement although she never said a word throughout the experience. I looked at the small red slit between her legs, and looked at Edgar's monstrous sausage and thought to myself that this act was impossible. Edgar got down on his knees and lowered himself onto Molly, and we watched his white, pimply butt moving, Molly hidden beneath him except for her thin legs that stuck into the air and managed almost to touch soles in the small of his back. Edgar was saying, "Aw! Aw! Aw!" as if he were being punched in the stomach. After a minute or two, he raised up on his hands and yanked out the portion that had been sunk into Molly, and we saw our first sight of that mysterious creamy fluid as it squirted onto Molly's stomach and formed a puddle on her navel, and in fact there was a bloody froth. "Boys," Edgar said, looking up at us, "that's how to fark." He put on his overalls and called the little fat boy over to him. Edgar made a fist with the middle joint of his middle finger rising from it like a chimney. He hit the fat boy a quick hard blow on the bicep. A knot jumped up on the boy's arm and started turning purple. We called it frogging. Edgar was an expert frogger. "Tomorrow's when you really get it," Edgar said to the fat boy, who was crying again. The next day after school the fat boy had to run a gauntlet of belt lashes. As usual when the victim was soft and had no tough friends, a few kids hit him with buckles. Then Edgar had the boy's pants taken off and thrown into a tree. It was a few days later when my parents had gone into Dallas and Brenda and I were being punished by being made to remain on the farm and miss the Saturday afternoon movie, that I came in and unsaddled Sam and rubbed him down with a brush, and walked up to the house and saw Edgar and Brenda emerging from the cellar with his big, freckled hand clamped around Brenda's thin pale one, and I thought with revulsion of Edgar getting down between Brenda's white spraddled legs while she took that sausage in her fingers and helped him cram it in, and he said, "This is how to fark." Whether that happened I never knew, as Brenda and I were not talking to each other much by then, and Edgar was not the kind who would tell you something about your own sister, because out in the country people got shot for that.

Edgar came up the steps from the cellar with the flashlight in an armpit and several dusty Mason jars in his arms.

"They tooken most of the stuff," he said. "I should of never left nothing for them Okies to look after." He put his load down on the ground and then gave two jars to my father and two to me. "Here's some real strawberry preserves for you, John Lee, and some real grape jelly made out of Mustang grapes. I don't guess you get too much of this real good stuff out in Hollywood. People say it's never as good anywheres else as what the home folks make."

"Thanks, Edgar," I said.

"Mr. Wallace, John Lee and me sure had ourselfs some times while you all was living on the place here. I mean we had fun, didn't we, John Lee? Remember down at the creek when we killed that huge old rattlesnake with a big rock? Snake was fat and full of babies, remember that?"

I nodded.

"Shee-it," said Edgar, "how 'bout that time we caught that mama possum and cut her open and took the live babies out? They was like little pink blind mice. You remember?"

My father looked at me curiously.

"We had a time, I mean!" Edgar said.

"Whatever happened to that little girl named Molly?" I said.

"Which one was that?"

"She went to school with us."

"You mean little Molly that used to be kind of wild?" he said. "She married some old boy and moved to Fort Worth, I heard. They said she was doing real good, too."

My father mashed a cigarette into the dirt and lit another.

"I'm gonna go look in the house for a minute," he said.

We watched him shuffle off.

"You remember little Molly, huh?" Edgar grinned.

"Sure do."

"I bet that old boy that married her would fall down in a fit if he

140

known what we know. Shee-it, she was wild! I don't guess they was a boy anywheres around that didn't fark on her."

I smiled to hear the word again.

"Say, I'd like to ask you a question that ain't none of my business," Edgar said. "But I've wondered about it."

"Go ahead."

"Is it a good deal to be a TV star?"

"Sometimes."

"Do you get a lot of poezy?"

"More than I can handle."

Edgar considered this information solemnly.

"That's good," he said. "That's real good. How come you keep taking my picture? You gonna make me a star?"

"You're already a star," I said.

My father came back from the house.

"I don't want to see any more of it," my dad said. "They carried off half the furniture and broke the rest."

"They was just a damn bunch of hillbillies," said Edgar. "They was real trashy. Just outright dumb, you know?"

"You ready to get back to town?" my dad said to me.

"Whyn't you all come over to the house for a while and we'll drink a bunch of beer," said Edgar.

"We better get on back," my father said.

We shook hands with Edgar. Looking through the rear window as we drove off, I saw him walking toward the grazing cows in the field by the barn.

"Your mother and I don't have anything much to leave for you and Brenda," my father said. "You know I never made any money. So take a good look at that piece of dirt. That's your inheritance." He glanced around with the cigarette hanging from his lips and the smoke twisting into his face as we stopped for me to open the gate. "Maybe you can make more out of it than I did. To tell the truth, I don't envy you trying."

13

My agent, Annie Nash, was on the phone from California. "John Lee, you darling man, I love you, I think you're brilliant. This latest ploy of yours is working like a dream. Norman Feldman is willing to tear up your old contract and write you a new one before shooting starts again. He won't call you personally, he's rather annoyed, but he called me this morning. It does him good to stew a little bit, find out the world doesn't revolve around him. Everybody's talking about you. Everybody misses you. Did you get the clipping I sent you from the *Hollywood Reporter?*"

"I got it," I said.

(John Lee Wallace, a leading light of the fast-climbing new TV western series, Six Guns Across Texas, *has gone back home on the range. Seems he missed his Texas ranch so much he had to grab a whiff of sagebrush. Producer Norman Feldman is concerned Wallace might injure himself at his favorite pastimes of bulldogging and breaking wild broncos. But Feldman dismisses the 26-year-old cowboy's vow to quit the series and lens his own flick. Feldman says Wallace will lope back to the TV gulch soon.)*

"You were planning to call me about this, weren't you?" said Annie.

"Sometime."

I could picture Annie Nash slid into her palette-shaped walnut desk in the room with the Miró prints and the novels, scripts and notepads stacked on shelves and chairs.

"I knew you hadn't forgotten that I live on this earth with you and love you and miss you. I'm working for you. I'm on your side, don't forget that. You still trust me, don't you?"

"Why would you ask?"

"Because you haven't confided in me! Between us, my darling, what is the idea of this sudden call of the wild? You can't possibly like Texas any more now that you've seen the outside world. How can you prefer heat, dust, scorpions and ignorant hicks to what you've got out here? Look out the window. Right now, do it."

"All right," I said.

"Do you see any trees?"

"I see three trees and a bush. It might be two bushes."

"Are you lying to me? Trees in Texas?"

"I don't know what kind of trees they are, but they're pretty tall," I said.

"Darling, the way your show has taken off, you're in for a good bit more money damn quick. Let's not kid anybody, you're the one who makes that show click. I told Norman this morning. The others are just actors, John Lee, you're real. On that screen you are a genuine authentic Texas cowboy! And why not? That's what you are. Down there roping and riding and getting healthy. The truth is, you were looking a tiny bit haggard. Women and booze have wiped out many a strong man before he was due. Stay clean, darling. I know you love your horse, but hurry back to us."

"Why don't you come to Texas?" I said.

"Is it hot there?"

"A lot of the time."

"Do people carry guns?"

"Some do."

"From my house I can see palm trees and fig trees and the Pacific Ocean," she said. "I have warm, friendly neighbors. We drink cold gin. I work hard. I have fun on the beach. You come here instead. John Lee, I demand you tell me why you left."

"The people out there stick their heads out the windows of their cars and howl like wolves," I said.

"And in Texas you're all so calm and laconic. You sit and whittle and pick at your guitars and croon to the cows. Have I about got the idea?"

143

"Ever heard of Big Earl?" I said.

"The fabulous billionaire Big Earl, of course," she said.

"There's a chance he might give me two million dollars to finance my movie."

"Darling! This could be a whole new direction for your career."

"I figured that out."

"But you don't know anything, really, about making films."

"With two million dollars I wouldn't have to know much," I said.

"When can you put your hands on the money?" said Annie.

"As soon as the man who's managing this project agrees with me about what kind of film it will be."

"What's the chance of that?"

"Slim."

"Oh, John Lee, if you would only grow up, you could be so wonderful. But you've hung onto your adolescence too hard and for far too long. My darling, you've made your point. Whatever it is, you've made it and made it. Now don't break your heart with this. Tell the nice Mr. Big Earl you will be glad to place his money in a good solid property, and we'll find one, the absolutely right one, for you to star in. A feature film. Meanwhile, let me call Norman Feldman back in a day or two and start negotiating a new contract."

"Don't call him," I said.

"He loves you. He's hurt."

"Norman's grown up. He can handle it."

"You think people can handle things they can't handle," said Annie. "Not everybody is a big, rough, straightforward cowboy with no weaknesses. Some people are able to feel despair."

"Annie, do you know me?"

"Right to the heart, darling."

"Then don't talk bullshit to me," I said.

I had met Annie Nash the first day I arrived in California. I found out later that the way I happened to be there seemed very unusual to many people, but I was so accustomed to weird things that it didn't strike me as any odder than my ordinary life. In the summer of 1961 I had interviewed a movie producer named Denny Spencer on a TV

144

show in Dallas, and I had mentioned working on ranches and riding in rodeos, maybe embroidering a bit on my experiences. Spencer said he was casting a Western feature, and he believed in hunches, and he had a hunch I'd be good in a fairly small role as some kind of a raunchy gunman. I didn't see any reason why I couldn't do it. I could ride a horse and pull a trigger and lie with a straight face, and I wasn't afraid of cameras. But I didn't believe Spencer would remember the conversation when he left Dallas. I was wrong. He sent me an airplane ticket and three hundred dollars expense money. I had three weeks' vacation coming, so I thought I would go out to California and have a few adventures to be paid for by Denny Spencer Productions.

I had expected Denny Spencer himself to pick me up at the airport. Instead, when I answered the page I was met by a pretty little black-haired girl who was very intense and serious and intellectual and had a knockout body.

"I am a production assistant for Mr. Spencer," she said. "Where's your boots and hat?"

"In the suitcase with my horse and saddle," I said. "Actually, he's just a pony."

"Come on then, Tex. Let's go to work," she said.

We were stalled in traffic on the freeway in her white Volkswagen convertible, and I found myself crying from the smog. My eyes stung, and I kept blinking and tears dripped onto my lapels. The girl, Peggy, looked at me with amusement.

"You're not very tough, are you?" she said.

"I'm sentimental."

"Tex, do you have an agent?"

"What would I need with an agent?"

"You're too old to know so little," she said.

I suppose Peggy was touched by the sight of a weeping cowboy, even if he was wearing cordovan loafers and a flannel blazer. We stopped at the Beverly Wilshire drug store for a bottle of eyedrops, and Peggy put in a call to Annie Nash, describing my situation. "Annie said to tell you to beware of Denny Spencer—he's not a nice man. And to bring you over pronto," Peggy said, after hanging up.

145

Annie Nash's office on Wilshire Boulevard was in a red-brick building with a marble front. "Annie is a very successful agent, but she might be willing to take you on," Peggy said as we rode up in the elevator. "She's looked after me ever since I came out here from Michigan three years ago. I lived with her for a while." Peggy looked at me to see what I would think about that, but it was all right with me who she had lived with.

Annie Nash came around her palette-shaped desk and kissed Peggy and shook hands with me. Annie was a handsome woman in her forties, with her hair cut short in Jane Wyman bangs. She wore a white silk blouse and dark slacks and her pearl ropes rattled when she shook my hand.

"The very first thing I have to tell you is Denny Spencer is a bastard," said Annie.

"He's nice enough to send me money."

"I think you need me, John Lee," Annie said.

Peggy smiled. I had started to understand that I would be in bed with Peggy before the night was over, and instead of being jealous, Annie Nash liked the idea, and I had probably misread her relationship with Peggy in the first place. After a few minutes of conversation I signed an agreement making Annie Nash my agent, and we shook hands again and all kissed each other, and then Peggy drove me to Spencer's office.

"Some people spend years out here without ever getting a good agent like Annie," said Peggy.

"Let's go to dinner tonight, and I will thank you for introducing me."

"You know what it is, Tex? As soon as I looked at you, I could tell it has never occurred to you that you might fail."

"At what?" I said.

"At anything you might want to do."

The fact was, it had never occurred to me I might fail at being a movie actor because I had not thought that far ahead. Of course, I didn't know Denny Spencer yet. He sent for me immediately when we arrived at the office. He sat with his feet on the desk, freckled arms folded across his chest, cigar sticking out of his freckled face, red hair standing an inch high.

"Wallace, I want you to get the sense of the total concept of the involvement of yourself as a creation of a rounded, coherent whole, as this film is," he said. "You won't have much to say in this film, but every word you say is loaded with meaning, dig? You delve behind the words, and discover the man who is saying them. You do exactly what I tell you, and you go deep, and you feel deep. You start to work Thursday morning. Peggy will tell you where to be. From now on, your life is in my hands."

"Don't I get a screen test?" I said.

"I've seen you on TV. That's enough. Just don't forget, I know what I'm doing and you don't. Have an agent?"

"Annie Nash."

"That fucking dyke, she's no goddamn good for you. Fire her."

"I can't fire her. I like her."

"She's a bad person, Wallace. How long have you been in Los Angeles?"

"About four hours."

"Fire Annie Nash. I'll get you a good agent."

"I'm not going to fire her, and I'm not going to give you back your three hundred dollars," I said.

"Think you're a stud badass, huh? You be there Thursday morning, hoss."

With only three hundred dollars in my pocket and no contract yet signed, Peggy persuaded me not to check into a hotel but to sleep on the couch in her apartment in Santa Monica until it was certain Denny Spencer intended to pay me. But I did take her to dinner at La Scala, promptly blowing a fifth of my entire bankroll. There were some actors I recognized at the red leather bar, and Peggy kept pointing out producers and directors in the booths. It made her horny to look at them. She talked about Raskolnikov—and I told her about the time Buster and I declared student day and wore ragged clothes and wandered around Dallas drinking wine and ripping pages out of *Crime and Punishment* and seeing if we could find exactly the right

147

old lady so we could persuade her to murder us, which was more like the way things work. Peggy smiled, but she wasn't listening. She talked about Raskolnikov, but she loved movies, and being in La Scala with these slick, magic people was making juice run down her legs.

I stayed with Peggy in Santa Monica for three weeks while I worked in the Western called *Ride, Comancheros!* Peggy adored for me to show up in the evening with my make-up on. We ruined her sheets. Annie Nash had got me a contract at a thousand dollars a week for the three weeks. That was eight hundred a week more than I had been making in Dallas, but this wasn't steady employment and it wasn't even easy. It was the most boring work I had ever done. Hours of sitting and listening to people argue about where to move a light. Every line I spoke and every bit of action I took, Denny Spencer told me it was wrong. He mentioned total concept over and over. I began to realize that Denny Spencer not only had no concept of the total concept, but was also very close to panic. I had seen *Ride, Comancheros!* twenty times under different titles, and I knew that all you had to do was say words and shoot your gun, and any discussion of this movie beyond that level was ridiculous. By the time *Ride, Comancheros!* had finished, my part had grown. A stunt man from New Mexico and I were the only ones who openly spoke of *Ride, Comancheros!* as bullshit, and this brought Denny Spencer to the verge of psychosis; he rode me harder every day. The more he rode me, the more I began to hate him, the better I got in my role as a killer, the bigger my part became. At last I put in my final day on the set and then went to Denny Spencer and told him if he ever saw me anywhere again, he had better run for his life.

My vacation was over. I was at Peggy's, packing to go back to Dallas, when Annie Nash arrived.

"You should stay here, John Lee. You've got a career ahead of you," she said.

"Anything that's waiting for me is in Texas."

"Peggy wants you to stay."

"She knows it's time for us to break up. She's got her eye on a screenwriter who lives in the hills."

"Darling, you're too smart to go back to Texas right now. The word is out on you. Everybody knows you're great. Everybody knows you saved Denny Spencer's ass in this film."

"Annie, do you people ever say anything believable? If I don't go back to Dallas today I'll lose my job. How long will three thousand dollars last?"

"I've got another part for you. I can get you fifteen thousand for it. And it's going to be shot on location in the Far East. Exciting?"

"What kind of role do I play?" I said.

"A killer," said Annie.

I phoned the TV station and told them they had lost me. Geraldine came out to see if I could convince her not to marry Herbert, but paying a hundred and twenty-five dollars a day for her bungalow was not the way for me to do it. The film was postponed twice, and I got very broke and took in a dope-fiend actor and a stoned sound technician to live with me in my rented pink stucco house. One afternoon I found several pieces of notepaper under the actor's window. He played pretty-young-man parts, but he thought he was getting ugly and was always throwing notes out the window asking for help. On one piece of paper it said TC. The next piece said TOO M. The printing covered the entire page. It required six pages before the actor could make his printing small enough to get his message on one sheet of paper. The message said TOO MUCH SPEED. I found him in his room with a needle stuck in his arm, just pumping blood back and forth, fascinated with it.

I was out of work again after we shot the film in the Far East. I owed two months' rent and Geraldine was threatening to jail me for back child-support. Annie Nash called and asked if I wanted to be Tarzan.

"Careerwise, this may not be a thoroughly super thing for you, but it pays twenty-five thousand," she said.

My work in the Tarzan film took eighteen days. People acted as if they expected me to be embarrassed about it, but I wasn't. We had a good time with it. In the back of my mind was the thought that nobody I knew would see this movie, anyhow. The day we wound it

149

up, we gave a party for Cheeta at the pink stucco house. The speed-freak actor, who had just been released from the hospital, jumped off the porch and broke his leg. A naked girl ran down the hill. The police came. The party made me nostalgic for Dallas. I called Buster and flew to Dallas the next morning and met Dorothy a week later.

Again, there was no work for months. Annie Nash kept calling about roles that didn't materialize. I got two good parts in pictures that were canceled. But Dorothy was living with me in Hollywood, and I had a little money, and I was feeling fine again and I knew my luck was on the rise. Then Norman Feldman walked up to our table at Steffanino's and introduced himself. He had seen *Ride, Comancheros!* He wanted to talk to me about a new TV series. He wanted me to put my hat and boots back on. He said he knew my background, and he knew what I really was and he wanted me on horseback.

"I want you to be John Lee Wallace," he said.

"You'll have to talk to Annie Nash about that," I said.

Book Three

14

There was a feint at autumn in Dallas before the hot weather returned. In October, the temperature was in the nineties. When you drove along the streets the city hummed and quivered with air conditioning. Car windows were kept shut, and people looked incredulously at me in Buster's little Morris Minor with the windows open and hot air blowing in my face.

Buster and I shot film at Neiman-Marcus, at a livestock auction, at a quarterhorse farm, at a revivalist church service, at the First National Bank, in a slum where several hundred Indians lived, at a night club, at a dress factory. We showed the film at the apartment and discussed possible ways to edit it, but we didn't yet know where we were going. Buster believed destiny would show us the path. He didn't take Big Earl's offer seriously, and he refused to allow me to brood about it. My funds were disappearing in a hurry, but we kept the Bolex working.

Most nights I sat on the couch and read magazines and smoked and occasionally peered at TV, rising from my seat to go to the kitchen for sandwiches, ice cream and glasses of wine. I gained eight pounds.

Jingo threw out Buster's stale food and restocked the refrigerator. She would come over about five in the afternoon bearing a Sara Lee coffeecake or a half-gallon of banana-nut ice cream. She would stay a couple of hours, leave for work in a haze of smoke and come back about two in the morning, by which time I was usually asleep. She spent the night in my bed without waking me. I would find a note from her on the dresser—*JL (smile) you ravished me again you Hollywood satire ha!* A doctor friend arrived with a quart of vodka one evening, wondered at the curious aroma in the apartment and gave me a prescription for a hundred Dexamyls. I took the prescription, of course, but I hid the pills away for some other time. I stayed off amphetamines for a week, and then for several days, and then for another week. I slept twelve hours every night. I began to feel I had blood in me again instead of spooks.

I dialed Dorothy's number several times and got no answer. Then one evening her mother Ina Mae picked up the phone and was full of apologies for her forlorn suicide attempt. "All in all, I guess I'm glad I'm not dead," she said. Ina Mae said Dorothy had moved into an apartment with three other girls. "The poor kid doesn't have any money. I don't know how she's getting by." I could guess. She gave me Dorothy's number and urged me to call her. But one day drifted into the next, and I didn't call, and when I thought about her it was with a sort of numbness. Her nightgown and douche bag were still hanging in the spare bathroom.

Buster knew a girl who worked as a waitress at a good restaurant that specialized in Chateaubriand. She began arriving at the apartment in the afternoon about the same hour Jingo showed up, bringing slabs of steak from the restaurant and cooking them for us and making a salad; then the four of us would sit down with a half-gallon of California red wine. Buster was busy shooting pictures for several magazines and doing a series of ads for a bank as well as operating the Bolex. He had a tiny studio and darkroom not far from the apartment, but he seldom did his own lab work, unless it was for nude photos of the girls he brought home. Women of all ages and stations would gladly peel once Buster promised he'd destroy the negatives and not show the prints to anyone other than themselves. Buster appeared by remote control in more than one series wearing a Lone Ranger mask and drooping black socks.

I had first encountered Buster when I was a TV news reporter toting a 16-millimeter movie camera that I had only a dim notion how to operate. In those days I was responsible for radio news also. I would start a working shift at five-thirty in the morning at the pressroom at police headquarters. I would check the desk sergeant's reports of the night ending and make rounds of various divisions—traffic, homicide, juvenile, vice, the general detective office, the jail sergeant, the radio dispatchers. If anybody interesting was in jail I would look up his record in the ID Bureau and always assume that if a record existed it was correct. Early in the morning I phoned hospitals and questioned emergency rooms about the night's activities and then talked to nursing supervisors about patients who might be good for feature stories —unusually gruesome operations, terrible hard luck, any number of oddities. I phoned the Fire Department every morning. Often the people I knew on my beat would call me if there was a story. Nearly all of them liked seeing themselves on television or hearing their voices on the radio. Sometimes I would rush out to shoot film at a hospital or a fire or a crash site, or at the scene of a murder or holdup. Always I had to phone the news department and tell them what was up and dictate the radio reports either live or into a tape machine. I hated dictating from the pressroom. I put on a dramatic radio voice for these reports, another self. It came across fine on the air, but in the pressroom it sounded as if I were auditioning for announcing class. Other reporters, those from newspapers, would listen and applaud. If they knew my broadcast was live, they would yell "fuck!" We constantly listened to the police radio. In the flow of talk we were alert for the dispatcher's voice cutting in with a Signal 19 (shooting),

18 (fire), 7 (accident), 14 (stabbing), 17 (gang fight), 20 (robbery), 20a (robbery in progress), and 27 (dead person), and we listened for him to say Code 3, which meant it was a top emergency. Upon hearing one of these signals we would phone the dispatcher for more information and then we'd run for our cars and race each other to the scene. Many stories washed out when we recognized the address as being in a black neighborhood, or if the dispatcher or detectives involved brushed it off by saying, "Nigger deal," just as the cop at Parkland had done on the night of Ina Mae Leclaire's stomach-pumping. Maybe the blacks were on municipal golf courses and in hotel lobbies now, but some things hadn't changed. Newspapers, radio and television did not report violence involving blacks unless it was against whites. They did not report much of anything at all involving blacks, with the exception of professional sporting events, unless it was humorous, like watermelon stealing. But if a black man killed a white man or raped a white woman, you would see detectives in the hall with shotguns, and you had a story.

One of the last stories I ever shot film on—this was after I had moved from police reporting into general assignments and was working out of the TV station—was a civil rights sit-in at a drugstore near the SMU campus. Twenty young Negroes and whites sat at the soda counter waiting to be served. The drugstore doors were locked and a fumigating company was called to spray the inside of the building with insecticide. The demonstrators withstood the white smoke for fifteen minutes or so. Then they came to the glass doors and begged to be let out. Police and firemen dragged out several who were unconscious. The drugstore owner shook his fist at the demonstrators and told them they had ruined the goods on his shelves. Some of the demonstrators were theological students. I interviewed the owner, the police, the demonstrators and the crowd and went back to the station with my film and tapes. The film was not used. The incident was never mentioned on the air or in the newspapers. If such a thing should be reported, I was told, it would encourage other radicals to cause trouble in a peaceful city.

In the pressroom, many days were tedious. I read paperbacks and played cards. There were only two narcotics officers on the force then. They had little to do. One of them sat on my desk almost every day and talked. Several times he gave me bags of marijuana he had taken away from people.

"This is low-class dope. Only people use it are niggers, Meskins, musicians and white trash," he used to say. I kept the marijuana in a desk drawer. I didn't bother to tell him that I sometimes smoked it. He didn't tell me that he was a morphine addict. Several years later he got busted by a state agent.

One morning Buster E. Gregory walked into the pressroom carrying a Speed Graphic camera and wearing a shoulder bag full of plates. He was in his early twenties, about my age. He was much thinner then, the way I still remember him, and very brown with thick black hair. Neither of us had been out of the Army for long. This was Buster's first job in journalism, as it was mine. We got coffee from a machine in the hall. He told me he had gone to photography school in the army and then had been assigned as a lifeguard and swimming instructor in Honolulu, where he became serious about photography as a potential hustle once he got out. He admitted that he was a great photographer and would prefer shooting 35-millimeter natural light with his Rolleiflex, but the Dallas *Morning News* insisted on Speed Graphic shots with flash, for fast news. Buster had come to police headquarters with a reporter who was also a rookie. They were supposed to do a feature on the radio dispatchers, a story that was done every eighteen months.

While we were drinking coffee, the police radio announced a Signal 27 in Oak Cliff. At that moment a homicide detective named Brady, a white-haired fellow who wore a snap-brim hat and flicked cigar ashes onto his tie and vest, hurried past on the way to his car. "Don't know, boys. Can't tell yet. White woman dead in her bathroom. Probably had cancer," he said. Buster and I and the rookie reporter rode with Brady, who was working alone because his partner had the mumps. It was a two-story white frame house with another family living upstairs. A junked washing machine lay in the front yard. The houses on either side were very close. The dead woman, who was in

157

her sixties, had lived downstairs with her fifty-year-old nephew and his wife. We stepped around sticky patches of blood in the hall. The woman lay back on the bathroom floor with her arms spread and one foot up on the toilet. But her head was turned so that her eyes looked at us in the hall. The cut went clear through her neck to the spinal cord. "This is a terrible thing, boys, terrible," Brady said. The Justice of the Peace arrived and looked at the body. Brady and the JP talked to the nephew and wife, who said the woman had been depressed. The nephew wore work khakis and had an Adam's apple the size of a lemon. Brady showed a double-edged razor blade he'd found on the sink. The JP pronounced the death suicide. Buster had taken a hundred pictures by then, three or four with the Speed Graphic. We pointed out that the woman's fingertips had not been damaged as she sawed through her throat. "Poor woman must of been desperate," Brady said.

The photos that Buster took and the film I shot did not appear in the newspaper or on television. Suicides ordinarily rated about a paragraph of newspaper space and no television time unless there was an angle more interesting than the distasteful death of a poor woman in a low-rent neighborhood. Buster brought back prints for the pressroom bulletin board. We thumbtacked them up with the caption SUICIDE OF THE WEEK. We had no sooner put up the photos than there was another dead person call, and we found ourselves in Brady's car again. He complained about having to work too hard with his partner loafing at home. Buster gave him a print of the dead woman, and Brady said he'd keep it for his scrapbook. When we arrived at the scene of the call, a swollen bundle was draining on the shore of White Rock Lake. A fisherman thought he'd hooked a record catfish. Instead, he had snagged the body of a young prostitute and narcotics informer, whose skull was crushed and whose hands and feet were bound with chains. Brady looked at the body for a long time, very annoyed, showering his vest with cigar ashes. Finally he said, "Boys, I sure do hate to say this, but I'm afraid it looks like foul play to me." That became a slogan around police headquarters and the bars where we hung out—*it looks like foul play to me*—and I suppose Buster and

I were both struck by the fact that our first two experiences together had been on the piquant side, and if we kept at it we might remain entertained.

Buster's full name was Buster Elam Gregory. He came from Grand Prairie, a small town between Dallas and Fort Worth. His father worked in a bank. Buster had played halfback on the high school football team and had belonged to the DeMolay and 4-H clubs. He had raised swine and calves and had been on the Grand Prairie shrub-judging team. He had boxed in the Golden Gloves, winning his first match by a knockout and losing his second the same way. He went to Arlington State College for a year and transferred to TCU, in Fort Worth, to get further from home. Buster married Alma while on leave after photography school and took her to Honolulu with him. She talked about Honolulu incessantly. Alma had a tremendous memory for detail. In the next five or six years I learned Honolulu street names, gasoline prices, distances from one point to another, shop-window decor and much more. In a lengthy, nasal description of sights along a Honolulu thoroughfare, Alma would drop in *you know*'s after nearly every phrase and before proper nouns. We introduced Geraldine and Alma to each other while drinking beer and eating pizza at Gordo's about two nights after I'd first met Buster. The two women didn't like each other much, but they had a common dissatisfaction leading to disgust with most of the things Buster and I did. Alma endured her life more stoically than Geraldine. That first night, while Buster was at the jukebox, she told us with a mild frown that Buster forced her "to play wheelbarrow." The worst thing, she said, was when they played wheelbarrow up and down the stairs. Afterward I was never able to get entirely out of mind the picture of Alma being wheeled around the apartment, up and down stairs, while she presented Buster a lecture on a scenic tour of *you know* Honolulu.

Shortly after we met, Buster and Geraldine had a romance that lasted for a week or two before they both, separately, told me about it. But I didn't care. I trusted Buster not to do me harm. Geraldine was in one of her spells when she thought I was getting along too well and needed humbling. One of her methods of moving in to break up a friendship of mine or otherwise cause me trouble was to use her considerable sexual powers in some devious manner. At times she set out to block me off from everybody else. Or she would encourage me to rush out and be free. I took some hard falls at the end of Geraldine's rope. Anyhow, I knew Geraldine didn't want Buster, and he wouldn't want her when he got to know her better.

A year or so after we met we all moved into the same apartment building. It was U-shaped, with grass in the center and the open end facing the street. Buster and Alma, who'd just had twins, lived in the front of the building. Geraldine, Caroline and I were in the rear. The apartments had a living room, dining room and kitchen downstairs, two bedrooms and two baths up. The apartments were owned by SMU, and the rent was one hundred thirty-five a month, unfurnished, utilities included. Buster and I were both making about a hundred dollars a week. Some months, Geraldine would make five hundred doing TV commercials, some months nothing. Alma got a job as receptionist and secretary at a furniture store for sixty a week. Alma and Geraldine each hired a Negro woman at twenty-five dollars a week to clean the apartments, do the laundry and look after the kids from about eight till five or six, five days a week. The maids would baby-sit for fifty cents an hour. That left the four of us relatively loose to roam. Buster was fooling with some girl from the circulation department he persisted in screwing on a bamboo mat on her bedroom floor. For two months his knees and elbows bled. He told Alma he kept falling into a rose bush. Then one evening Alma came to see Geraldine and me, weeping, and said she'd been carrying on with a guy at the furniture store. Buster had found a rubber in the car. I would have been nearly as surprised if my own mother had confessed to an affair with Mickey Mantle. Now that all four of us were known to have moral failings, Buster and I began to devise elaborate schemes for wife-swapping. But Geraldine said it was wicked and corrupt to think of such a thing, and Alma said we ought to get right down on our knees and tell God we were sorry for our dirty minds. Since we knew that Alma had fooled around and Geraldine had even screwed Buster in the car parked by the tennis courts, it didn't make sense that

160

we couldn't get it going among the tight little family we had become. One midnight at Gordo's, Buster and I thought up an idea that seemed so simple and beautiful that it could not fail: when we returned home, I would get into his bed and he would get into mine. In the dark the two women would be relieved of whatever they considered their moral responsibilities. I crept up Buster's stairs and saw Alma lying in the moonlight in her short chiffon nightie. Knowing from her own complaints that she was accustomed to being mounted at any hour, I crawled into bed with her and went straight to work. Somehow, Alma planted a bare foot against my forehead and thrust me onto the floor. "John Lee Wallace, if you don't get out of here I'm going to call your wife!" she said. I went back to my own apartment and sat on the porch to drink a can of Falstaff while Buster explored Geraldine upstairs. I heard Geraldine yell from the window, "You wretched ass, you're worse than a goat!" Buster came down and sat on the porch with me, and we drank and talked until the Venezuelan woman law student across the way stepped out in a nightgown for her morning paper.

One summer Buster and I went to the landlord, a dean, to complain about the condition of the paint and the landscaping. We were evicted. I bought the gray-brick house in North Dallas. Buster and Alma bought a red-brick house, nearly identical to ours, with a GI mortgage, a few miles to the west. Discounting separations, when Geraldine would flee with Caroline to Houston or I would find a room someplace, we lived in that house for three years before Geraldine packed me that final bag. We'd had a fight, I don't remember how it started, that had lasted too long and gone too far, and there was no way to come back from it. I brought home a Chevrolet convertible and two bottles of champagne as birthday gifts for Geraldine, but she pointed out that she'd already packed the bag and I may as well pick it up and keep moving. Geraldine kept the car, but I took the champagne with me.

Buster and Alma had me over for dinner a few times. I was doing the TV news on camera by then. My notoriety was spreading. Geraldine had detested the idea that I was recognized and often pandered to when we went out. She'd been recognized for years because of her TV commercials, but now people knew her name: Mrs. Wallace. Alma, however, seemed to enjoy it when she went out with Buster and me. People in clubs and restaurants would stare at us, and Alma would babble, taking short gasps for breath. Alma was pleased not to have Geraldine around, although she continued to say that Geraldine and I would be getting back together. I think I believed it then, sort of took it as a matter of course that Geraldine and I were thoroughly mismatched, unsuited, exciting together and inevitable.

Before long Alma actually contrived to catch Buster in their own bed with a neighbor whose laundry was in Alma's dryer. As a reward not only for her enterprise but also for her refusal to leave the room while she telephoned her father and her threat to phone the woman's husband, Buster broke Alma's jaw in seven places with one punch. He was sorry he had done it, and he took flowers to her in the hospital. As Buster was entering the hospital, Alma's father, a prominent Episcopal layman with a sturdy old sense of crime and punishment, assaulted him and smashed a vase across his head, whereupon Buster knocked him down and threw the roses on him. Buster was strong that week. Since early in World War Two, Alma's father had been an aircraft-design engineer in Grand Prairie, but he decided he had seen all of Buster he wanted and moved to Seattle to work for Boeing. Alma and the twins followed her parents out there. The twins came to Dallas once a year for a visit of precisely three weeks and lay beside the apartment swimming pool pining for the forests and the soft green hills and the ocean. By the time they adjusted to Buster's life, and he to their presence, Alma called to remind the twins to come home. Every few months Alma phoned Buster to tell him how happy she was and to threaten to have him put in jail if his child-support payments were ever late again. She would talk for an hour and would wind up bitching at him and getting hung up on.

Each time Buster came to see me in California, usually when he was on some magazine assignment, it was a flashing, smoky speed-run of events that never would get sorted out in my mind but never needed to be. Buster seldom went to the movies, and he watched television

162

only when in a quietly addled condition, and thus the names of actors or directors he met meant nothing to him. The Polo Lounge and Gordo's were all the same to Buster. We carried pocketfuls of amy poppers and did them in nasal inhalers in strange places at unlikely times. Many of the people who met Buster grew confused at first at not being recognized and avoided him as though he intended to destroy their investment in analysis. He paid no attention to this, either, and soon some were drawn back to find out what was wrong with him. I began to hear Buster described as "real." At a party at the pink stucco house above Sunset Boulevard, I heard an actor telling another, "This cat that is a friend of John Lee's is so funky that he doesn't know what the word means, and he can write his name on the porch in piss." After Buster's first visit, each time he returned, more and more of my peers would rush to lay grass, coke and pills on him and buy him drinks and offer him their flesh in return for it being known around town that they were capable of keeping company with a real person. Buster knew all this was going on, of course. He just didn't give a damn.

Lying around Buster's apartment after running off from my pink stucco house in Hollywood, I read the newspapers every day, starting at the top left of page one and finishing at the bottom right of the last page. Dallas is a city of more than a million people but only two major newspapers—the *News* in the morning and the *Times-Herald* in the afternoon. The papers have a fortune in advertising to divide, and each owns its own TV and radio stations. Occasionally the papers made a show of competing for news, but this was often the work of a new young reporter who either moved on or settled back to a life of nolo contendere with low but regular pay. Because of the large amount of advertising there were a lot of odd columns to fill up around the ads, and so I had plenty to look at.

Billy Bob Teagarden had his picture in both papers as his trial proceeded fitfully through a legal thicket. He smiled and looked confident for the cameras and said he was innocent at heart and optimistic that the jury would agree. Little Earl was summoned to the witness stand, but hardly any of his testimony appeared in the papers. Big Earl was reported ill with strep throat and still unable to testify. A front-page story said Governor Connally had met with President Kennedy in Washington to warn that the Democrats could expect a hard fight in the Texas elections. The President promised to come to Texas in late November to pull the Democratic Party together and meanwhile attract himself some votes. A luncheon was announced for him at a downtown hotel in Dallas but was later canceled because a charity ball had been scheduled for the same room. I read these stories because they were in the papers, not because I much cared. I read the politics with about the same interest that I read about the Dodgers winning the World Series in four straight (I watched on the TV as Koufax pitched against Whitey Ford in the opener). Negro churches were bombed in Alabama. A Mafia hoodlum was revealing intimacies of his trade. The British government broke apart in a wormy confusion of hookers, dope, spies and nude parties that were like a dream of Hollywood. The sister-in-law of the South Vietnamese President was touring the United States denouncing Buddhist monks as Communists and calling for an increase in the fifteen thousand American soldiers in her country. I wondered if Big Earl would receive her, after all, and if, in some mad stroke, he might go out to greet Kennedy with his tale of brain-wave attacks. Perhaps inspired by the amount of publicity gathered by the Billy Bob Teagarden affair, the Senate voted to investigate Bobby Baker, who seemed quite surprised, but confident that his old friend the Vice President would protect him. Wrestling matches between midget women were the attraction at the Sportatorium in Dallas. Rockefeller said the President's handling of the Cuban missile matter had been a flop and had placed the country in jeopardy. All this stuff sounded to me like the singing of America, a medium-level insanity, goofing, but not out of control. Sitting in Buster's apartment watching *Lassie* on TV, drinking half-gallon jugs of California wine and eating pineapple cheesecakes, hearing Jingo's accounts of her disputes with her boss, venturing out to shoot film with the Bolex, waiting for my forces to straighten out, I was more concerned with *Mary Worth* than I was with Madame Nhu. Buster felt the same way, but one morning he saw that a high school friend

164

of his, who had become a captain in the Green Berets, had been killed in the Mekong Delta. Buster phoned the young widow and went over to console her. I was reminded of kindly Herbert and lay on the couch speculating on Geraldine's potential widowhood. Buster refused to talk about the dead captain's wife when he returned. "I can't help it, I knew her before he did," is all he would say.

Sitting in front of an air-conditioning duct on a hot afternoon, I was turning the pages of the *Times-Herald* when I noticed a name that attracted my curiosity. Mexican and U.S. Customs agents had grabbed 125,000 rounds of ammunition bound for the interior of Mexico in six automobiles. The ammunition was of various kinds: .22 shorts, .30 for M-2 carbines, three thousand rounds of .30-06, fifteen thousand rounds of .38 Super and .38 Special, and assortments of .270, .25 and .30 caliber cartridges. The drivers of the cars of this traveling supermarket all told the same story. They had been hired in Nuevo Laredo and paid a hundred and twenty dollars each. They were to be intercepted somewhere along the highway toward Monterey and told where to deliver their loads. Upon delivery they were to be paid another hundred and twenty dollars each. Customs authorities were searching for a thirty-two-year-old American named Erwin Englethorpe for questioning. It was now my turn for news of old school friends. Except that it was not really correct to describe Erwin as a friend. Old antagonist was nearer the truth.

Erwin Englethorpe had given me my first puppy when I was five years old. He lifted the growling mother off a squirming litter in a cardboard box in his garage and gave me a black-and-white male that I kept for two years until the dog was run over in front of my house. When the dog got killed, Erwin hit me in the eye. He said he'd warned me he might want that dog back. Erwin taught me to play a game, which had a summer of popularity in the neighborhood, of bumping peckers. It was especially important to do it with little girls watching, which was not difficult to manage, as they were never reluctant for a show of that sort. But it was no good for mothers to see the game, although it might have been esoterically satisfying for Erwin. My mother observed us one afternoon, and it was all over for me, threatened with turning piebald if I ever did it again. Erwin was never allowed back inside our house. His daddy, the milkman, gave Erwin a terrible, noisy beating that started on the sidewalk with an audience of several kids. We admired Erwin for fighting back, running, cussing, kicking, but his daddy won the fight. Erwin knocked out most of my baby teeth with his fists at one time or another. At the age of ten we fought to the death with butcher knives, using garbage-can lids as shields. I slashed Erwin's arm, knocked him down and was whanging on his shield with my butcher knife, intending to kill him, when the man who lived next to the vacant lot rushed over and threw us apart. I was fascinated with myself for the way I had acted in that moment of extreme violence and almost looked forward to another encounter with Erwin. But a few months later Erwin broke my nose in a fistfight, and we were nearly back to where we had started, but not quite. We had our last fight in junior high, and Erwin won again, chipping two of my front teeth and purpling an eye.

Erwin tried out for the football team in high school, as everyone was expected to do, but he wouldn't accept the discipline and didn't have the desire to stick it out. He might have been a good guard if we hadn't had to practice every day. The coach kept demanding that we "pay the price." Erwin was caught cheating on his laps. The coach ordered him to stand on the fifty-yard line, and every boy on the squad lined up to tackle him. By the time I hit him, we had driven him over against the water fountain, and he was swinging his fists when I ran at him. I hit him hard and knocked him against the stone fountain. Erwin was bleeding from a dozen scrapes and cuts, and a boil had burst on his elbow and his uniform was torn and dirty. I told him I was sorry for tackling him. He glared at me and said, "Shit on you, Wallace." Erwin came back to a few more practices and was doing well enough to be promoted to the first string, but then one day he didn't show up. He began wearing a black leather jacket with silver studs and a black cap and riding to school on a motorcycle. He hung around the other side of the building from where my group loafed. The motorcycle jocks never went to the drive-in cafés many of us frequented. If a motorjock did show up, he would probably have to fight at least one football player. Erwin moved into a different world from mine. Although we lived in the same neighborhood and went to the same high school, I had no idea what he did with his time. I don't recall seeing him at the party on graduation night. While I was in college I heard Erwin had a job selling seat covers and spare auto parts.

I next ran into Erwin at police headquarters when I was a TV reporter. He'd been arrested on suspicion of burglary. I saw him on his way to the property room to retrieve his bag of tools. "Got to have my tools so I can make money to pay my lawyer," Erwin said. "It's a circle they catch you in." Erwin had become what is called a "police character." The cops used to pick up known characters on sight, stick them in jail on suspicion of whatever burglaries, thefts or armed robberies were current, kick them around a bit and parade them at line-ups for each changing shift before letting them go. At a line-up, Erwin would be forced to walk back and forth while a sergeant or lieutenant would say, "This is Erwin Englethorpe. No-billed three times for breaking and entering, two arrests with no convictions for armed robbery, one arrest with no conviction for sodomy, no-billed for showing his cock to a minor female, several arrests for drunk and disorderly and simple assault, several arrests for aggravated assault. Erwin is a known burglar and armed robber. He says his trade is salesman and auto mechanic. Last known employment was eight years ago. Take a good look at him. He's one of our Dallas boys. You know we don't like you here, Erwin. Do you hear me? We don't like having you on our streets. Every time we see you, we are going to bring you down here for a visit. Why don't you leave town, Erwin?" Sometimes a particularly bothersome character would be sneaked out of the jail in the company of a Texas Ranger, with no arrest report having been filed, either to be hidden so he would not be released on bail while a crime was being investigated, or to be persuaded to move to another state. Being a character was not a life to grow old in. But Erwin seemed very cheerful and asked if I could put his picture on television. "I want to show all the folks I've made good," he said. I shot some film of him and tried to get him onto the late news in one of those desperado-nabbed-again stories, but it was a busy night for news and Erwin was rejected. Preparing the story, I looked up Erwin's record. He had been arrested twenty times but had served less than thirty days in the county jail. His lawyers' fees had amounted to far more than my total salary. I saw him in the hall or in the tank or the line-up or in an interrogation room several times more, and we exchanged a few words if we could. His right forearm still had the scar I'd put there with the butcher knife—a raised white welt about four inches long—and on his large right bicep the words DEVILDOG and USMC framed the tattoo of a bulldog wearing a tin helmet.

Then I didn't see Erwin around any more. The last I'd heard of him was that he had married a stripper.

When Jingo arrived I asked if she knew Erwin Englethorpe.

"From New Orleans?"

"I don't know where he's from now. He married a dancer named Bumpy Rhodes."

"Curvy Rhodes, you mean! That whore! What a goddamn mean junky slut!"

"I guess you knew her, then," I said.

"The mob had to work overtime to bring in enough dope for her to get straight enough to say hello. She shot up her toes so it wouldn't show. But how many toes has a person got? I mean the bitch whore had to run out of toes." Jingo put a jar of honey and a loaf of rye bread on the kitchen bar and then reached into her leather bag and pulled out a coconut cake. "She shot up the soles of her feet! John Lee, you should have seen her number. Like she was dancing on sponges. What she wouldn't steal, nobody has ever bought yet. Put it down and blink and Curvy had it at the hock shop. Before she got so far out of it she couldn't talk, every word she said was a lie. She worked for me on Bourbon Street."

"You had your own place?" I said.

"Well, come on, man, you know what I mean. I sort of had four places down there for a while, was out front of them, you know, all within three blocks of each other, before that son-of-a-bitch District Attorney Garrison, that big tall lump of do, put on a crusading

168

clean-up face and ran me out. I mean I was a big stah, and a certain police official had given me my new Cadillac, so Garrison picked on me. But that Curvy Rhodes, she was a foul ball even for Bourbon Street. She had some crooked sucker for a husband—must have been the guy you asked about—and what a time he had! She'd steal his damn shoes!"

"Erwin was making his way toward being tough when I knew him," I said.

"Goddamn, I guess he'd better have been tough. I used to see him with Mexicans and Cubans that were solid killers."

"Where's Curvy Rhodes working now?"

"Nowhere, I hope," said Jingo. "She's dead."

"What did she die of?"

"Who knows? When you get that heavy, you don't live too long. How about if I make you a sandwich with honey and butter on this good bread while you go get us some milk?"

About dusk I was pushing a wire cart through a supermarket when I rounded a stack of pork-and-beans cans and saw Big Earl engaged in a dispute with an old woman in the Dietetic & Health section. Ginger Pops yapped sharply from the basket of Big Earl's cart.

"You can't bring a dog in here," the old lady was saying.

"Clearly Ginger Pops is in here already, so you are wrong about that," said Big Earl.

"I'm right right right," the old woman said.

"Wrong wrong wrong," said Big Earl.

His angel hair fluttered and he had his furious baby look. I expected Mr. Clwyd to spring out from behind the Ry Krisp and remove the old lady, but Big Earl seemed to be alone, except for Ginger Pops.

The old lady took one step back and two fast steps forward and crashed her cart into Big Earl's cart, causing Ginger Pops to yip with rage.

"Who sent you here?" Big Earl said.

"I come here every day," said the old lady.

169

"You've been sent here to pick on me," Big Earl said.

He stamped his foot. With his gray suit and blue bow tie, he was wearing black railroad shoes.

"You retired old idiots with your dogs and cats make me sick. There are people starving in the world, and you put a ribbon on your dog," said the lady.

"I could hit you. I used to be a boxer, you know," Big Earl said.

"I used to rope steers," said the old lady.

"I could knock you out with one punch, probably," Big Earl said.

"I could kick you in the leg and break it."

"I could pull your hair."

"I could get your nose."

"Not my nose, you couldn't!" cried Big Earl.

I walked over to them. Ginger Pops twirled around barking in the basket.

"Are you the manager?" Big Earl said.

"No sir, I'm John Lee Wallace."

He frowned at me angrily, his blue eyes squinting, and then he smiled.

"You're Clive Riordan," he said.

"Yeah, I'm him, too."

"Clive, tell this old crank to get his dog out of the store," said the lady.

"This is Clive Riordan from *Six Guns Across Texas,*" Big Earl said.

"I know who he is," said the old lady. "That's why I know he believes in doing the right thing. The sign on the door says no pets allowed inside. This fuzzy little animal is a pet, from the looks of it. It sure don't work for a living."

"Clive is my personal friend," Big Earl said.

"He's my friend, too," said the old lady.

"Clive, you make this woman leave me alone," Big Earl said.

I looked at the old lady. She was thin and tall in a cotton dress and cardigan sweater, and she regarded me with ferocious trust.

"Tell her to get out get out get out!" said Big Earl.

"Tell him to take his dog and run," the old lady said.

170

"Listen, ma'am, if you would just let the gentleman finish his shopping," I said.

"You're siding with him?" said the old lady.

"Well, now, it's kind of . . ."

"Can't you read either?" she said.

"This is just a little dog," I said.

"I'll never watch you on TV again, you young snake," said the old lady. "You act like you're so great but you won't even protect a lady from a nasty idiot and a noisy illegal animal. I can't tell you how disappointed I am in you."

The old lady yanked her cart loose from Big Earl's cart and wheeled away, shaking her head.

"Good job, Clive. You know how to handle these rough people," Big Earl said.

He tottered along, pushing Ginger Pops in the cart, while I walked gloomily beside him.

"How is our movie progressing?" said Big Earl.

I almost told him my idea for the film. But Franklin had warned me about that. Instead I said, "There are a lot of things still up in the air."

"Of course there are. Life is uncertain. We have many problems. It is very important that you and I be wise and strong and make people feel good. When life is in peril, the people need to sing."

Big Earl hopped away from the cart, stood against a backdrop of frozen spinach, and began to sing:

A road winds through the wilderness
leading who knows where.
And on that road a traveler
come from the county fair.

He meets a boy with an armload of pies,
says, hark! what have you there?
The boy says, sir, these pies are for you.
I baked them with tenderest care.

171

Oh, what a nice young lad you are
to think of this old gray head,
and how I long for pies these days
now that my mama is dead.

Then the boy he looked at me so sad,
he said, sir, they're ten cents each.
I said, boy, they're not worth more than six.
He said, sir, that's cheap for fresh peach.

Get on down that wandering road, my son.
You can't do business here.
For pies are not so precious when
I know that heaven is near.

Show me the bird, show me the deer,
Show me the way and I'll take over here.
Give me some spinach, give me some cotton,
Give me some oil, and I'll never be forgotten.

Several people gathered among the stacks of canned goods to listen. Big Earl gulped a breath and continued:

Then the boy said, sir, before I baked
the pies you see on my tray,
I worked as a motorman all night long,
and I work for starvation pay.

Oh, boy, I said, do you really think
a story like that me would sway?
For on this wandering road I hear
a tale like that every day.

The boy said, mister, I know you do,
and I've only a dime in my pocket.
But I'll take it out and give it to you,
if you'll let me play with your rocket.

Into the Army, boy, you must go
or the Marines in Vietnam.
A wise young lad like you should know
I am a superior man.

172

Then the poor little boy spoke up and said,
sir, you're exactly right.
And if you'll just let me run on my way,
I'll be a corporal by tonight.

Show me the monkey, show me the coon,
Show me the gold and I'll own it soon.
Give me some corn, give me some broccoli,
Give me a truck and I'll have a monopoly.

Big Earl started to drop to a knee like Al Jolson but seemed to fear he might not be able to get up.

So on down that wandering road I roamed,
hearing the wind on the land.
And next thing passing before my eyes
was a skinny gypsy man.

Ah sir, he said to me so soft,
I've got my guitar here,
and if, sir, you'll sit and ask me a puzzle,
I'll whisper truth in your ear.

And to him then I said, dark fellow,
if a puzzle you would know,
then you must figure out for me
where did my mama go?

Oh, sir, a question that profound
I'm hardly fit to answer,
I'll tell you only what I know
She went off with a terminal cancer.

But, sir, let me pose a question to you,
your clothes are so fine and neat.
How does one find the place where you come from,
the house and the name of the street?

I can't rightly tell you where I come from,
except it's the end of this road,
and through these lonely woods I wander,
carrying this psychical load.

Oh, sir, if I had a horse or a mule
or even a lowly cow,
I know, sir, I would follow you,
but I just can't do it right now.

Give me a president, give me a king,
I'll write a song they'll have to sing.
They'll do a dance, they'll do a hop,
They'll look to me to know when to stop.

So by myself I trod alone
along this lonely road.
And should I ever reach my home,
I wondered if I'd know?

As I walked on down this road,
so long and narrow and steep,
I found it was approaching an end,
my heart did an acrobat's leap.

Who's that old fellow with his hair so long,
so snowy, and he's got no shoes?
I walked straight up to him, and I said,
Fellow, what's the news?

The road stops here, the stranger said,
you cannot go no further
except through me or into this thicket,
where last I saw your mother.

Well, I had to laugh, though it be my last,
for that was not what he should have told me.
I took out my gun and I gave him a blast,
on life's road you got to move boldly.

Then I walked on along, and I'm walking still
as I sing this song to you,
and if there's a message to many, I guess,
it'll be a plague to a few.

Show me the bird, show me the deer,
Show me the way and I'll take over here.
Give me some spinach, give me some cotton,
Give me some oil, and I'll never be forgotten.

A little girl clapped. Big Earl smiled sweetly and shyly.

"I wrote that one myself," he said.

"I supposed you had," I said.

Big Earl pushed the yapping Ginger Pops in the cart over to the meat counter, ignoring the crowd he had attracted. He picked up a two-pound package of steak. He showed the meat to the dog.

"See, for her's a dood durl," he said.

At the check-out counter the clerk punched the cash register, put the meat into a sack and tried not to see Ginger Pops. Big Earl tucked the meat under one arm and the dog under the other. He started toward the door.

"Hey, sir, that'll be a dollar eighty-seven," said the clerk.

Big Earl glanced back at me, annoyed.

"Well, pay him!" Big Earl said.

I paid for the meat. Outside, Big Earl was behind the wheel of the old Hudson I had seen at his house. His eyes barely peeked above the dashboard and he was licking his lips as the ignition whirred.

"Tell your daddy hello for me. Such a decent man," said Big Earl.

The old Hudson crept off across the parking lot with the poodle yapping from the rear window. A black Chevrolet pulled out behind the Hudson. I saw Mr. Clwyd in the Chevrolet. He looked at me and solemnly nodded his head one time.

15

Jingo was sitting on the edge of the wash basin, facing the mirror, with her feet up on the counter in the dressing area of her motel room. She was naked, and her orange hair hung down her back to below the level of the counter as she leaned close to the mirror to glue on her eyelashes. Standing behind her, I had a view of Jingo from front on, beginning with the bottoms of her bare toes against the glass, and then of myself watching her, and of the shower curtain and white tub through the open bathroom door behind me.

"These son of a bitches," she said with a shrill giggle. "It's hard enough to put the bastards on anyway, but when you're really straight it's damn near impossible." She used the word straight to mean high. "Don't you want to get straight, John Lee?"

"Not yet. I'll wait a while," I said.

She thrust one eye up to the mirror and blinked rapidly.

"Oh Christ, you should have seen me the other night," she said. "I waltzed into that club just as straight as a goose and I kept tripping over things and people were looking at me weird. Christ! I drove down to the club wearing nothing but my mink coat and a pair of high-heeled shoes, I was so zonked I couldn't put my dress on, and I stopped by this fellow's apartment that I know, and we did up about a spoon of coke in about three snorts, and, Jesus, was I flying when I hit the door of the club, I was saying you fucking Jack Ruby you better not give me any shit tonight, man, my head is in no shape to stand it. Christ, I could barely see, I was so stoned, and finally I got in my dressing room, and boy did it smell like shit from those goddamn dogs all over the place, and I couldn't see to put my costumes on or anything, and finally I tried to look at myself in the mirror, and what do you think—I had my goddamn eyelashes on upside down! Man, it was like trying to look through a bush!"

"You got anything to drink?" I said.

"You know I don't drink. You shouldn't drink either. You should take better care of yourself. Christ, I sound like your old lady or something. Did you like having a wife to tell you what to do?"

"No, I didn't like that part of it," I said.

"Christ, when I was a kid all kinds of different people kept telling me what to do," said Jingo. "My father was a bandleader. He went to Princeton. He was smooth. My folks busted up when I was eight, and they put me in a boarding school. My mother got killed that same year in a taxicab wreck in Central Park. Every summer and Christmas and Easter I went home with friends from school, or sometimes to some relative's. I ran off from boarding school when I was sixteen and got a job in the mail department at NBC. A few months later I started dancing at the Copa. Then I found out I could make four times as much money taking my clothes off slowly instead of starting out practically naked like we did at the Copa. It's been a circus, John Lee. A fucking freak show every day."

"Where's your father now?" I said.

"He lives somewhere in New Jersey. I've never seen him again since my first year in boarding school."

"Lousy father."

"Watch your mouth! There's nothing wrong with my father. He's just not a family man."

"Why don't you take off from work tonight? A few people are coming over to the apartment to swim and eat barbecue."

"Ruby's already threatening to sue me for missing work when I had to go to Chicago," said Jingo. "First he threatened to beat me up. What a laugh that is! I said listen, you fucker, you think you're rough, I know some people that can hang you on a hook, you're not the only one that carries a gun and knows how to shoot it. He said would I really cool him and I said lay a finger on me and find out, you fucker, and he went over and started cussing Donald, the MC, but he hasn't said any more about punching me."

"That's an elegant place you work in."

"A rat hole, a goddamn rat hole! When I dance I kick up dust from the stage and it makes me sneeze. It's not a fit place for a stah. I got two more months on this contract and then I'm going to a club in Minneapolis for a month and then San Francisco if those topless bitches don't put me out of business."

"You wouldn't do topless?"

"Baby, look at these," she said, squeezing her rather small breasts. "People don't come to my show to see tits, they come to see art. Why don't you watch my first number tonight? I'll hurry it up. Then you can take my car to the apartment and come pick me up later, or I'll get a cab to your place."

I don't know whether I was more interested in seeing Jingo dance

177

or in driving her bronze Cadillac Coupe de Ville convertible with less than two thousand miles on it. But anyhow I went downtown with her and we left the car in a garage on Commerce Street next to the Carousel Club. Hundreds of conventioneers with name tags pinned to their coats were on the sidewalks in front of the two big hotels at the intersection, waiting for something to happen. At this intersection there were fistfights, thrown bottles and a jam of people and vehicles every year on the night before the Texas-Oklahoma football game, and it was here that a crowd had harassed and jostled Lyndon Johnson and his wife for taking up with Kennedy in 1960. But when the conventioneers caught on that most nights nothing at all happened at this intersection or hardly anyplace else in downtown Dallas, they would investigate the neon lights of the Carousel Club. They would see Jingo's photograph with her stuffed tiger in the display case by the door, and they'd climb the dank stairs and enter a dark room with tables crowded together and a small platform stage against the far wall. When Jingo and I came in, it took a few seconds for my eyes to accept the purple lighting. Four waitresses were sitting at one table, talking. Up on the stage a man was tapping on the drums. At another table I saw Jack Ruby and two men. There was some kind of argument going on. Jingo led me to a table where I would have a good view of the stage but would be outside the spotlight. She ordered a Coke for herself and a water setup for me and told the waitress to bring her bottle of Scotch from her costume closet. The waitress brought my setup in a large glass instead of the small ones they ordinarily used. The argument had become louder, and Ruby's voice was rising toward shrill, and I saw him looking at the waitress as she passed his table with the large glass.

"Jack can't go through one night without a beef," Jingo said. "If a beef doesn't walk in here, he'll go find one. Those two guys at the table, the short one is an MC Jack fired and the other is his agent. They claim Jack owes them money. I don't know who's right. Ruby's got to make a living, too."

"Does he do well up here?"

"Who the hell knows? He's always bitching about going broke, but

178

he makes money off of me, you can bet your ass. He's into a lot of things. He gambles. He does business with people. He's got that jazz joint over on Oak Lawn that his sister runs. I don't know what all else. He won't use a bank. Does everything with cash. Some creepy people come in here to see him, but I don't ask what they want. You got to expect a few creepy people in a place like this."

Ruby and the two others stood up from the table. The agent was tall and lean and athletic looking, like a YMCA swimmer, and the unemployed MC was slight and somewhat shorter than Ruby, who was about five feet nine. Ruby was wearing a beige suit with wide lapels and padded shoulders. In the purple light, the suit made him appear stockier than he really was. He stood with his hands in his coat pockets and his chin thrust out in a portrayal of a gangster out of a movie. He was scowling, his cheeks dark, hair slicked back like George Raft's, profile surprisingly clean and sharp, dark eyes seeming to gaze at some point between the men he was concluding the argument with.

The MC said something to indicate they were leaving.

Ruby walked around the table and hit him on the mouth with a left hook.

The force of the blow made the man sit down hard in his chair. He put both hands to his mouth and coughed. Then he looked down into his cupped palms with an expression of astonishment. His tongue probed his bloody lips and gums as he looked up at Ruby and then back at the pieces of two teeth in his palm.

"You knockth out mah theeth," he said.

"You're lucky if that's all that happens," said Ruby, rubbing his left fist.

"Mah theeth," the man said in wonderment.

"I'm not a goddamn dentist," said Ruby.

The tall young agent helped his client up. At the door, the agent looked back and said, "We'll see you at the courthouse, Mister Jakey Rubenstein."

"You don't ever want to see me again!" shouted Ruby.

He started toward the door, and we heard the pair running down the stairs. Ruby laughed and came over to our table, still performing his ruffian number, scowling at me and then glaring down at Jingo.

"You're a big shot so you get a big glass for your big friend," he said.

"Cut the shit, Ruby, it's only a glass of ice," she said.

"You invited me here, anyhow," I said.

He peered at me in the purple gloom, struggling to identify the face that had taken on ornamental shrubbery since last he had seen it.

"John Lee Wallace?" he said. "Well, hey, glad to have you."

He gave me a delicate left-handed shake and sat down.

"I jammed a knuckle on that guy," he said.

The top of the forefinger on his left hand was gone—bitten off, I had heard, in a fight. He wore rings on both hands. I offered him a drink from Jingo's bottle, and he shook his head. Half a dozen young men who looked to be soldiers on leave thumped up the stairs and into the room. "Check their ID," Ruby said to a waitress. He looked at me. "These damn kids. You got to be careful. They got no sense of responsibility. They don't give a shit if they get me closed up. Well, John Lee, you and our star here have got to be pretty good friends, I hear."

"None of your business who my friends are," Jingo said. "I'm going to get dressed."

She bounced across the room between the tables and disappeared into a dark hallway.

"That girl has caused me a lot of trouble. A lot of personal trouble," Ruby said.

"Why do you keep her?"

"She's good for the place. Draws people. But I'm afraid she's going to bring the heat on me. She's about half crazy, you understand. She makes up terrible lies, and the tantrums she puts on around here are embarrassing sometimes. She comes in here loaded and pulls some raw stuff on that stage. I had to turn the lights off on her the other night. What she was doing with that stuffed tiger was against the law to see. It was plain vulgar. I'd have hated for anybody in my family to have been in this place that night. A damn drunk got so excited

I had to throw him down the stairs. But Jingo does attract people in here. How good friends are you?"

"I like her."

"Just don't believe anything she tells you," he said.

"Jack, you bastard, this is the last straw!" Jingo's voice screeched from the darkness.

"That bitch!" Ruby said, jumping up. I followed him across the room and could see a bar of light in the hallway, and Jingo standing in the door of her dressing room wearing a G-string and gold pasties. The hallway was heavy with the smell of women's clothing that had been splashed with perfume far more often than washed, that sweetly sweaty whorehouse smell, but as we reached the dressing-room door the odor thickened into a goulash of odors, one of the most pungent of which was dog manure. I could smell face powder, perfume, perspiring feet, liniment, frying onions and milk chocolate, and, cutting through on its own plane, some freshly released gas.

"Those dogs are in the kitchen again! I can hear the son of a bitches whining and barking, not even to mention smell their shit!" Jingo said furiously.

From her seat at an old vanity table that looked as if it had been rescued from a railroad-station hotel, another woman looked at us without expression. She was naked and had a lipstick in one hand. The walls of the dressing room were covered with mirrors, pieces of hanging costumery and eight-by-ten glossy photos of the strippers.

"I'll keep my dogs where I want to," Ruby said.

"It practically makes me puke," said Jingo.

"Frankie, can you smell dog shit?" Ruby said to the other woman. She shrugged.

"See, it don't bother Frankie," said Ruby.

"What does bother Frankie? You could set off a bomb and she wouldn't know it!" Jingo said. "I'll get my things and beat it out of here. If your customers want a show, let them go in the kitchen and smell your dogs."

"If you walk out, I'll have the law on you!" Ruby said.

"Oh, man, what a threat! Wait till I let the judge in on the news

181

about your pocket pool games in here! At least you could have the nerve to just whip it out and let us watch you get off! What are you scared of girls for?"

"You lying slut!" Ruby shouted. For a moment he seemed about to hit her, but something held him back. I wondered if it was my presence behind him, or the resolute defiance with which the little orange-haired, purple-eyed Jingo stared at him or the power of her connections in the world they operated in. Or if it was something else entirely, a feeling for her that he didn't know how to express otherwise.

But clearly this was a ritual for them, a warm-up bout for the evening. The other stripper didn't even turn around. With the impression that I had intruded, I left them yelling at each other in the dressing room and went back toward my table. At the entrance to the main room, I almost collided with a thin, worried-looking man in a maroon dinner jacket and black tuxedo trousers.

"They at it again?" he asked, as if hoping I would deny what his ears plainly told him. I nodded, and he looked out at the room, where about one-third of the tables were filled. "I don't want to get stranded up there again," he said, with a nervous smile. "Last night when it was time for Jingo to close the early show, she and Jack were back there fighting for half an hour. I did five introductions, and the trio played a number and I told every joke in the last two Robert Orben books. Guys started booing and throwing swizzle sticks at me. Orben ain't that bad, either, but when guys want to see skin it ain't my skin they want to see. Is Frankie ready?"

"I don't know whether she's ready or not. But she's naked, if that'll answer your question."

"Yeah. Funny. You tell the jokes tonight, huh, buddy?"

He was pacing in the hallway as I went back to the table. I poured a large glass of Scotch. A row of soft yellow stage lights had been turned on. A red velvet curtain was drawn across the back of the stage to conceal the musical instruments until the show began. I sat there and sipped the drink, thinking for no discernible reason about Dorothy. I had heard nothing from her now in weeks, and was starting to

182

miss her. Around me male voices rose into the mumble of a barracks just before lights out. I could hear more people coming up the stairs, and a waitress clattered her tin tray on the next table. Then a chair scraped and I felt someone sitting down.

"Hi, Bubba," he said.

Bubba is a name I was called until I entered the first grade and had to register as John Lee Wallace.

"Erwin Englethorpe!" I said.

"You don't have to talk so loud," he said, glancing at the other tables.

"I read about you in the papers."

"Which thing was it?"

"About the six carloads of ammunition in Mexico."

"Did that get in the papers? Too bad. It's a good thing cops don't read stories that ain't got their own names in 'em."

Erwin opened a brown paper sack he had been carrying, unscrewed the cap off a bottle and fixed himself a drink of bourbon and water. He lit a filter-tip cigarette with a paper match and grinned at me. There was a scar on his upper lip that I hadn't seen before, and his face seemed a bit rounder and heavier and his eyes were almost as dark-ringed as those of a raccoon. His thick blond hair was combed at the sides with plenty of oil to sweep around his ears into ducktails at the back of his head, and he had long sideburns like a country musician's.

"You a pal of Jingo's?" he said.

"Yeah."

"She's all right, that girl," said Erwin. "I saw her a lot in New Orleans when I was down there working with some fellows on a deal. I might of made a run at her, but her old man was hanging around for a while."

"Her husband?"

"She's had five or six husbands is what I hear. That last one, I think she divorced him in Mexico. He was a jealous wop that didn't have any sense. He wasn't no good to be with for a girl like her, you understand? That girl gets around, takes a lot of trips, delivers packages for people. If I was you, Bubba, I'd kind of watch it. I don't mean stay away from her or anything like that. She's a good-hearted girl. But I wouldn't be a old friend if I didn't tell you to keep your eyes open with her, and be sort of careful with Ruby, too. He don't look like much, but he ain't the safest man in town to be with. Especially right now. He's doing some business with some boys, and he's kind of agitated. He swallows damn pills by the handfuls and gets to whirling around like a hummingbird."

"Ruby doesn't bother me," I said.

"That's right." Erwin Englethorpe grinned and squeezed a wedge of lemon into his drink and sucked his finger. "You've had experience with these mean boys. Learned it at the cop shop, didn't you?"

"Maybe I never could whip you, Erwin, but I'm sure I could handle Jack Ruby if it came to it."

"Think so? You got him outmatched for size, but he can be mean as a snake and he claims he can punch like Joe Louis. You never were mean enough, Johnny. I remember that time we had that fight with butcher knives when you cut me on the arm. You looked like you might kill me that day. Really scared the devil out of me for a while. But them other fights we had, one reason you couldn't win was you wasn't trying to hurt me, you was just fighting to defend yourself and hoping I'd stop. That ain't how to win. The day with the knives, I guess you understood that you was in serious danger, and you went sort of berserk, and you got so vicious it defeated me. The other times, you didn't figure I was going to kill you but only black your eye or something, and you wasn't quite scared enough to be cold mean and keep your mind on what you was doing."

"Sounds like you might have swallowed a few pills tonight yourself," I said.

The piano player, trumpet player and drummer stepped onto the stage in the yellow lights and began their early set with "Lullaby of Broadway."

"I got kind of a runaway talking mouth from snacking at that meth powder to keep awake on the road driving into Dallas," Erwin said. "But what I'm saying is that some of these boys do real stuff that can make you dead. It ain't like your movies, Johnny. I've seen all three of your movies. I thought they were great, except Tarzan wasn't too great but it was okay. I've seen your TV cowboy show, too, and it's great. You're always shooting and beating up people and talking wise. I keep wondering whether it's more fun to do it on the screen than it is for real. It's very strange to do it for real. It can be a kick sometimes."

"I can see that it might be," I said.

"When we were kids playing wars and cowboys and gangsters, and shooting each other with rubber guns or BB guns or just with toy guns or our fingers, that wasn't all that different from real life for me. I believed in our games, man, I really was a soldier or a gangster, not no playlike. But the result was different, you see. Now it ain't different from real life, it is real life. When you was that dope smuggler in that movie with all them Chinamen, I sat back and thought, well, there's Johnny on that movie screen playing like he's his friend Erwin. It made me proud to think I might of taught you something. That dope smuggler in that movie, you played him just right, where he was living on the true edge, right where I live. Of course when they shot you down you got up later and went home from work and had a drink, more than likely. But when they shoot me down, I ain't going no-where."

We both finished our drinks and made others.

"I got an idea," Erwin said. "Why don't you make a movie about a guy that smuggles guns and dope? Make it real authentic. To get the facts right, you get a haircut and come along with me on my next deal in a few days. You can find out for yourself what it's really like. It ain't all that different from in the movies, except it's seedier and there's a lot of waiting around, but it's got to be more exciting than doing it playlike."

"You want me to help you smuggle guns?" I said.

"This trip'll be dope," said Erwin. "Marijuana is all. Maybe some coke if I run into the right guys. I don't never deal heroin. I don't have no use for guys that deal that shit. The fact is, I don't really like dealing any kind of dope. I don't smoke weed. Did it one time so I could lay a beatnik girl that thought I was square if I didn't smoke reefer, and I didn't feel high but just kind of went to sleep before I could open my fly. Also, with guns it ain't too bad if you get caught on this side of the border, but if they catch you hauling dope in Texas you can forget what the street looks like for a long time. But you can haul a lot more dope than you can guns in the same amount of space. I can go down to a little town north of Acapulco and buy reefer for eight dollars a kilo. I got a pickup truck with a camper rig on it and a false bottom that'll hold close to a thousand pounds. My rig is so good I don't worry about checkpoints and lead cars and decoys. I just drive."

With a ballpoint pen, Erwin wrote the figures on a paper napkin. The MC had come onto the stage and was telling jokes to scattered laughter and a few jeers.

"Say I get four hundred first-class kilos. That costs me $3,200 in Mesko. If I want to drive that reefer all the way to New York I can unload it wholesale to some beatniks up there for $100 a pound. Shit, they sell it for $200 a pound without no trouble, maybe $300 a pound if it's good gold. The demand for reefer is picking up all the time, new people getting involved that don't know much about it yet. I give them a good deal, like $210 for a kilo, and every brick they have a few extra ounces thrown in for free, and they love me. So that comes out to $84,000 for the load, or about $80,000 clear for me. It don't ever come out quite that good, what with bribes and cheating and one thing or another, but you see the point. I can wholesale the weed for $150 a kilo in Dallas or San Antonio if I don't want to drive all the way to New York. Now, you go along and help me drive the truck, and I'll put you in for a full half. No, hell, it's my truck and my contacts and my know-how, so I'll put you in for a full third. That's somewhere about $20,000 for your share. The whole trip won't take more than two or three weeks. You dress up like a bird shooter or something, like some kind of redneck hick, or get you a gas-station uniform with Bubba sewed on the pocket, and the Customs won't never look at you. Take along a movie camera and shoot a bunch of film of the road and some of the places and use the film in the authentic dope movie. I just wouldn't pull out the camera in front of them Meskin dealers if you don't want to get punctured."

"It sounds easy," I said.

"It takes nerve, don't forget that. Then when we get back from New York, I'll put most of my money into buying guns and ammunition from boys I know that steal from the National Guard and the Army Reserves and sporting goods stores. I already got a bunch of guns stashed down in Mesko, but they knocked off my bullets like you read about. I can sell all the guns and bullets I can get my hands on in Mesko City or in Guatemala. I could sell 'em in New Orleans, but I don't like dealing with them people over there. It's better just to skip them and go on down south. I might make myself quarter of a million dollars in the next year, Johnny, and think what a good true-life kind of movie you could tell about our adventures after we got back safe."

"Erwin, aren't you being sort of offhanded about this?" I said. "I mean, telling me all this stuff couldn't be a good idea for you."

"Look here, Johnny, I keep telling you this is real life I'm dealing with. I've heard you smoke that reefer yourself. People that smoke it learn who to talk to. A guy like you, people like to tell stories about him, anyhow. Make it sound like they know a lot about a star, you understand? I know you ain't going to turn me in. We both think it's glamorous, and I saw your eyes when I started counting up the money. Ever'body wants money they don't have to work all their lives for. I guess you make a hell of a lot of money for playing like you do what I really do, but it seems to me you'd like to get out and experience it one time instead of keeping on playing-like."

"I'd have to think it over," I said.

"Aw, Johnny," he said, disappointed. "I'm sorry to hear that. It means you won't do it."

"They might recognize me at the border."

"What would that hurt?"

The MC gave up and retreated to the wings, where he stood to reach out for the garments the first stripper discarded as she slid around the stage. A waitress whispered to me that Jingo said she hadn't quit, after all, and I should please wait for her number. Erwin and I sat in silence and watched the first girl.

"Just do me one favor," Erwin said as she finished and the second girl came out. "Don't tell Jingo none of this, and for God's sake don't tell Ruby. He could mess me up."

The second girl was the placid Frankie. She danced with the same enthusiasm with which she had applied her lipstick. The MC told a few more jokes and introduced Jingo.

"In the second show the MC does a drag act," Erwin said. "It don't go over."

The room went dark. A blue spot picked up Jingo holding to a curtain. A recording of Martin Denney jungle music was playing, with a lot of caw-caws and monkey chatter filling in behind the trio on stage. Jingo glided into view wearing a tiger mask with ears and a tiger cape with a long tail. She frolicked around, leaping and hopping, in a clearing in the jungle, and she began to purr and growl and rub herself between the legs with the tiger tail. Then she let out a shriek that made me almost drop my glass. I thought she might have stepped on a nail. But she continued to leap and hop. She grabbed a prop tree, wrapped herself around it and started sliding up and down it, shrieking again. I happened to look back toward the entrance just as the door opened and shut, and in that instant I saw two uniformed police come in. I told Erwin. "They like her show," he said. Now the recorded rumbling of a tiger growl was heard. Jingo shrieked. The tiger growled louder. She tore herself loose from the tree and with some fast ballet bounds covered the stage in a frenzy, whipping off her tiger outfit and shaking loose her hair until at the very moment the tiger himself appeared, thrust from the wings by the MC, Jingo the animal seductress stood revealed nude except for an almost invisible G-string and one pastie, the other having fallen off in her leaping. She danced coyly around the tiger, advancing and withdrawing, cleverly grasping its ears to pull it to the center of the stage, where, at last, in a crescendo of growls and shrieks, she heaved the great stuffed beast onto her body, hugging and kissing the tiger and falling backward beneath it and closing her legs around it in a fit of lust. I was blinded by the pop of a flashbulb in the front row and then heard scuffling and saw Ruby wrestling an Instamatic camera away from a conventioneer. Jingo had rolled the tiger over now and had placed her head between the tiger's legs. "I told you not to do that!" Ruby shouted, holding the camera high and pushing the conventioneer down into his seat. Unperturbed, Jingo uttered one long shriek of contentment and lay back satiated as the lights dimmed out.

The applause was tremendous. The yellow stage lights came on again, with the blue spot shining on Jingo as she bowed and asked for a hand for the tiger. Hers was no act that demanded encores to build it up. On her toes, she came to the front of the stage and curtsied deeply. She winked at me and looked at Erwin. By the door, the conventioneer was insisting that the cops make Ruby give his film back, and the cops were suggesting that the man leave with no further disturbance.

"Quite a show," I said.

"She's a trouper," Erwin said. He yawned. "I'm coming down, Johnny. I been driving twenty-nine hours straight, and I got to catch some sleep. I'll call you in a couple of days. Where you staying?"

Erwin wrote Buster's number on the napkin. He tore off the part of the napkin with the figures on it and gave that part to me.

"Erwin, they've got plenty of crooks in Hollywood," I said. "I could throw a rock from my porch and it would bounce off three or four thieves before it hit the street. I don't need to smuggle dope and guns just to get mixed up with shady dealers. By the law, I'm already a felon."

"Aw, Johnny, you know the difference," he grinned. "I ain't a crook, I'm an adventurer. I took all that stuff serious we used to see in the movies on Saturday mornings when we were kids. I might of done some stealing a few years ago, but that was mostly just from churches and beer distributors and big chain drugstores, redividing the wealth, you understand. I'd never steal from you unless I was in awful bad shape, just the same as you wouldn't cut me with a knife unless you felt like you had to. So let's go adventuring together, like old times. We can point our fingers at Meskins and go bang-bang and won't have to argue with 'em about whether they're dead or not."

"Those cops are still at the door," I said.

"I seen 'em. They're young and don't know me."

"They could pick you up anyhow if they don't like your looks," I said.

"It ain't exactly rare for a rough-looking boy like myself to be in the Carousel Club," Erwin said. "Cops don't come up here to hassle Ruby's friends and customers. He loves cops. Why else would he give 'em money?" Erwin laughed, put his cigarettes in his pocket and screwed the cap back on his bottle. "It ain't me they won't like the looks of. Until you get a shave and haircut, you're too dangerous to be seen with."

16

At noon I was stumbling around the apartment, stepping over crumpled paper cups, and puddles, and trying to avoid looking at glasses with cigarette butts floating in them. I had taken a sip of instant coffee and was reading a front-page newspaper story with the headline TEAGARDEN GUILTY, WILL FILE APPEAL when I started thinking about phoning Geraldine.

I took my Alka-Seltzers, aspirins and vitamins and on impulse swallowed one of the Dexamyl spansules that I had lifted from my mother's medicine chest. I dialed Geraldine's number. I was surprised when she answered.

"We got back yesterday," she said.

"But you should have been back two weeks ago. I've been calling."

"They gave Herbert extra leave time, and we were enjoying ourselves so much we stayed down there. Caroline caught some kind of a red-colored fish. She was so proud of it. I almost wished you could have been there to see it."

"I'll come over this afternoon."

190

"Not this afternoon," said Geraldine. "We're leaving for San Diego on the four-thirty plane. The mover is here now."

"Then I'll come now."

"John Lee, you can't. Caroline is having a farewell party with her little friends. They're being collected in a few minutes and are going to have ice cream and see the movie at that place in the shopping center. We're picking her up when the movie's over and going straight to the airport."

"You can't do that!"

"I know how you're going to claim you feel. But really, you should have called last night."

"I didn't know you were home," I said.

"You could have called us in Houston or Galveston at any time for the last few weeks."

"I didn't know the number."

"John Lee, I can distinctly remember you telling me many, many times that you were a great reporter when you did that TV news thing. Surely, such a great reporter could have found a dozen phone numbers for his former wife's relatives in Houston. I mean, they are listed in the Houston telephone directory at the public library, and for the illiterate there is a service known as long-distance information."

"If there's any little favor I can do for you, Geraldine, if I can help you break into TV in San Diego or anything like that, I hope you'll let me know," I said.

"I don't intend to do any more television. Or watch it, either."

"How will you keep up with what the rest of us are doing?"

"I don't have an adolescent need to keep up. I'm much more content with myself than you are," she said.

"That's something different in your life."

"I'm satisfactorily married to a nice man. That is indeed something different."

"You've never told the truth."

"I've always told the truth about myself. You've never believed me. Of course there's much more to it than merely what I say and how I act, but you never have understood or really tried to find out what it is."

"What's your motivation, Geraldine?"

She laughed. "I am motivated by a strong desire to keep any thought of you from intruding on my happier and more worthy thoughts."

"You won't like being happy."

"When your movie project has fallen apart, and you finally decide to come to San Diego to visit your daughter, take a look at me," said Geraldine.

"I could take a look at you right now."

"I'm busy with the movers."

I drove to the ice-cream parlor in the shopping center nearest to Geraldine's house. The place was empty except for housewives who had sneaked in to get a fix for their sugar and chocolate addictions. Behind the counter a woman in a paper hat was plunging an ice-cream scoop into a sink of soapy water.

"Where's all the kids?" I asked.

She looked at me suspiciously. "They're in school," she said. The housewives looked up from hot-fudge sundaes, banana splits and strawberry malteds. They were thinking the word pervert so vividly that I could almost see it printed in the air. It was good that I wasn't wearing a raincoat. I ran out to the car and drove a hundred yards to the movie theater. I was buying a ticket before it struck me what film was playing: *The Joy Train*. I felt dizzy and flooded with cold. Stupidly, I touched the painted figure on the poster that, with short hair and no mustache, looked somewhat like me holding a .45 automatic and sneering as I bashed a Chinaman off the rear platform of the Kowloon-Canton Express. Above the title it said *starring* and some names, and below it said *with John Lee Wallace* and some more names.

It had to be an absolute fact that Geraldine didn't know what movie Caroline had taken her friends to, and whatever mother delivered them to the theater must have thought *The Joy Train* was something cheerful and wholesome.

"Did a bunch of little girls go in here?" I said.

"All the time," said the woman in the ticket booth.

Inside, fighting down a rush of alarm, I bought a box of popcorn and a Mounds bar. Breathing slowly, I stood at the entrance, reassuring myself that this was going to be all right, and then I went into the darkened theater and groped down the aisle and took a seat in an empty row midway back. On the screen in color as bright and startling as Hong Kong itself an airplane was banking around the harbor and the green mountains, with the blue bay incredibly cluttered with boats. The camera was coming down low over the city, and you could see people living in tents and blankets on the roofs of the buildings, and washing hanging everywhere. That meant the film had barely begun, and I was not to be spared the first sight of myself on a movie or television screen since the night that had so shaken me.

Now I could see that eight or ten rows further down, nearly at the very front, there were half a dozen children together. I could hear them giggling and talking. I kept looking at the backs of their heads, avoiding the screen, but I could not make out which one was Caroline. Then I heard a strange voice that was my own saying, "One more run, and then you can give it up, eh, Richard?" The children down front shrilled at that immortal line delivered in that scratchy voice by that oddly familiar man. "That's him, Caroline!" one of them cried, and they giggled and bounced in their seats and threw popcorn at each other. My face filled the screen as I glanced at the NO SMOKING sign on the plane and snubbed out my cigarette. Richard stared straight ahead without speaking. The skin on his face was slack, as if he had recently lost a lot of weight (he had caught dysentery and held up filming and in these studio close-ups was sweating and close to a faint; in the next scene, shot earlier in Hong Kong airport, he looked robust and healthy again). Once more we saw the crowded rooftop refugee camps with the shadow of the airplane on them, and hundreds of signs in Chinese. "I won't let you down, old man. You can count on me," I said with a shifty smile.

I thought about going to the lobby for a smoke until I was dead, but I didn't smoke cigarettes any more except on the screen. I slid down in my seat as far as I could, like a child at a horror film.

The person on the screen had nothing to do with me, I was assuring myself, as I had through most of my time as an actor. He was not me. I didn't recognize him as being how I thought of myself as being. In appearance he was familiar, like someone I had seen before but could not recall exactly where. But the voice was surely too raspy and nasal to be mine, and his movements too awkward. It reminded me of when I had first grown the long hair and mustache and would see my reflection in a store window on the street and think: who's that? and be surprised to find it was John Lee Wallace. I remembered when Denny Spencer had hired me an acting coach. The coach said if I was to be a great actor, it meant revealing myself in public, exposing my soul for all to see. I let him talk, but I was not about to do what he said, not for a minute; I had known better than that nearly all my life. So when I was called upon to act for the cameras, I fell back upon something I was already good at, and became a different person. It was easy to become another person. If I'd had to stick with my own self for the camera I would not have done it.

On the screen now I was in the penthouse bar of the Mandarin Hotel, making a deal with a sinister Oriental. I turned away again and put my forehead on the back of the seat in front of me and stuck my fingers into my ears. While *The Joy Train* was being shot, I had done some very authentic research by smoking opium in Hong Kong, in Singapore and in Kuala Lumpur—each time in places very much alike: lying on wooden platforms with wooden blocks for pillows, in smelly crowded rooms among alleys and passages of many turnings, with little men in undershirts and pajama pants looking on curiously and helping me with the pipes and sometimes sharing packets of opium and bottles of Tiger beer I bought. One great thing about opium dens was that they looked like opium dens. The actor who played Richard went with me on one of these occasions and was quite nervous and finally left me lying on my wooden platform speaking dreamily with several Oriental gentlemen. Richard insisted later that he'd caught dysentery from a bottle of orange crush in the opium den, and I said it was his fear of the place that had ruined his bowels. He

194

was about equally afraid of the opium, which he did not smoke, and of getting knifed. He didn't know that I had already taken acid many times, and that opium by comparison was a mellow drug that made the mind sharp and clear and removed all fear.

I first took acid in New York in a friend's apartment, shortly after my first cowboy film was completed. The friend was solemn about it and set up candlelight in a dark room, and someone read to me from the Tibetan *Book of the Dead*. An hour after I had swallowed the acid I knew I was too high to pay attention to the *Book of the Dead*. I felt golden, and my heart burst in a golden shower. I had an experience of the white light the book had spoken of, but the light for me was pure gold. I felt I was caught in the instant between what I was and what I was going to be—the instant of becoming—and if I wished I could continue to exist in that golden light beyond thought or other sensation. But the golden light passed and I returned into being. I sat in a corner absorbed in introspection and speculation; I learned that time and space are not just words, and that in considering them we are like babies playing with dynamite, and for days afterward I remembered what I meant although I could not put it into words and did not even want to try (in those days many people felt compelled to discuss their acid adventures at confused and boring length, and each new switch of perceptual cartoons meant further hours of intense gabble). That night, listening to the music on the phonograph, I recalled the theory that smoking reefer slows music down to a speed that can be more clearly understood, but I knew instead that reefer speeded up the listener's senses so he could keep up with the music. Reacting to the acid, my senses began operating so much faster and more efficiently that I caught up with more than I could handle and for hours sat in catatonia, with every sense so overloaded with impressions that I had to indulge them rather than bother about moving or talking. I found myself going through many types of doors—swinging doors, revolving doors, sliding doors, double doors, single doors—in and out of rooms and lobbies, and my body did not leave the couch, and I was not the least bit afraid but only curious as to what I would discover, which, insofar as the doors were concerned, was nothing.

195

Over the next year and a half I took acid on an average of at least once a week, perhaps more, in liquid, sugar cubes, capsules, pills, litmus paper—any form in which it was offered, and nothing memorably disturbing occurred. Occasionally I took it as a challenge to see how high I could get and still get away with it, how extraordinary and complicated my daily life could become and remain functioning. There were days on the set and nights in bars and theaters when I must have appeared very strange. When I sensed monsters and felt their presence creeping along the canyons after me, I called them by name as my own weaknesses and ancient dreads, and they could not harm me but could only amuse or sometimes annoy. Hallucinations were theater with my mind; I saw a friend at a party become a seventeenth-century minstrel and watched with delight the play he put on, knowing all the while that though he looked in truth like a minstrel and his performance was truly Elizabethan, it was the acid that was showing me this event in this light. The first lesson acid teaches is that there is no authority for any belief. What is perceived in one condition to be one thing may in another condition be something else altogether, and in neither case are you certain. But this didn't bother me either. My childhood God had blown off, and I had learned to be without and had built suitable structures from which to make necessary judgments while I waited it out. I didn't discover in acid the erotic glory that some maintained was there. Sex was far out in the interests of my mind. When I could sit on the couch alone and have orgasms throughout my entire body hour after hour, the physical act was of no importance. I had no tormented struggles with myself to speak of, only a few brief and illuminating bouts. One thing I didn't like about acid was that as I kept burning my strength in the rounds of my goings, the drug began to outlast my endurance for it and my interest in it; there was always a time when I looked in the mirror and saw myself ugly and deranged, and was tired and wanted to sleep, and the acid would not let me go.

Some premonition had kept me from taking acid and then watching myself perform on the screen. I had perched outside myself and watched me in my conduct with people and situations, but never on the screen. But one night in my pink stucco house above Sunset Boulevard I swallowed some acid in blue liquid from a test tube. Even before I did it, I knew I shouldn't. I was tired and had been feeling disagreeable. But some people had come out, and I'd had three or four martinis and started to relax.

A visiting dealer from Cleveland produced the acid out of a sampler kit of vials in a briefcase, and all of us took it. An hour later nothing much was stirring inside my head, so I drank another vial, and then the first one began making itself felt. Sometimes the temptation to down a bit more is like the temptation to stay a few more minutes under a sun lamp.

The heavy loading of sensations on acid vastly increases whatever tiredness I might feel. In a while I was very weary, although my mind was madly busy. I knew the people I was with intended to go to a club on the Strip, and I took two Dexedrine spansules in order to get my body to moving. I went into the living room—which was whirring with golden hues, the woodwork swimming—my arms and legs tingling with blood and electrical storms, feeling orgasms cresting without ever quite exploding all through me. I sat down and without knowing what I was doing found I was watching John Lee Wallace on television.

My impulse was to laugh. But when I had been laughing for a moment, I knew I was laughing because I was anxious and afraid. Once I discovered this, the fear began rising. I don't know what brought it on, what brain valve failed me or what conception flew apart, but suddenly the pink stucco house where I had felt so comfortable was a strange cold place. A painting I liked had become a lunatic scrawl. Walls seeped with fissures. I could hear timbers rotting and crumbling. Roaches crept through the house in search of my life. There was something in the room that I had not known before, and I was terrified of it. It was a presence of madness. It was a horrible, murderous lunacy. It had no rational quality but sprang from the deepest dread in my memory. That it was real and was truly present there could be no doubt. But I thought it was coming only from me and touching no one else. So I looked at the others in the room, and every one of them was comically insane, faces contorted, mouths wrenched into hideous grins, eyes flicking with fear. Their flesh was yellow and they looked poorly made-up, overdone, hair dyed in colors that missed register, eyebrows drawn in heavy pencil, nostrils vast and thick with hairs. A friend named Tommy was sitting at my feet, his head jerking in sharp wooden movements like a clockwork doll, tongue popping in and out of his mouth, and he was groaning in guttural grunts for speech. The presence of madness had weight and texture: it was exceedingly heavy, and thick as cold dew. I was paralyzed with fear. I knew that at any moment madness could strike any one or all of us with terrible harm, and that we were helpless because we ourselves were its agents. Someone screamed in the kitchen, and Tommy leaped up and went running around laughing wildly, and I sat clutching the chair and wishing desperately that this nameless dread would come forth so that I could face it before it destroyed me without ever being seen. I felt death in everything, and I saw everything dying, and madness unloosed. I looked directly into the heart of nature, and it was terror and chaos, and there was nothing that could be called sanity.

In this state I looked again at myself on television. That thing on the screen was me, or as close as I could ever come to a being. I was exactly that and nothing more. I was what I was doing. I tried to rip my eyes away from the screen, but I could not move them. I saw the cameras and the sets and heard the directions and the rollers of moving machinery. The structures of it were as bare to me as bones, and I was as fake a clockwork mechanism as Tommy's head in its little puppet jerks. The creatures on the screen were taking actions that were meaningless, and speaking nonsense. Someone came up and asked me a question, and I looked at her and saw this question as a pitiful and artificial attempt to keep a structure moving that had no need at all for moving and that might as well cease and fall into dust. I went outside and stood on the porch looking down at the neon lights on the Sunset Strip shining red and orange on the low smog clouds: the lights were jumping and flowing, and roaring in pairs, and close all around me it was very cold. I went down the steps and crunched up the dark gravel driveway beside the house and then climbed the outside stairs in back and crouched down on a screened-in porch behind an old refrigerator. There I waited, shuddering, smelling dust, with my forehead on my knees. What I wanted was some authority that would hold up against the dread. But each prop my mind summoned quickly fell apart. I could not think of my name, or my mother's name, or my address, those simple things you count on. I seemed no longer to exist. I remained alone, insane and dying, without significance.

I sat there throughout the night. I heard them calling for me but could not answer. In the morning I could feel the dread like the flames and power of the earth beneath the thin crust that I walked on. In the daylight each thing I saw was strange and new, but enough memory and will had returned to make me at least semifunctional, and I drove to the studio to finish filming an episode of *Six Guns Across Texas*. The people at the studio were like dolls to me. Their mechanisms and fears, their efforts to make themselves coherent and worthy of living, were so obvious and pathetic and simple as not to be worth my interest. All the unconsidered underpinnings that had held myself together were suddenly seen in what I took to be a clearer vision, and were disposed of. I knew the unknowable. My own life was useless chaos, wired together by idiots, and pretending otherwise was ridiculous whether there was a camera on me or not. That night I went home and took my .38 Police Special pistol out of a bureau drawer and returned to the upstairs porch and sat behind the refrigerator with the pistol in my hand, in the darkness, for hours. I tasted the oily muzzle, sucked on the barrel, placed the cold wet muzzle against my temple and into my eye sockets, and kept this up for a very long time, until I was quite sure it would be easy to pull the trigger. I had succeeded in fooling myself and others for many years, I thought, and now that I had been found out, I could easily remove myself. When I had decided that, I could see no further need to be afraid. Once I discovered I could kill myself in an instant, life began to seep back. But I was still apathetic, bored with the trappings of my life and with the behavior of others. Although I could feel rumbling in my heart that came with the power of the knowledge that I could rub myself out as easily as wiping chalk off a blackboard with a wet cloth, it was not until I thought of making my own film to please myself and explain my sense of things, that life began to come together into a functioning whole, and I could see other creatures as having spirit again, and that infernal insight into cosmic pandemonium began to recede from the front of my mind.

Sitting now in the movie theater behind the giggling children, one of them what is known as "my own," I could feel the dread and craziness inside me not to be tampered with again. I rubbed my wet hands together and felt sweat down my ribs. I'd had to move very near death to restore life, and death was nearer now than I wished to consider, and my footing was treacherous.

"Richard," I was saying on the screen, "you know it wasn't me that stole the opium. I'm your pal, Richard."

We were having dinner in the open courtyard under the palm trees at the Raffles Hotel in Singapore. Candles on the tables sputtered in the wind. One of Richard's hands was beneath the white tablecloth.

Pfffffttttt!

I looked amazed—one of my better expressions as an actor—and dropped a fork of prawns and lowered my face into the salad like a young executive toward the end of a long lunch. Richard finished his glass of white wine and slipped the pistol with silencer beneath his coat.

"My friend is ill. Don't disturb him. I'll go to the suite and fetch his pills," Richard said to the waiter, rising and wiping his mouth with a napkin.

"Cool!" yelled one of the little girls down front.

When the movie ended I was waiting in the lobby. The first two little girls to emerge did not recognize me, but the third squealed, "Caroline!" Then Caroline came out, and her freckled face broke into such unexpected joy that I felt chilled and started to cry. She ran to me clumsily, knees and elbows flopping. I hugged her and picked her up and kept hugging her. The woman at the candy counter was watching, and the little girls were giggling.

"Daddy, I was afraid I wouldn't see you," Caroline said.

"Baby," I said.

"I caught a huge fish."

"Your mother told me."

"We're leaving today. Oh, I'm so glad you came," she said.

"Mister Wallace! Mister Wallace!" the little girls were saying. I put Caroline down and let go of her hand so I could sign my name on the pieces of paper the little girls had gotten from the woman at the candy counter.

"Caroline, you're so lucky!" one little girl said.

Caroline smiled and looked at them proudly, and it was all I could do to write my name.

"Mr. Wallace, can't Caroline stay here?"

"We don't want her to move away."

"Is this Caroline's real daddy or her other daddy?"

"Stupid, her other daddy's not named Mr. Wallace. He's named Herbert."

I finished the autographs. Caroline took my hand again.

"Come on, honey, it's getting late," someone said.

I looked up, and there was Herbert, looking embarrassed.

"Sorry, John Lee, but the airlines won't wait," Herbert said, chuckling.

I knelt down and kissed her, and she put her arms around my neck. She smelled like chocolate-covered coconut.

"I love you," she said. "Please come see me."

"I love you, too," I said.

"I don't want to go to California," she said.

Then she tore loose and ran to Herbert, who was holding the lobby door open. "Okay, Daddy," she said. She waved at the other little girls and looked at me for a moment, and ran to the car where I could see Geraldine looking at her watch in the front seat. Surrounded by little girls, I walked outside and leaned against *The Joy Train* poster and watched Geraldine's yellow Chevrolet convertible drive off. It hadn't occurred to me to wonder why they weren't driving the car to California, but there was no more reason why I should care.

17

On a Saturday afternoon Buster and I parked his Plymouth station wagon in a reserved lot by the front entrance to the Cotton Bowl and walked down a long concrete tunnel, past ambulances and policemen, toward the bright grassy field marked off with stripes and colored designs. Noise boomed outside, but we could hear ourselves walking in the tunnel. We emerged onto the grass in the sunlight. The concrete stadium rose up on all sides, and seventy-five thousand people were making a vast incredible whisper. Then one entire section exploded with sound. Shielding my eyes against the sun, I watched University of Texas cheerleaders tumbling about, and looked into the stands at thousands of orange and red pennants. Buster had got me a sideline pass as his assistant while he photographed the game for *Sports Illustrated*. I was filming with the Bolex. I went along shooting the rows of invalids waving pennants in their wheelchairs and patients on stretchers who had requested themselves borne to the game. At the north end of the stadium I switched to a long lens and shot the Texas team running out of the tunnel between files of cheerleaders and organized Cowboys in orange outfits, while the band struck up "Texas Fight" and the stadium shook with noise. The ground trembled as if a subway train were passing beneath. I was standing in the very place where some thirteen years earlier, as a student, I had found myself a seat on the grass with some friends—the Cotton Bowl being more than merely sold out for that Oklahoma game, as usual—and we had brought along a gallon Thermos jug of a drink we used to call Purple Jesus, which was one-third each of gin, grapefruit juice and grape juice. We arrived at the stadium two hours before game time and sat on the grass in the sun, drinking from the Thermos. We started to sing some of the old songs we liked, like "My Gal Sal," and, hearing a terrible roar, I looked up as a Texas halfback hit the ground with a grunt and a whack of leather and rolled against our feet, where he sat up, the football clutched in his arms, and looked at us with a peculiar dazed expression, as though events were too swift to comprehend, and a cannon blasted. Later I discovered the halfback had been scoring a touchdown in the third quarter. That was all I noticed of the game.

The band played "The Star-Spangled Banner" and the Oklahoma school song and "The Eyes of Texas." Seventy-five thousand people stood, many of them singing, many with hands on hearts and eyes on flags. I trotted along with Buster during the first half, squatting down when he did, getting an idea for shooting positions from his anticipations for the game. At half time I sat on the bench and filmed the majorettes and dancing girls and marching bands. At the beginning of the second half I moved just outside the chalk stripes that marked the Texas team area, and knelt and aimed the Bolex at Darrell Royal, the young Texas coach, as he paced in front of the boys who were holding the attention of two states and a good part of America that afternoon. Royal was wearing football shoes and white athletic socks and had rolled his pants legs up above his ankles. He wore an orange baseball cap and a short-sleeved white shirt with a necktie. It was surprising how young the tense faces with the black smudges beneath their eyes were in the viewfinder. Watching from the stands, or on television, I never really remembered that the players were boys of eighteen and twenty; seeing them move on the field with grace and power, hearing them crash into each other, watching them throw and catch and run and tackle with skills that had taken all their lives to develop, I thought of them as being of no particular age, but men, surely.

By the time the game was ending, with Texas the winner by three touchdowns, the field was in shadow, although I could feel my face was sunburnt, and there was a sense of nervous exhaustion from this outpouring of strength and desire by so many people. Buster and I ran to his car, beating most of the crowd out of the stadium, and drove to the airport to ship his film to New York. We smoked a couple of joints on the bank of Turtle Creek and then went to a small Mexican restaurant called Villa Lopez, a narrow room, rather dark and shabby. Buster and I ate there often. We ordered a plate of nachos and two Carta Blancas and followed with beef tacos, chili con queso, guacamole salad, enchiladas, refried beans, an extra dish of jalapeñas and chopped onions, all of it sloshed with plenty of hot sauce, a stack of hot tortillas with butter, and a pitcher of cold sangria. Hector Lopez came in. He was in his early twenties and had been a busboy, a waiter and a cook at a Mexican restaurant in Austin before he put all his savings into his own place. Nearly everybody who worked for him was a relative. Hector made the University of Texas victory sign—the forefinger and little finger extended, the middle fingers and thumb folded down—and yelled, "Hook em, babies!" He got himself a beer and sat down with us. "Man, we kicked hell out of that Oklahoma," he said.

"Who's we?" said Buster.

"Texas, man!" Hector said. He was never sure whether Buster was kidding him. "Darrell Royal, man! We're number one in the whole country. We're the greatest!"

"I didn't realize you went to Texas University," said Buster.

"Man, I lived in Austin, didn't I? Wasn't I born in Austin? Texas is my team," Hector said.

"You're a Dallas businessman now. You ought to be for SMU," said Buster.

"SMU can't beat any son of a gun. Texas, we're winners. We're number one in the whole damn U.S."

"Is that a bruise on your chin?" I asked.

Hector rubbed a blotch the size of a quarter below the corner of his mouth.

"Them damn cops whipped on me again last night," he said.

"That's twice in the last month," said Buster.

"I know it! We had a few beers, you know, while we were cleaning up, and when I went outside about midnight the cops stopped and said, 'Hey, you damn greaser, what you trying to steal?' I said, 'To hell with you, you damn cops.' So they got out of the car and knocked me down. One son of a gun held me and the other one kept punching me in the stomach and ribs. Man, am I sore!"

"Same cops as before?" I said.

"No, man, different cops. I told them this was my place and they said, 'You're still a damn greaser.' "

"You should have told them you're a friend of Darrell Royal's," said Buster.

"Shoot, man! They wouldn't believe that!" Hector pointed to the big University of Texas pennant hanging on the wall beside a straw sombrero. "Number one in the U.S.! Man, I'm happy today! I like to beat that damn Oklahoma! I'm gonna put a Darrell Royal Special on the menu—Mexican pizza."

"Business getting better?" I asked.

"Pretty good!" Hector said. "Little Earl and Mr. Franklin and their wives were in here last night. They had some more people with them so I had to push three tables together, and they ate a lot. If those big shots keep coming, we'll be rich." He yelled to a waiter and tapped the empty sangria pitcher. "Hey, Buster, can you get me a big picture of Darrell Royal? I want it for my wall, man."

"I'll get you one," Buster said.

"I been thinking," said Hector. "Do you know if they have any age limit for playing football at Texas? I might go down there and play for Darrell Royal. I could be a good halfback. I'd like to run over that damn Oklahoma's ass one time."

"The other day you said you were in training to become the middle-weight champion of Texas," I said.

"Man, Gloria don't go for that. She said if I got up in that ring and looked like a monkey she would go off and leave me. I blacked her eye for talking to me that way. I need her to run the cash register."

"I wouldn't fool around with playing for Texas," said Buster. "You have to enroll in college and carry books to classes."

"I don't mind going to school," Hector said.

"But you could skip all that and turn pro. Both the Dallas teams need halfbacks," I said.

"Shoot, that's not the same game. You don't get to run over Oklahoma," said Hector.

"You could run over New York or Los Angeles," I said.

"They're too far off. I got nothing against them."

As Hector lifted his glass we could see the Pachuco cross in the wedge between his thumb and forefinger.

"I've been to Oklahoma," Hector said. "Up there they think I'm a damn Indian. If I trompled their ass in the grass I'd get a good laugh."

"Buster and I are both part Indian," I said.

"Is that what makes you so crazy?" said Hector.

The telephone was ringing when we walked into the apartment about dark.

"What are you doing home on Saturday night?" Dorothy said.

"Saturday is the only night I don't go out," I said.

"I have a date, myself."

"You're going to the ballet, I guess."

She brayed. "You wouldn't know this guy, John Lee. He works in an office. He drives a red MG. He went to Notre Dame. He has a crew cut. He's really sweet. He buys me steak for dinner. And wine. He belongs to another private club besides the one in his apartment building. He's got a good build. He doesn't have a fat stomach. He never reads or watches television. He'd go to the ballet sooner than you ever would."

"Is he taking flying lessons?"

"Guys like you think guys like him don't have anything to offer, but you don't look at it from a girl's point of view."

"If you could see what Buster's doing right now, you'd know why it will soon sound like I'm holding my breath."

"I'd like to be over there with you all. I miss you," said Dorothy.

"I miss you, too," I said.

"Why don't I have my date deliver me over there tonight? About one-thirty or two, after the clubs close."

"I don't know what'll be happening."

"Well, I could make him drop me earlier."

"Come on over now."

"I can't do that."

"Look, Dorothy, who the hell knows what we'll be doing by one-thirty or two?"

"What would you think if I wanted to move in over there?"

"It would be okay," I said.

"No more than that?"

"We can set up a bed in the den, or maybe you can sleep with Buster, I couldn't say."

"Who is it?" said Buster.

"Dorothy."

"Tell her to hurry."

"She means she wants to stay for a while."

"Oh. We could put a bed in the den."

"I heard him," Dorothy said. "You guys are really friendly."

"We've offered you your own room."

"And you'll want me to clean the place up," she said.

"Did you ever before?"

"At least my Notre Dame man isn't tired all the time."

"Dorothy, I've got to hang up now, I'm getting dizzy. Do you want the den or not?"

"I'll stay where I am," she said.

"Do you need some money?"

"Yes."

"All right. I can let you have a couple of hundred."

"When?" she said.

"Right now."

"See you in a few minutes."

Using five or six cigarette papers, Buster was rolling an Austin Torpedo. He had taken the airline flight bag from the closet, and out of that had taken the paper sack the musician's wife had left, and had strained a handful through the flour sifter, and then had scraped that in a shoebox lid with a match folder to remove the tiny seed husks. Jingo had brought us a gift of two pounds of clean weed in a Girl Scout cookie tin, but we stuck it away on a shelf for later, thinking maybe to bake an extravagant chocolate cake for Thanksgiving, if we got around to it. When weed was scarce we had been reduced to grinding seeds in a pepper mill, and to digging the lint out of coat pockets to roll toothpicks, but it was always the case that when more weed showed up hard times were forgotten and the joints grew into Camels, chalk sticks, Thumbs, Torpedoes and even Corona Supremes.

We did off with the Torpedo and then sat staring at television for a few minutes. Finally I got up to take a shower. On my way into the bathroom I noticed the phone had been ringing again. I picked it up and a voice said, "Is that you, Bubba?"

"Erwin?"

"Is this phone tapped?"

"Why would it be?" I said.

"Always assume your phone is tapped. If you're wrong you're still ahead."

"I'll try to remember," I said. "Should I call you X?"

"Don't call me nothing. Just say if you want to go along on that deal we talked about."

"I figured you'd have already gone."

"I got held up."

"Who did it?"

"I don't mean hijacked. I mean delayed. I did a little thing with that guy you know from downtown."

"Listen, X, I appreciate the need to be mysterious, but I don't follow you."

"You stoned?"

"This phone might be tapped," I said.

"Bubba, you're still kind of wise, ain't you?"

"What is it you want, X?"

"I want to know if you're going with me on that deal."

"To Mexico?"

"Goddamn, Bubba, why don't you publish it in the newspaper?"

"I don't think I can go with you this time," I said.

"It's probably just as well for you, and better for me. But I promised I'd give you a shot at true-life adventure."

"I don't really want any more adventures right now."

"You had your chance, anyway. Maybe I'll see you again when I get back."

"You be careful, X."

I hung up the phone and looked at Buster.

"I'd swear I heard you call somebody X," he said.

The phone rang again, and I picked it up.

"What now?" I said.

"John! I've combed the planet for you, baby. This is Norman Feldman. I've got to see you. Really, babe, it's very very urgent. I've just stopped off from the Coast and I'm taking the red-eye to New York in a few hours. Let me grab a cab and come on over there."

I felt like sitting down on the floor and covering my head with a blanket.

"Babe, you're a hard man to locate. I called up that entertainment columnist—Jimmy Widgin, you know?—and he gave me this number."

"The Annie Nash Agency knows where I am," I said.

"Annie Nash is trying to hold me up. She's trying to rob me. I'm not speaking to her this week. How far is it to your apartment?"

I looked at Buster, who was sitting happily on the couch, looking at the television through a 300-millimeter lens.

"It would be better if I met you someplace," I said.

I gave him the address of the End Zone and said I'd be there in an hour.

"Promise? This is not one of your jokes, ditching Norman Feldman in a beer joint?"

I stood in the shower for a while, soaping up several times, steaming the mirror and the half-open window, and was washing my hair with Big Earl's Perpetual Beauty lotion when the curtain was pulled back and Dorothy peeped in.

"This is a treat for you to see a naked celebrity," I said.

"My date's waiting in the car," said Dorothy.

"Invite him in."

"Are you kidding? I told him my ex-roommate lives here, but I

209

didn't tell him my ex-roommate was two male dope fiends. Hurry up, John Lee. The steam's making my hair fall."

"You don't have to stay in the bathroom and gape at me."

"If I don't, you'll be in the shower for hours."

A horn honked outside.

"Please, John Lee! My God, I hope he can't see in that window. Why do you and Buster want to show yourselves off all the time? Somebody's going to call the cops one of these days."

"The people out there could avert their eyes."

I rinsed and stepped out of the shower. Dorothy tossed me a towel.

"You look gorgeous," I said.

Her skin was the color of pecan meat from the sun, and her eyes were big and walnut-colored, with diamonds in them. She smiled quickly, her tongue curling up in front of her crooked upper teeth. She was wearing a fawn dress with matching shoes, and gold bracelets and earrings with the pearl ring.

"It would be hard to guess you are without funds," I said.

"That's the advantage of living with four other girls," she said. "The only things I've got on that belong to me are my brassiere and the ring. I even lifted the girdle out of somebody else's drawer."

"I never knew you to wear a girdle."

"There's lots you don't know."

She followed me into my bedroom. The airline flight bag lay on the bed with the brown paper sack sticking half out of it. I opened a drawer and dug into a shirt—folded and packaged by the laundry— to find my cash next to the cardboard. I had six or seven hundred dollars in there, and maybe three thousand left in the bank. I was in the wrong kind of trade to be allowed to keep much of the money I had made. In the past year I had made enough money that once I would have considered myself rich, but this was all that was left. I gave Dorothy a one-hundred-dollar bill and five twenties.

"This is the first hundred-dollar bill I ever had," she said.

"Stick with me, kid."

"I would have."

"Got a better deal?"

"I don't have any deal. Am I hearing an offer?"

"I believe that was a bat that flew through the room," I said.

Dorothy put the money into her purse. One thing about her, Dorothy never acted embarrassed about taking something she wanted.

"Thanks," she said. She kissed me on the mouth with a loud smack. "I love you for this."

Buster drove me to the End Zone and decided to stay. There were three wooden tables out in front of the place, on the grass, with a string of lights overhead, and across Lemmon Avenue in a grassy park was the water of Turtle Creek down to the right through the trees as you faced out. Buster sat at an outside table with some people we knew. I went inside to look for Norman Feldman.

The jukebox hit me a blast. I went along a narrow aisle between dark booths, toward the bar, looking around, saying hello to people. A hand reached out and tugged at my sweater. Seeing the big hat in the dim light, at first I thought it was some cowboy, and I had an adrenaline rush, but then I saw it was Norman Feldman sitting there in the noisy gloom in his Topanga Canyon wrangler outfit. As I slid into the seat across from him, Norman took off his Stetson XXXX Beaver hat with the carefully rolled brim and saddle crush, and put it out of sight on the leatherette.

"I thought you Texans wore your hats indoors," he said.

"Not in the company of ladies."

"Are there ladies here?"

"You better call them ladies," I said.

Norman grinned and showed me the label on his bottle of Lone Star beer.

"Do you like it?" I said.

"Tastes just like beer to me," he said.

I put my bottle of Scotch on the table.

"Have some of this poured out of an authentic brown paper bag."

"Better not, John Lee. I've got miles to go before I sleep."

211

Norman popped open a pearl snap on the breast pocket of his Western shirt and offered me a cigar.

"Not a Havana, I hope," I said. "You could get arrested for smoking a Havana cigar in Dallas."

For a moment he believed me. Then he smiled and lit both our cigars.

"Being a Jew smoking a Havana cigar is more than they'll stand for, huh?" said Norman.

"I'd lower my voice if I were you. All they know about Jews down here is that's what the Neimans and the Marcuses are supposed to be. But don't say Havana."

"I have the feeling they hate Jews in Dallas," said Norman.

"That how come you're disguised in a bandana?"

"Where's all the other Jewish cowboys?" Norman said.

"Watching television," I said.

"I have the very definite feeling in my gut that this place is full of bigots."

"This is a foreign country, Norman. There's a lot of people down here who don't speak English. Even most of the people who speak English don't speak English," I said. "You may fly across America every week and think you understand what we're doing down here on the ground in these villages between New York and Los Angeles, but your ideas about us are about thirty-seven thousand feet off."

Norman sighed deeply and rubbed his palms together, looking troubled. He was a short, plump man with a high forehead and curly hair that bobbed like springs. He looked like a bright young professor, though he was in his late forties.

"Let me read meaning into this, babe," he said. "You are telling me that as producer of *Six Guns Across Texas* I don't know shit about my subject?"

"Your subject doesn't have anything to do with Texas. That title just sells better than *Six Guns Across Iowa*. I mean, all those ice-cream peaks and redwood forests we ride through chasing those thousands of Indians and rustlers every week. One time I'd like for us to have a chase through the cedar brakes and wind up murdering a Mexican for eating one of our cows."

212

"That's Commie talk, babe," Norman said. Quickly he raised his hands. "Now don't look at me that way. Have you lost your sense of humor?"

"Not yet," I said.

"John Lee, may I say it? Your trouble is you react before you think. That can be wonderful for an actor, but a producer can't afford such a luxury. You are a creative genius with your emotions. That's a fine thing for you to do. Me, I am like a great editor who knows how to put it all together into a solid product, with quality. Let me tell you, if there's one thing I know it's how to make a Western. Have you seen our ratings? Maybe you think *Six Guns Across Texas* isn't art. But maybe also you can't tell me what art is. I can tell you that when a story has the power of myth, you got art. Take a look at *Six Guns Across Texas* sometime. Examine it in your mind. Read more of the script than your own lines."

"Is this another test of my sense of humor?"

"In our show, here's what you find week after week—good is stronger than evil, shooting and fighting don't really hurt although you might get killed so you have to disappear, women are pretty unless they're old and then down deep they're warm hearted, whores don't put out for bad guys, the landscape is beautiful, Mexicans are picturesque, Negroes are loyal and polite, Indians are either innocent or evil, a man is free to make up his own mind about anything and change his destiny, nobody is poor and hardly anybody is rich, everybody is violent except for yellow chickenshits, and if something is wrong a good man will come along to straighten it out. Americans believe this stuff about themselves, John Lee. They don't want the story changed. If I changed it, they'd hate me and throw me out of their living rooms. Listen, don't you think I'd like to have a good tough Jew for a hero sometime instead of all those white Protestants and closet Catholics? I'd like to change your name from Clive Riordan to Manny Rosenstein, but America would reject me and my poor wife would have to look for work. It's hard to find work in Palm Springs."

"How about Lance Birnbaum for a hero?"

"Now you're joking, now you see the truth. This is a very big thing

213

we're doing with our little show. Again, may I ask? Is there honor in being an American? You grew up believing without a question in your head that an American is superior to anybody—a better fighter, more resourceful and ingenious, better at sex or at least preferable, handsomer in a wholesome way, unselfish, morally certain. We've got a responsibility. We can't make a television show that tells the American people that all these things they believe are a pile of rat turds. They don't want to hear that. In fact, these things they believe are closer to the truth than not. That's my opinion. So you want to give the whole country an inferiority complex? No! In *Six Guns Across Texas* we are sure of our virtue. We don't mind killing our enemies because they're wrong and we're right, and there's always more of them than there are of us."

Norman sucked on his cigar, which had gone out.

"You tell me I'm an idiot because *Six Guns Across Texas* isn't realistic. So our mountains have got snow on them instead of cactus. So we got a lot of shots of Wyoming and Colorado in there, not to mention the studio ranch. Is that a big deal? So one time we moved Fort Worth to a half a day's ride from the Rio Grande and you jeered at me and said I'd get a million letters calling me a fool. Well, I got not one letter saying we were wrong. Nobody cares about a thing like that. I say maybe our show doesn't have chickens scratching in the dirt in front of some peon's shack like you've got here, and maybe we don't have any poor spades slaving in the cotton fields. Mox nix! This show is not about Texas, as you were intelligent enough to perceive. This show is about America, and I don't care what kind of romantic ideas you damn Texans have about being different, you are Americans just like the rest of us. You got here on a boat just like we did. If there's anything unusual about Texas, it's that you might be more American than most places, even. So tell me, babe, what is this I'm hearing that you are thinking of running off from our show?"

"It's no big problem for anyone but me," I said.

"Wrong! If you leave, the whole show is changed. How can it ever be the same if Clive Riordan isn't in it? The problem is for sixty million Americans who love us."

214

Norman lit his cigar again.

"We could kill you off," he said. "We could have you bushwhacked by a hundred sneaky cattle rustlers allied with a mob of Apaches and the Mexican Army. But I don't want to do that. You have a contract."

"I have the creeping sensation that you are threatening me," I said.

"John Lee, I love you. I think you're wonderful. You know how it is with most actors. You show an actor a hundred-page script and say baby this is a great part, you're on ninety-six out of a hundred pages, and the actor will want to know what happens on the other four pages that he's not on them, too. But you don't behave that way. Sometimes I think you don't even realize you're an actor. I love that. I'd cut off my tit for you. But you should tell me the truth. In less than two months' time we start filming again on *Six Guns Across Texas*. You do understand that an option has been exercised, a legal matter is continuing, a great deal of money is involved, many people's lives and livelihoods are at stake, scripts are being rewritten and rewritten, machinery is being hired, electrical companies are screwing in their bulbs, bankers are conferring, big executives whose names you'll never know are pouring energy out of their brains. It's like building a cathedral, and if at the last minute one cornerstone should say to me, Norman, I know I am helping hold this mighty edifice in the air, but fuck you, baby, I am having no part of your attempt to commune with the American soul, I am going away to play by myself for my own amusement while your structure smashes down—I would have to regard you as irresponsible if you said that to me."

"So if I don't come back you'll sue me," I said.

"Wait! Have I said that? I'm still talking. While I'm talking, I must ask. How could I help but hear that you intend to make your own movie? How could I not be embarrassed when people ask me about it, and I know nothing? You drink. You talk. You have said it at the Polo Lounge, and at La Scala, and at the coffee shop at the Beverly Wilshire, and at too many other places for me to count on my fingers. I don't go to those places any more, as you know, since my last divorce and my new marriage I couldn't afford it, but people who go to them come to me. I told them: don't bother, John Lee is just being frivolous.

215

But I do have a TV set, John Lee. When you chose to tell this plan to all of America on the *Tonight* show, I happened to be looking straight at you and hearing every word. Am I supposed to believe you? Let me in on the secrets. What is the concept for your movie?"

"It's not entirely settled yet," I said.

"And the script? Is it so obscure you can't have a script?"

"I don't have a script at the moment," I said.

"The money, then. Where did you raise the money?"

"I don't have any money," I said.

"What I heard you say on the *Tonight* show is you are going to make a real movie about the real true Texas, telling the truth for the first time, and so on, as if *Six Guns* were not visible to America one night every week. Is it to be a documentary, then?"

"Sort of," I said.

"So all you have for this movie, in fact, is one actor."

"I'm not sure if I'm going to actually be seen in it," I said.

"But how could you have a real movie about the real true Texas if you, as a real true authentic Texan who claims to have his roots planted in Texas, are not in it? I'm asking."

"Norman, I don't know if you can hear your own voice, but you're starting to play movie Jew," I said.

"Now we are hitting the truth again," said Norman. "I must tell you that what you said about Jews in Dallas could not be true. You can't know about Jews in Dallas unless you are one. Jews in Dallas suffer while you eat cheeseburgers and fried onion rings. You tell me this and that about Texas. Well! You have a right. But don't tell me a gentile's view of a Jew's situation and proclaim it as the truth. A Jew is a Jew wherever in the world he is. Your last remark has proved this. We sit here in this beer joint and you tell me Dallas is not full of bigots, and all the while you are looking at me and thinking Norman Feldman sounds like a movie Jew."

"While ago you were talking about a sense of humor," I said.

We sat quietly and smoked our cigars while the jukebox noise crashed around us.

"All right. I'm laughing at myself," said Norman. "Ha, ha. Do you hear that?"

"Spontaneous good humor always cheers me up," I said.

"Then tell me one more thing while we are both cheerful instead of evading my question. I have heard from Annie Nash that Big Earl the billionaire is willing to finance your movie. Is this correct?"

"It's partially correct. I can't explain it to you," I said.

"I appreciate that big-time operators like yourself must have secrets," said Norman. "And you have already been shooting film?"

"We've shot a lot of 16-millimeter."

Norman shrugged. He regarded 16-millimeter as something a schoolteacher might use to film her vacation in Mexico.

"Could you introduce me to Big Earl?" he said.

"I'm afraid Big Earl doesn't like Jews," I said.

Buster appeared in the aisle and put a shoebox down on our table. He asked us to keep it for a minute while he went to the toilet. The box had a few small holes punched in it. Written on the box in crayon was ALLIGATOR INSIDE DO NOT OPEN.

"I wonder what's in here?" Norman asked.

"Probably an alligator," I said.

Norman chuckled and stuck his cowboy hat back atop his large head.

"Waaaal, podnuh," Norman drawled, "ah been thankin this town ain't big enough for me and them damn ally-gators."

Norman removed the lid. A mean caiman lizard, about ten inches long and looking very much like an alligator, leaped out of the box with jaws clacking. The caiman scrambled across Norman's arm, jumped to the floor and scurried along the aisle to screams and shrieks that pierced the clamor of the jukebox.

"I suppose you'll put that in your goddamn movie!" Norman said.

Book Four

18

On United Nations Day, toward the end of October, Buster and I drove to the Municipal Auditorium to shoot some film of Adlai Stevenson, who was then the U.S. ambassador to the UN, on his visit to Dallas. We went because we had nothing better to do that day, and we got up and went for a swim and looked at the paper and saw that Stevenson was in town. Stevenson's arrival was told in a few inches of type among stories that Madame Nhu was speaking in Austin, and there were rains and floods in central Texas, and the U.S. had refused Castro's request to lift the economic embargo on Cuba despite Hurricane Flora having blasted a good bit of the island into ponds of rubble. Neither of us was interested in hearing what Stevenson had to say, but we figured an

221

hour or so of activity would make us feel better about the days of indolence.

The night before, there had been a right-wing rally at the Auditorium, with a speech by General Walker. According to the paper, there had not been much of a crowd to listen to the General, but the ones who did attend were enthusiastic. When Buster and I got to the Auditorium, we saw a couple of thousand people, perhaps less, gathered outside the building. We jumped out of the car, and Buster stopped to film a man in an Uncle Sam suit who was yelling that the blackbird must be kept apart from the other birds. About a hundred people were in groups with banners from the Indignation Committee, the Young Americans for Freedom, and Alpha 66 and other anti-Castro Cuban organizations. One large sign said UN RED FRONT. I heard a woman excitedly telling a friend that Stevenson had said in his speech that the U.S. could no longer dominate the UN. "Why, that's just as Communist as it could be," she said. Back in the crowd I saw Annabel Withers.

Then Stevenson began moving out of the Auditorium. He glanced for a moment at the cops who were protecting him, and he sort of straightened up and headed into the crowd toward his car. Most of the people were cheering and clapping for him, but a few were loudly heckling, and there were scuffles, and the police wrestled two men away. Buster dived into the crowd with the Bolex, shoving people aside, closing in on Stevenson. A man leaned past the camera and spat on Stevenson. Buster kicked at the man and kept shooting. A woman moved in with a placard on a wooden staff. It was hard to tell exactly what happened, but the people up front were shouting "Red!" and "Communist!" and the crowd was pressing forward, and the placard came down while still in the woman's hands and rapped Stevenson on the head. It was not a vicious blow, more of a cardboard whack, but Stevenson felt it, and he looked around at the hatred in the woman's face and he kept going toward his car. Buster was surrounded by hecklers. One of them reached for his camera. Buster jammed it into the man's face and jerked it back again. I grabbed the man by the

222

collar and pulled him away, tearing his shirt. At the sight of my hair and mustache the man seemed to turn blue with rage and fear.

"Anarchists!" the man cried.

"Red beasts!"

"Go back where you come from!"

A policeman stepped in front of me.

"He tore my shirt!" the man said.

"You making trouble?" the cop asked me.

"Hey, Darden, that guy was trying to break my camera," Buster said to the cop.

"Hidy, Buster, you shooting for television now?" said Darden.

"For the movies," Buster said.

"Newsreel, huh? Go on, you folks, get back! These men are reporters from the newsreels," he said.

"Communists!"

Darden walked back to our car with us. He took off his cap and wiped his face with a handkerchief.

"What theater will this newsreel be in?" Darden said.

"Never can tell," said Buster.

"This won't look good for Dallas," Darden said. "It's a shame we got people that act that way."

"We got a lot of them," said Buster.

"I haven't been to the movies in a long time," Darden said. "I didn't even realize they still have newsreels."

In the next couple of weeks Buster went off for a while to do a magazine assignment on bass fishing in Arkansas, and I played golf twice with Gordo and went out to the farm of a friend named Pete Dominguez. Pete owned a restaurant called Casa Dominguez which had been one of our hangouts until it got so successful that we began going to the Villa Lopez. At Casa Dominguez one night while Buster was gone, I drank tequila with Pete for several hours and he gave me a quarterhorse named Nancy. The next morning I didn't remember it until Pete stopped by the apartment pulling a horse van behind his pickup truck and wanted me to go with him to bring Nancy back to town. I told him the landlady wouldn't like me keeping a quarterhorse tied by the pool. Pete said we could take Nancy to my parents' farm. I could tell that Pete was very fond of Nancy and was not especially happy that he had given her to me, but he was too proud to go back on his word and would have been offended if I had refused the gift. We made a compromise. Nancy was mine, but she was to stay on Pete's farm, and I was to go out and ride her now and then. I went out there with him that morning and rode Nancy while he rode a new quarterhorse he had just bought called Black Thunder. Nancy was a trained cutting horse with a tender mouth and fast feet. At my first touch on the reins while she was moving, she turned so sharply that I lost a stirrup and dangled for a moment from the saddle like a wounded Indian. From then on, I rode her with my knees. Pete and I drank a lot of tequila at Casa Dominguez again that night, and he decided that rather than break up Nancy and Black Thunder, he would give me both horses. But we agreed that he would continue to keep the two horses on his farm. In the course of all this I gave him my gold wristwatch, and he gave me an umbrella.

Annie Nash called to say Norman Feldman was behaving in a peculiar fashion.

"What did you do to him down there? He says everybody in Texas is crazy, and Dallas is a city in foment."

"We let Norman hold our alligator," I said.

"I can't stay hep with your slang, so I don't know what that means," said Annie Nash. "But I do know that Norman said you had better be back in Los Angeles before the end of November. When I asked about a new contract, he started muttering about the current contract and obligations and responsibilities and fundamental decency and so on. He sounded like he was at the edge of a snit. Do you think Norman is a homosexual?"

"He's as straight as you are, Annie."

"I'm a eunuch. He's not a eunuch. But I don't think he's very sure of himself sexually. Anybody he makes out with, he's afraid it's because they know he's a producer."

224

"Norman has a sense of these things," I said.

"John Lee, you have to make up your mind what you're going to do."

"I've told you what I'm going to do."

"Have you considered analysis? I could recommend a good psychiatrist."

"Send him down here and you won't know him when he comes back."

I phoned Franklin in another attempt to get him to agree with me about a documentary movie, but he had gone to Washington on an errand for Big Earl. I started writing a script but threw it away. There was nothing yet to say. By the time Buster returned, we were well into the planning of our Thanksgiving party.

Our Thanksgiving party was held on the third Thursday of November, due to a long-standing tradition that went back three or four years to our first Thanksgiving party, when we thought that was the correct date. We called our party the Annual Head Stretch Held Yearly. Instead of turkey, Hector Lopez was to bring nachos, tacos, enchiladas, tortillas, refried beans, refried rice, a tub of chili and whatever else he might think of. Buster and I bought cases of beer and California wine and a few bottles of whiskey, but whiskey drinkers were expected to furnish their own. The announced boundaries of the party were that it would start about dark and be over by about noon. Swimming was available if weather permitted, and the evening of the party came out warm and sweet-smelling, following a few days of rain.

With the help of Jingo and Buster's waitress friend, we swept out the apartment. I put the trash into garbage cans behind another apartment house farther down the alley, in case something should occur during the evening that would cause our trash to be investigated. We carried in fifty-pound sacks of ice, stacks of paper cups, cases of soda, tonic and Cokes and bags of Fritos. The waitress prepared bowls of cheese, onion, crab and sour-cream dips. Jingo baked a supercake with six ounces of powdery grass. We opened all the doors and windows and turned on the air conditioning and

225

sprayed the kitchen constantly with pine scent room deodorant. Jingo peppered the cake with raisins, pecans, cherries and mincemeat. We each ate a small piece, and it tasted like green weed with nuts and fruit on it, but we put the cake in a cake tin on top of the refrigerator. Jingo rolled up a dozen Austin Torpedoes and hid them under the socks in Buster's top bureau drawer. Buster kicked his laundry into a pile on the floor, removed the jock strap from the lamp and the tennis shorts from the night table and pummeled these items into the closet that held the rest of his clothes, the flight bag, paper sack and what remained of the contents of the cookie tin. We discussed ways of locking the other closet, where the Baby Giant flourished in its plastic wastebasket. Jingo suggested we hang Christmas ornaments on the Baby Giant to disguise it. Instead we merely pruned the plant again so it would continue growing fat and bushy rather than tall and graceful. We put the clipped leaves into a shoebox lid to dry on the shelf above the infrared lamp, and took out a few dried leaves to roll into a thin cigarette which we, of course, smoked. "It must be like your kid making All-American," Buster said, holding his breath.

Jingo went back to her motel to dress. Though Jack Ruby didn't know it, she had no intention of showing up at the Carousel Club that night. She had a date with a night-club comic who was passing through town, and she was going to bring him to the party. The comic's name was Harry Lockwood. They called him One-Line Lockwood for his ability to keep shooting one-line gags until even Milton Berle or Henny Youngman would have to go back to the filing cabinet. He played in Las Vegas, Miami Beach, Reno, the Copa, the big hotels and did a lot of guesting on television. I had invited Jimmy Widgin, the columnist, and had called around to a few of the clubs in town to invite performers, only to discover that Jimmy Widgin had already invited them. That was how it was with our parties. It didn't matter who offered the invitations, nobody was turned away. Buster and I invited several pro football players, two newspaper reporters who were relatively trustworthy not to invent scandals about us for print, photographers, a congressman, a herd of millionaires, a great

226

many airline stewardesses and secretaries, college professors, a few dopers (there were not very many in Dallas at the time and most had concealed themselves in stockbroker outfits and hid their stashes in garages and locked desks), groups from Gordo's, the End Zone, Casa Dominguez and Villa Lopez, several musicians and folk singers, a few beatniks, a pair of outright hoodlums, two golf pros, a sculptor, two doctors, a dentist, three or four bankers, an airline pilot, an assistant district attorney who had kept Buster out of jail when Alma tried to have him locked up for being late with a child-support payment and so forth. We liked having a mix. Thinking it over, we realized we had not invited any preachers or Negroes. We didn't know any very well. There was one Negro girl who came to the apartment now and then, but she was always moving and we didn't have her latest phone number, and one black civil rights worker who was off on a march in Alabama. Preachers were never considered. In days and nights of running around, you didn't encounter preachers.

At dusk, Buster and I were in the living room with the doors and windows open to catch the sounds and odors of air that felt like spring. The phonograph was playing the album from *Kismet* —we liked the line about peacocks and monkeys in purple adornings, and the song about kief—and we were pleasantly stoned. Buster had mounted a light on the Bolex to shoot party scenes, and we started talking about the movie. We talked about doing the obvious and hiring one of the *Six Guns Across Texas* writers to retire to the Hollywood Hills for a few weeks to knock out a script that Big Earl would like and Franklin would approve, and our lives would be money, gin, blondes and tassel loafers from then on. As Norman Feldman had said, maybe his TV series came as close to the truth as anything else. Which real Texas did we mean, anyhow? Another suggestion was that Buster would sell me 10,920 of his Texas photographs for one million dollars. We could project the photographs at a rate of sixteen per second for two solid hours. People in the audience would leave with headaches, but for months they would be waking up in the middle of the night with some strange picture burned into their brains and

227

would think: if I've never been to Mineral Welis, how come I know what the Crazy Hotel looks like?

We were folding a couple of paper hats out of the afternoon *Times-Herald*—using the front-page stories about President Kennedy arriving in San Antonio to be met by a crowd of a hundred thousand and Jackie Kennedy speaking to them in Spanish while a few pickets chanted "Cuba!" and the President then moving on to Houston where two hundred thousand cheered him while an airplane flew overhead dragging a banner that said COEXISTENCE IS SUICIDE. A small story inside the paper said Richard Nixon was in Dallas on business for Pepsi-Cola and predicted Lyndon Johnson would be dropped as Vice President. Furthermore, the University of Texas football team was number one in the nation again this week and Governor Connally had refused to invite Senator Yarborough to a reception for the President at the Governor's Mansion in Austin on Friday night, and the President was to meet with Lodge on Sunday to discuss pulling more U.S. troops out of Vietnam, and on and on, these confusing affairs—and in through the patio door stepped the first arrival at our party, Jack Ruby, looking very angry, the coat of his rumpled gray suit hanging open, the butt of a nickel-plated revolver held by his belt against a navy blue sports shirt. He wore a snap-brim hat.

"Where's Juliette?" he said.

"I don't know," I said.

"If she's at home, she won't answer the door," said Ruby. He stared at us. "You guys making paper hats?"

"It's Thanksgiving," Buster said.

Ruby nodded.

"Could I have a glass of water?" said Ruby.

"Make yourself a drink," I said.

"I don't drink. I just want to take some pills." Ruby got himself a Coke and a glass of ice and swallowed a large pink pill. We watched with interest. "It's a diet pill," said Ruby. "It's called Preludin, 75 milligrams. I don't have time to eat, and these pills help me keep moving. I could get you some."

"Okay," I said.

228

"Come down to the club next week and remind me." Ruby handed each of us a card showing a girl with a champagne glass. The cards would get us into the Carousel free. Ruby drank half of his Coke and walked around in agitated circles. "I don't never bitch," he said. "I don't complain about nothing. I might of had a hard life and come up from a slum and not had a proper education and had to fight like hell all the fucking time to get something for myself. I might of had to support a lot of people including some that try to cheat me. But I don't complain. But you tell that goddamn Jingo that if she keeps taking advantage of me, I will put a end to her career."

"You better tell her yourself. She's got a bad temper," I said.

"I got a temper of my own! You remember that!" said Ruby. Ruby snatched his Coke off the counter and drank the rest of it.

"You seen them signs?" he said.

"What signs?" said Buster.

"Them signs that say IMPEACH EARL WARREN. There's a big billboard on the Central Expressway that says it. And somebody is passing out handbills with a picture of the President like a police poster, and it says WANTED FOR TREASON. It's enough to make you wonder what kind of fucking idiots live in this town. Goddamn, I'd say it's embarrassing. President Kennedy shouldn't have to see that kind of shit."

"He won't see it," I said.

"What do you mean he won't see it?" said Ruby.

"The motorcade won't be on the Expressway. If he sees one of the handbills, I imagine he'll want to keep it as a souvenir," I said.

"I could send him a Polaroid picture of the billboard," said Ruby.

"Send it to Earl Warren," Buster said.

"Fuck Earl Warren! I'm talking about the President of the United States!" Ruby slammed down his Coke again. "You guys give Jingo my message, and come see me when you want them pills."

In a rush to get out the door, Ruby collided with our second arrival —Little Earl. They danced from side to side, each blocking the other's path, and then with a cry Ruby grabbed Little Earl by the shoulders and walked around him. Little Earl came in, filled a glass with ice and our Scotch and leaned on the counter.

"Was that Jack Ruby?" he said. "Why was he carrying a gun?"

"It's protective ornamentation," said Buster.

Little Earl had arrived early, he said, because he had been playing golf at Brook Hollow, and this was more or less on his way home. He downed his first drink and went into the kitchen to make another. We heard a clang, and Little Earl emerged with a glass of Scotch and ice in one hand and a piece of Jingo's cake in the other. "Weird cake," he said, chewing. "Tastes like it's got sand in it." In a moment he went to the phone and called his wife and said the party had started and for her to come on over. He called Franklin and told him the same thing. "My dad was talking about you, John Lee," Little Earl said after he put down the phone. "He was sort of confused about your name, but it was you he meant. You in with him on some kind of deal?"

"No," I said.

"I didn't see how you could be. You're not the type he likes to deal with. But he was telling me how strong and brave you are, and I told him you're about half Socialist, and he jumped all over me. He said he admires your whole family. How does he know your family?"

"Your daddy's ways are a mystery," I said.

"You telling me! That old man is into so much stuff that he won't even give me a hint about. His damn old house and office are crawling with foreigners. He acts like I'm not smart enough for him to let me in on everything. Hell, I went to Yale, and he didn't go to any college at all."

"He may have an edge on you there," said Buster.

"I studied economics and sociology and all that shit. I could do just about anything," Little Earl said.

"Speak up to him, he's your daddy," I said.

"He says I don't have any ESP. They didn't teach ESP when I went to Yale," said Little Earl. "He says you have it, John Lee. How'd you get it?"

"I was born lucky," I said.

"I wish I'd been lucky," said Little Earl.

By then, a half dozen others had wandered in through various doors. One was a pro quarterback who at once tore off a hunk of Jingo's fruitcake and fell into conversation with Little Earl about the stock market. I hid the rest of the cake in a cabinet after Buster and I each ate another piece. Then I took two spansules, hid the pill bottle, fixed a Scotch and water in a tall glass with a lot of ice and walked into the living room feeling quite contented, anticipating the finest Thanksgiving Head Stretch we'd ever had.

By eight o'clock, walking across the living room was like trying to move through the crowd at a football game. The phonograph was thundering, and cigarette smoke formed a layer three feet thick down from the ceiling. The crowd and the fruitcake and the Scotch were working together to transform the party for me into hundreds of fragments of conversation, hundreds of disconnected scenes, as with a puzzle that had been dumped on the floor and the pieces kicked around. There were scenes in every room, bits of talk, strange sights and groupings. I talked to Jimmy Widgin and scarcely knew what I had said. He walked away shaking his head. People ran back and forth to the pool, sloshing and splashing and yelling. There were groups of people in both bedrooms and in the den. A great many of them I did not recognize. The other apartments in our building emptied in defense against the noise, and the occupants came to our party. The landlady threatened to call the police. At that moment, Little Earl was staggering past, smiling like an idiot. I introduced him to the landlady, who congratulated me on my nice friends. Little Earl just stood there with his forefinger on the tip of his nose, grinning.

"I feel wonderful," he said.

Buster had taken up a position in the corner of the kitchen, his back against the wall, within reach of ice and whiskey, and was talking to anyone who stopped. I seemed to see him through a curtain and heard voices banging around and skidding off, as if I were inside a glass bell.

I stood for a while and listened to him lecturing to a couple of young dope heads, about twenty years old, who were drinking Coca-Cola and had remarked with scorn on the fact that Buster was drinking what looked to be gin and tonic. Both the young heads appeared to be very stoned. Their eyes were red and sleepy. In an alarmingly loud voice, Buster was saying: "The damn gin-drinkers think I'm a criminal for smoking weed, and you rookie weed-smokers think I'm backward for drinking gin. But what I know that you don't is that one's good for some things, and the other for others. Gin and whiskey are good for parties, talking, singing, fighting, moving around, going places and making girls lose their inhibitions. Weed is good for music, TV, movies, sitting down, sunsets and for eating. When I'm drinking, I never want to eat but I might want to fight. When I'm smoking weed I never want to fight, but I'll eat anything I can stuff into my mouth." I noticed that several strangers were listening. "Whiskey makes me want to have adventures. But if I'm home when I smoke a reefer, I'll stay home."

"What happens when you do both at once?" asked one of the heads.

"I have a good time," said Buster. "Gin is a narcotic, anyhow, don't you know that? It cuts out the world. Has something to do with juniper berries, is my theory."

I moved on into the den and looked at my watch. It was only nine-thirty. What might be going on by midnight was an awesome prospect. Dozens of people had commented on my hair, and on the TV show, and a few had called me Tarzan, but nobody had gotten mean. I saw Charlie Withers and Annabel in a group with Franklin and Little Earl, and somebody was passing around the handbill that called Kennedy a traitor, but I heard many people saying they planned to watch him drive through Dallas in the morning, or attend the luncheon for him at the Trade Mart. Annabel Withers intended to be among the pickets to jeer the President at the Trade Mart, she said, and she was proud of having been in the crowd that had booed Adlai Stevenson, but when Laureen and Leroy told me about it I shrugged. Who the hell cared or expected anything else of Annabel Withers? I moved along, jostling, smiling, coming in and out of lucidity, and was trapped by four or five women (one of whom I had fairly recently been to bed with but whose name I could not recall) who demanded to know when I was going to get married again.

"When I meet a good-natured psychiatric nurse who knows accounting and loves to give massages," I said. It was my routine answer, and women always giggled because they knew I meant it and would never meet such a person.

"How about just a big old tall girl of uncertain character?"

It was Dorothy. In an Empire gown of a light turquoise color, cut low over the breasts and falling in folds of cloth to touch the floor, with her hair worn in coils at either side of her head, and no jewelry and little make-up, her skin lightly tanned, she was good to look at but seemed a little different somehow, in a way I could not identify: heavier, a little more flesh in the face and arms, a deeper look to the eyes. I was very glad to see her, felt myself moved again by her presence. The truth was that I had hardly thought of her since I had given her the two hundred dollars—what with Jingo being around most of the time, and the script to fiddle with and our daily events of one sort or another.

I saw Franklin glance at us, and then look away, and then I went into a fruitcake flash and wasn't sure what was going on, but when I came out of it Dorothy was leading me toward the bedroom and saying something about turning her on. Everyone stared at us as we passed through the room. She was braying with laughter and dragging me along. I steered her into the bathroom, thinking it would be the best place to smoke, but the quarterback was in the shower with someone's wife, both naked and soapy, and so we went into Buster's bedroom, which was full of people, and into my bedroom, which was also crowded. Finally we went outside and walked along the sidewalk. Street lamps shone off dozens of cars parked along either side of the road. It was nice being with her again. A man and woman passed us on the sidewalk, and I cupped the joint in my hand, and we tried not to breathe on them. Then Dorothy gasped and winced and sort of bent over for a second.

"What's wrong?" I said.

233

"Just a little cramp," she said.

"Are you all right?"

"Fine."

"You look kind of odd," I said.

"Thanks, John Lee."

"I mean, you're as beautiful as ever, maybe even more so, but there's some kind of weird change, I don't know what. Your face is fuller. You look like you've been sitting by the pool thinking too much."

"Nobody can think in the sunshine," she said. "The truth is, I've done a lot of exercises. You want to feel my muscles?"

"I sure do."

"Not right now, though," she said.

"You're always bluffing."

"No more than you."

"How much of me do you think is bluff?"

"About sixty percent," she said. "The rest is sheer bravado."

"You're in good spirits tonight. When you're like this, I love you."

"How often do you think I'm like this?"

"About sixty percent. The rest is sheer bitch."

"So you could live with me six days out of ten, and then take a holiday," she said. "That might be the perfect formula for enjoying each other."

"You can still have the den."

"John Lee, your style of living is shitty."

"Compared to what?"

"To anything good."

"I've been thinking about moving out to the farm."

"This is another one of the hundred things you've been thinking about doing," she said. "But nothing changes except time goes by."

"You wouldn't like it on the farm."

"Neither would you."

"We'll do that when we're sixty."

"You'll be sixty. I'll only be forty-eight and in my sexual prime."

"Are you still only twenty? Come on and grow up," I said.

234

Dorothy grabbed my arm and dug her fingers into my bicep.

"Another cramp?"

"I think I have to go to the bathroom," she said.

On our way back to the apartment we passed a police car at the curb and two cops on the sidewalk. The quarterback and a lawyer were talking to them, promising to turn down the music. The quarterback gave me the forefinger-and-thumb circle sign, an appropriate gesture. Inside, Dorothy had to wait for a moment at the door to the back bathroom. She bit her lips. When she went into the bathroom, I went over to where Jingo was sitting on the arm of One-Line Lockwood's chair. Jingo had washed her orange hair and let it blow free so that at times you could hardly see her face, and she wore a very tight red sheath dress with spangles and red high-heeled slippers. She was smoking a gold and ivory pipe which smelled like nothing but pipe tobacco. One-Line Lockwood was surrounded by fans. He glared at them like a goldfish and continually smoked cigarettes and growled for someone to get him a drink. Charlie and Annabel Withers were at his feet, waiting to collect some of One-Line Lockwood's wisdom. Jingo introduced me to him.

"Noisy fucking party," he said.

"They get this way," I said.

"Lots of broads, though," he said.

"Enough."

"That photographer tried to give me some dope. He want to make trouble?"

"He was kidding. He doesn't have any dope," I said, glancing at Charlie and Annabel Withers.

"I never seen your show. I hear it's hot shit," said Lockwood.

"Mr. Lockwood, how about coming to our house for dinner tomorrow?" Annabel asked.

Slowly he looked her over, from her shellacked blonde hair down along the pancake on her face to her bony breast and fingers. Sunk in the chair in his shiny brown suit, One-Line said, "Why?"

"Well, for dinner and cocktails. A little party, you know," said Annabel.

"Naw, forget it," One-Line said. "A little party—that's a midget with a kazoo."

Each time he spoke, Jingo screeched a laugh. Pretty soon, I was laughing at him too. I had seldom heard anyone as unfunny as One-Line Lockwood. He kept rolling his eyes up at me as if he feared I might be insane.

"What you doing in this shit hole of a town?" he said.

"I'm going to make a movie about it," I said.

"They made one already. Randolph Scott was in it. One's enough," he said.

"There's plenty more to say about it," I said.

"Like what? Broads and money, that's all. Forget it."

"It's got good hotels," said Annabel.

"My room is so small I have to lean out the window to scratch my nuts," One-Line said.

"Against the side of a passing bus," I said.

One-Line scowled.

"It's okay as long as the driver don't punch me a transfer," he said.

A girl touched me on the shoulder.

"Somebody wants to see you back here. She says it's very urgent," she said.

"Vegas. There's my idea of a good town," said Lockwood.

The girl pointed me toward the back bathroom. I knocked on the door. I heard Dorothy's voice inside. When I opened the door, she was sitting on the floor with her back against the wall, clutching her stomach. Her hair had broken loose in wisps, and she had chewed her lips until they had started to bleed. I knelt down beside her. She looked at me with terrible dark eyes, full of pain.

"Please, John Lee, take me to the hospital," she said.

"Are you sick?" I said stupidly. I put my hand behind her neck, and it was wet with sweat, and I was telling myself this was truly happening and I had best start to move.

"I'm having a baby," Dorothy said, moaning. "Oh damn, John Lee, it hurts!"

236

19

While Buster called a doctor friend who phoned ahead to Baylor Hospital, Jingo helped me get Dorothy to the car. Dorothy had put a towel over her face so that no one could see her pain, and I carried her through the crowded room. People thought she was drunk. We took Jingo's car. My mind was very clear now for such functions as driving and dealing with people, but all this seemed to be happening to someone else. The contractions had started coming fairly rapidly by the time we reached the hospital. Dorothy was crying. I carried her into the emergency room, where a nurse and an intern helped me lay her on a stretcher. The doctor's phone call had prepared the hospital for Dorothy's arrival, but it had not prepared the people in the emergency room for the sight of Jingo and me. The nurses, interns and cops looked at the lovely young Dorothy, sobbing in her labor as she was rolled off down the hall, and then looked at us with no attempt to disguise disgust and hatred. I had a charge of paranoia and was certain we were about to be attacked or arrested, but instead I was called forward to fill out papers. Jingo said she would be back in a few minutes. I didn't blame her for leaving.

Dorothy had asked me not to tell her mother, so I gave the nurse the names and particulars that I knew. The nurse went ahead and wrote down that Dorothy was Miss Dorothy Leclaire and then looked at me and said, "Are you the father?"

"No ma'am. I'm just a friend."

I could feel the tempers of the others in the emergency room closing around me as surely as if they had laid hands on me.

"Will you be financially responsible?"

"Yes ma'am."

At least he has a fleck of decency, they thought.

I sat on a chair in the corner and hid myself behind a newspaper. The fruitcake should have worn off by now—it was nearly midnight —but the paranoia hit in waves.

"She wants you," a nurse said, as if to say, *I don't know why.*

I followed the nurse along a corridor and into a labor room where Dorothy lay on a bed in a white cotton nightgown, her fingers clawing the sheet. Already she had rubbed red raw splotches by grinding her legs against the sheet, and bits of skin hung off her lips, and her eyes were crazed. Her voice came in breathy mumbles. I bent down to hear but could not understand her. She seemed to recognize me, but distantly, as if I were some relative she had not seen since she was a child. I sat beside the bed and held her hand until she tore it away and clawed at the mound of her stomach. Freed now of whatever had bound it, Dorothy's abdomen had expanded into a rather small, but definite, lump of pregnancy. I was wondering what she must have been going through all these months, hiding it, and I considered the night she had asked me to marry her—she must have known it then —and her strangeness when I had first returned from California, and of course I speculated if the baby might be mine, and near as I could figure it might be barely possible but not if the baby was at all premature. Then I felt myself contemptible for thinking about such a matter while Dorothy lay here crying.

A fat Negro nurse came in.

"I'll take over now. You done enough to this poor child," she said.

I didn't argue. As I was leaving the labor room, I heard the nurse saying soothingly, "Now, now, honey, you gone be all right, that turble man is walkin out the do' and you gone be all right now here with me."

Jingo was in the maternity waiting room. She had driven to her motel and had brought back several nightgowns and a case of cosmetics for Dorothy. We drank coffee out of paper cups from a machine. In less than an hour, a doctor appeared from a hallway and summoned me.

"Miss Leclair has given birth to a little boy," the doctor said. "The baby is quite premature, about two months so, I would guess. Weighs four pounds, eleven ounces. He's in an incubator, of course, and I can't promise what may happen. But if you'd like to see him . . ."

I went with the doctor along a hall to a room with a large plate-glass window. Looking through the window, I saw a tiny red monkey lying inside a barrel with a window in it, his tiny fists clenched and tiny mouth open as he fought hard for breath. I looked at the little red creature and found myself crying. I couldn't help myself. The poor little bastard had such a long way to go. In a moment a nurse said, "Miss Leclaire is sleeping. She had a bad time. You had better wait until morning to see her."

On the way back to the party Jingo said, "I had a kid one time. Court took him away from me. He lives with his grandma on his daddy's side. Kids get along." I looked around at her. "What can I do about it?" she said. "When I go see him, they howl and scream at me. The kid's embarrassed by the sight of me. He doesn't like me, and I don't really like him. I send him money, but he's their kid now, not mine."

If anything, the party was more crowded than when we had left. The entertainers from the clubs were arriving, and drunks had come in when various bars closed. Aluminum plates of Mexican food lay all over the place, with paper boxes of Gordo's pizza, and paper cups, bottles, bags of melting ice, record jackets, pieces of clothing, people. We managed to get inside without One-Line Lockwood seeing us. Frankie, the imperturbable stripper from the Carousel, was standing at the counter.

"Jack is pretty mad," Frankie said to Jingo.

"He's not coming over here, is he?" asked Jingo.

"I don't think so. He's all upset and busy. I think he tried to screw some of them rich Florida Cubans on some kind of deal, and he's got to watch where he sticks his head at."

"Does he know about this party?" Jingo said.

"Sure. I told him. You think I'd lie to Jack?"

Buster came out of the bathroom, grinning, with his arm around another stripper who was famous for the size of her breasts. With

239

them was a thin blond fellow who looked like a pool hustler. When he saw me, Buster left them for a minute.

"How's Dorothy?" he said.

"It was a boy," I said.

"I'll be damned," he said, shaking his head. "She really had a baby? Where'd she been keeping it?"

Jingo was talking to the pool hustler, and I saw One-Line Lockwood approaching with his lips puckered. There was a loud rip of a needle across a record. I heard a club operator assuring two girls that if they stayed around a while Buster would take off his clothes.

"You seen my broad?" One-Line asked me.

"Not lately."

"There she is," he said. "With that pimp."

"Is he a pimp?"

"Don't he look like a pimp?"

One-Line went over to speak to them.

"That guy says his name is Corbett," said Buster. "He's trying to raise a thousand dollars. Five hundred to buy an old car, and five hundred to buy weed in Mexico. He said if I'd put up five hundred he'd pay me back with twenty-five pounds of weed."

"You going to do it?"

"What do we need with twenty-five pounds of weed? I just laid a couple of joints on him and told him *hasta luego*."

In the kitchen, among fifty empties, I found several fresh bottles of Scotch that had been brought in by the late crowd, and I knew there would be other bottles hidden in cabinets, so I poured myself a drink that must have had a half-pint of liquor in it. I wanted to get up for the party again. While I was digging in a bag for ice, Franklin held out his cup. He looked very tired and drunk, a stubble on his face, his wattles loose.

"I heard Dorothy got sick," he said.

"She'll be all right," I said.

"Anything I can do for her?"

"She'll let you know if there is."

"You pissed about something?"

240

"I lost my spark is all," I said.

"Little Earl got terrible drunk. He was giggling and acting crazy, and then he turned into a zombie and finally went to sleep on the floor."

I filled Franklin's cup with ice.

"How you coming on that scenario or script or whatever?" he said.

"Have it ready any day now."

"I wish you'd get your ass to moving on this thing, John Lee."

"It's moving right this minute," I said.

I decided to get one of the Torpedoes Jingo had rolled and go out in the alley and smoke it and maybe stay out there for a while until the party had thinned or until my mood had improved. But when I went into Buster's bedroom to seek out the Torpedo from under the socks, the fellow called Corbett was standing by the window smoking a joint.

"Put that thing out," I said.

"Take it easy, man. I got the window open to handle the smoke."

"I could smell it from the door. Put the goddamn thing out."

"Listen, man, I got a radar in my head," said Corbett. "It works in concentric circles starting at thirteen blocks out and coming right down to three feet from my nose. My radar picks up every cop within thirteen blocks. I got them all spotted right now. Ever'thing's cool."

I took the joint out of his hand and mashed it in an ashtray.

"You sure are tense," he said.

"If I get busted, I don't want it to be for somebody I never even saw before."

"I'm an old friend of Jingo's."

"Go smoke at her place," I said.

"Man, those people out there don't know what grass smells like. I could walk through the room puffing a number and they'd think I was smoking like tobacco from Turkey."

"I ain't going to argue with you. Just don't smoke dope in here," I said.

Buster came into the bedroom then and said, "Corbett, where's the joint?"

241

"Your pal put it out. He thinks the house is full of cops."

"John Lee's in a bad humor," Buster said.

I gave them back the roach, found a Torpedo, and went out to sit in Jingo's car in the small concrete parking lot off the alley behind our apartment building with a cigar and the big drink of Scotch. At first the Torpedo did not help to smooth me out. I reacted to every sound and movement in the alley, nearly leaping out and running for it when a dog turned over a garbage can. A man and woman began undressing in a lighted window across the alley, and I was convinced I would be arrested for window-peeping as I sat in Jingo's car watching them. But after a while I could no longer remember what I was supposed to be worried about; I had to keep reminding myself of the troubles and dangers. The anxiety remained, but it had no name, and as the Scotch went down, so did my fears. I sat in the car while a thunderstorm struck, with rain so thick I could not see the end of the hood.

A little before daylight I woke up and got out of the car and went back into the apartment across puddles of rainwater around the pool. It looked as if a battle had been fought inside between several platoons armed with cigarette butts, buckets of water, cups and bottles, record jackets, tinfoil, cardboard, paper bags and other refuse. A strange girl was asleep on the couch, another girl and the quarterback were asleep on the carpet in the den, and One-Line Lockwood was snoring in a chair in front of the flickering TV set. Buster's bedroom door was shut. I switched off the turntable and opened my bedroom door. Jingo was lying across my bed. I tried to move her over, and she awoke and sat up.

"Where's One-Line?" she said.

I pointed toward the living room.

"I got to get out of here without him seeing me," she said. "One more line out of that son of a bitch, and I'll murder him."

She slid open the lower panel on my front window and got down on her knees to crawl out, but her long orange hair tangled in the shrubbery. Jingo unsnarled herself, pulled back inside and took off her shoes. Then she stood up and wriggled her spangled red sheath dress up to her waist to allow her legs freedom of movement. She wasn't

242

wearing any underwear. She sat her bare self down on the floor again and stuck her feet out through the panel. Slowly Jingo began easing through the window and the shrubbery.

Looking out the window, I saw the newspaper boy riding his bicycle along the street in the early light, his paper bag slung over his handlebars. He was lobbing papers into yards on either side of the street. As I watched him, he saw Jingo. She had planted her feet and thrust up her naked crotch as she worked her shoulders and hair through the window and bush, and the dress had gotten pulled up to her breasts.

The bicycle went up a curb and smashed into a tree. Newspapers spilled onto the wet lawn. The paper boy rolled over and lay staring.

Jingo stood up, pulled down her dress, put on her shoes, patted her hair and said, "See you later, John Lee."

She walked around the paper boy, gave him a twitch and I fell down on the bed. It seemed I had scarcely closed my eyes when the phone began ringing. I staggered out and answered it.

"Aha! Sleeping in! Double-crossing an old friend!"

"Who do you want?"

"You, John Lee! This is Leroy. You're supposed to be at the Breakfast Brigade in forty-five minutes."

20

I had a powerful thirst and drank three or four glasses of water and felt drunk again, and disoriented. I swallowed three Alka-Seltzers and three aspirins, went into my usual vitamin ritual, and then washed down two spansules with two Cokes and watched through the bathroom window as One-Line Lockwood left in a taxi. After my shower, I was standing in my bedroom, giddy as if I had been holding my breath, peering at two jackets, unable to decide whether to wear the green one or the brown one. The telephone rang again, at this peculiar hour of twenty minutes until eight.

"Let me speak to Juliette," the voice said.

"She's not here, Ruby."

"I'm gonna give you a warning," the voice said in a fine gangster snarl that put me in mind of John Lee Wallace in *The Joy Train.* "If you know what's good for you, you'll keep away from that girl. I won't tell you this again."

For a moment I considered what he had said.

"You punk son of a bitch, is this supposed to be a threat?" I said. An unreasoning anger had suddenly crept into my rather strained and delicate mental state.

"Aw, now, John Lee, listen, I didn't mean I was threatening you."

"Then what did you mean?"

"All I meant was that girl will get you into trouble if you keep associating with her."

"If she does, that's my tough luck. But I don't need any advice from you about who I associate with," I said.

"Did she tell you she's put me under a peace bond? The little bitch has got me under a thousand-dollar peace bond that says I got to keep away from her. How can she work for me? I'm thinking I might have her arrested for indecent acts."

"So call a cop," I said. "But don't ever call me again."

I hung up the phone and went back into my room to resume staring at the green jacket and the brown jacket. Suddenly I shoved both of them back into the closet and dug out my suitcase. I put on cowboy boots, faded Levi's, a khaki shirt with epaulets and snap buttons, a belt with a big buckle, and my black felt cowboy hat. I don't know what caused me to do this. Whether I thought the cowboy outfit would protect me from the Breakfast Brigade, or would further enrage the sturdy business leaders, I am not sure, but putting on a costume was an impulse I had to follow.

I walked into Buster's room to find his car keys. When I opened the door he was sitting in the middle of the bed, sweating and smoking a cigarette, between two waitresses from one of the clubs. One of the girls tried to cover herself with the sheet but couldn't yank it out from under Buster. The other girl smiled at me.

"You just missed the rodeo," said Buster.

"I think you look real cute," one of the girls said.

Buster hugged the two of them.

"My new motto is 'Let it happen,' " he said.

"How does that differ from your old motto?" I said.

"Word for word, exactly the same," he said. "What is our mission for today?"

"Our mission is to shoot the President after I make my miserable speech to the Breakfast Brigade."

"You take the Bolex," said Buster. "I'll borrow another camera. I'll catch Kennedy at the airport or over on Lemmon Avenue by the End Zone, and then while he goes downtown I'll drive out to the Trade Mart to get the look on Annabel Withers' face when she sees Kennedy and lust overcomes hatred."

"The President is a stud doll," one of the girls said.

"I'll shoot some film downtown. Maybe I can get Kennedy at Dealey Plaza with the Dallas *Morning News* building in the background," I said.

"Try not to be too ironical," said Buster.

I said I would meet him later at the Villa Lopez. On the porch I picked up the Dallas *Morning News* and turned the pages rapidly. The front page was full of Kennedy's reception in Texas, the size and warmth of the crowds, comments by politicians and so forth. I didn't read it. Inside the paper I saw a full-page advertisement, bordered in black, that said WELCOME MR. KENNEDY TO DALLAS. This seemed an odd thing to be in the Dallas *News,* so I read more of the ad and found its reason. The ad assured the President that Dallas was a town of Conservative Americans, an "economic boom town" that had "rejected your philosophy and policies and will do so again—even more emphatically." The ad demanded to know why Latin America was turning Communist, why there was no freedom in Cuba, why Kennedy was selling wheat to enemy soldiers when "Communists are daily wounding and killing American soldiers in Vietnam," why

Kennedy had entertained Tito, why he had "let Cambodia kick us out after pouring four hundred million dollars into their leftist government," why he allowed Argentina to "seize our property," why the CIA was "exterminating staunch anti-Communist allies of the U.S.," why did he "permit Bobby to go soft on Communists, Fellow Travelers and Ultra-Liberals in America but persecute loyal Americans who criticize you," why he had "scrapped the Monroe Doctrine in favor of the Spirit of Moscow." There was more. I looked down to the bottom and saw the ad was signed by The American Fact-Finding Committee . . . "Citizens Who Want the Truth."

I tossed the newspaper onto the couch where the strange girl was still sleeping amid the wreckage, and drove to the Tropical Island Motor Hotel. Listening to the radio as the Morris Minor moved through the early traffic, I heard that it was to be a warm, sunny day, the rains gone, temperature about seventy. Vast crowds were expected along the route of the President's motorcade through Dallas. Now, as I was driving, Kennedy was presumably finishing breakfast at the Texas Hotel in Fort Worth, and as I was addressing the Breakfast Brigade the President would be making a speech of his own before getting on his plane at Carswell Air Force Base to fly roughly fifty miles to Love Field in Dallas. I couldn't figure why he didn't drive to Dallas—from the Texas Hotel to Dealey Plaza was only thirty minutes on the toll road—and have the plane pick him up later, but I had more urgent concerns than presidential transportation. There was Dorothy in the hospital with that little red baby, and *Six Guns Across Texas* hanging out there, and Caroline in California, and my movie unsolved and what was to be done about Big Earl? On top of all that, I felt purely awful. And the least of my problems was the most immediate— what to say to the Breakfast Brigade. The two Dexamyls were down inside someplace, scrapping around, dredging up babble that I doubted my mind would bother to censor before the words leaked out through holes in my brain and landed upon the ears of two hundred leading citizens.

The lock was broken on the car, and I took the Bolex inside with me. Leroy met me in the lobby with a look of relief. "Just about on

246

time and in uniform and barely even staggering. Not bad," he said. We entered at the back of the banquet room and had to travel a long aisle between rows of tables, and then force men to slide in their chairs so that we could find our places at the speakers' table. Above the head table hung a banner:

THE BREAKFAST BRIGADE
SELLING DALLAS TO THE WORLD

I had heard comments about my odd appearance as I walked to my seat, and voices had called out my name. I had begun to regret wearing the cowboy outfit. I kept on my smile but tried not to look at anyone. Once seated, I looked at them: two hundred solid faces, with hair cut short or no hair at all, not one mustache in the entire room, no one without a necktie, nearly all in business suits enough alike that they could have been in the same regiment.

I neglected to remove my hat.

While a Methodist preacher spoke the opening prayer with a fair amount of feeling, considering the time of day, I looked at the two fried eggs and two strips of bacon on my plate. The eggs were filled with little puddles of milky matter and without noticing what I was doing I stared at these blobs until suddenly I thought I was going to vomit. I put my napkin to my mouth, swallowing hard, trying to think of something pleasant, imagining that I was walking between trees on a golf course on a cool bright morning. I glanced around at Leroy, who understood at once what was wrong. He looked away from me, as if he knew that once I started he would do it also. But the nausea passed in a moment, and then I felt very warm, my ears red and burning and my breathing difficult. With the napkin I covered my plate. Leroy was standing at the lectern, adjusting the microphone, making jokes. Mild laughter rolled back in rows from the front, where they could hear better. I heard Leroy talking about various club members and covering each critical remark with a grin so that everyone could laugh at the man who had been mentioned. The faces looking up at us seemed very cheerful and healthy. Among those I could see, the closest ones, there was not a trace of a hangover. They appeared to be mostly of an age, about fifty, a few younger and a few older. They were drinking coffee and had lit cigarettes when I heard Leroy say my name.

". . . too thick to be a mop, too tall to be a sheepdog, too short to be a palm tree, too smart to be a prophet, too dumb to be Einstein, too much alive to be Buffalo Bill, too old to be a beatnik, too crude to be Liberace, and he's not even Tarzan any more, but when Greer Garson is out of town he's our longest-haired movie star, and we love him—John Lee Wallace."

Hearing the applause, I got out of my chair without knocking it over and walked to the lectern, where Leroy's shining perfumy face was smiling at me.

"That was a lot of cheap-shit stuff," I said, smiling back.

"Be charming, Tex," he muttered.

I turned to the crowd and gripped the sides of the lectern and those two hundred balls of flesh tilted slightly upward to keep aim on me, and I could feel a great sense of anticipation and good-natured wonderment coming from them, as if they were a crowd of Victorians viewing a Hottentot. Gazing down at the crowd, I realized I hadn't anything at all to say. My mouth was dry, my lips were stuck together and my mind felt as though it had been seared—it was like a painting of the sun with little strings of thought radiating out from it but not one of them worth talking about on its own. It is a common trick for a speaker to pause before speaking, drawing his audience into straining to communicate for him, but certainly you can't go on with this for very many minutes. I wished I had made some notes, at least. I thought about faking a brain attack. Chairs began to scrape.

"Thank you, Leroy," I said. The audience began laughing, relieved that I had spoken at last, and expecting me to reply in kind to Leroy. "If I ever have a chance to introduce you to the bottom of Lake Dallas, I'll be glad to do so." More laughter. "I'm surprised you could even be here today, Leroy. With the President on his way, I figured Laureen would have you out on Lemmon Avenue sweeping up the nails." A good laugh. "As the only Liberal Democrat in this club, Leroy, you ought to be wearing an arm band that says ME NO DALLAS

248

NEWS." Silence. Missed them with that one. "I guess you saw that ad in the *News* this morning. Leroy hasn't had time to read it yet, because Liberals don't usually get up very early. But I understand someone showed it to the President, and he said, 'Lyndon, would it be all right with you if we sell Dallas to Germany?' " Utter silence, except for a couple of coughs. Well, that wasn't funny, anyhow, but it was something to say. I looked at Leroy, who seemed nervous again.

"So here I am at the Bacon Brigade," I said. "Hidy, ever'body."

I realized Clive Riordan had said that.

"Breakfast Brigade," Leroy said, smiling, and there were a few chuckles.

"I get mixed up. The idea is to bring home the bacon, isn't it?" I looked down at the faces. A few of them were faintly smiling. "As long as it isn't Polish bacon." A sprinkling laugh. I had a terrible inspiration to start clucking like a chicken. The desire was almost more than I could bear, and thinking about it I started laughing, a sound that did have certain clucking qualities.

"Some of you may have read in Jimmy Widgin's column that I'm going to make a movie about Texas. A good place to start that film would be right here in this room. With a shot of all your faces out there."

I picked up the Bolex, raised it to my eye and knocked off my hat. Big laugh. I put my hat on again and began shooting the faces, panning the tables. The Breakfast Brigade sat up with interest. Several men removed their glasses.

"These faces are certainly representative of one aspect of Texas life, all right," I said, laying down the camera. "If each man here will now just write me out a personal check for five thousand dollars and deliver it up here to the head table, I can practically guarantee your faces will be in my movie, and that's another aspect of Texas life that you understand quite well."

Scraping, rustling, disappointed laughter. They hadn't wanted me to be kidding about their faces in the film.

"When I've got these checks, we'll be in business," I said. "In a Texas minute. You know what a Texas minute is—that's sometime between immediately and never. It takes foreigners a while to learn that when a Texan tells them he'll do something, they better demand to know exactly when. A Texan probably means it when he says it, but as my good friend Francis P. Franklin says—anybody who does everything he says he's going to do is short on imagination."

I put on my best smile to show them it was all right to laugh at this joke about ourselves as a group, and they did. I had it going pretty well again, but I didn't know where to go next, and I felt a touch of panic.

"I'm sure the Bacon Brigade isn't short on imagination," I said. "It takes a bushel of smart apples to think up a deal like this, where two hundred guys go eat a lousy breakfast at eight o'clock in the morning at some fruity looking motel to hear a dope fiend blabber at them about nothing." With horror, it occurred to me that I had said the words dope fiend out loud, and I smiled again to demonstrate that it was a joke. "That takes some sharp thinking. I suppose the secret is that nobody in the world really knows what he's doing."

They didn't laugh at that. In fact, I heard murmuring at several tables, and two or three men got up and walked out. The black waiters were lined up against the back wall with their towels and trays and were looking aghast in the main, though perhaps a few were grinning. The black waiters didn't like me either.

"If you bunch up and act grotesque like those people who put that ad in the paper this morning, you can make believe you know what you're doing, but when you wake up in the middle of the night you know you don't really have any idea about any of it," I said.

The Methodist preacher seemed irritated, so I said, "What about that, Parson?"

"When I wake up in the middle of the night and feel lonely or confused, I say a prayer," he said.

"Say one for that Communist," said a voice from the crowd.

I looked to see who had said that. I thought I located the table, because a number of people had looked in that direction. Three men at the table appeared somewhat embarrassed, but the fourth had a flushed face and was leaning on his elbows with both thumbs in his mouth.

"You talking about me or the President?" I said, looking at him.

His head rocked back and forth, and he bit on his thumbs, but he didn't answer.

"Tell us what happens on *Six Guns Across Texas* next week," someone shouted.

"I think that's the one where Clive Riordan shoots a loudmouth," I said.

There was a lot of nervous laughter. I picked up the Bolex, looked at my heckler through the viewfinder, imagining it might be a scope, and pressed the button.

"Might get shot yourself!"

It was a different voice from another part of the room, and the man I had been filming smiled around his thumbs.

"Stand up, Preacher, and tell them what Jesus said about being rude," I said.

"Taking their picture without their permission is rude," said the preacher.

I filmed a close-up of the preacher's nose.

The preacher covered his nose with both hands.

"Tell me one thing about yourself that makes sense," I said to the preacher.

"Sit down, cowboy!" someone shouted.

"Fuck the pile of you," I said, and sat down in my chair.

I said it in an offhanded way, and not very loud. Probably not more than fifty of them actually heard me, but they started repeating it to those farther back, and then it was rolling all around the room—fuck the pile of you, fuck the pile of you, until even the waiters were repeating it to each other, and the amazing thing was at least half the Breakfast Brigade and nearly all the waiters started laughing. It struck me that some did indeed think it was funny, and others would swallow nearly anything from Clive Riordan. But there were about a hundred very sour faces out there. The balance teetered for a moment before the sour faces glared the laughers into silence, and as Leroy stood up and walked toward the lectern someone in the crowd stood up and led the occupants of his table out of the room, and that set off a general standing and milling and talking, and by the time

251

Leroy said into the microphone, "If I still have anything to do with it, next week's speaker will be Helen Keller," there were only twenty or thirty people remaining.

The Methodist preacher looked at me and shook his head and walked out. I stood up again, watching the room clearing, with the banner SELLING DALLAS TO THE WORLD at my back. The president of the Breakfast Brigade, an old man in a gray suit, stopped in front of me and said, "Thank you, Mr. Wallace. That was very unusual."

"John Lee is a real pro," said Leroy.

"I apologize for people yelling at you. I don't approve of that," the old man said. "By the way, do you frequently eat breakfast wearing your hat?" Then he turned and was gone before I could comment.

Leroy walked with me to the car. In the parking lot with the Buicks, Pontiacs, Oldsmobiles and occasional Cadillacs that the Brigade drove to breakfast, Buster's Morris Minor looked depressing, like something left over from the Dust Bowl.

"I've got to go out to the Trade Mart now and help Laureen and her friends get the place ready for the President's luncheon," he said. "I won't even get to see the motorcade. There's going to be twenty-five hundred people in that hall to hear Kennedy. I hope he's better prepared than you were."

"I guess I made your life a little harder," I said.

"They'll get over it. They're not as bad as you might think. They're just a little uneasy about things."

"You're either a saint or a dangerous schizophrenic," I said.

"I'm no crazier than you are, you've proved that," he said, grinning. "But I'll promise you that if anybody spits on the President or hits him with a signboard, I'll put sugar in their gas tank."

21

"You can't see the baby right now," said the nurse. A curtain closed off the big glass window, and I could make out only the shape of the incubator behind it. "But Miss Leclaire is awake." The nurse walked swiftly in padded white shoes, and I shambled in my boots in an effort to keep up. At Dorothy's door the nurse turned and said, "Do you feel all right? You look ill."

"It's been a long night," I said.

The nurse frowned and walked away, her starched white dress making a switching sound. Dorothy's bed was behind a hanging screen in a room she shared with three other young mothers. She was combing her hair using Jingo's comb and mirror, and was wearing one of Jingo's pink silk negligees with blue ribbons. Dorothy smiled drowsily at me with chewed lips and eyes half shut.

"I should have brought flowers, but I forgot," I said.

"Where did I get this gown? It barely reaches my crotch, and when I move I'm afraid I'll tear the shoulders out."

"It's Jingo's," I said.

"That was nice of her, considering that she hates me."

"She doesn't hate you."

"I screwed up your party."

"Not to make you feel unimportant, but the party went right on without you. Having any pains?"

"I just had a shot while ago. I'm so stoned. I feel wonderful. But goddamn, it's creepy in this room. The girl in the next bed cried for two hours this morning because her husband has run off, and the one across from me has been bitching about having a girl instead of a boy.

253

The other one's whole family came in here and got into an argument and left. Did you see the baby?"

"Early this morning," I said.

"What did he look like?"

"Well, he's very short," I said.

"What color hair?"

"Kind of brown or black, I don't know. He's awful red, and he sure does want to breathe."

"Do you feel like he might be yours?" Dorothy said.

Her eyes kept that sultry, doped-up look as she regarded me.

"I feel like he couldn't be mine, but maybe he is. I don't know. I feel like he really needs somebody to look out for him. I'm not sure what all I feel about him."

Dorothy put the mirror on the night table beside an ashtray and a drinking glass with a bent glass tube in it. She held out a hand, and I took it. Her hand felt cold and rough and her fingers began to squeeze.

"I wanted him to be yours, but he's just not," she said. "I don't really know whose he is. I tried not to have him. I couldn't stand to go through another abortion, but I drank castor oil and jumped up and down and tried not to have him." She was still smiling, but her lips trembled and tears appeared on her cheeks. "I kept thinking something would happen to stop him from coming, but he came anyway. He couldn't even wait till the party was over, he wanted to come so bad."

"Nobody at the party knew except Jingo and Buster and me."

"Is he a cute baby?"

"I wouldn't describe him as cute, but maybe you would. Girls have a funny way of looking at babies."

"I wish I could have seen him," she said.

"You can see him soon."

"No," she said, her voice cracking.

I was suddenly alarmed. He had looked so tiny and so thoroughly outnumbered, but I hadn't supposed he might not make it.

"Did he die?" I said.

254

"The doctor was in here a while ago and said it will be two or three days before they know for sure, but he thinks the baby will come through."

"That kid seems pretty determined," I said. "He'll be yelling for you by this afternoon."

I didn't know why, but that remark set off the tears in an abrupt flow, although the only sound Dorothy made for a time was a sort of choking. I reached over and wiped her face, feeling awkward and loutish.

"The doctor was in here a while ago," she repeated, "and I signed a paper for the baby to be adopted. Some organization will pay all my hospital bills and see the baby gets a good home with people that want him, right straight from the hospital, but one rule they've got is I'm not allowed to see the baby ever."

"I'll find the doctor and tear up that paper," I said.

"I signed the paper because I think it's the best thing to do. If I saw the baby, it would just be harder for me."

I felt a strange mingling of relief and sorrow, and the guilt that was often my companion. I hadn't known what I would do about this baby, but I felt that I was somehow to blame for his arrival, and it would be necessary for me to do something. Now there was nothing for me to do. I could have asked Dorothy to marry me then, and gone and talked the doctor out of the piece of paper, but I sat there with my mouth shut and held her hand while she cried for a minute.

Finally I stood up and said, "When you get out of here, I'll take you someplace. We'll go to Mexico and have a good time."

"That's always your answer," she said, trying to smile again.

"It may not be the best thing that could possibly be done, but it's available."

Dorothy was slipping into some reverie that did not include me, so I said I would visit later and kissed her on the forehead. "Thank you," she murmured. Going out, I passed a counter where several nurses looked at me, and I heard my name mentioned. One of the nurses came to the elevator and asked for my autograph for her little boy, who watched the TV show, she said, and wanted to grow his hair to look just like mine. "God forbid," she said.

I went to the apartment to change clothes and try to catch Buster, but the gray Plymouth station wagon was gone from the curb, and when I opened the living room door I saw why. Ina Mae Leclaire was sitting on the couch with her legs crossed, smoking a cigarette. She looked very different than she had the night I carried her out of the hospital. Her hair had beauty-shop waves, and her eyes and mouth were thick with cosmetics. She wore high-heeled shoes and showed a shiny reach of handsome nylon legs.

"Some wreck," she said, gesturing around the apartment.

"Hidy, Ina Mae."

"How come you don't invite me to your parties? I'm more fun than Dorothy."

"Have you heard what happened?" I said.

"Yeah, I knew she was pregnant, and Buster told me she went to the hospital, so I figured it out. Now I'm a grandmother. What a goddamn joy."

"It's your secret," I said. "Dorothy signed a paper for the kid to be adopted."

"My poor little girl," said Ina Mae, apparently meaning it. "How is she?"

"Hanging on. Why don't you go see her?"

"We don't get along, John Lee. We fight all the time. I'd only upset her. But I'll tell you one damn thing, there's a certain person in this town who ain't going to get away with making my little girl suffer like that. I'm going to have this certain person beat up so bad his pecker will bleed ever' time he looks at another young girl."

"That's a little harsh," I said uneasily.

"You're too soft. That's one reason I like you so much."

Then it wasn't me she meant.

"But your friend Franklin ain't soft," she said. "After they kick the crap out of him, he will be."

"Franklin?" I said.

"It's his baby, you know. Dorothy told me."

"I don't believe it."

"Would she lie to me about that?" said Ina Mae.

I looked at her and nodded. Ina Mae thought it over.

"You really don't believe it?" she said.

"I don't think Franklin ever got close to Dorothy that long ago, and if he had he would have handled it better. He'd have sent her to Paris or something."

"Jesus, I better use the phone," said Ina Mae. I saw the flash of inner thigh as she got up, and watched her walk to the phone, and couldn't help but admire her body as she dialed. Once again I reminded myself that although she was Dorothy's mother, Ina Mae was only thirty-eight, and there was more to her than the pitiful gray-skinned slobbering creature who had gone down the corridor in a wheelchair at Parkland. "Hello, George," I heard her say, "listen, baby, call it off about doing that guy I asked you to do. Tell you later. Love ya. Bye-bye." She put down the phone. "Wouldn't want to make a mistake in a deal like this," she said to me.

"Want a Bloody Mary?" I said.

"You flirting with me?"

"I'm glad you weren't here last night. I could have really got bizarre. Today it's too late."

"I'll make the drinks, anyhow. I like to keep practicing my trade."

She pinched me on the ear and went into the kitchen. In the back bathroom I brushed my teeth again and placed my hand on my chest to feel my heart bumping and felt a speed rush that told me to keep moving. I looked at the place on the floor where Dorothy had been sitting when the little fellow had started knocking his way out. A handkerchief and an earring were lying on the tiles.

Ina Mae shook several drops of Tabasco and Worcestershire into the drinks and sprinkled in a lot of pepper on top of the ice cubes and stirred them with her finger.

"Good-bye to hard times," she said, clinking her glass against mine.

Usually I avoid Bloody Marys because the tomato juice sticks in my mustache, but there are occasions when no other drink will quite suffice. I took a swallow and happened to look into the den. On the floor was a blue suitcase that I had last seen when I checked it at the airline counter as Dorothy was leaving California.

"Dorothy's things are in there. I kept some of her stuff for myself that she never wore anyhow," said Ina Mae.

Staring at the suitcase, I finished my drink.

"Her rent was up at the other place, and I'm moving to Detroit," Ina Mae said. "I've got a real good job up there, honey, as a cocktail waitress. I can make two hundred dollars a week. Dorothy won't be sorry to see me go."

"Yes she will," I said.

"Not in the long run, she won't." Ina Mae looked at her watch. "Kiss my little girl for me, John Lee, and tell her I love her. I know you'll take real good care of her. I kind of wish it was me you loved instead of her, but I know how men like young girls. Listen, baby, I got to run see the President. Ain't he beautiful? I'll send you my address. Bye-bye now. You make a real cute cowboy."

Quickly she kissed me on the mouth, with her lips open, and I got a smell of a good delicate perfume, and then she was out the door into the sunlight.

I sat down on the couch and started pulling off a boot, but it would not come off, and the effort made me dizzy. I stamped my foot back down into the boot and put on my hat and ran for the car with the Bolex. I had trouble starting the Morris Minor and feared I might miss the motorcade, but the engine finally caught and the radio came on. Because of the cleared weather that caused me to stop and roll up my sleeves, the bubble-top had been removed from the President's black Lincoln, the radio said. Plenty of Dallas cops had been at the airport, where the President had touched hands with admirers, and hundreds more were spotted along the route—a map of which had been printed in the newspapers—where three hundred thousand people were waiting to see the Kennedys ride past in the open car with Governor Connally and his wife, and Lyndon Johnson riding a few cars behind. I drove fast and parked the Morris Minor by the Texas & Pacific Railroad tracks on Pacific Street in a brown-brick warren of warehouses. As I stepped over railroad tracks and around boxcars,

I saw a few people sitting on loading platforms eating sandwiches out of paper bags, but most of the workers had gone over a couple of blocks to Dealey Plaza to watch the President. The sidewalks at Elm and Houston beside the School Book Depository Building were crowded, and I didn't immediately see an opening in the crowd across Elm in Dealey Plaza, so I trotted on along Houston to Main Street, going past the Criminal Courts Building, looking for a view for the Bolex. At the corner where the cars were to turn north off Main onto Houston, I squeezed among people at the curb as I heard cheering and the motorcycles coming amid a roar that boomed toward me along Main like the roar of a football crowd. People flinched back from me, but it didn't matter. I leaned out and saw the motorcade approaching very close, first the motorcycles and then a pilot car of cops, then six more motorcycles and the white lead car with the Sheriff and the Police Chief and the Secret Service boss, and finally four or five lengths back came the black Lincoln. Through the viewfinder I saw Connally's wavy blue-silver hair. Mrs. Connally was in the other jump seat, hidden from me. Now I found John F. Kennedy. He was on the side of the car nearest the curb, his eyes crinkled and puffy underneath, an arm on the rim of the open car, shirt cuff showing, wearing a dotted necktie, looking at the people along the curb as they applauded and called out to him. Kennedy was smiling a very good smile with very white teeth, and his wife was smiling almost the same way but without as much heart in it. His hair looked thick and healthy, and his face was tanned, and his eyes were clear and seemed to be enjoying what they saw. I was struck by how much like a movie star he looked, what an air of ultimate celebrity there was about him, everything put together exactly right and a good heart showing from that smile and the eyes, with his wife sitting there beside him trying to smile in the same manner. She had the look of celebrity, too, but more distant from the people and from life, a movie star's smile that was like a fence between her and the crowd; where her smile said *keep away I'm doing all right,* his said *we've got it going and I love it all.* They both looked as if they had been made up for the cameras, whites of the eyes sparkling, teeth polished, skin tinted copper, grander than the rest of us, but his face shone with intelligence and humor that broke through the celebrity mask without apology for the mask itself.

As the car pulled abreast, I didn't want to see him through the viewfinder, but the movie might require this vision. I lifted the camera and the President's gray eyes looked directly at me leaning out from the curb, took me all in with an instant's deep gaze, and looked squarely into my lens, and his lips moved a bit, the smile broadening, and he raised a finger and pointed at me, and I took my eye away from the viewfinder and looked straight into his eyes, and a communication flashed from him to me that said *there you are you freak what a time you must have among these people I like you for it don't give up.* At the same second he was sending me that message I was receiving it and thinking as well, with surprise and embarrassment that I would have such a thought, that if I'd wanted to hurt the man, I was so close I could crack his skull with a five-iron or couldn't conceivably miss with a pistol. But I could tell this perverted thought never reached him. He had trained himself to tune out small paranoias. I smiled at him as he looked at me, and his right eye squinted very slightly as if it occurred to him that he had seen me before but could not recall where. Then his eyes left me and held their place in the crowd that was moving past the car, and he said something to his wife, and she looked back, smiling with the flowers in her arms, but our eyes never met, and then the black limousine was going on down the road and I was looking at the back of the President's head.

I didn't wait to film Lyndon Johnson or any of the others. To me they were just politicians, not great men, just part of the crowd the same as me, and I still didn't care for all this big-ass politics, but I knew a great man when I saw one. Reflecting on the sensation of having connected in a mental relay with the President, and repeating to myself *there you are you freak,* I ran and caught up with the car as it turned onto Houston Street. I flipped on the long lens and got the Lincoln in my magnified sight again as the motorcade turned once more onto Elm at the red-brick Depository Building and started down toward the triple underpass and the railroad trestle.

POP

I knew it was a rifle shot. The sound is so common as to be quite distinctive. Later, many said they thought it was a firecracker, or the popping of a paper bag, or a backfire, but I knew at once that it was a rifle shot and I heard myself moan as I looked through the viewfinder and saw Kennedy raise his hands toward his throat and Connally starting to turn back toward him.

Pigeons flew up from the Depository Building. The car kept moving slowly. I was expecting the car to leap ahead and disappear through the underpass, but it moved so very slowly.

POP

The car had passed an oak tree, and now people were screaming and had begun running around in Dealey Plaza, and the pigeons were circling in the sky, and cops in helmets on motorcycles were looking back and forth, wondering where the shots were coming from. Through the viewfinder I saw Connally sliding down, and Kennedy leaning to the left toward his wife, and the black Lincoln almost seemed to be stopping, edging down from slow motion into stop-frame.

"Go on!" I cried. "Goddamn you, go on before they kill him!"

Someone shouted into my ear. I kept my finger on the button. I was waiting for another shot. The first two shots echoed through the Plaza, bounced off the county jail and the Depository, caroming around the Plaza, and people were running, falling, dodging, throwing themselves onto the ground as in war movies. On the grassy knoll I saw figures scattering, and Kennedy continued to lean in the creeping Lincoln.

POP

Pieces of skull sailed out of Kennedy's head. A red spray flew out, as if a stone had been thrown into a pot of tomato soup.

"No! They've got him now!" I yelled.

At last the car moved. As the President's wife began scrambling out the back of the car, out of this blood and madness, at last the car moved forward, carrying its passengers too late down into the underpass.

I knew he was dead.

For a moment I kept the camera on the tumult around the Plaza, on the stunned and frantic crowd, and then I took the camera away from my eye and began trotting toward the Depository Building for no special reason other than that my car was over in that direction.

"He's shot! He's shot!" a voice cried.

Beside me a woman was screaming.

A man with a transistor radio at his ear said, "Well, I'll be damned, they've shot them all."

By then the Plaza and the sidewalk in front of the Criminal Courts Building were blurred with people running and milling, and voices rose in wails and sobs, and police with riot guns and helmets scurried in the smell of motor oil and exhaust fumes and human breath, and many people were shouting. I didn't look at the rest of the motorcade now passing, at the press buses or the cars of the functionaries. I jogged toward my car, my mouth open, staring straight ahead.

He's shot!

I jogged on.

"Grab that long-haired guy! Get him!"

He's shot! Who did it? Where are they now? Jogging along, I looked at the underpass, at the banks of green grass sloping down to the street. I looked up at the windows of the Depository and at the big Hertz sign on top. A weeping woman in a flowered hat looked at me and said, "I didn't want him to die." Jogging, I felt possessed by anger and terror, and the old dread was coming back, the knowledge of the presence of madness and murder as the forces that ruled us. Our truth was lunacy and our destination oblivion, and I had it in the Bolex.

He should not have tuned me out.

"Officer, get that long-haired fellow!"

"What's your name, Buddy?"

"Wallace."

"What's your business here?"

"I came to see the President."

"What kind of work you do?"

"I'm a cowboy."

"Okay, move along."

262

"Who shot him?"

"How the fuck do I know? Get moving."

I went across the street and passed beside the School Book Depository Building. A man came out of the building carrying a Coke, and we looked at each other, and I went on down the narrow street among the warehouses and boxcars and railroad tracks, and the Morris Minor started at once. I put the Bolex on the seat. I didn't want to touch it any more right now. I turned on the radio. There was a report that the President, his wife, John Connally and Lyndon Johnson had all been shot. They were all in Parkland Hospital, the radio said. My God, all of them rolling on slabs down the hall where Ina Mae Leclaire had sat looking at the concrete with foolish attention. Listening to the radio, shivering, with a hot knot in my stomach, I drove out Cedar Springs to the Villa Lopez. Shot!

Hector, his wife, a busboy and two waiters were sitting with the two club waitresses of Buster's morning bed. They were at a big table, with bottles of beer around a radio.

"He won't die," Hector said.

But I knew he was dead already. I saw his brains fly out.

I got myself a beer and sat down. By now the radio had explained that the President and Connally had been shot, but not the others. We kept sitting there, with our elbows on the table, listening to the radio. No customers came in, and nobody made a move toward the kitchen. Each of us recounted where we had seen the President that noon and how he had looked, as a sort of liturgy to reestablish his presence, a juju against death. In their minds the broken head was healing, the bullets becoming part of a myth, but I knew better. I told them the President had sent me a message, and what he had said, and they smiled, not understanding. Then the radio said Kennedy was dead. One of the club waitresses began to moan, and tears spurted from Hector's eyes. Everybody in the room was crying. We knew we were helpless. We knew what was waiting for us.

And we had a new king.

"That man can't be dead," Hector said with tears pouring down his face.

A new king in the land of death. A new Caesar from the provinces.

"God, he was pretty," said one of the girls.

"He was a good son of a gun," Hector said.

The new king was out there now at Love Field on that airplane waiting for the coffin, to take it back to Rome.

Sunlight burst in as the front door banged open.

"Kennedy is dead!" a boy shouted.

The door shut again. Hector went into his small office behind the cash register and came back with a bottle of tequila. He put the bottle in the middle of the table and then brought more beer.

"We can't do nothing else about it," he said.

That was the truth. Things go away.

We had been drinking tequila a few minutes when Buster came in. His khaki shirt was smeared with sweat. He drank from the tequila bottle and picked up a beer.

"Were you at Dealey Plaza?" he said.

I nodded.

"You got it?"

I nodded.

"Christ in heaven, I wish we didn't have it," he said.

"I'll rip it out of the camera," I said.

"It happened," Buster said. "We've got it. It's real now."

He swigged down the beer and picked up another.

"At the Trade Mart they had yellow roses and organ music and everybody was eating steak," he said. "Annabel and Charlie Withers were at a table. They didn't have a banner. Then I went to Parkland and shot the reporters and the cops. Now I'm going to the police station. But first I'm going over to Turtle Creek and beat the hell out of the first right-wing bastard I see."

"I'll go with you," I said.

"You're crazy," said a waitress.

"It was those right-wing bastards that did this," Buster said.

"I'll fight the son of a bitch, you show me who!" shouted Hector.

"Let's go," I said, needing to do it.

"I'll get my pistol," said Hector.

"No guns," Buster said.

"They'll shoot us down right off," said Hector.

"We'll fight, though," Buster said.

Murder was loosed, and lunacy was unburied, and there was no other way.

In the Plymouth station wagon with the bottle of tequila, we started driving down Cedar Springs toward Turtle Creek. The day had a strange dreamy quality, cars moving silently, people frozen on sidewalks in yellow sunlight, the dusty beery smell in the station wagon, our senses loaded beyond capacity to reason as we had been trained to do.

"There's two son of a bitches," Hector said.

In front of a tall gray mansion at the back of a green lawn, two men in business suits were talking. As we looked at them, they started laughing. I wanted to kill them.

"I'll get these guys myself," said Hector.

"We'll stomp their grinning fascist butts," Buster said.

Then the radio announced that the Dallas police had information that the suspect in the Kennedy murder was a Communist who had recently returned from Russia. More details were forthcoming.

We sat in the car and looked at the two men in business suits.

"The government is saying this to stop people like us. They know it's all about to come apart," said Buster.

One of the men on the green lawn went to the porch of a big gray house, and the other walked across the driveway toward the house next door.

"So let's get them," I said.

A police car slowed as it cruised past. The cops looked at us. Seeing my cowboy hat, one of the cops smiled. The police car went on. Both men had gone inside their houses, where, in Dallas in that neighborhood, they presumed themselves safe.

"So much for frontier justice," Buster said. "We don't even hit back. What the hell has happened to us?"

Not being working reporters any longer, and unable as yet to face what might await at the police station, we drove to the End Zone.

Someone had strung up an old parachute as an awning out front. We sat at a wooden table under the awning and the light bulbs. People wandered in and out, getting very drunk, and always the portable radios and televisions, and the large television inside, were turned on until you could finally feel the city trembling with electricity, and all the minds in the city connected into the circuits, and the minds and electric machines connecting in expanding networks with broader webs of mind and machine until the entire world was linked into us sitting there in Dallas, and then those outside feelings of hate and fear began to overwhelm our own feelings of shock and anger and disgust with ourselves, and we became the receptacle for the guilt of all the world. We didn't want it, we couldn't stand it, and we couldn't refuse it. After that burst of motion and fury, that moment when we might have acted without regard for opinion and worked off our rage with blind violence against those we knew deserved it, after that moment we retreated into stunned revulsion at ourselves. The world was grieving—the television showed us so, the weeping faces in Europe, the people asking why we had done it. The country was outraged. We were becoming paralyzed. A man sat on the grass in front of the End Zone and wept and then stood up and said he was selling his jewelry store and moving to New York, and an advertising executive hit him on the jaw. "This is my town, this couldn't have happened," the executive said, crying. We cursed ourselves and defended ourselves. What did I do? How am I to blame? There were rumors of the city in flames. The new king spoke to us, and we knew from his voice that it was all different now, the old government overthrown. His hound's eyes gazed out at paranoia worse than his own. One move would have torn the society apart, but the move never came. The tissues were stronger than we realized, holding back the move. Conspiracies crept among us, phantom gunmen and mysterious airplanes, threats from all sides as we huddled together. The death was our failure.

By now we had heard of the murder of the policeman, Tippitt, and the arrest of Lee Harvey Oswald, who had hidden—where else?—in a movie theater.

At last Buster and I got up to drive down to the police station.

266

Buster locked my film of Dealey Plaza in a metal box in the rear of the station wagon.

"I don't like this movie, John Lee, but we've got to see the end of it," he said. "It's the movie we've been making."

22

Buster already had a Dallas press card. I had no trouble getting one, because the officer handing them out remembered me. We went up to the third floor with both cameras. Oswald, we were told, was being held in the jail on the fifth floor, but they were bringing him down often on the elevator to the third floor where the chief's office and the homicide bureau were located. The pressroom was also on the third floor, and Buster and I thought to go and wait in there. But when we reached the third floor, the entire crucifix-shaped corridor was totally jammed with movie and television cameras and cables, tape recorders, reporters, Texas Rangers, the FBI, Secret Service, sheriff's deputies, Dallas detectives in Stetson hats, newspaper and radio reporters, dozens of photographers. They kept shouting, "Where's Oswald? Bring him out here, the little shit! Show us the killer!"

"Give us Barabbas!" yelled Buster.

"Where's Barabbas?" someone shouted.

"Where's that goddamn Barabbas?"

Getting behind a Texas Ranger, Buster and I fought along the hall, shoving hard, elbowing and pushing and stomping on feet. Many of the people in the hall wore red badges that showed they had been part of the Kennedy motorcade. We worked to an arm of the cross near the chief's office. Along that arm were the water fountain, coffee machine and a dispenser that sold soft drinks and milk. The machines were empty. Buster and I wedged in beside the coffee machine and found ourselves beside our old friend Brady, the homicide detective who years ago had furnished us with the SUICIDE OF THE WEEK. Brady's cigar was crushed, and his hat was flattened against the wall.

"Looks like foul play to me, Brady," I said.

He stared at me.

"John Lee!" he said. "John Lee and Buster! Ha yew boys?"

He tried to shake hands with us but could not lift his arm in the pressing bodies.

"Have you seen him?" I said.

"No, I just been trying to get to my office," said Brady. "He's up in one of those security cells."

I knew the place. Small rooms with a wall of steel and wire mesh, a bunk, a faucet dripping into a sink, a hole in the concrete floor for a toilet.

"Look at all these New York boys," Brady said. "All they want to do is give Dallas a bad name. If I was chief, I'd throw their ass out of here. Move them downstairs. Don't quote me on that." He looked at me. "I didn't know you were still in the news. Hell, I just saw you the other night riding a horse in that outfit you got on."

"This is special," I said.

"Tell the people we didn't do it. We did all we could to protect that man. It wasn't our fault," said Brady.

"He's dead, though," I said.

"The Communists did it," said Brady. "Don't quote me on that."

The corridor lit up as if by a prolonged flash of lightning. Hundreds of voices were shouting. The mob swayed toward the elevator.

"Did you kill the President?"

"Is this the bastard?"

"Why did you shoot him?"

Buster climbed onto my shoulders and got a shot of Oswald as detectives in Stetson hats forced him through the crowd into the door in the glass wall of the homicide office. I got a quick look at Oswald's surly face and balding head and the bruise on his left eye.

"Let us have him!"

"The world wants to see him!"

"Show us Oswald!"

Then he was gone into the homicide bureau, and Buster slid down my back.

"He looks like the guy whose name you never knew in high school," Buster said. "To think what he did, what he has caused, it's unbelievable."

"He did it, not us," said Brady.

Buster and I shoved our way back down to the pressroom. It took half an hour to get there. Inside, a reporter I knew from the Dallas *Morning News* was talking on the telephone. I said hello to the others I recognized.

"What are you doing here?" said one. "You turned into a coppie?"

"First time I ever saw you in cowboy drag," said another.

"This is to cover up my Batman suit," I said.

"In chapter thirteen, Kennedy gets up and says, 'They just winged me after all,' " said another reporter.

"Everybody's gone crazy," the Dallas *News* man said, putting down the phone. "The hospitals are full. Suicides, beatings, accidents. Hysteria."

We heard them shouting in the hall as Oswald was moved through again.

"John Lee, did you see that Commie creep? That dirty little turd. Goddamn this city," said a high whining snarling voice. It was Jack Ruby. He carried a paper bag. His gray suit coat was open. I wasn't surprised to see him at the police station, since he knew a lot of cops and was attracted to violence, but I was surprised to see the butt of his pistol sticking out of his belt.

"How'd you get in here, Ruby?" someone said.

"I'm a reporter for the Israeli press," he said.

Several people laughed.

"That little shit, what he's done to our city! I'm closing my clubs tonight, boys. You hear me? I'm the only guy that's got class enough to close my clubs out of respect for our President and his wife."

"Our late President?" someone said.

"I loved that man," said Ruby.

"I didn't know you could carry a pistol while you're under a peace bond," I said.

"I got a right to protect myself. By God, a man needs a pistol in a city like this," said Ruby.

Buster and I fought our way down the hall again and got to the door of the forgery office, where reporters were yelling at a slim young woman in a headscarf and plaid slacks. She was holding a baby in her lap. She looked confused, unable to understand them.

"Why'd your husband kill the President?"

"Who helped him?"

"Where'd he get the rifle?"

"Are you a Russian spy?"

A large stout woman wearing glasses and a white uniform, looking like Big Nurse, pushed through the crowd of reporters and photographers and cops. Oswald's wife jumped up and showed her the baby.

"I'm a grandmother again!" Oswald's mother said with surprise, hugging her daughter-in-law.

Oswald's brother, grim and distracted, went into the room.

"Lee didn't do this," said his mother. "He was working for a big organization. It was very secret. He took his orders from high up."

I made it to the water cooler and took another spansule. By now I was having my second hangover of the day. Buster looked like a drowning victim. It was somewhere around ten o'clock when the police chief, the homicide captain and the district attorney appeared together in the corridor, staring into the lights.

"Speak up!" shouted the reporters.

"We want pictures!"

"We demand a press conference!"

"The world's got its eyes on you!"

On a portable TV screen, I saw the three Dallas officials who were standing ten feet from me.

"Bring the killer out!"

"We demand to talk to Oswald!"

Sometime after midnight we got the word to go to the basement assembly room. Reporters crashed into the long narrow room, knock-

270

ing over chairs. There was a cable in every electrical outlet. The light was like a Texas summer noon. Jack Ruby was standing on a table pushed against the wall near the front of the room. Buster and I climbed up there with him.

"You seen Jingo?" Ruby said.

"I've been here all evening."

"I'm going to fire that bitch," he said.

A wedge of detectives bashed into the room with Oswald between them, like tackles escorting a little running back into the converging mob on a kickoff. Oswald's sullen mouth turned downward and he raised his two hands, manacled in handcuffs, above his head.

"The Commie salute," Ruby hissed.

People shouted for quiet while others shouted questions. From the table I could see Oswald very plainly as he stood on the floor in front of the rostrum. Microphones, like gun barrels, were shoved in his face. His left upper eyelid was swollen with a blood bruise. He looked sort of ratty-mean, scared and defiant. I remembered seeing Erwin Englethorpe walking in a circle on that rostrum while the cops told him to get out of town. I tried to feel sympathy for Oswald, but it was very hard. The reporters were yelling at him.

"I was questioned . . ." I heard Oswald say.

I aimed the Bolex at his face.

"Talk louder!"

"You guys shut up so we can hear!"

"Did you kill him?"

"I don't know what this is about," said Oswald. "I'm accused of murdering a policeman."

"You kill the President?"

"No," he said.

Through the viewfinder I saw his eyes lower, then raise again to look into the hostile crowd.

"How'd you hurt your eye?"

"I got hit by a policeman," Oswald said.

"You saying they beat you up?"

"Did they beat you in jail?"

271

"You yellow bastard, are you crying brutality now?"

"They ought to kick your head in!"

Suddenly the detectives in their white hats pulled Oswald away and led him out of the room. The district attorney, Wade, a tall man with a big jaw and white hair, a tobacco chewer, began to talk about the charges and the evidence. Oswald was charged with the murder of the President. I could not hear Wade very well, but I heard him say he was certain Oswald would be convicted. Someone yelled a question about politics.

"He was a member of the Free Cuba Movement," said Wade.

From beside me Jack Ruby shouted, "It's the Fair Play for Cuba Committee!"

"Was he in Russia?"

"Is he a Communist?"

"Is this an international conspiracy?"

As Wade was answering, I turned and looked at Ruby. His eyes were wide, staring hard at the district attorney, a distinctly speedy urgent concentration in his expression, his breath fast and short, shaking with excitement and emotion.

"How did you know, Jack?" I said.

He kept looking at Wade. I nudged him, and he jumped and glared at me.

"How did you know the name of that committee?" I said.

"I get around. I got friends. I know things," he said.

"Do you know Oswald?"

"A creep like that? I wouldn't know a creep like that."

23

Tiny threads of coconut hung from Mother's lips as she chewed a piece of cake at the coffee table in her living room while I sat on an antique chair that was covered in faded red velvet.

"Honey, I feel as terrible about Mr. Kennedy as you do, but I don't see how you can blame anybody but the Communists," she said. "That fellow Oswald is a Communist spy, it's as much as said so on the television, even got a wife that speaks Russian, and he did the shooting with a foreign-made rifle. You can't say Dallas is to blame. Oswald is from Fort Worth, anyway, hadn't been here very long. Fort Worth has so many roughnecks. But it's sure terrible. I hope Mr. Kennedy finds peace in heaven. Like the Bible says, there's no peace on this earth, we know that."

"I may leave town for a while," I said.

"I've been reading in the newspaper about the movie you're making here. Your daddy and I are so glad you're going to stay around, so we can visit. Tell me what your movie is about."

"I can't think about it right now."

"Well, I hope it's a good movie that the whole family can see. I know it will be, honey. People are so tired of all that filth and sex. Walt Disney does the best movies of anybody. I don't mean those cartoons, I mean those real cute movies that teach you something about animals, or those comedies about real American families. Those movies with drunkenness and obscenity are so distorted. I just won't look at one of them."

From the next room we could hear the television.

"Your daddy has been right in front of that set ever since yester-

273

day," Mother said. "He slept in there on the couch last night, and he was up watching television when I came down this morning at six-thirty. I just had to shut the door, it was driving me crazy."

"Does he know I'm here?"

"I told him. Why don't you go in there?"

"I don't want to see any more television at the moment," I said.

"Have some cake, Johnny, this is really good."

"No, thanks."

"Honey, these are evil times. We're very close to the end of the world, just as it prophesied in Revelations. The figs are returning to the tree—that's the Jews going back to Israel. The bear is menacing the children of God—that means Russia is after us. Oh, there's so many things coming true. It's thrilling to be alive in these days, because as soon as Armageddon is over God will raise up the dead and we'll have peace for a thousand years."

My father came out of the television room. He was wrapping adhesive tape on the handle of his putter.

"They've got it all tied up now against that bozo. He's as guilty as he can be," my father said. "Old Lyndon Johnson says there's nothing to worry about, the country is in good hands. I wonder if the golf courses are open."

"You'd play today?" I said.

"You mean because it's crowded on Saturday?"

"You know what I mean."

"I don't see how it could help Mr. Kennedy for me not to play golf," my father said. He poured a cup of coffee. "The truth is, I didn't like him very much. I thought he was kind of a smart aleck. But I didn't want him to get killed. I don't want anybody to get killed. If you can tell me how I can bring Mr. Kennedy back to life by not playing golf, I'll throw down my clubs and never pick them up again."

"Brenda called," Mother said.

"Yeah, she called from Kansas City and acted like ever'body in Dallas had all got together and pulled the trigger," said my father. "I don't feel like I had anything to do with it. You can't blame a whole town for what that crazy Communist did. Listen, Johnny, Dallas is

274

a real nice place. Your maw and I have had it good here, and we didn't have no college education or rich relatives pulling for us. If you treat people right in Dallas, they'll treat you right. We've got this house all paid for, and plenty of food to eat, and I play golf on the same course with niggers, and I never shot a gun in my life. You're the one that did all the gun-shooting, but far as I know you never shot a person except in the movies or on television. Some of these fellows on television are talking like Dallas is running wild with idiots and murderers and ever'body is a millionaire. I might know a few idiots, but I don't know any of the other. Your maw and I have worked hard all our lifes and haven't made any more mistakes than most people anywhere else, and I don't like it for that wise sister of yours to set up there in Kansas City and tell me I'm supposed to be ashamed of myself because some crazy no-good Communist shot the President in Dallas. What would ever'body say if the President had of got shot in Kansas City or New York or California?"

"Fletcher, don't get yourself worked up," Mother said.

He lit a cigarette and with his lips rolled it into a corner of his mouth and sat in that pose that was one of my earliest and steadiest memories of him, squinting through the smoke, tapping the blade of his putter against the toe of his shoe.

"Johnny's working on his movie," said Mother.

"Why don't you make it out at the farm?" my dad said. "Get them to build us an Alamo out there." He grinned. "We'll put Edgar Bramlett in a Mexican uniform, and you can knock him off the wall ever' afternoon for the tourists. Maw can sell cake and get fat as a hog."

"Oh, Daddy, you shut up about me being fat," she laughed. "Isn't he terrible?"

Mother's car was in the garage for repairs, so I agreed to drive her to church for a memorial service. While she put on lipstick and a hat, my father and I stood on the lawn, and he swung a six-iron, knocking up bits of grass and dirt. His swing had gotten shorter and very stiff because of the pain in his back. He said he hit a six-iron barely a hundred yards any more, where he used to hit it a solid hundred and forty. Across the street a man and woman had put their television on their front porch and were eating sandwiches and watching the screen while their terrier rolled in the grass with a bone. I told my father I was going to leave town for a while, and he nodded and said it might do me some good. "You look like you been drinking too much. Lord, your mother's terrified you'll wind up an alcoholic. I think Brenda was drunk when she called here. Things do change, don't they?" He looked at me, ducking his head, and we shook hands as Mother came onto the porch.

Though she bumped her knee and knocked off her hat getting in, Mother did not complain about the Morris Minor other than to comment that foreign people were small. The streets and sidewalks were pleasantly empty, looking bright and washed, most of the shops closed, but still that feeling persisted that the city was whispering with electricity. I felt chemically burnt out, could hardly bring myself to speak. At the church Mother asked if I would go inside with her. I said I couldn't stay for long because I had to visit a friend in the hospital. But I walked in with her clinging to my arm and realized it had been close to twenty years since we had last entered the church together. It was smaller inside than I had remembered, but nearly a thousand people, about half the capacity, were standing between the dark polished pews, and their voices burst upon us singing "Rock of Ages" as we came into the auditorium. Mother gave me a hymnal in black paper binding from a rack on the back of a pew, and then I heard her thin sweet voice singing with the others. She smiled at me and patted my hand before turning her eyes toward the choir director in a white robe up behind the pulpit between the two banks of robed singers with the organ in the middle.

"Dear God, we are gathered here today to ask Your divine mercy on the soul of John F. Kennedy," said Brother Sloane, the preacher, into the microphone. With his black, wavy hair and horn-rimmed glasses, Brother Sloane looked like a clarinet player. "Lord, this was a man who asked not what his country could do for him . . ." and so forth. I looked up at the stained-glass window of Jesus in purple garments gently beckoning to the sheep, and then noticed I could see

276

no other head raised but my own. After an interminable prayer, we were allowed to sit down. Brother Sloane's memorial-sermon topic was that we were beset by enemies, especially Communists, but with help from heaven we would stick it out until Jesus came to fetch us. "Jesus is coming," my mother said. Brother Sloane said Kennedy had been murdered by a notorious atheist from Russia. After a few minutes I told Mother I had to leave, and kissed her on the cheek. "Can't you wait till the sermon is over?" she whispered. I shook my head. She was disappointed in me again, but I slipped out of my seat at the end of the pew and walked out the closest door, aware of the heads that swung in my direction.

At the hospital, Dorothy and I talked about the assassination for a few minutes in a desultory way, as though we'd already heard more of it than we could bear. She said the doctor had told her the baby was surviving, and every day his chances were better. The other three mothers were watching television. Dorothy had been watching, but drew her curtain when I came in. Finally, I told her Ina Mae had gone to Detroit. She accepted this news without surprise.

"My daddy was stationed in Detroit when he was in the Navy," she said. "Mother always liked Detroit. Did she say what dresses of mine she took?"

"No."

"That whore."

Dorothy's color had returned. Jingo's egg-blue nightgown fit her in a manner that was good to behold, and we sat for a while without saying much, listening to the television.

"I'll be back tomorrow," I said.

"You don't need to come every day. But I like it. Buster was up here this morning. He wouldn't take off his shades, and he asked the nurse for a dish of ice cream." She laughed and touched her tongue to the crooked front teeth. "John Lee, will you still take me on that trip?"

"Soon as you get out of here."

"I've never been to Acapulco."

"That's where we'll go."

277

"And you won't bring Jingo along?"

"Hadn't thought of it."

"Have you asked Buster to come?"

"Not yet, but I intend to."

"He can find a girl, and we'll have a great time. You'll like me again."

In the afternoon I took a nap and was dreaming about a Christmas party in a two-story house that I seemed to own, when I was awakened by Caroline phoning me from San Diego.

"Daddy, are you safe? I've been so worried."

"I'm all right, baby. Nobody's going to hurt me."

"Mama says Dallas is full of terrible people."

"You know some nice people in Dallas, don't you?"

"Yes, but not grownups."

"In no time at all, I'll be a grownup, and I won't like to hear things like that."

"Oh, Daddy," she giggled. "I don't mean you or Buster or Grandma or Granddaddy."

"How do you like San Diego?"

"I hate it. The school is terrible, and the teachers are mean, and the kids are dumb. But I've met a neat boy who's going to teach me how to surf, and they do some great dances out here."

Oh God. I suddenly got a picture of my little Caroline, brown as a gopher, her hair bleached and long, dancing on the beach in a bikini with those hard brown blond beautiful brainless boys, and whipping along the coast with a surfer in a red sports car while the sun set on the ocean, and getting Southern California hip, and I almost cried out.

"You watch out for those people out there, baby," I said.

"I'm all right, Daddy. If you can take care of yourself in Dallas, I guess I can take care of myself in San Diego."

"Those people are not like you."

"Well, I do look kind of strange to them, I think, but I've bought some neat clothes and the kids are getting more friendly. But, man, are they dumb. This one boy I know drank two cans of beer last night. He thought he was so cool, but he just acted crazy. He tried to feel me."

"Caroline, you keep away from that boy!"

"Daddy! I guess I shouldn't even have told you."

"I didn't mean to fuss at you, baby. I'm sorry."

"I thought I could tell you things. All the kids out here watch your TV show, and they're really impressed. I kind of feel like you're here. You're more like one of us, you know?"

"You're right," I said.

"Mama doesn't like the weather out here. She says it's too perfect. Isn't that crazy? She's taking Yoga classes and has got a groovy teacher. He came over last night and stood on his head. He's got a motorcycle. Herbert's going to Vietnam next week. We've got a neat house that's sort of up high where we don't need air conditioning, and we've got a nice yard and a barbecue pit, and it's only a mile to the beach, you could practically walk there. But this boy, he's fourteen and his daddy bought him a car. He's a real neat boy, honest, Daddy."

"I'll bet he is," I said.

"I've got to go now so I don't run up Herbert's telephone bill. When are you coming back to California?"

"I don't know."

"What's wrong? Are you mad because I told you about that boy drinking beer?"

"Nothing's wrong, baby. I love you," I said.

"I love you, too. Bye."

I went into Buster's bedroom and turned off the infrared light on the Baby Giant in the closet. I was staying by the phone at the apartment because our detective friend Brady had promised to call if anything dramatic occurred at the police station. Buster had gone to the lab of a photographer he knew to develop the Dealey Plaza film. We didn't have time to print all the film we had shot in the last few days, the party scenes and Breakfast Brigade and all, and there were still many feet of undeveloped film from the last two months, but we wanted to find out what we had from Dealey Plaza.

I smoked, sat on the couch trying to read a magazine and then left the door open and went out to the swimming pool and watched a girl's portable television for a while. They were saying it was a terrible dark time in the vilest of cities. All over the world people on the streets were being interviewed and detesting us. They said our souls must be boundless with evil. Well, I knew that, so I went back inside where our television was playing with the sound off. I looked at the sports section of the *Times-Herald* and waited for the telephone to ring.

Buster came in with a 16-millimeter projector and cans of film. We took some paintings off the wall. People from around the pool came in. Everybody had a beer or a drink. A dripping girl in a bikini drew the curtains and turned off the lights. In the square of colored light projected against the plaster we saw the motorcycles coming down Main Street, and we saw Kennedy looking at me, looking straight into my lens and pointing his finger, and we saw the motorcade turn onto Elm and Kennedy's hands reach for his throat, and we saw Connally begin to slump and Kennedy leaning and cops leaping off their motorcycles with pistols drawn and the bone fly off Kennedy's skull and the red spray from his brain. We saw it all. We saw it over and over. We saw people falling in the Plaza and running on the grassy knoll. In our darkened living room, looking at the square of colored lights on the wall, people began to cry again. You could not look at it without wanting to cry. As the night came, more people arrived, and we showed our film for them. Some sat very close to the wall, too close really to see the figures clearly, and studied what they saw. Some did not watch it all the way through before they walked out.

I was too tired to get drunk or stoned, and I could not watch the film any more. So I went in and lay on my bed. Buster came and leaned on the door frame.

"I promised Dorothy I'll take her to Acapulco as soon as I can," I said. "We want you to go with us."

"I know a guy with a studio in Acapulco. We could put together a rough cut of our film," said Buster.

"We could sell this Dealey Plaza film right now to some magazine and make enough to finance the rest of the work," I said.

Buster shook his head.

"Let's keep the Dealey Plaza part intact for the film. We'll show it when we're ready," he said.

24

Brady called early on Sunday morning and said Oswald was going to be moved sometime before noon to the county jail on Dealey Plaza. He said he had driven past the Plaza that morning and it was crowded with mourners and sightseers, and the slopes of grass were piling up with flowers and religious trinkets. We started loading the Bolex and the borrowed Arriflex, but the phone rang again. It was Franklin, saying he had to see me, that it was imperative we have a conversation at his house.

"Go ahead," said Buster. "I'll shoot the flowers and the people in the Plaza and then handle the Oswald transfer. It'll be routine."

"I don't mind missing that jam of reporters," I said.

"I feel sorry for the poor bastards. It's no wonder they get so vicious," said Buster. "What're you going to tell Franklin?"

"That we've got a movie he can't ignore."

"Tell him to shove Big Earl's money up the butt of his favorite A-rab," said Buster. He dug into a leather bag and started unscrewing the tops of film cans that went with the 35-millimeter Leica he usually carried. He found the can he was looking for. Buster wrote D on a piece of tape and stuck it to the can.

"I got Mexico in my heart, John Lee. I'll be ready to fly as soon as Dorothy can move her feet," he said. "Some of the greatest farming in the world is done around Acapulco."

When I pulled into Franklin's semicircular driveway, I saw his Ferrari and his Cadillac limousine in the garage, but Margaret Franklin's Cadillac convertible was gone. I went across the patio to a side door where Franklin was waiting, barefoot, his head scraping the top of the frame.

"Glorious day for football," he said.

I followed him into the den. A clay pot of chili was smoking on a table. The gold foil necks of six bottles of Tuborg beer stuck out of a bucket of ice.

"Is the Cowboy game on television?" Franklin asked.

"I assumed the pro football games had been cancelled."

"The National League is playing. I know the Cowboys are in Cleveland because a friend called me from up there while ago. He tried to mail a package to Dallas last night, and the clerk at the post office refused to take it. Wouldn't touch a piece of mail headed for Dallas. People are damn fools, old cock. Stick a spoon in that green chili. It'll clear your head. Meanwhile I'll turn on the TV in case Little Earl wants to give me a quiz after the game."

He turned on the television but turned off the sound. The smell of the chili made my eyes water and for a moment I thought I would sneeze. Franklin tore open a bag of Fritos and pushed some of the chips into his bowl of chili. Before sitting down I looked again at the framed photos on the den wall—Franklin with various politicians and movie stars, Franklin and Margaret, their dead son with a tennis racket, Franklin in a leather jacket standing beside his bomber, Franklin a head or more taller than the rest of his bomber crew.

"How'd you ever fit into that airplane?" I said.

"Tightly."

"I don't see how you got in at all, the planes were so small then."

"It wasn't any worse than sitting in that Ferrari," said Franklin.

"But you'd have to stay in the bomber for ten or twelve hours in a row."

"I admit it did make my knees ache some," said Franklin. "But when you're as tall as I am, you learn to fit into things. Where would I be if I couldn't? People are always asking how I do this or that—sleep in a motel bed, ride in a sports car, know if my shoes are polished. This world wasn't built for me, old cock, but I've made do with it."

"You could have been 4-F," I said.

The way he glanced at me when I said that, I knew I was wrong. Francis P. Franklin could not have been 4-F.

I sat down and spooned out a bowl of chili and opened a Tuborg.

"How's this stuff grab you?" he said.

"I like it hot," I said, sweating from the first bite.

"I mean Kennedy getting shot."

"I'm still sorting out all my feelings about it, but I think it was a disaster for humanity, and I think it happened in an ugly place."

"I liked Jack Kennedy. He had style," said Franklin. "His brother went around the block to get rough on Billy Bob Teagarden, but you can't win 'em all. I'll tell you this, I'm not very excited about Lyndon Johnson taking over. But Godalmighty, what if Nixon had won that close election and it had been Nixon who got shot while he was pulling the party together in Ohio, and now we had that guy for President that ran on Nixon's ticket. What was his name?"

"I don't remember," I said.

"There you go, that's a good citizen."

"Which side do you think helped Oswald do it," I said, "the left or the right?"

Franklin looked surprised at my question. "Well, nobody has proved that Oswald did the shooting, but let's suppose the district attorney is correct and they've got the evidence on him. Oswald is some shade of a Red. I don't believe the Cubans sent him, or the Chinese, or any of those people. Oswald is one of those crazy little home-grown Reds we turn out in this country. I'm not worried we'll ever turn out a big Red, other than the famous soda pop, because we don't have any use for a man like Lenin or Mao or even Castro. We're better at turning out movie stars like you and Nixon who'll keep giving us what most of us want. So I suppose Oswald did it by himself." He poured a glass of beer. "I didn't know the right wing was being said to have any connection with Oswald."

"A lot of people feel it was a right-wing plot," I said.

"Some people just won't ever believe anything is what it seems to be. I guess there'll be people saying Big Earl is mixed up in this. He's kind of a right-wing crank, I suppose I'd have to concede that, but he rated Kennedy as a pretty conservative man at heart when it came to getting business done. You might remind your show-biz friends of that while they're making Kennedy into a saint and Johnson into a clown."

"Nobody is making Johnson into a clown," I said.

"They will when they get to know him better. Lyndon just can't help it, he's got the biggest ego of any Texan I ever met and all but three or four Frenchmen. He thinks he's snowing people when he hugs 'em and calls 'em mah fren, so he believes he can get away with anything he wants to do, and a lot of people are going to dislike him very much. Personally, I wish he'd stay down there in Hye, Texas, on his peach farm. But Big Earl will do fine no matter who's in charge. Big Earl may not be as sharp as he used to be. In fact, sometimes he's about half dotty. But he's never been fooled by Lyndon Johnson. Big Earl didn't get where he is by being a weak dealer and not knowing how to take advantage of greedy people."

Franklin went into the kitchen and came back with a plate of jalapeña peppers.

"Do you think I could work for a man who killed Jack Kennedy?" he said.

"Not if you knew it."

"I doubt if he even knows Kennedy is dead, the shape his mind is in." Franklin chewed a pepper, drank a swallow of beer and wiped sweat off his face with a napkin.

"Not a soul in the house," he said. "Ever'body gone to church. I kept thinking Wilburn was here to answer the phone while ago and I almost missed the call from Mr. Hoover."

"Herbert Hoover?"

"J. Edgar Hoover," said Franklin. "I've known Mr. Hoover for many years. He likes to watch Little Earl's horses run. He called me to ask what the people in Dallas are saying about this thing. I told him people are confused, and the FBI ought to clear it up as soon as they can. He said the case is sewed up against Oswald. There's no plot."

"Do you believe Hoover is telling you the truth?"

"If you think the head of the FBI is a liar, then there's nobody in the government you can believe," said Franklin. "Of course I believe

Hoover. Wait for Oswald's trial. He'll open up at the trial and tell us why he did it all by himself because he's a psychotic little bastard. That'll cool your suspicious friends."

We watched faces mouthing silently on television.

"Did you know Dorothy is pregnant?" I said.

"Damn, John Lee, I got a mouthful of chili."

"Had she told you about it?"

"I gave her a thousand dollars the first of last week," said Franklin, pinching the flesh beneath his chin. "When she got sick at your party, I figured it might have been from her operation. She was getting pretty close to the time limit for an abortion."

I laughed.

"I can't see why that's funny," Franklin said. "She must have been more than three months gone. I promise you, I never touched Dorothy until shortly before you came back to Dallas. When you were serious about her, I didn't even wink in her direction."

"Dorothy's mother was going to have some hoods beat you up, but she changed her mind," I said.

"I pay my bills with money if I can," said Franklin. "How's the girl?"

"She'll be out of the hospital Tuesday morning."

"She had it taken care of?"

"Yeah, it's all gone," I said.

"Tell her I'll send somebody down there early Tuesday to handle the hospital bill."

"She's paid it," I said.

"Already?"

"She left a deposit."

"Then I'll send her some more money. You don't mind?"

"Give her all the money you want," I said.

"That's a reasonable attitude." He smiled and seemed relieved. "Now let's talk about your movie. The sooner you come up with an idea I can approve of, the better off you'll be. Big Earl has convinced himself this movie is already being made, and he sees it as *No, No, Nanette* with cowboys. But if you just give me a good outline of the

285

story you want to shoot, you can come by my office tomorrow morning and sign the papers and shake the money tree. Let's hear your ideas."

"I don't have anything against Big Earl except that he couldn't have got to be a billionaire without doing damage to a lot of people," I said. "It might take decades to figure up how much ruination Big Earl's greed has been responsible for, and you intend to keep operating in the same way when the old man dies. I'm not trying to stop you. I admire certain things about you. But I don't like your attitude that for two million dollars you can turn me into a light-running asshole."

Figures were moving on the television screen. A news announcer appeared, speaking solemnly without sound, and then a crowd of men and cameras and lights squeezed into a small area.

"We need fifty thousand dollars to finish what we've started," I said. "I want to make this into a fictional documentary, using actual people when we can, inventing a few things to help it stick together, re-shooting some parts to show myself in all these places involved in all these things that have happened to me since I've been back in Dallas. Let this be one good, true, fair thing we can do."

"You'd use ever'thing?" said Franklin. He frowned and looked at the TV screen. "That makes me kind of goosey. There's so many contradictions. How are you going to pick what's true and fair and still have me and Big Earl like it?"

"I'll pick what's true and fair for me," I said.

"Things happen so damn fast," said Franklin. "It makes me feel very temporary. You can't keep up with things doing a movie like you're talking about. Get yourself an old standard authorized sure-fire plot and take the two million."

Franklin leaned forward and turned up the sound. We heard the announcer saying Oswald was expected momentarily in the basement of the police station and would be moved in an armored car to the county jail. I saw Buster struggling in the crowd with the Bolex.

"There's no authority when it comes to making movies," I said. "Nobody knows any more about making movies than they know

286

about death. You know how to raise money and put deals together and hire lawyers and bookkeepers, and somebody knows how to ship films to theaters and put ads in the papers and turn on the projector. But you're no expert at whether what I'm doing is good or not. The very highest authority on that is me."

There was a great deal of movement on the screen, and clatter and shouts, and then we saw Oswald in a dark sweater with his shirt collar turned out walking between two big cops wearing suits and Western hats, and then a man in a gray fedora and dark jacket stepped into the picture, moving past Buster, and we heard a rap of a noise, and yelling and high voices, and police were grabbing the man in the gray fedora and Oswald was falling with his arms across his chest and a look on his face as though it hadn't been supposed to turn out this way.

"That's Jack Ruby," I said. "He shot Oswald."

Franklin and I sat there staring at the screen. He was eating Fritos, dipping them in the chili, and drinking beer.

"I warned you two months ago that your notion about a true-life movie was too far-fetched," Franklin said. "I think you better hire a writer."

25

"Christ, I've got to get out of this town, it's too goddamn strange for me here," Jingo said. She was doing a circuit of the living room of our apartment, looking at each painting, photograph and patch of skinned-off plaster as if they were new and odd. She wore a white linen suit and white high heels, with her orange hair flowing around her face and down her back. "I'm gonna go get married. Jesus, that I would come to this!"

"Who have you decided to marry?" I said.

"This guy in New York, this big-shot advertising executive, he's been after me for two years to marry him, so I'll just shock the son of a bitch and do it. He's weird, but around here he'd look sane. I sent him a wire I'd be there at seven. Can you imagine Jack Ruby? So Jake Rubenstein gets famous! Who would have thought it! One of the girls told me Oswald was in the club a while back, but who the hell can you believe these days? I wouldn't remember a nothing guy like that anyway. Now the FBI is looking for me on account of that goddamn Ruby. They don't scare me, but I wouldn't want them poking in my purse."

"That wouldn't be very good," I said.

"You bet your ass it wouldn't! They'd have me now if it wasn't for the switchboard girl at the motel. I called her up from Corbett's apartment to see if I had any messages, and she said the FBI had been in my room. I sneaked back there and grabbed enough clothes to make it look like I hadn't left. I had a suitcase full of grass and pills under the bed, I know they didn't open it because the hair was in the lock, so I put it in the trunk of the car."

"I thought Corbett had gone to Mexico," I said.

"You know how these dealers are, man, if they say Wednesday they mean maybe Sunday." From a cigarette case she took out what appeared to be a commercial filter-tip cigarette. "I stuffed some of these to smoke on the plane to make that food edible."

"People will smell them," I said.

"Not these they won't. This is my special batch. One time I hid a couple of ounces of weed in a Baggie under the refrigerator at this house where I was staying in Chicago, and I forgot about it for four months. When I got it out, the weed had turned white. From being damp, or next to the coil or something, I don't know." She lit the cigarette. "But I decided to smoke it no matter what color it was. Not only had it turned into dynamite, but it doesn't smell."

The odor was faintly disagreeable, resembling that of a mild cigar. The taste was somewhat moldy, and the effect was immediate and sensational.

"I smoked this stuff in a pipe in a front-row box at Wrigley Field and fell out of my chair I was so stoned, and nobody knew what I was doing," she said.

"You should make more of this stuff," I said.

"I never have been able to leave it under any damn refrigerator that long again!" she screeched.

After the smoke was gone, we sat on the couch puzzling among our thoughts for one that was worth saying aloud.

"You have a theory on why Ruby shot that guy?" I said.

"You let a nut that takes a lot of pills carry a pistol, anybody is liable to get shot at any time. He's been close to shooting me, but he's scared of me. I got friends, Oswald didn't have a friend. Ruby would think he's a hero and go to jail for shooting Oswald. If he shot me, the only place he'd go would be to hell in a hurry."

I heard someone knocking on the patio door, but I neglected to act on this information until they knocked again. As I was opening the door, I remembered it might be the FBI. But the door was open by then, and there stood the tall solemn Mr. Clwyd holding a white felt cowboy hat. Peeking around from behind Mr. Clwyd was the pink baby face of Big Earl, mouth puckered, eyes wary, fine white hair delicately waving. Seeing me, Big Earl smiled and prodded Mr. Clwyd.

"May we come in?" said Mr. Clwyd.

I backed away from the door. Mr. Clwyd glanced at Jingo and began looking inside every room of the apartment. Without waiting, Big Earl shuffled in, stooped and smiling.

"This must be the little lady," Big Earl said to Jingo. "Pleased to know you, ma'am. You've got a fine young man here, a fine man. See he gets plenty of rest and good food."

"This is Big Earl," I said.

"Christ!" said Jingo.

Big Earl pulled a bottle of cologne from his pocket and gave it to her.

"Girls always like toilet water," Big Earl said. Mr. Clwyd closed the patio door and stood against it with his arms folded, the white hat against the chest of his black suit. "Francis tells me you're having a

hard time making up your mind about our movie," said Big Earl. "I
know how easy it is to be confused when you're young. So I've been
writing some things that I'll let you use in the movie free of charge.
I'm not telling you exactly where to put them in. You're an artist,
you'll know how to do that. But all you really need to do is fill in some
words around these numbers of mine, and your movie's all done!
Except for taking moving pictures of it, I mean. Anybody can do that.
What do you say?"

"That's very kind of you," I said.

"I can't stay but a few minutes today. There's so much excitement!
But I will do one of my numbers for you." Big Earl held out a smooth
pink hand, and Mr. Clwyd gave him the white hat. Big Earl put on
the hat, which had a wide brim and a tall peaked crown. Then he held
out a hand again, and Mr. Clwyd gave him a shiny silver pistol. I must
have flinched at the sight of the gun because Big Earl chuckled and
said, "It's a cap pistol, my boy, not the real thing like you're used to
out on the range. Now you sit down and listen to my number."

I sat beside Jingo. Mr. Clwyd looked at us as if daring us to laugh.
Big Earl shuffled into the middle of the room. "This number is called
'My Mama's Elm Tree,' " he said. He composed his face, lost the
smile, lifted his tiny blue eyes above our heads as though looking out
from a stage into an audience, or perhaps into some other distance
that was beyond our seeing.

He sang.

Moonlight on the elm tree outside my
Mama's door.
Have I ever seen a vision that promised
To me more
Than tiny angels dancing round my blessed
Mama's floor
While Mama hugged me tightly and kissed
Where it was sore.

Don't you 'member
Don't you 'member
How the roses smelled so sweet

290

Now it has come December
And can nevermore repeat.

Pop! He fired the cap pistol.
"Jesus God!" said Jingo.
Big Earl kept singing.

I loved my Mama dearly and my brother
and my sis
And later on my baby cuddled
in my arms like this

He rocked his arms as if holding a baby.

While my darling Sarah whispered who
shall ever know such bliss.

Don't you 'member
Don't you 'member
How the roses smelled so sweet
Now it has come December
And can nevermore repeat.

The patio door opened, knocking against Mr. Clwyd's head and sending him stumbling forward. Big Earl turned quickly with the cap pistol outstretched.

"Reach for your iron!" squeaked Big Earl.

Pop! Pop!

Buster ducked in astonishment.

"I got you! No fair now, you're dead!" Big Earl said. He looked back at me. "Who was this fellow?"

"He's all right," I said. "He's my friend."

"I expected we would be alone here," Big Earl said petulantly.

"You scared me worse than I scared you," said Buster.

"It's a good lesson for you to learn. Never try to sneak up on me. I'm faster than you think. There's always you young gunslingers trying to knock me off. Well, I got you before you could even touch leather."

291

"Go ahead with your song," I said.

"I don't like people jumping on me from behind," Big Earl said. He returned the hat and cap pistol to Mr. Clwyd and looked at Buster. "See where it gets you? Dead!"

"I'd like to hear the rest of the song," said Jingo.

Big Earl reached up for the hat he no longer had and then bowed to Jingo.

"I'll sing it for you, little lady," he said. "Where was I?"

"Can nevermore repeat," I said.

"Mr. Clwyd, where is my hat?"

Mr. Clwyd gave him back the hat and cap pistol. Big Earl jammed the hat down on his head, looking like a little boy about to be photographed on a pony. I wanted to ask him to help us with our movie, but I knew I couldn't reach him.

"I can't remember anything," he said in a curious small voice, and then his tongue peeped out of his mouth, and he sat down on the floor and closed his eyes.

We waited to see what he was up to. His shoulders began to twitch.

"He's having a stroke," I said.

Mr. Clwyd grabbed Big Earl under the armpits and lifted the old man to his feet.

"We better call an ambulance," I said.

"I know where to take him," said Mr. Clwyd.

"He might die," I said.

"He wouldn't want the publicity," said Mr. Clwyd.

A horn honked out front. Big Earl's head was jerking.

"That stamps the ticket for me," Jingo said.

She picked up her white overnight bag and white make-up kit and walked out with us while Buster and I helped Mr. Clwyd carry Big Earl to the old Hudson. The taxi driver stared at us and smoked a pipe. Big Earl lay in the back seat of the Hudson, his hat askew, Ginger Pops yapping in the rear window. Mr. Clwyd put the cap pistol into his pocket and drove off without another word to us.

"That tall guy in the black suit, he was in the club last week," Jingo said. "I've been doing a stunt lately where I haul a guy on the stage

292

and get a Polaroid picture taken with me. I tried it on that tall guy and he had a fit and ran out. Christ, I'll have a fit, too, if I don't escape this town. Good-bye, Buster." She kissed him and then kissed me. "Good-bye, John Lee. You guys be careful, hear?"

Jingo stuck her head out the window as the taxi began to move.

"My car's parked in your place behind your building," she said. "I'll collect it one day when things cool off."

She waved a white glove.

We went out to look at her car, thinking maybe to move it behind some other building, and realized she had locked it and taken the keys. Knowing the FBI was looking for the driver, I saw her bronze Cadillac as immense and glowing in the sunlight, shooting signals a thousand miles into the air. The suitcase full of weed and pills was probably still in the trunk. On the driver's door the gold letters still said JINGO. But she had done one thing to outwit the FBI and conceal her car. She had removed the license plates.

Dorothy was asleep when I entered her room at the hospital that evening. Two of the other beds were empty, and the third had a new occupant who was in her teens and seemed very happy. Just as I walked past her bed and smiled back, her husband came in and they fell to kissing. He looked like a hubcap thief. I pulled Dorothy's curtain and sat beside her without waking her. Her lips were slightly open, and she bubbled a bit as she breathed. A big vase of flowers stood on the table, an arrangement. The card said *good times follow bad.* I sat there for a while, listening to the kids at the other bed talking about their unbounded futures, listening to the sounds of the hospital from the hall.

"How long have you been here?" Dorothy said. "I hate for people to watch me sleep."

"Do you ever wake up smiling?"

"Not if I'm being spied on." She yawned and stretched and looked at the flowers. "Thank you for those. They're beautiful."

"I didn't send them," I said.

"Who could have done it?"

"I could guess."

293

"I could, too," she said.

I sat quietly while Dorothy drank a Coke.

"Hear anything about the baby?" I said.

"I've been thinking, I wonder if it's too late, if they'd give me back that baby after all. I could go someplace where they don't know me and raise him up."

"You could ask."

"But I don't know what to do. I don't know if I'm thinking this because I want the baby or because I feel so guilty. Goddamn it, I'm only twenty years old. I want to go to Paris and London and New York and San Francisco. I haven't had my fun yet. I may not be ready to get strapped with a kid to raise."

"Your mother was eighteen when you were born."

"Maybe she wouldn't have turned into such a bitch if I hadn't come. Probably a woman shouldn't have a baby any more until she's at least thirty. She'd miss too much. What should I do?"

"Sounds like you've answered your own question," I said.

"I haven't answered anything," said Dorothy, sighing. "I'm just barely even asking. Damn, I wish I was somebody great so I'd know what to do. The people who care say they don't know what to do either, and the rest just tell you a lot of bullshit. I went to a priest four or five months ago. He told me so much bullshit that we never got down to talking about the real problem. It was just useless bullshit and rules and the Pope and stuff I know would never have occurred to Jesus. The only useful advice the priest gave me was to get married. But there wasn't anybody I would have been willing to marry except you, and you didn't want to, and I didn't blame you. Marriage might have made it worse. But if I took that baby I'd have to get a rotten job as a waitress or a filing clerk, or be a whore, or marry some rich guy and be a whore that way."

"Maybe you could marry a poor guy."

"A rich whore is better than a poor whore. I don't know any poor guys I like except Buster."

"I'm rapidly becoming poor," I said.

"You won't be poor, you'll just be broke, and you won't stay broke unless you really screw up, and you don't want to marry me anyhow."

"It's funny you'd think of Buster as poor when he has two cars and makes good money when he works."

"Well, that's the class of poor I'm talking about. It's out of the question that I'd ever marry some migrant farmer or coal miner or some guy who worked in a factory and brought me his paycheck."

"You'd never even meet a guy like that."

She laughed. "What I'll do is wait until the kid is about twenty and then tell him about all these guys I wouldn't marry and ask him if it turned out I did the right thing." Dorothy lay back against the pillow, looking at a cigarette. "But the trouble is, I won't know his name."

26

By Monday morning the amateur assassination-investigators had begun arriving in town. Several who were friends of friends called me up and asked questions and confided that the President had been killed by a Batista Cuban conspiracy, by a fanatical Fascist faction in the CIA, by an international opium syndicate afraid Kennedy intended to interfere with their sources in Indochina, by a German intelligence organization with ties to the Nazis, by the Mafia, by a secret right-wing group with headquarters in Dallas and Alabama and by combinations of these. I thought it was interesting that none of the amateur investigators believed the President had been murdered as the result of a Communist plot, or that Oswald was alone in the crime, or that Ruby had acted on his own, or that the FBI or any government commission would ever reveal the truth. One investigator, Harrison Jones, the son of a film producer in Beverly Hills, crept up as I was sitting in an aluminum chair beside the pool and said, "John Lee Wallace, I'm on the track of something very important here. Is Buster Gregory available?"

"He's asleep," I said, putting down *Passage of Arms* by Eric Ambler. Buster had worked most of the night printing his film of Ruby shooting Oswald.

"Listen, you don't know me but I got your name from Norman Feldman." Jones sat down beside me and straightened the creases in his lemon-colored pants. He was a small, dark man, his face rather purple with whisker, his sharp nose red and sounding moist. I was certain he must have something incredible to tell me, because he was wearing brown-and-white wing-tip shoes, a navy blazer, a pink shirt, a blue-and-white ascot and a straw hat the color of a cigar with a narrow brim and a yellow feather in a brown-and-yellow polka dot band.

"I have reason to think Oswald and Ruby were working together in this with an organization based in New Orleans dominated by homosexuals," Jones said. "Oswald was on his way to Red Bird Airport when he was intercepted by Officer Tippitt. He was to fly to Mexico in a private plane. Red Bird Airport is in Oak Cliff where Jack Ruby's apartment is."

"Two hundred thousand people live in Oak Cliff," I said. "You want a drink?"

"A ginger ale, please."

Jones's brown-and-white wing tips had taps that clicked and scraped on the flagstones as we walked toward the apartment. The manager opened her door and scowled at me. I'd heard that one of my friends had kicked her bulldog into the pool and had threatened to do the same with her husband, but she wouldn't let me get close enough to apologize. Harrison Jones, as an investigator, looked in our den, front bathroom, kitchen and living room and was anxious to enter the bedrooms but didn't yet dare. To my surprise I found a bottle of ginger ale in the pantry among fifty empty bottles of various kinds.

"You sure this is all you want?" I said.

"A small bowl of potato chips, please."

I put a record on the phonograph and sat on the couch with a cup of coffee, watching Jones with his glass of ginger ale and small bowl of potato chips. Buster staggered out of his room naked wearing sunglasses, went into the back bath and slammed the door.

"Did you ever meet Oswald?" asked Jones.

"We didn't run in the same crowd."

"You must know Jack Ruby," Jones said.

"Very slightly."

"If Oswald did shoot the President, why do you think he did it?"

"To fuck everything up."

"Why then did Ruby kill Oswald?"

"Ruby was ready to kill somebody."

Jones smiled. "Not very sophisticated theories," he said. "I'd prefer to operate on a more complex level."

Buster came out of the bathroom still naked and wearing shades, but now he had put on his Hester Prynne hat and was smoking a joint. The hat was a University of Arkansas baseball cap he had been given while on an assignment, white with a red bill and a big red A on the front. He sat in a chair across from Harrison Jones and offered him the joint.

"I don't smoke that stuff," said Jones.

"You don't mind if I do?" Buster said.

"It bothers my sinus," said Jones.

"Bothers mine too," Buster said, holding his breath. "But for the head in general, it does wonders."

Harrison Jones began explaining his theories to Buster. While Jones was talking, Buster got up and closed the door and the curtains.

"Why the darkness?" Jones asked nervously.

"You can watch this while you talk," Buster said, flipping on the projector.

The two murders were spliced together for convenience. The film started with the motorcycles coming along Main Street and ended with the camera being bounced into the back of a detective as people grappled with Jack Ruby in the police-station basement. There was

297

one clear shot of Oswald as the bullet struck him.

"Remarkable!" Jones kept saying. "Incredible!"

He asked Buster to run the film again. When the motorcade turned onto Elm, Jones rushed to the wall and pointed to the trestle above the underpass.

"There, do you see it?" he cried. "Three Cubans with rifles!"

We backed up the film and showed it again in slow motion and stop-frame. When the President's hands reached for his throat, when Connally slumped, when the brains flew out, Jones said, "They're shooting at them!"

We saw some dim figures on the trestle.

"No doubt about it," said Jones. "Kennedy was hit in the front of the head by rifle fire from the trestle. See the police running up the grassy knoll? They knew where the shots came from."

"I'm willing to believe it, but I don't see it," Buster said.

"Run it again," said Jones.

I left them and went to the hospital to see Dorothy. She was up and walking around and seemed cheerful. I told her I had the reservations for Acapulco and had wired a woman to try to find us a house to rent for a month. Dorothy clapped her hands like a little girl and said, "Neat!" in a way that reminded me of Caroline. There was another vase of flowers beside Dorothy's bed. Wearing a robe I had dug out of her suitcase, and holding my arm, she walked with me around the halls. We heard televisions as we passed each door. Soon we could no longer talk about Mexico, and Dorothy went back to bed. The baby had not been mentioned.

When I got home I had to park the Morris Minor at the curb nearly a block from the apartment. Buster and I would not use the parking lot behind the building, feeling if we didn't see Jingo's car maybe the FBI wouldn't either. Corbett, the dealer, his hair clipped like a convict's, came out of the courtyard entrance. Without knowing quite why, I stepped off the curb and stood behind a car while he got into a wrinkled old Ford and drove off.

The first thing I heard when I opened the sliding door into the den was Harrison Jones blowing his nose and saying "Remarkable!" Then a familiar screeching voice cried, "I haven't come to the remarkable part yet! Jesus, don't look at that snot, throw it away!"

In the living room, Jones was clutching a wadded paper towel, and Buster, having added tennis shorts to his outfit, was drinking a large martini with eight or ten olives in it from a Mason jar, and both of them were listening to Jingo, who still wore her white linen suit and high heels but looked as if she had been wrestling with a mechanic.

"John Lee! God didn't want me to get married!"

Jingo recounted the story while Buster prepared me a martini like his. She had arrived at Idlewild and had taken a taxi to her fiancé's apartment, for which she owned a key. Letting herself in, she went into the bedroom and saw, hanging from a bedpost, a garter belt and hose, a brassiere and black lace panties. Two startled figures looked up from the bed.

"It was my fiancé and another guy," said Jingo. "He thought my telegram meant seven A.M. instead of P.M. The idiot! But I told him I don't care if he has boy friends, who gives a shit about that? About that time—I'm high as a skunk—the door opens and in comes a reporter and photographer who start shooting my picture and asking questions. The taxi driver had seen my act in Chicago and had read about me in a story on Ruby, and he turned me in for a ten-dollar news tip! Christ, here I am a stah! Giving interviews! Posing with my skirt pulled up! And my fiancé is furious! He's stomping around, trying to throw the newspaper guys out, claiming I'm trying to ruin his reputation! He's got a bad temper, likes to beat up small women, so when the newspaper guys left I left with them. Threw that key on the carpet and said to each his own, daddy! I went to the newspaper office and posed for some more pictures and gave them a story on Jack and then went over to visit a musician friend, and this morning there's my picture on the front page!"

She showed us the front page of the *Daily News* with a photo of herself sitting on a desk with her legs crossed.

"And this big story on page three!"

"Then I remembered the FBI is looking for me and I thought, well this ought to confuse their ass, me being in New York, so I took off for Dallas again."

Not having slept in a couple of nights, Jingo showered, put on one of my shirts, crawled into my bed and was promptly unconscious. Harrison Jones was trying to persuade Buster to take a photo with a 500-millimeter lens of another School Book Depository employee who was said to have resembled Oswald. The more Buster drank, the more interested he became in Jones's theory about the anti-Castro New Orleans homosexual ring. Finally Buster got up and found the long lens and a tripod.

"Don't you worry, Harrison, you and me will get to the bottom of this," Buster said.

"Did I see Corbett leaving?" I said.

"He came over to get some weed. I laid about an ounce on him," said Buster.

"The dealer's out of personal smoking weed?"

"He said he's been intending to leave for Mexico every day but hadn't got around to it yet," Buster said. "Come on, Harrison, you point out the other Oswald and I'll blast him."

"Shouldn't you wear trousers?" said Jones.

While Buster was putting on Levi's and a sweater, Harrison Jones looked into the mirror and tilted his straw hat down at an angle that covered his right eyebrow. He fluffed the ascot up over his Adam's apple.

"It's been a fabulous day, John Lee," he said.

"Just a run-of-the-mill day around home," I said.

After Buster and Harrison Jones had gone, Norman Feldman phoned from Van Nuys.

"Get out of that sick town, baby," he said. "Your home's here now. Come back to us. We love you."

"Did you send me Harrison Jones?"

"I knew you'd want to hear what he knows about this thing. Those goddamn Dallas bastards. I start to cry every time I think about them killing Jack Kennedy. What goddamn gall they've got, baby! Rednecks in business suits, racist Jew-hating bastards, get out of there before they massacre you, John Lee, you're not one of them, you don't belong there, they'll start shooting down oddballs on the streets of Dallas any minute, and you'll be the first to go."

"It hasn't quite come to that," I said.

"You don't see it, baby! You're too close. You're the bird who doesn't know he's in a cage because it's made out of glass. Dallas is stinking up the entire earth. May I say it, baby? Forget that true-son-of-Texas crap and come back out here where you belong. I'm finding you another house to live in. That pink stucco freak den was no good for you, it was always full of dope fiends and bums, you couldn't find any peace there. You know what people call that house now? They call it the speed museum! I'll find you a beach house in Malibu, good clean ocean, sand and sunsets, moonlight on the water, jazz on the Victrola. That's what you want, not that goddamn Texas where an alligator jumps out of a box at a man. Listen, your car. I've located your car. Some dope addict left it right in the middle of Rodeo Drive, just walked off from it when it ran out of gas, and the Beverly Hills cops phoned the studio. The top is ripped and the radio and spare tire have been stolen, but I'm getting it all fixed up for you. See what I'm saying? We want you back."

"Norman, you are obligating me."

"I'm not doing it just because I love you but also because you're a decent human being and you got talent, and if you stay down there any longer I know they'll destroy you. There's a big difference between Texas and California, baby. Texas is where they killed Kennedy, and don't you ever forget it!"

"I suppose you'll change the name of the series now," I said.

"We'll have to watch the ratings," said Norman. "We might do a poll to see how people feel. 'Guns' and 'Texas' are very emotional words these days. You're not going to sell anything with Texas on it for a while."

301

"The President of the United States is from Texas," I said. "Just the same as I am."

"John Lee, I feel you're slipping away from me when you say things like that. I fear for you. They can kill you more ways than with a gun. They can catch your soul. Get out of that place. Don't spend another night there, I beg you. Fly straight out here, I got an apartment on Doheny you can use until we find your beach house, the apartment's got a view like of the whole town and the ocean on a clear day, I'll stock it with Johnnie Walker Black Label Scotch, I'll even get some damn marijuana up there—pot, I guess you hepsters call it—and there's a telescope for you to voyeur with, but come on!"

"I'm going to Acapulco tomorrow," I said.

"That's in Mexico."

"I know."

"You can fly from Acapulco to Los Angeles. You could even ride a boat."

"Norman, things are whizzing around right now. I'll go to Acapulco and lie in the sun for a few days, and then I'll call you."

"I know how you call people. I've had experience."

"I promise I'll call you."

"I should tell you, I hate to say this, believe me, but if you are not out here by the end of next week I will consider you delinquent on your contract and sue the piss out of you."

"But you love me."

"That makes it hard, I admit. But I've done all I can do to make you wake up. Could I do more than this? Tell me where I'm wrong."

"I appreciate your position, Norman."

"As an extra personal incentive, when you come, bring that film with you that you and that wild man have been shooting and I will stick together a documentary that you can narrate and we'll peddle it to one of the networks. We might have to cut out the actual shootings, or clip them in real fast, too much violence, you know, not good for people to see."

"Where did you hear that we've got the shootings on film?"

"Harrison Jones called me. He said it knocked him out. I'm dying

302

to take a look at it, babe. I don't really know if we can do anything with it, but I'll try."

"Norman, you're not going to touch my movie," I said.

"Okay, I was doing you a favor. I can exist and be a happy man without doing you a single favor. Come on out here right now!"

"I'll call you."

"I'll hold my breath," he said, and hung up.

During the evening a number of people dropped in, some of the End Zone crowd, strays from here and there. Several sat on the floor in front of the television set, close enough so that they could hear it despite the phonograph music. At one point, when a girl was using the dishwasher to clean glasses and someone else was mixing daiquiris in the blender, I realized that every electrical outlet in the apartment was operating, every light turned on, the phonograph and radio playing, the television, the refrigerator. The air conditioning rumbled in an effort to clear out the smoke, and infrared light shone on the Baby Giant in Buster's closet. Three bulbs burned out within ten minutes of each other, dousing the lights in the den and one lamp in the living room, but nobody flipped off the switches, and I could feel the power moving. Buster and Harrison Jones returned without a photograph. They had been parked down the street from their target's house, and the police had come and told them to move on. Buster hadn't known either of the cops, and his magazine credentials did not impress them.

"Now will somebody try to tell me the cops aren't in on this thing?" said Jones.

Buster was drunk and angry, wearing his werewolf look. For the moment, he had accepted Jones's theories and was fitting in extra pieces of his own. Now Buster was convinced there had been at least five shots, maybe six. Arguments were developing, other theories and suspicions being offered, the lone-assassin belief being defended, the Dallas police condemned and approved of. I went into my bedroom and shut the door. Jingo sat in the middle of the bed wearing my old blue shirt and rolling a joint. I lay down beside her, and she scratched my chest gently with her long orange nails.

"I've got some money saved," she said. "It's stuck away in safe-deposit boxes nobody knows about but me. Tomorrow I'll get rid of my car somewhere, and then I'm going to Rome. You want to go with me?"

"I can't go to Rome," I said.

"I've got plenty of money. We could last probably two years on what I've got stuck away. You could write your movie over there. It doesn't have to be about Texas, does it? Jesus, do an Italian Western, do Tarzan with clam sauce."

"Thanks, Jingo, but I don't have any business in Rome."

"Okay, it's your loss. While I'm smoking in a café in Tangier, I'll maybe write you a post card if I can hold a pen." She popped the joint into her mouth, pulled it out slow and wet and looked at me rather sadly. "I'm not coming back for a long time. But when I do, you'll hear about it."

We heard a thump like a slamming door, and people shouting in the living room. I rushed out there and saw Charlie Withers trying to get up, holding a bloody forearm to his mouth, with Leroy tugging at Charlie's shoulders and pushing a hand against Buster's chest. People sat in front of the television or stood, posed, around the room.

"No call for you to do that, Buster. He didn't say a word," said Leroy.

"He put his foot through the wrong door," Buster said.

I moved between Buster and Leroy while Charlie managed to reach his feet. Blood poured down his chin from a split lower lip. Leroy gave him a handkerchief.

"We better go get you fixed," Leroy said to Charlie, sounding drunk. Leroy looked back at Buster and shook his head.

"Acting like a beast won't make the world any better."

"If the world got rid of Charlie Withers, it would be better," said Buster.

27

On Tuesday morning Franklin phoned to ask about the encounter between Charlie Withers and Buster. He reported with pleasure that eight stitches had been sewn into Charlie's lower lip. He also said Big Earl would be laid up a few weeks with a mild stroke.

"Right now he can't do much but slobber. Mr. Clwyd said Big Earl was singing one of his numbers for you Sunday afternoon when he fell over. Now you know why you better get an idea pretty quick. We need something dramatic. I am not going to put even fifty thousand dollars of Big Earl's money into a film of a string of absurd events that a lot of my friends would resent seeing. When you get back from Mexico, have me a real story."

"You've talked to Dorothy."

"I sneaked down there last night disguised as a middle-aged gentleman. She's happy about this trip. Dorothy's a good kid. I wish I was going to Mexico with her, and you were sitting beside Big Earl's bed. It's hard to beat the devil, old cock, and I don't want to try."

I packed for Dorothy and me both, using her suitcase and the airline flight bag that had once held a paper sack of weed but now was nearly empty. I put the sack and its remains into the closet where the Baby Giant was growing. With Jingo gone, there was no one we trusted to take care of the plant. But Buster had rigged up a relay that would switch the light on and off at four-hour intervals, and mounted a five-gallon water bottle with a rubber-glove nipple to drip water into the soil, which had been fed vitamins. He placed a small electric fan to blow across a sack of salt onto the Baby Giant, claiming that this sea-breeze effect would strengthen the Baby Giant's resin. Buster helped me select what to pack for Dorothy. Occasionally he would

305

rub her garments on his person and growl. For myself I packed only a swim suit, a pair of sneakers, rubber shower slippers, two pairs of khaki Levi's, two wash-and-wear shirts, my toilet kit and my movie notes. With the seersucker coat, polo shirt, slacks and loafers I was wearing, I'd have more clothes than I needed for a month in Acapulco. Buster was going to wear a linen jacket so he could carry two ounces of refined weed in the pockets. Taking grass into Mexico might have seemed like taking kangaroos to Australia, but Mexican Customs were no problem, and this way there'd be no hurry about scoring after we arrived. I snapped the suitcase shut. Buster stacked film cans, tied in a bundle, beside the door.

"I've got some errands to run while you pick up Dorothy," Buster said. "I'll meet you at the Villa Lopez at noon."

"The flight's at two."

"I know, but this will be our last chance to get good Mexican food for a long time."

Tied to our patio door we found a small brown-and-white goat that at the sight of me tumbled onto his back with his legs sticking into the air and began trembling and moaning in terror. Around the goat's neck was a note that said *I'm counting on you boys to give my goat a good home. Raise him like he was your own goat and he will return your love & affection I didn't have nowhere else to turn.*

"Franklin couldn't let us get away easy," I said.

We discussed cutting the rope and allowing the goat to depart into the wilds of Dallas with the note on his neck. But being a goat on your own in the city could be a perilous life. Buster said he would load the goat into the station wagon and deliver him into Franklin's yard.

"If I knew where to get them, I'd take him a dozen armadillos as a bonus," Buster said.

Dorothy was waiting on the front steps of the hospital, wearing a yellow blouse, white slacks and sandals that I didn't remember having brought to her. She stooped and slid into the Morris Minor and pounded her fists on her knees and laughed.

"Faster, faster," she said. "I want to get to Mexico before I get bored."

She put up an argument about stopping off at the Villa Lopez but quickly saw I was going to stop anyhow, and dismissed it from her thoughts so as not to spoil the mood. There was a line of people at the door of the restaurant, but Hector had saved us a booth at the rear beneath Buster's huge color photograph of Darrell Royal. When Buster hadn't arrived by twelve fifteen, I phoned the apartment and got no answer. I thought that meant he was on the way. It could have taken longer than expected to get rid of the goat. Hector offered to cook the goat and serve it to Franklin as *carne asada* some future night. Waiting for Buster, I started ordering dishes from all over the menu—chalupas, tacos, enchiladas, refried beans, chili con queso, guacamole salad. I phoned the apartment again. At ten to one, with Buster's food cold, Dorothy suggested he might be driving straight to the airport because he was late. He would figure us to be sensible enough to go to the airport without his needing to phone us, she said. Between the crowded tables we shook hands with Hector, and hugged him, and carried on as though we wouldn't see him again for years. Though his restaurant was flourishing, and he planned to open another one soon, Hector had seemed quieter since the weekend of the murders, and he no longer spoke of being a boxing champion or an All-American halfback.

At the Braniff counter, Buster still had not checked in. I got the tickets and the tourist cards, and we walked around the lobby, expecting Buster to burst in stoned and yelling, and we would all run for the plane, and get on board sweating and out of breath, and that's how a good trip would start. Dorothy stood beside the big statue of the Texas Ranger in the lobby between the coffee shop and the magazine counter, searching every face—the young soldiers with their shaved heads, women in toreador pants bulging with child, West Texas ranchers and merchants in boots and hats and gray gabardine suits with pearl buttons, the country boy in his straw hat and Levi's and beat-down boots with a wad of tobacco in his mouth, young stewardesses, salesmen in metallic-brown suits, the family of Mexicans putting their frightened grandfather on a plane for the first time, men with vests and briefcases.

With ten minutes to go before the flight, we went down a long hall to the gate, where we could see the airplane through the door. The agent gave the final call and said we would have to get on or stay off.

"We could leave his ticket. Maybe he'll show up as we hit the door," Dorothy said.

"We could see him coming down the hall if he was going to make it," I said.

"He can catch the next plane," she said.

"So can we."

"Damn, John Lee, this is my chance to go to Acapulco."

"Here's your ticket. *Buenos días.*"

There was a terrible struggle behind her eyes. Dorothy wanted what she wanted when she wanted it. I held out the ticket, but she wouldn't take it.

"There's another flight in five hours," I said.

"We won't get to land in Mexico City in the daylight."

"You could hardly see it for the smog anyway."

"Goddamn Buster, he better have a good reason for this," she said.

I phoned the apartment again, and there was still no answer. We went back to the Villa Lopez. By now the lunch crowd had cleared out. Hector was sitting in the booth under the Royal portrait. He looked worried.

"A man called here for you," said Hector. "He told me for you to stay right here if you come back and to not go home whatever you do. He told me it's very important, and Buster's in trouble. I told to him I would come help Buster, but he told me to keep out of it."

"He's been in a wreck," Dorothy said.

For another half hour we tried to think up other explanations for Buster's disappearance, but I knew what had happened. The other explanations were reasonable and even probable—a car wreck, an assault charge by Charlie Withers, jailed by his ex-wife, a misfired scheme by Harrison Jones, violating some city ordinance pertaining to goats, a sudden urge to make love, another fistfight and more. But I knew, and I wasn't surprised when the man called me back and turned out to be a lawyer I had last seen at our Thanksgiving party.

308

"I don't have the details as yet, but a state undercover agent and the city vice squad grabbed him at the apartment," said the lawyer. "Buster has some friends down here, and I think I can get him out of jail in a couple more hours. I haven't seen the warrant and don't know who else they might be after. There's nothing you can do for Buster at the moment. I'll make his bond. He says for you to wait there for him."

"First offense possession, he'll get a suspended sentence, won't he?" I said.

The lawyer chuckled. "It's a bit early to guess at sentences, John Lee. That depends so much on the judge. But Buster isn't charged with possession. He'll be charged with dealing. He's liable to get forty years at the Big Rodeo."

"That's insane. He never sold dope in his life."

"Look, I said I don't know the details of the case. For all I know, Buster might have stepped on too many toes. But from the way the cops are talking, they don't have any doubt the apartment was cramfull of marijuana. They found at least a pound. I don't know anything about the stuff, but what would a guy be doing with that much unless he's a pusher? On top of that, the cops are saying Buster was operating a marijuana factory, growing the stuff in his closet. It looks pretty damn bad."

I went back to the booth and told them. Dorothy started crying. Hector scowled. "Buster wasn't hurting nobody but himself. Why couldn't they leave him alone?" Hector said.

I felt I was going to be sick, and went into the bathroom and stood at the commode but lost the urge. Back at the table Dorothy said, "John Lee, you've got to get out of here. They're bound to arrest you next."

"No damn cop is going to get you in here," Hector said.

"Are you holding now?" said Dorothy.

"No," I said, but I felt in my pockets and found a roach.

"I warned you the first day you came back here you'd better cut your hair and straighten up," said Dorothy.

"You're not the only one who told me," I said.

"I'm sorry, I don't mean to bitch," said Dorothy. She sniffled again. "I just hate it about Buster, and I'm afraid for you."

"I'm scared enough for all of us," I said.

We sat gloomily drinking beer and an occasional shot of tequila until I began talking wildly and optimistically of wading the Rio Grande with Buster and hiding in a Mexican mountain town. When Buster finally came in we all embraced him as though he had returned from headhunter country. He seemed calm and very sober, but he immediately drank a tequila and started on a bottle of beer, and he kept making a smacking noise with his lips during pauses while he told us what had happened.

"Right after you left I was trying to drag that miserable goat to the Plymouth," he said. "Corbett showed up with two guys I recognized from the vice squad and pulled a gun on me and flashed a warrant and handcuffed me while they searched the apartment. You should have heard the vice-squad cops when they found the cookie tin, and they nearly lost their minds when they found the Baby Giant. You'd think it was a plantation. They wouldn't let me read the warrant. But I saw my name was on it. Yours wasn't on it, John Lee. Maybe the JP who issued the warrant is a TV fan. I don't know. Maybe Corbett doesn't even realize you live there. The son of a bitch isn't very smart, and he's been stoned every time we've seen him. But he did ask where you were, and I told him you'd gone back to Los Angeles. The cops wrote it down. Good thing Jingo left when she did. They're looking for her. Corbett says she's a courier for the mob. But I wouldn't believe anything Corbett says. I heard him tell the vice-squad cops that I'm a major dealer for the Dallas area."

"How can they charge you with dealing?" I said.

"That weed I gave Corbett. Giving it away is the same as selling it, according to the law. Can you imagine, they got me down at the station and tried to make me tell them where the weed came from, and the pills in the medicine chest. I showed them the speed is on prescription and I didn't admit you'd got some of it from your mother. I said I'd never seen the weed before, somebody must have dropped it at the party. I said the Baby Giant had been delivered by a florist as an anonymous gift. They had a spade down there they were whipping with a wet towel. But they were a little wary of hitting me. Now, you two had better take off for Mexico and stay gone a long time."

"Come with us," Dorothy said.

"They won't let me leave the country. I'm on a ten-thousand-dollar bond."

"I'll stay here with you," I said. "Anything they think is wrong, we did it together."

"That would be stupid," said Buster. "If they're not looking for you now, they will be pretty soon. No use throwing yourself away. It won't help me. Keep out of sight, they'll probably forget it. They'll see you on television and remember you're a cowboy. Everybody knows cowboys are good Americans and don't traffic with dope. In fifteen or twenty years, after I've learned to make license plates and bead belts, we can open a shop."

"That's too long to wait," I said.

"They could give me life for being such a criminal," said Buster. "But one of the cops said realistically I probably wouldn't get more than twenty years. So I could be out after serving only eight. Eight fucking years in Huntsville behind that wall for smoking a native weed that grows wild." He shook his head. "Goddamn, it's starting to sink in. Eight fucking years of chopping cotton on the prison farm because I gave away an ounce of dried leaves that cost me nothing to a lying underhanded son of a bitch who smokes the stuff all day long and gets paid five hundred dollars a month for putting other people behind the wall for doing the same thing."

"Damn cops," Hector said.

Buster was fiddling with a cigar and staring at his tequila. "If I go to jail, I'm not going to take any goddamn pictures for the prison newspaper or work in any lab or office," he said. "They're not going to reform me. They're not going to teach me I'm wrong to smoke weed. I've seen what they do in this town. I know who's wrong. I'll wake up every morning hating their ass, and soon as I get out of jail I'll light up another joint. The only difference will be I'll hate their ass worse than I do now."

By six o'clock, we were all very drunk. I called a taxi to take Dorothy and me to the airport. Hector and Buster followed us out to the sidewalk. Traffic stalled along Cedar Springs in the dusk, horns honking, exhaust rising amid gasoline fumes. We had begun having hazy sunsets like that.

"I might decide not to go to their jail," Buster said. "Keep watch for me around the plaza. I might come to Mexico and find a man to teach me how to do a revolution."

"I'll find a man," I said.

Buster shook my hand and held it.

"I didn't have the heart to tell you this until I'd had a few drinks," he said. "When the cops searched the apartment, they tore open all the film cans and scattered the film around the living room."

"We can just roll it up again," I said. "We'll get that damn movie shown somehow."

"John Lee, I don't think we will. While I was handcuffed in the bedroom, Franklin's goat chewed up the film."

Book Five

28

In three hours we were over Mexico City. We could not see the volcanoes in the sea-blue night, or the great brown slums down below, but the bowl was sprinkled with lights. For an hour we waited in the airport bar, glum and hung over, until our plane for Acapulco was announced. In less than an hour more, we came down across the mountains, with the Pacific Ocean laid out in a silver swatch. Stepping off the plane, we at once were drenched in warm thick air and the smell of vegetation and warm piss fermenting in the night.

We passed through Customs with a fast chalk-scrawl on our blue suitcase and wandered, sweating, through the lobby of the new airport. At the front door a dozen children, taxi drivers and guides gathered around in a babble of offered services, brown hands reaching

315

for the suitcase, gesturing arms urging us toward automobiles.

"*Habla inglés? Habla inglés?*" I kept saying.

"Hokay, I speak!"

"*Sí señor,* you come!"

A short, heavy man in sweaty khakis and leather sandals pushed out of the crowd and grinned with a gold tooth.

"I take you where you want to go," he said. "I am very good to speak English. I gone to school when I was a little boy in Albuquerque. My name is Ramón."

I surrendered the suitcase. Dorothy was holding her elbows, looking at the children dancing around in an effort to sell Chiclets.

"Give these kids some money, John Lee," she said.

"I don't have any Mexican money."

"You don't have to give them nothing," said Ramón. "*Vamos, muchachos! Vamos!*"

The children followed us to the car, crying for money. Ramón tossed the suitcase into the trunk and slammed the lid. The children jumped up and down just out of his reach.

"Where you go?" he said.

"Any hotel where we might find a room," I said. "Try the Hilton last."

"I find you a good place," said Ramón.

Ramón's old Buick roared along the highway into town in the moonlight, passing the dark palm shacks along the road, honking and swerving wildly to miss a man with a donkey, careening around a truck on a curve going up a hill and turning at the last instant to avoid hitting another car coming head on, Ramón laughing and honking and blowing pungent Delicado cigarette smoke into the hot wind that blew back into our faces. From a height above Puerta Marquez we looked down at the lights of the hotels in the old port, and out beyond at the long ribbon of unbroken beach stretching south for miles outlined by the white breaking surf, with the jungle and copra plantations on one side and the ocean on the other. We sped along the road past the Las Brisas Hotel which climbed the cliff like a Mediterranean town, and went swiftly above the Las Brisas residential section where

316

lights from the villas of rich Anglos and Europeans shone through the shielding palms, jacaranda trees, bougainvillaea and shrubbery. At the top of a bend before the road plunged down around the Mexican Navy moorings and into the town, we could see freighters and cruise ships anchored in the bay, and the lights of Acapulco beginning high up on unseen mountains and swinging down in almost a circle around the bay, broken by the passage to the ocean, and the hump of Roqueta Island darkly glowing with the Pacific beyond. The sudden disloca-tion from Dallas to Acapulco made it difficult for me to comprehend that we were actually here rather than viewing it all on a screen, but Dorothy seemed to accept it at once. Recovering from the sullen humor that had taken us both since the news of Buster in the after-noon, Dorothy squeezed my hand and presented this spectacular sight with one of her finest heartiest hee-haw laughs, torn up from her by the overwhelming beauty before her and the notion that she had finally reached Acapulco.

"Why you don't like the Hilton?" asked Ramón.

"Too expensive, too ugly, too many gringos," I said.

"Hokay, I know where then," he said.

He mashed on the horn and twisted the Buick through a crowd of people who were peering at a big mound of something in the street.

"Dead elephant," explained Ramón.

"They have elephants here!" Dorothy said.

"He was from the circus. He run away. He make a real traffic jam, you bet. A truck hit him and the police shoot him. Now who will drag him away?"

Ramón drove past the tall tourist hotels on the bay and then went along the *malecón* past the freight docks and came to the plaza across from where the charter fishing boats tie up along the concrete dock. Dozens of people moved barefoot in the darkness among the smells of fish and blood and water under the hanging posts on the dock. Men sat at tables in the open air of the brightly lit cafés on the plaza, drinking beer in the heat, and hawkers peddled blankets, puppets and straw baskets on the narrow sidewalks in the continual dry stench of sewage from the gutters. U.S. sailors in white uniforms stood on a

317

corner beside a café, watching the girls and tourists, loudly fending off the peddlers, tossing coins to the children with Chiclets. An Indian woman with a baby sat on the sidewalk begging with both palms. The Moorish towers of the church at the back of the plaza behind the bandstand climbed into a purple fusion of the lights from the cafés and saloons and the dark creeping down from the jungles of the mountains above the town. Ramón drove up a hill to a white hotel across from the jail that had a fine view of the bay, but it was full. We descended again and took the road around the brow of the bay toward the bullring, and turned up a steep drive that led up past a high stone wall topped by trees and shrubbery, and came into a gravel parking lot between several old stucco buildings. What seemed to be the main building had a large veranda with a red-tile floor and a portico of arches, and people were sitting at tables just off the veranda, out of the lights, having drinks near a swimming pool. We could see the bay far below, and across to the lights of Las Brisas.

Ramón banged the bell on the counter. A young woman appeared from a doorway. I gave her five dollars. Yes, there was a room for us, for three days only. There had been a cancellation. The season had begun, we were to understand, and unless there was another cancellation we would have to move soon, but perhaps there could be an arrangement. I went back to the car with Ramón and a boy to fetch the suitcase. Ramón asked for one hundred pesos, and I gave him eight dollars, the equivalent. He grinned.

"Thank you, Tarzan," he said. "I have been thinking where I saw you. Even with the mustache, I know! Even with the bigger stomach than you had then, I know! I saw you in the Tarzan movie here two months ago. It was a very good movie I think. You are a very tough hombre."

"That wasn't me," I said.

"You don't fool Ramón," he said. "The girl, is she what you call a little star? She is very pretty. She could be a star for me, you bet!"

Our room was in a building past the pool along a narrow stone walk made into a tunnel by vines, dark and smelling of flowers. It was a large room with a double bed that creaked and a shower that dripped into a puddle around the drain. The entire wall facing the bay was screen wire with a canvas curtain rolled up at the top. A ceiling fan turned slowly a few inches above my head, making a soft sound like the wings of birds. Dorothy and I returned to the patio for a drink. At the other tables the couples and small groups were all men, most of them wearing bathing suits and unbuttoned shirts and talking quietly, except for one table where a middle-aged woman in a blonde wig laughed loudly at comments made by the two handsome young men who sat with her.

"A girl could do all right here," Dorothy said.

"Don't count on it."

When we went back to the room we were mildly drunk again. We undressed in the light from the moon through the screen-wire wall. I crawled naked into the bed. Dorothy stood at the wire wall, looking out, in panties and a pajama shirt, and then came and sat on the bed.

"John Lee, you know I can't do anything this soon," she said.

"Not anything?"

"I don't like to do that other."

"Oh."

"I will if I really have to," she said.

"I won't make you earn your keep."

"All right. I'm sorry." She lay down with her head on a pillow and her eyes looking straight up, and I rolled over with my back to her, my face toward the block of moonlight on the floor. "I don't really like to do any of it," she said. "I think I hate it." I didn't answer. I heard her crying. Then after a time I heard her breathing in the regularity of sleep with a slight rattle in her throat, and I lay listening to the shower dripping, the ceiling fan turning, the chirps of lizards and droning of crickets and smelling the sweet scent of flowers in the breeze of the fan. Dorothy's hand in sleep flopped over against my bare hip, and I was to the point of exploding. Well, I thought, I might go outside among the tables and have it taken care of, but instead, with hardly much more than a touch or two, it took care of itself.

I had a bowl of ceviche on the terrace for breakfast while Dorothy slept. Ceviche is best made of sea bass cooked by soaking in lime juice, with chopped onions, tomatoes and avocados. It made me feel clean to eat it, as if I had done myself a favor. I drank several cups of coffee and phoned the woman I had wired about renting us a house. She had not received the wire, which is not unusual in Mexico, but said we might be lucky. She knew of a house that could become available in a few days. It belonged to a rich Philadelphia banker and was managed by his cousin, Norris.

I wrote post cards to Buster, Caroline, my parents, Annie Nash and Norman Feldman.

Dorothy emerged, yawning and sullen, about noon. We took a taxi to town and walked through the hot narrow streets around the plaza before siesta time. In one of the shops, Dorothy ordered two bikinis, two pairs of shorts and a blouse to be made for her. All afternoon we lay in the sun by the pool or sat in the shade of the veranda. Many of the men at the hotel wore bikinis and rubbed their brown bodies slick with oil. Dorothy was very white compared to them. They kept glancing at her and then at me in curiosity.

In the evening we had dinner on the veranda and drinks on the terrace and watched the summits of the green mountains become purple, the color spreading like a stain down the slopes until the lights popped on. A white yacht of about eighty feet cruised out from its slip at the yacht club below us and circled a U.S. submarine in the bay as night leaked around it. After Buster's trouble, and depressed to the edge of nausea by the loss of the film, I had no further desire to smoke anything but cigars. I had been getting tired of being out of my head so much, anyhow. It was wiping out a large piece of my life that I occasionally thought I missed. There seemed to be no way to keep from crossing the line. Dorothy didn't care one way or the other as long as she had Winstons. On the terrace, beholding the spectacular performance put on by the bay, I found myself wishing I was high so I could look at this. But of course I was already looking at it, with a highly trained eye, and gradually began to reconcile the view for myself.

The second morning I rented a small boat at Caleta Beach and fished offshore for black tuna, wallowing in waves that smashed

320

against great rocks and foamed onto the perches of the gulls. At night I took Dorothy to a club and pretended to be her partner while she danced. She laughed and rolled her eyes, all flashes, and people began to imitate the new steps she was doing. The third day we didn't leave the hotel grounds. Dorothy was already brown, but I was sunburned and my stomach was uncertain how it intended to behave. The following day the real-estate woman phoned, and I agreed to rent the house without seeing it. The woman drove us to it with our suitcase and Dorothy's extra clothing. We went on a road around the bullring and up onto the cliffs above the Pacific and then turned onto a dirt road under an enormous palm tree guarded by a crippled dog and bounced in the ruts until we came to the garage of the house. From the garage we walked down steps through an overgrown garden, seeing the red-tile roof of the house below. It was a crumbling white stucco villa with arched doorways and an open *sala* with the garden behind it and a view out front of a blue-water channel and then of Roqueta Island like a green-and-brown dragon rising from the water. There was a small swimming pool just below the *sala,* and down another fifty steps was a concrete landing where you could see many different kinds and colors of fish down in the water around the rocks as the channel sloshed against the landing.

Norris lived in a little house up by the garage. He showed us a photograph of himself in the uniform of the Coldstream Guards. He was a tall man whose flesh had gone soft. A wave of yellow hair fell into his left eye. He came down the garden steps to introduce us to the cook, houseboy, laundress, two maids and two gardeners who staffed the house, and to the dozen children who lived with them in another house along a dirt path through bushes set with iguana traps. Finding my movie notes on a table in the *sala* while I was mixing gin and tonic for us, Norris said, "I was told you're an actor, but I didn't realize you're a writer as well."

"Those are just notes for a project," I said.

"I hope you don't plan to do any serious work on it in Acapulco," said Norris. "Nobody can do creative work in a place like this. It's too blasted lush. It's like floating on the old lotus to live here. I came to Mexico eighteen years ago to write a novel. The first few months I lived in a village in the mountains outside Mexico City and wrote fifty pages. Then I came to Acapulco. In the past seventeen years I've written somewhat less than fifty more pages."

"Why don't you leave Mexico?"

"Oh, my, no," Norris said. "I love it here. You come here to do something, but you can't do anything here, and soon it all just melts away. It's so pleasant here from one day to another that you forget why you ever wanted to do whatever it was. I'm sure Acapulco has saved the world from thousands of bad writers."

It was true that in a short while the days became all the same. In the mornings we drank coffee in the *sala* or on the pool terrace and watched naked divers paddling in the channel, clinging to their drifting boats and suddenly upending themselves with a flip of white buttocks and plunging out of sight to return with a fish on a spear or a few oysters for the bucket in the boat. Laborers working to build a villa next door came in the evenings to wash themselves just outside our wall. They stood naked in a muddy puddle beneath a single spigot. As I floated in the pool with my big rubber ball I could see the laborers through a gap in the wall, and could hear them laughing and talking after work. Soon days began to pass between trips to town. We learned to anticipate the tourist tour boats that came along the channel. The boats would be full of people and music, and we could hear the guide on the loudspeaker identifying the houses of the wealthy and famous; our own house was said to be the residence of Dolores del Rio. At this, people would peer at us and wave and I, looking at them through binoculars, would wave back. Creatures of all sorts crawled and jumped and flew through our grasses and up our walls and across our ceilings: lizards, scorpions, snakes, fireflies, weird little bugs with winking red and green lights, mosquitoes, flies, moths, butterflies, now and then a darting furry ball, dogs, cats, an odd little possum. We had several good unseasonal afternoon rainstorms that rattled the awnings and ripped coconuts and avocados from the trees. We slid along through the days, listening to Mexican music on the radio, reading the *New York Times* once or twice, listlessly inspecting the collection of

322

paperbacks and old magazines the house had acquired, and then, one morning about six o'clock, I was standing in the *sala*, listening to roosters crowing, and I decided to go to town and buy some weed.

I called a taxi and went to the dock. Walking among the coils of rope and rumbling engines, I looked closely at the boat captains who stood beside their crafts crying their virtues, and the percentage agents who hustled beside me promising vast herds of sailfish and marlin. At last I picked one of the agents, a slim boy of about nineteen, and said I would rent his boat for the day if he would guarantee to sell me a bag of marijuana when we came in. The captain took the boat out of the channel to a riptide of purple water that had approached within a mile from shore, and we trolled for five hours back and forth between Roqueta and the beach at Pie de la Cuesta without seeing anything more than other boats, gulls and the sun on the water, although the coastline changed as a continual show of cliffs, trees, bare brown bluffs, clusters of mansions, roads being cut through the mountains, palm and scrapwood shacks, brown boys fishing from the rocks with hand lines, the ruin of a hotel abandoned during building and falling apart in the hot wet air. I became hypnotized watching the baits skipping in the wake and the outrigger poles dipping against the dark water and rising against the bright sky.

"Pretty soon, pretty soon," the captain said. I sat beside him in a wooden chair on the flying bridge. Beneath an old blue cap, his eyes kept moving. He whistled between his teeth and slapped a wooden railing. "*Pesca! Pesca!* Come here, feesh!" From a matchbox the captain pinched out a fat cigarette and offered it to me. I shook my head. The cigarette remained in front of my face until I understood. The captain watched and nodded as I lit the cigarette, but he would not accept a puff of it. "*Más tarde.* Too strong for now." I smoked it and was thinking it was ineffective until I realized I was pulling on my lower lip and staring at the water with my mouth open and the sound of the boat engine was right in my ears and everything seemed to have shifted about three feet sideways. Then I saw the fin coming up behind the boat, like a dark blade in the far bubbles of the wake, cutting toward the splashing bait that was connected to the rod in the chair socket between my legs.

I was hoping the fish would pass on by, but with a ping the line ripped off the outrigger, and the rod bent throbbing in my hands, and automatically I rocked back to set the hook as the reel whined. The fish made a long deep run before he stopped and I was able to gain line by pumping and reeling, and he ran again, and again I took back the line. I was sweating furiously and my left arm ached from holding the rod. I wished the line would snap. The fish broke water in a showering shaking leap thirty yards behind the boat. Then came three more jumps, each one a little feebler than the last, until on the final jump only his bill, eyes and first crest of fin rose out of the water. The captain backed the boat toward the exhausted fish while I cranked in the line. In a few minutes I was looking down at the long purple-green body shining in the water beside the boat, one round glass eye peering back up at me.

While I was admiring the fish, a crewman grabbed the wire leader in a gloved hand and swung a gaff.

"Stop that!" I shouted.

"Good feesh," said the captain, leaning over me to look down.

Blood streamed into the water as the gaff pierced the fish, and the crewman raised a club.

"Quit it!" I yelled.

The club pounded the fish's head with three or four hard whacks that sounded like cracking a melon, and a rope was wrapped around the tail to secure the fish to the boat.

"Good feesh. Nine foot. We mount him for you, only eighty dollars, special price," said the captain.

"I don't want him mounted. Let him go."

"But he's dead," the captain said.

I looked down at the dark glass eye.

The captain shouted and pointed. Swimming toward the boat were two big sea turtles. A bait boy in khaki shorts grabbed a knife, dived into the ocean and swam out to the turtles. With their heads lifted like periscopes, their four feet paddling, the turtles kept coming. They must have been swimming on the surface in the sun for a while, and their shells were too hot to allow them to dive. The bait boy threshed onto one of the turtles and dragged the creature to the boat, where the other two crewmen heaved it on board. The turtle flopped and slithered on its back on the deck, opening and closing its beak. The bait boy turned toward the other turtle, which made no effort to escape but continued paddling. Quickly the second turtle was thrown onto the deck. The club fell on both turtles and while they flopped and gasped, still alive, knives sank into the rims of the belly shells and blood spurted and the crewmen began removing the shells as if opening cans. The internal organs were exposed, purple and red and blue and pink, the hearts still beating, the wadded viscera unfolding. The bait boy cut out a liver and began eating it, blood on his mouth and chin. They tore eggs from one turtle and swallowed them raw.

"I want to go in now," I said.

"You have one more hour."

"No, I've had enough."

Going in we drank beer, and the sailfish flag was run onto the rigging. I watched the water whirling white around the sailfish. At the dock the fish was strung up by its tail to the crossbar of a hanging post. Blood dripped onto the concrete in the smell of fish and salt. Other sailfish hung from posts, and turtles swam just off the dock, pulling at ropes tied to their legs. The green-and-purple bodies of the sailfish had turned black and rubbery. Holding their rods like spears, grinning dentists and their wives posed for photographs beside their catches. Barelegged children raced along the dock among a parade of tourists. Sandals salesmen and sunglasses hawkers gathered around as I paid off the captain and again declined to have the sailfish mounted. It seemed incredibly hot on the dock. Flies swarmed around the dead fish and patches of blood.

"How about the stuff, you know, the cigarette?" I said to the captain.

"Maybe today," he said.

He told me to wait at the café across the street in the plaza. While I was drinking a beer, the boy agent sat down and began scratching with his thumbnail at a blotch of food on the tablecloth. "Tomorrow," he said. "You be here. I have the stoff."

"You promised for today," I said.

He shrugged. The game had started. For the next four days I met the boy at various places, and there was always a reason why the person we were to deal with had not come down from the hills just yet. The boy did score me six packs of cigarette papers, which are harder to buy in Mexico than grass or speed, but the mysterious man from the hills kept evading us. One afternoon I waited with the boy in a hot, white, narrow, dusty alley, beside a new chrome tortilla machine, while drunks and cripples in astounding numbers slithered through clouds of flies. The man was said to have gone to a cantina. Hunting him, we were sitting in a dark and fairly cool bar when the swinging doors clattered open and in walked three men wearing sports shirts, with pistols stuck in the belts of their slacks. They ordered a drunk to leave his table and pulled up chairs for themselves and a fourth man, a short heavy fellow with a mustache and glistening skin. He began to flirt with the waitress. One of the men sat with his back to the wall, so he could view the room, and held his pistol in his lap. The agent nudged me to finish my ale.

"Theese man is a politician," he said on the sidewalk. "No good to get too close. Too much bang-bang." He laughed. "Plenty of bang-bang here. Last summer a bunch of drunk police shoot each other on the street right here where we are. Too many police still not dead though."

I was to meet the agent in the plaza at ten o'clock in the morning, and when I got there the square was full of people, flags and flowers, marching children in uniforms playing drums and bugles. The sound of bugles always made me shudder. A voice boomed and echoed around the plaza from a loudspeaker. Platoons of soldiers and sailors with rifles shuffled in cadence into the plaza. People looked down from second-floor balconies lined with flower pots. A corridor had been cleared in the concrete area between the bandstand and the church. I saw men and women walking on their knees, many with heads bowed, many weeping, edging toward the church. Some carried

326

flowers, others held up photographs. I asked a man what was going on. He looked at me as if I were a fool and said, "Guadelupe."

I phoned Dorothy and told her to come see this pageant for the Virgin of Guadelupe, patron saint of Mexico. Dorothy and I had spoken little in the last few days. She had been reading, sleeping or lying in the sun while I performed the weed protocol. When dinner was over at eleven, she had been going to bed, complaining of headaches, backaches, cramps and stomach rumblings. We slept in the same room, up a flight of steps from the *sala,* but it was a big room with two double beds. When I went out after dinner to the Zona Roja, to prowl for adventures among whores in the dirty back streets, she didn't ask where I was going nor mention it when I returned crashing into furniture in the dawn. So I was surprised, and pleased, when she not only came promptly to the plaza but arrived smiling and energetic, as though she might have pried into the bottles of Dexedrine I had bought at a *farmacía.*

"Look at them on their knees," she said. "Would you walk on your knees?"

"If I believed in it," I said, "I'd be happy to."

"Let's get closer."

We pushed in into the fringe of the crowd around the pilgrims. Little schoolgirls in white uniforms were singing. A fat woman at our feet clutched a tinted photograph of a young man, and a girl of five or six unrolled a piece of carpet for the woman to place her knees on as she journeyed across the plaza into the church. Hawkers moved through the crowd selling religious medals and crucifixes. The church bells rang in a tremendous bonging that shook the square and sent birds flying, and the voices of the little girls were lost in the noise.

"John Lee, those children, they're so sweet," said Dorothy.

Taking my hand, she led me up the steps of the church, skirting the pilgrims' corridor. She placed a lace handkerchief atop her head and stuck it there with bobby pins.

"What are you doing?" I said.

"Going inside."

"You're not a Catholic."

327

"Stay here if you don't want to go in," she said.

Dorothy crossed herself as we entered the church. Pilgrims knee-walked along the center aisle toward the altar, where they placed their flowers and photographs and lit candles in prayer. Hundreds of candles burned among the banks of flowers and ribbons beneath a large image of Our Lady of Guadelupe. Dorothy knelt in a side aisle with her hands clasped against her breast. I looked up at the inner dome and the stained glass and gilding, listening to the praying and moaning of the pilgrims and the people kneeling in the pews. Once, at the Basilica of Guadelupe in Mexico City, while I was married to Geraldine, I had been struck by a column of gold light inside the church and had felt a swelling of the heart greater than the bongs of the bell, and a giddy joy had grasped me with a sort of terror I had not experienced since I was a boy in the Baptist Church—a terror unlike that which had come with acid, for this terror was of my own unworthiness before the unexplainable mystery of God, not a dread of nothing. Then I had gone down to my knees as though hands were pressing my shoulders, down beside Geraldine who had looked around astonished as I said aloud to the golden light and the presence of the church, "I'm sorry. Please forgive me."

Now Dorothy's mouth was trembling and she began to cry. I knelt beside her. Seeing me there, she sobbed. "I'm a terrible shit," she said. "I'm terrible. Nobody knows how terrible I am."

"You're not so bad," I said.

"Oh God!" Dorothy said, putting her hands to her mouth and weeping in coughing bursts. Her shoulders shook. Even a few pilgrims glanced around. Sobs exploded from her. She began to sound as if she were choking. She drooped forward and put her forehead on the floor and wept. I wanted to touch her but didn't. Then she suddenly stood up, a smudge on her forehead, her eyes red and tear marks on her cheeks. I got up, too, and went with her out the side door into the heat and cotton-candy smell of the street. She pulled off the handkerchief and blew her nose in it. A man thrust a thin wooden T-bar at us. There was a green bird at one end of the bar and a yellow bird at the other. Their wings were clipped, and they were tied to the bar with strings.

"These bord tale your fortune for five pesos," the man said.

"Are those real birds?" said Dorothy, wiping her eyes.

The man thumped the handle and the birds hopped.

"Two pesos," I said.

He nodded and grinned at Dorothy.

"Will John Lee ever love me?" she said.

"You esk these bord?" The man thumped the handle, and the birds hopped again, the green one nearly falling off the T. "The bord say chess! He lofe you right now!"

"Which bird said that?" I said.

"Is that another question?" said the man.

"Ask if Dorothy loves me," I said.

"Two pesos more?" He thumped the bar a third time. The birds hopped. "Chess! She lofe you right now! Five pesos for the two questions, special deal."

All three of us laughed, and I paid him, and Dorothy and I moved along the jammed sidewalk with our arms around each other's waist, in a peculiar mood. I felt very much moved by her and wanted to make myself responsible for her. I felt her sorrow and her weakness and wished them to mingle with mine, as though in finding my own way into becoming I could also find the way for her. I sensed that she was flowing with good will and desire for me, and was ready to accept me without holding back and that she was thrilled by what I was thinking. She hugged me as we shoved toward the corner of the plaza by the *malecón* to find a taxi. The drums of a cadet band were tapping, and bugles blew in tinny squeals.

"A green bird never lies," said Dorothy.

"You can trust a yellow bird every time," I said.

It is useless to suppose what might have happened had we not run into the boy reefer agent in front of the café on the corner.

"Hey, Tore-zan, I am looking for you. We got your stoff in the car in the next block," he said.

"Why do you call me Tarzan?" I said.

"You got hair like Tore-zan, and we think where we see you, and now we know," grinned the boy. "You are hokay! Get your stoff."

329

Dorothy looked at me.

"After all these days of trying, I better get it," I said.

I put her in a taxi and sent her home. With the boy agent, I walked down to the bus station and turned up a side street and got into an old Chevrolet driven by the boat captain. *"Buenos días,* Tore-zan," the captain said. The starter whirred and the old car bounced and jingled into the area of town behind the plaza, through the markets and into a maze of narrow streets and unpainted houses with naked children in doorways and TOME PEPSI signs peeling from walls. I saw a road marker that said PIE DE LA CUESTA. We were rolling north out of town.

"We go in the heeels. To my house. We smoke and drank beer," said the captain.

"That's good of you, but I don't want to go today," I said.

The captain scowled.

"You come drank beer and smoke," he said.

"No!" I said. "Stop the car."

"Tore-zan got a pretty gorl waiting for he," said the boy agent.

"Haw!" the captain said. He pulled the car off the road and stopped. "Hokay, Tore-zan, you rather have gorl than me, eh?" He laughed. "Hokay, get out."

I opened the door and got out, and the boy handed me a brown paper bag. It felt as if it might contain a loaf of bread. I peeked inside at a tangle of dust-colored leaves and twigs and smelled the sharp hay odor.

"How much for this?" I said.

"You pay what you theenk," said the boy.

I gave him fifty pesos. The old Chevrolet rattled off, flinging dirt on me. With the bag tucked under my arm like a football, I hitched a ride back into town in the rear of a pickup truck full of copra workers wearing white pajamas, rubber-tire sandals and sombreros and carrying machetes. They were amused at the sight of me. I kept nodding and smiling and saying, *"Bueno."* Near the big market I caught a taxi and returned to the house.

Dorothy was lying beside the pool in a blue bikini. Out in the channel a tour boat was passing, and I heard a recorded orchestra playing "Bahia." Dorothy looked inside the bag, smelled it and clapped her hands. Upstairs I rolled a couple of Austin Torpedoes and put on my bathing suit and made two gin and tonics at the bar in the *sala* and lay down beside Dorothy. Listening to a gardener clipping a hedge somewhere in the jungle growth around the house, we smoked and drank and I rubbed the golden hairs on Dorothy's smooth brown thigh, and then the old curtain came down before our eyes. Dorothy's thoughts went off somewhere I would never be able to locate. My own thoughts got scrambled amid long contemplative stares at distant fishing boats, gapes at the action of the waves against the prow of Roqueta Island, studies of a hawk in the clear sky. I was vaguely anxious over what to do next, but unable to speak. Floating in the pool with my arms wrapped around the big red-and-yellow rubber ball, I saw an old man appear at the spigot in the gap in the wall. There was no work that day on the neighboring villa, so the old man had come just for a bath. He stripped off his dirty cotton trousers, turned the handle and stood naked under the pouring spigot. He bent his head under the spigot, and he looked at Dorothy, who was calmly watching him, and his eyes looked squarely into mine as I floated in the pool with the rubber ball, and I thought with a sudden shiver that when throat-cutting time came back to Mexico I would wish to be somewhere else.

Before those first two Torpedoes could wear off, Dorothy rolled two more. We each had two more drinks, and I discovered myself to be lurching around the grounds in the sunset, observing insects and cats and children moving in the vegetation as the warm thick evening settled close and the sky rippled with lightning. The air smelled like a botanical garden in the rain, a thousand mysterious odors drifting separately and at once. At least, I reflected, the fishing-boat captain had not stuck me with any inferior product. For a while I leaned against a palm trunk and looked at the white stucco house where the servants lived. Several hammocks were strung up inside the house, and chickens strutted in the doorway. Hearing the dinner bell, I went back along the path. On the radio we listened to static interspersed with snatches of music. We stared at a dish of paella in the center of the table.

"It's got too many arms and legs," Dorothy said. "I can't eat anything that looks at me."

She lay down on the couch in the *sala* and went to sleep. I had a theory that girl babies born during the years of World War Two had some inherent impairment of seed that made them sleep as Dorothy did. Ever since I had known her she'd been able to sleep fourteen hours at a stretch and hardly blink. Our first two weeks in Mexico, she was seldom awake. At any rate, watching her asleep on the couch with a fly crawling on her cheek, I knew that the fancy which had struck us outside the church had gone up in smoke for this day. I went up to the bedroom and dug out the paper bag again. Noticing my book of traveler's checks in a drawer, I counted and found I had seven hundred dollars left in the world, with the rent paid for two more weeks and Geraldine still waiting for this month's check. So I did the best thing I could think of at the time. I sat on the terrace with my bare feet up on the rail and smoked and drank a bottle of wine and watched the lanterns of the fishing boats dancing in the night at the entrance to the channel. I was still sitting there when Dorothy got up and went to bed.

The following evening, in an attempt to restore whatever had touched us, I arranged a mild celebration. First we phoned Buster in Dallas. I had tried several times before and had not gotten through, but this call went through in half an hour. The grand jury had indicted him, he said, and he had lost a lot of friends. Franklin, the waitress, the models, Leroy, the pro football players, most of the End Zone people, had quit calling or dropping in.

"Alma phoned and said she always knew I was a degenerate," Buster said cheerfully. "My mother cried and wondered how she could have failed. The bank has called in my notes. The landlady has given me two weeks' notice. My lawyer wants five thousand dollars. Ad agencies have quit hiring me. Charlie Withers has threatened again to ruin me. I told him he'd have to get in line to do that. All in all, I feel pretty righteous when I look around town. This place is coming apart, John Lee. You can really see the cracks in it now. Dallas is so full of nuts it rattles. They don't know why God doesn't like them any more."

"From a distance they seem to be fatter than ever," I said.

"No, it's all falling down. It's breaking up. I can feel it."

"Where are you going to get the five thousand?"

"Somewhere. I'm not worried about it. I'm a dangerous felon now."

"I'll send you what I've got left. It's not much."

"Spend it down there in my name and I'll fantasize about it," said Buster. "I met a guy the other night who says he likes to watch himself screw in the mirror because that makes it seem like it's really happening, so I'll put a mirror by the bed and wear a sombrero for a few days. But you better not come back for a while. I don't think the cops are looking for you, but you ought to stay away until we're sure."

He talked to Dorothy and made her smile. Then I took the phone back.

"Before my pre-trial hearing I went into another court and watched them send a spade away for eighteen years for stealing a television set," Buster said. "The whole thing took about a minute. The lawyer pleaded him guilty, and the judge said good-bye, Rufus, you can watch TV in the dayroom for the rest of your old black life. I wish we had something to put on the screen for that man to see."

"Could you save any of our film?"

"I've got hunks and scraps. The two murders are pretty well chewed up. It would take a lot of work and money to put that movie back together, and the money all seems to be in other peoples' pockets. I've had to sell the Bolex and some other equipment. But the good news is not all mine. I signed for a registered letter for you from a lawyer in Los Angeles. You want me to open it?"

"Throw it away," I said.

"Yeah, there's no use going to hell in the tropics with a bothered mind."

The call had not been much of a start on a celebration, but at least Dorothy had smiled and Buster had sounded so far unbeaten, and it was up to me to make the celebration. We went to a restaurant in town on a roof above old stone walls. Our table was in a garden with a fountain. A candle flame popped and fluttered inside pink glass in the middle of the white tablecloth. Violinists in tuxedos strolled under the palm trees. We had smoked across the street before going up. The grass was heavy, and my anticipation lost its edge, but I ordered a bottle of champagne to begin with. The glass was good and cold to the touch. As the bottle settled into the ice bucket, and the violin music roamed through the garden, I raised my glass and looked at the candlelight on Dorothy's maple-syrup skin, and tried to select some suitable thing to say in these glamorous trappings that would not sound like a line from a film.

"Well, John Lee, we can be quiet down here and not have a lot of people around all the time, so we can get to really know each other," Dorothy said.

"I think we know each other about as well as we're ever going to," I said.

She withdrew the hand that had been touching mine on top of the table.

"Forget it," she said.

"What's wrong?"

"I shouldn't have tried to be romantic."

"Dorothy, do you remember that time we were very high and were making love and I said I saw silver things flying through the air and it was like a tremendous explosion with showering colors? You said you saw the same things."

"If I said that, it was a long time ago."

"All right, then, let me put it this way," I said. "From now on, regular as clockwork, once a year, you got to come across and no excuses. Call it romance."

She smiled again and patted my hand and yawned.

"You don't have any idea how to treat a woman," she said.

After chicken tacos, fried potatoes, steak Diane, two bottles of champagne and several brandies, we walked along a dark street and I smoked a joint and then we went to a café toward the back of the plaza, across from the church, for another drink before going home.

334

I was fairly well muddled by then and had the inspiration that perhaps we would find the man with the birds by the church, and the birds would be good for us. We had a table at the edge of the sidewalk in the open air just under the overhang of the roof. Children selling Chiclets and shoeshines gathered around at once. I handed out coins, and soon there were twenty children. Dorothy laughed and talked to them, and I took this as progress. My back was to the bar and most of the other tables, but I could tell by the noise that the place was very crowded. Drunks were arguing, and the jukebox was playing. The voices stopped. As I sat pondering, someone tapped me on the shoulder.

I looked into a mouth that said, *"Maricón!"*

A squat, bow-legged man in short pants leaped past me into the street and crouched, clawing his fingers into his thick black hair to mock me.

"Maricón!" he repeated. Behind me there was laughter.

The man bobbed up and down on his toes halfway between me and the side door of the church. In the light from the café his dark Indian face looked full of hate. The children hushed and waited. The man beckoned to me and let his long arms drop, crouching, fingers touching the ground like an ape's.

"Maricón!"

In my mind I fancied stepping out there and kicking away the knife he would come up with, and chopping him down with a right elbow, but in fact I sat perplexed and a little frightened by this strange event, yet seeing the man with a sort of detached curiosity.

"What's he calling you?" asked Dorothy.

"A queer."

"Hit him."

The man turned his back, waggled his butt and walked slowly off into the darkness. The drunks and the children laughed.

"Aren't you going to hit him?" Dorothy said.

"It appears not."

"Well, shit, John Lee!"

"You want me to chase him?" I said.

"They'll think you're afraid."

"I don't give a damn what they think."

"Yes you do. You're an actor."

"I'm not an actor right now."

"How can you pass yourself off as a goddamn Tarzan cowboy gunfighter dope gangster if you let a little Mexican call you a queer?"

I drank a shot glass of tequila and started to feel my neck redden, and began to feel ashamed of myself for not grabbing a bottle and attacking the man, which would have meant that by now I might be stabbed or embarrassed, or triumphantly explaining the incident to the police, most likely in the jail, where I might even deserve to be and where they might ask me to account for what they had found in my pocket. But Dorothy had expected me to attack the man, and the drunks and children had hoped to see it, and a part of me had considered it, so why hadn't I done it? I hadn't been afraid of being hurt, only of being made to look foolish and of some mystery that awaited the moment of action, and I didn't feel there was sufficient reason. Or was any of that the truth?

Before daylight I was awakened by a bubbling cramp in my stomach and heard Dorothy in the bathroom throwing up. I ran for another bathroom. For three days I tasted chicken tacos and could not go as far as the pool. We were miserably sick. I thought I had polio, malaria, the flu, typhoid and hepatitis all at once. There was a terrible greasy odor around the house. I moved into a different bedroom. On the fourth day, early in the morning, I was at the big oak table in the *sala* tentatively eating a bowl of soup, and Dorothy, pale now and with streaks beneath her eyes, was smoking a cigarette and softly cursing Mexico, when the houseboy trotted down the steps from answering the bell at the gate. He said we had a visitor. I looked up half expecting to see Buster or Franklin or Jingo or Norman Feldman or Dorothy's mother or a cop with an extradition order or even Big Earl in a wheelchair with another song for me.

"This is the way to learn about a country. Come to Mexico and live just like a native," our visitor said, walking into the *sala.*

It was Erwin Englethorpe.

336

29

It took about thirty minutes for Erwin Englethorpe to ask me to drive with him up to Zihautanejo to trade a truckload of guns for a truckload of weed. First he told the houseboy in fast crude Spanish to bring him a cup of coffee. Then he said to Dorothy, "You can play on my team, honey." He walked to the edge of the *sala,* looked out at the channel and the island, flipped a cigarette down to the grass by the pool and turned and grinned. Since I had last seen him, one of his bottom front teeth had been chipped, and there was a trace of swelling at the side of his left eye, concealed by reflecting sunglasses with gold wire rims. His dirty blond hair was combed back slickly over his ears. He wore a checked sport shirt, wrinkled khaki pants and brown shoes, looking as if he might be on leave from one of the freighters in the bay. "I heard in the plaza that Tarzan lived up here," he said. While I had thought I was skulking along the *malecón* like a secret agent, they had all known about me. "You got to face it, Bubba. You don't have an anonymous appearance."

Erwin picked up my movie notes from the table where they had lain since Norris had put them down

"Still making up stuff?" he said.

"Still using my head," I said.

"Sometimes that's the dumbest part to use," said Erwin. He looked at Dorothy, who seemed fascinated by him. "There's other parts. You know what I mean, honey? Now, Bubba, don't be so overjoyed to see me. You'll make me blush."

"You plan to be here for long?" I said.

"John Lee never has really liked me ever since we were little kids

and used to bump peckers and fight, but he's usually not so rude,"
Erwin said to Dorothy.

"He's been sick," said Dorothy. "It makes him cranky."

"Don't drink water anywhere, or use any ice, or eat anything that
ain't been cooked, and take plenty of Lomatil pills, that's my advice,"
said Erwin.

"It's too late for advice," I said.

Erwin laughed and sat down. He lit another cigarette. Dorothy
stared at his biceps that moved like rolling grapefruits stamped with
tattoos. I noticed the welted scar that my butcher knife had carved
on his right forearm. He gave Dorothy a cigarette and lit it for her.

"Bubba, I got another real experience to offer you," he said. "You
remember that dope deal we talked about at Ruby's club that night?
It didn't come off quite as big as I'd hoped for, but I did move a bunch
of reefer across the border"—he glanced at Dorothy for her reaction,
which was one of admiration—"and made a little money. Then I
bought guns from some fellows in Arizona and Texas. You're acquainted with one of them, but I won't mention no name. He ain't a
burglar, though, like the other fellows."

"Who is he?" said Dorothy.

"It wouldn't be good for me to say. But he done an awful strange
thing recently. I expect he won't live too much longer. Maybe I'll tell
you later, honey, if you ask nice," Erwin said.

"What is this wonderful experience you're offering?" I asked.

"I didn't say it was wonderful, I said it was real. It might be
wonderful, it might not. What I did was bring my guns down and
make a deal to sell them to some goddamn revolutionary son of a
bitches in Mexico City. Well, to cut the story short, I showed up with
the guns, and they showed up with a bag of money, and when I started
to walk off with the money they slapped me aside of the head and
grabbed the money back and kept the guns. It's a risk you got to take.
Matter of fact, I'm lucky they didn't shoot me. But you remember
those other guns I had, that you read about in the paper when the cops
stole my bullets? Those guns were still stashed, so I went and got
them. Now I'm going to swap them in Zihautanejo for a pile of dope,

338

and I want you to come with me. I drove up there yesterday to arrange the deal. One of these guys is another goddamn revolutionary like Mexico is full of, and I ain't going to have anything more to do with one of those son of a bitches by myself. You can't trust a man that starts telling you a lot of political bullshit. He don't believe a deal is a deal unless it fits in with his scheme. I'll do business alone with dope dealers, but not any more with political bastards."

"You want John Lee to be your bodyguard?" asked Dorothy.

"You sound like you think he couldn't do it," Erwin said. "Don't you watch television, honey? This boy can ride and rope and knock fire off a wild pig's ass."

The houseboy brought Dorothy a glass of water. Erwin removed it from her hand.

"It's bottled water," she said.

"Honey, bottled water comes out of a hose that's connected to a faucet," he said. He glanced at the houseboy. *"Verdad, hombre?"* The houseboy went into the kitchen. "We don't want you getting the runs. You can ride up to Z with us."

"Can we, John Lee?" asked Dorothy.

"All there is to it is you all come up there with me right now in my truck," Erwin said. "We'll meet these guys at a little café on the bay in Z and then go outside of town someplace and do the trade. Then we might stay in a hotel if they ain't all full up, or we can drive back down here. The drive takes about six hours, and that road ain't safe at night for a man by hisself. There's a hell of a lot of damn crooks in Mexico that don't hesitate to hold you up and maybe kill you. But with John Lee riding shotgun, we'll be safe as in the arms of Jesus. Z is a real pretty town. It's like a minor-league Acapulco, not so built up. Tough place, too, man. The road ends there. From Z north, up through Michoacán, it's pure Wild West. Ever'body that's rich enough to have a gun wears it and there ain't no telephones, and a cop or doctor is liable to be three days away by horseback and scared to come anyhow. You'll feel right at home there, Bubba. I've seen you chase those Meskin bandits and beat their butts more than one time."

"All right, let's go," I said, looking at Dorothy.

339

"To show you what a good guy I am, I'll mention money even though you've already spoken up," said Erwin. "I'll give you a thousand dollars when I get back here safe to Acapulco."

"John Lee doesn't need money," Dorothy said.

"It's a deal, Erwin, for a thousand dollars," I said.

"You shouldn't take his money. That's how he makes his living," said Dorothy.

"Shut up, Dorothy, you don't have any idea whether I need money or not," I said. "All you do is lie on your ass with your mouth open."

She looked at me as though I had inexplicably stomped on her foot.

"See there, honey, that's the John Lee that nearly killed me one time. I know that boy," said Erwin.

"Let's get moving," I said.

"I'll roll some joints," said Dorothy.

"Not for this trip," I said.

"A few nips of tequila is more like what we need," said Erwin. "I still can't figure out why anybody smokes reefer. It makes you act so damn stupid. Tequila makes you invincible and reefer makes you a pushover. You can bet this political son of a bitch won't be smoking no reefer."

Erwin reached into the hip pocket of his khakis and gave me a snub-nose, nickel-plated, double-action .32-caliber revolver with a black plastic grip.

"Stick this inside your shirt someplace or hide it in your pocket," Erwin said. "I got a big .44 hogleg that I'll wear in my belt where they can see it. With that .44 I can make a Meskin climb a cactus in the desert."

Erwin grinned at Dorothy with his chipped tooth.

"Don't worry, honey. If we showed up without wearing a firearm, these fellows might think we was so crazy we'd be willing to give them our goods without making them go through with the trade."

"I don't like guns," she said.

"Ever'body likes guns," said Erwin. "That's how I happen to still be in business. Like you said, it's my living."

I went upstairs and put on socks, sneakers, a pair of olive Levi's and

340

a polo shirt with the tail out to conceal the pistol. I flipped out the cylinder, unloaded the pistol and inspected each shell. I found the thumb safety, flicked it a few times, and was aiming into the mirror, squeezing the trigger and snapping the hammer, when Dorothy walked in.

"Don't you feel silly doing that?" she said.

"It's the way I make my living," I said.

I reloaded, put the safety on, shoved the pistol into my right hip pocket and pulled down my shirt tail, looking into the mirror. I could see Dorothy behind me stuffing a bathing suit, comb, brush, toothbrush, toothpaste, coconut oil, clean blouse and clean shorts into a flight bag, as though we were off to a resort. She turned her back, removed the shorts and halter she was wearing, and put on clean underwear, her yellow trousers, a yellow-and-white striped T-shirt and a pair of rubber sandals. I leaned against the wall for a moment, feeling dizzy and weak. The spell passed, and I took a Dexedrine and tossed the bottle into the flight bag.

"Are you sure you want to do this?" asked Dorothy.

"Don't you want to?"

"It could be fun."

"That's right, it could be."

"You're pissed at me," she said.

"No, I'm just ready to go. I've been getting ready all my life."

Erwin's vehicle was parked under a jacaranda tree outside our garage. It was a camper mounted on a Ford pickup truck. Erwin showed me the bolts that could be removed so that the camper could be lifted with a winch to reveal a compartment that would hold four hundred kilos of marijuana bricks.

"I won't bother with a winch until I get up to my stash place this side of the Texas line," he said. "We'll pick up six hundred keys of reefer tonight and just load it into the camper and lock it up. No need for more precautions than that until I get near Customs at the border. My rig looks so good I don't bother with lead cars or decoys—just hand over a little cash at the interior checkpoints and keep traveling. If we come back here tomorrow morning, I'll be in San Antonio five

341

days from right this minute with my pockets full of cash again."

Erwin unlocked the camper door and opened it. The windows were locked and the shades drawn. He nudged me and I leaned in through the door. Inside the hot, musty camper was a smell of oil, and in a moment I could make out about ten wooden crates. The crates that I could see were stenciled with the words:

LOS MELOCOTONES DE MAZATLÁN

"I don't know if peaches grow in Mazatlán or not, but it sounds good," said Erwin. "What we got in these crates is twenty M-1 rifles, fourteen M-1 carbines, two thousand rounds of .30-caliber ammunition, fifty hand grenades, six .45 automatics and five hundred rounds of .45 ammunition." He looked at a notebook in his shirt pocket. "Those fellows up there agreed to pay me a hundred dollars for each rifle and carbine, ten for each grenade, twenty-five cents for each round of .30 caliber, fifty cents for each round of .45 caliber, and a hundred and twenty-five dollars for each of them macho .45 automatics. That political son of a bitch has got a .45 automatic and one small carton of bullets that look like they was made for World War One. He can't wait to get this new, modern Korean War stuff."

"That sounds like a lot of money," I said.

"It comes to forty-nine hundred dollars, but I'm taking it in reefer at eight dollars a key, so I told them just to make it an even six hundred keys. I expect the political son of a bitch will hold up a bank or kidnap somebody to pay the dealer, but that's not my affair. I've made an agreement to turn this reefer for a hundred and forty a key in San Antonio, whole load to one guy."

"In that case, a thousand dollars isn't enough for me," I said.

"John Lee, what's got into you?" said Dorothy.

"I knew you'd figure it out!" Erwin grinned. "If I can get this reefer to San Antonio I can turn it for a profit of better than eighty thousand U.S.A. dollars. But I'll have to make two trips from my stash place to San Antonio with the weed hid under the camper body. Plus the drive from here to the stash place, which is kind of dull after you've done it a while. So if you go all the way with me, and drive the second load from the stash across the border up to San Antonio by yourself

342

after I make one round trip by myself, I'll cut you in for a third."

"Half," I said.

"A third is generous," said Erwin.

"I can hardly believe they'll pay you a hundred dollars for an M-1 rifle or carbine," I said. "You can buy a perfectly good reconditioned Mauser in Dallas for less than twenty."

"Dallas ain't exactly in the Guerrero-Michoacán wilderness, and these people can't exactly walk into a gun store and buy whatever they want," said Erwin. "Besides, they're only trading me a bunch of crushed-up bushes that grow all over the mountains. It's the guns that are valuable."

"Half," I said.

"A third," said Erwin. "But I'll tell you what else I'll do. I'll keep a third for myself and put the rest of it in on that dope-dealer movie we talked about. With your third, that'll give you more than fifty thousand dollars to work with. Can you make a movie for that?"

"I could," I said, thinking it would not be exactly the movie Erwin expected.

"Somewhere at the front of the movie it's got to say 'Erwin Englethorpe helped with this.' "

"How about if it says 'Produced by Erwin Englethorpe'?"

"You want to shake hands on it, or bump peckers?"

We shook hands. Norris came out of his cottage, yawning.

"Here I am, a goddamn artist," said Erwin.

"I think you're a natural producer," I said.

"Going camping?" said Norris.

"Just for the night," I said.

"Be careful. This isn't Yosemite," said Norris.

With Dorothy in the middle and Erwin at the wheel, we bucked along the ruts in the dirt road above Norris's villa, past brown shirt-less laborers carrying bricks in slings to the new villa next door. The day was already warm and very bright, with the ocean flat as a prairie and tiny white boats looking nailed to the horizon. In the confusion of tight streets and many cars and buses obscuring traffic signs, Erwin made an illegal turn in the area around the market and was whistled

343

at by a traffic cop in a brown uniform. The cop's smiling, sweating face appeared in the window on Erwin's side.

"Buenos días," said the cop. "Toureest?"

"Sí, amigo. I'm sorry we missed that sign. I'll pay the ticket right now." Erwin pressed five ten-peso notes into the cop's palm. The cop touched the brim of his cap in salute, stepped back and stopped traffic so Erwin could move the camper into the street in the proper direction. "In Mexico, always deal with a cop right on the spot," Erwin said. "If you let them take you to jail, you got a lot more people to deal with and you're liable to get so wrapped up in red tape and macho feelings that you won't see daylight for years." Seeing the PIE DE LA CUESTA marker, Erwin swung the camper in front of a honking truck loaded with chickens. "There was some beatniks, four boys and three girls, that got busted by the Federales up in Z last summer. They had close to a thousand pounds of weed drying on their roof. The Federales offered to let them go for a hundred dollars. The beatniks stood on principle and asked for a lawyer and the American consul. Cops don't like beatniks, anyhow. So they raped the girls and beat up the boys and threw them in the back of a cattle truck and drove them to the next state over east and kicked them out. Cops picked them up there and did the same thing. The beatniks kept going that way until they got to Texas." Erwin chuckled. "They didn't even save their hundred dollars. The cops took all their money right off."

"The American government must have done something about it," Dorothy said.

"Honey, if you're a beatnik you ain't got a government."

Small shops and cantinas began to fall away from the road, and soon we were passing palm-frond huts built on bamboo frames with open walls. Hammocks hung in shade inside, and women swept dirt in front of their huts while children and dogs gazed at our camper.

"Another thing," Erwin said. "If you're a gringo and got money, they'll snap shit at the big hotels in Mexico City or Acapulco or any resort. But if you're a gringo out in the country, you sleep with one eye open."

We rolled for hours through tall copra forests with mountains

344

rising beyond. Oxen pulled carts with wooden wheels, and men in sandals trudged along with machetes and occasionally there was someone on a horse or a donkey. We crossed a crumbling concrete bridge over a wide river. On the banks of the river hundreds of women were bathing or doing laundry, their clothes spread in blotches of red, blue, green and white on the stones. Eventually we stopped in a village. Erwin and I went behind the cantina to pee on the ground, and Dorothy went behind the grocery store, where the proprietress pointed her. Several children ran to watch, wondering if the tall gringa did it the same way they did. We bought hot Cokes and drank them with a Dexedrine for each of us and watched a boy trying to pull his squealing pig by a hind leg out of the shade of a bush. On the hill across from the cantina stood a pink church with an impressive steeple. As in all the villages on the Z road, the two most prominent constructions were the church and the cemetery.

I drove for a while, and we began to see the ocean again, on our left, surging softly against bluffs and rocks that reminded me of the Monterey Peninsula in northern California. Erwin was telling Dorothy stories of our childhood and of our later meetings at the police station when he was arrested for burglary and other misadventures. He told several anecdotes about himself, and mentioned that his wife was dead. He stretched his scarred left arm across the back of the seat, a stain in his armpit, his left thumb casually scratching Dorothy's shoulder. Listening to him, she seemed to have lost her repugnance for guns, and now that I had agreed to help Erwin transport the dope all the way to San Antonio, I sensed that it was more than all right with her for me to take the money. I guess it was the difference in amount now that mattered, or perhaps it was the commitment. Trading for weed in Zihautanejo was merely a game to her, but selling it to a dealer in San Antonio transformed the affair into dramatic outlaw business.

Outside Zihautanejo I got out to remove a rock from the road, and when I came back I noticed Erwin's right hand on Dorothy's thigh. She looked at me as though wondering if I'd heard what had been

345

said. In Erwin's reflecting glasses I saw a weird small image of myself as if trapped in a bottle.

"All this jouncing gives me a damn hard on," Erwin said. He climbed down from the truck and walked into some trees, adjusting his pants and walking spraddled, as if he'd been riding a horse.

"Erwin's cute," Dorothy said.

"One of the very cutest."

"You're in a beautiful mood. What have I done?"

"Nothing out of the ordinary."

"I've said I'll try to do for you, but you'll have to tell me what you want me to be," she said.

"I can't ask you to be anything but yourself."

"Maybe you're wrong about that," she said.

We could see Erwin zipping up his pants behind a palm tree.

"Don't you know what you want me to be?" she said.

"It's like the bear dance."

"The what?"

"That Lord Buckley line about the bear dance. 'Two sniffs, three snorts, four turns and a grunt. It was so simple it evaded me,' " I said.

"Well, crap then."

The road smoothed again coming into Zihautanejo. Beyond a small landing strip cut into the forest where a red windsock dangled from a pole atop a tin shed, we turned left and drove into a gathering of stucco houses and palm huts. Then I began to see HOTEL signs with painted arrows, and signs that said FARMACÍA and TOME PEPSI.

"You may not of guessed it, but we're in the middle of town," said Erwin. "Right up there by all them palm sheds is the bay. Park over on the left by the police station. The truck will be okay there for a while locked up. The café we want is by the beach."

Siesta was over and the shops had opened again. The main street and the beach were crowded with tourists from the United States: young engineers and families from California or Texas, bohemians outfitted by Saks, beatniks, homosexuals, here and there a stray middle-aged woman in a print dress and carrying a camera. The tourists argued with shopkeepers and spoke in Spanish when they ordered

346

oysters and beer at the seafood bars at the end of the street. They seemed to take themselves fairly seriously, as though by being in Zihautanejo they had become classed in all eyes as aficionados rather than tourists, *muy simpático,* or else they were in a part of Mexico they were afraid of. I could feel the pistol in my right hip pocket as we walked toward the café. I had stuck a rag in my pocket and let the end hang out to explain the bulge. Erwin had locked his .44 in the glove compartment. He held Dorothy's elbow as we crossed the street, and they walked ahead of me, Erwin moving squarely along the middle of the sidewalk, forcing the people to part for them. I saw people glancing back, annoyed at Erwin, and remaining to look at Dorothy. Some of her color had returned. As if to match Erwin's belly-forward swagger, she straightened up a bit from her habitual slump and lifted her head, and I could hear Mexican men muttering to each other about her.

Two of the three Mexicans we were to meet were drinking beer in the café at a table near the sidewalk where they could see the people on the beach. They frowned when they saw Erwin had brought Dorothy and me, but they rose for Erwin to introduce us.

"This here's Nunio."

Nunio took off his straw cowboy hat, looked at Dorothy through a pair of drugstore shades and shook hands with me. His fingers felt like corncobs. He wore dirty khakis that smelled like peat, and he seemed a little drunk. I guessed him to be about fifty.

"And this here's old Carretera. They call him Loquito."

"Señor Carretera," I said, shaking his hand.

"Loquitho ith hokay," he smiled. I could see his gums, and his tongue in the gap where four upper front teeth should have been. He too wore a straw cowboy hat and khakis, and he was small and thin, with a stubble of graying beard, but his eyes were strangely opaque, the color of green grapes, seeming almost sightless until he moved them to look at me. He plunged his fingers into an extra glass of beer where his bridge was soaking. Replacing his teeth, he smiled again and said to Dorothy, "I am sorry I forget. I buy my teeth in Sante Fe, New Mexico. They hurt sometimes and I scrape them with a knife but it is too far to get them fixed."

"You sure talk good English," Dorothy said.

"I have been many times to the United States. I was in jail for a year in Texas for being a wetback and for three years in New Mexico for having mari-hwana"—he blew a hard breath on the h—"and I got much practice. I learn how to say boss."

"We could set down," said Erwin. "I need a *cerveza* and some of them shrimps."

The two Mexicans whispered together. From the table I could see Mexican women splashing in the surf in their dresses, modest amid male gazes, and a number of gringas smeared with oil lying on blankets in bikinis in the sand. Mexican men in tightly defining bathing suits strutted for the gringas, whose own men fiddled with surf boards and inner tubes and watched the wet dresses stuck to the bodies of the Mexican women.

"Cut it out," Erwin said to the two men. "John Lee here is my partner, and he don't handle Spanish very good. Where is Carlos?"

Loquito shrugged.

"I told him to be here on time. This ain't no goddamn political rally where we can hang around all day."

"He is coming now," said Loquito.

We looked up the street and saw a tall black man riding toward us on a burro, his dark bare feet dragging in the dirt. He was taller than I and wore a bandana around his head, and a vest with no shirt, and as he came closer I saw a silver St. Christopher's medal in the wiry black hair on his chest. A blanket roll was tied onto the burro's back, and a canteen dangled on the animal's right hip.

"Politicians like to dress up," Erwin said.

Carlos dismounted by swinging one long leg over the burro's head while the animal was still walking. With Carlos off, the burro stopped. Carlos came to the table and nodded to us but did not offer to shake hands. He took a chair from another table and sat with us. Carlos looked at Dorothy for a moment, ignoring Erwin and the other two Mexicans, and then he looked at me.

"Where you from?" Carlos asked me.

348

"Dallas," I said.

The three Mexicans looked quickly at each other. Carlos leaned his elbows on the table and scowled, his eyes touched with red in the corners.

"Dallas killed Kennedy," he said.

"About one more remark like that, Carlos, and you can hump a pig for your guns," said Erwin.

"Were you for Kennedy or against him?" Carlos asked.

"For him," I said.

"He don't have to tell you who he's for and who he's against," said Erwin. "We're here to do business. The goods we brought ain't got any politics."

"The goods you brought are politics," Carlos said. He spoke English very well, with an odd accent, a mixture of accents, partly Mexican, partly New York, partly southwestern U.S., rather like a California Negro from a big city.

"The way I look at it, Kennedy getting shot was tough luck for him," said Erwin, also leaning forward and placing his reflecting sunglasses close enough for Carlos to see his own eyes. The red-and-blue tattoo of the helmeted bulldog and USMC jiggled on Erwin's right bicep. "But it didn't hurt nobody at this table. It's good for us."

Loquito translated what had been said for Nunio, who shrugged as though the talk was too banal for a response.

"Man, if it was my country I would get rid of you," Carlos said.

"It ain't ever going to be your country," said Erwin. "Hey, *señora, más cervezas por favor* and a plate of them *camerons*."

Carlos sat back and struck a kitchen match to a short black Mexican cigar that looked as if it had been twisted out of a pot of tobacco and dried like a piece of taffy. Holding the cigar in his teeth, blowing out smoke that smelled of burnt hair, he turned toward me again.

"I have seen you before," he said.

"It's possible. I've been to Mexico before."

"You think I haven't been to Texas? Man, I've been to Texas. In Texas I'm a nigger."

"Yeah, and in Mexico you're a noble goddamn champion jungle

prince. I can see how well you been treated judging by your Cadillacs and them fine clothes you got on," said Erwin.

Carlos laughed. "He keeps thinking I want money. He's very stupid."

"I must be stupid to set here and listen to you, Carlos. I ought to go on back to Acapulco," Erwin said.

"You won't go until you get the mari-hwana," said Carlos. He looked at Dorothy. "You couldn't be his girl. You're too beautiful. You must belong to this person with the mustache and the pretty hair like a woman."

Dorothy smiled and started to speak, but I interrupted.

"She's her own person," I said, "but if you find my hair so attractive you sound like a *maricón.*"

"None of this macho shit now," Erwin said.

"I didn't mean to insult you, Texas," said Carlos, smiling at Dorothy. "I much prefer girls to men, hundreds of girls could tell you that."

"Are you a Mexican?" Dorothy asked.

"I live outside a town down the coast from here," said Carlos. "A slave ship wrecked there a hundred years ago. Most of the people in my town are dark."

"Looks like a colored town in Louisiana," Erwin said.

Carlos shook his head. "You are nearly the worst gringo I have ever met, and I met many bad gringos when I was working in hotels," he said to Erwin. "You are so bad I nearly admire you."

Loquito kept translating for Nunio, who occasionally would grunt and lift a beer bottle to his mouth with big fingers held away from the glass by calluses.

"Loquito here is a *brujo,*" Erwin said to me.

The grape eyes rolled back and forth, examining the café and the sidewalk.

"Don't say that in here," said Loquito.

"John Lee might like some of your mushrooms. He's taken about ever' kind of dope a man can swallow," Erwin said.

"I don't have no mushrooms."

"You always say that," said Erwin.

"I could find some mushrooms maybe. They are not fresh but not bad. Like the mari-hwana is not fresh this late in the year but not ever bad," Loquito said.

"Something wrong with the dope?" said Erwin.

"Not a thing wrong with it," Carlos said.

"I'll have your black ass if it's not good reefer. My partner here is a expert smoker," said Erwin.

"He looks like it," Carlos said.

While I was trying to decide how to understand that, Loquito asked me, "You have eaten mushrooms?"

"I've taken psylocibin."

"Yes," he nodded, "a famous American professor was in a hotel here and he gave me some of that and some LSD in trade for mushrooms and mari-hwana. The LSD made me feel plenty strange. I walked in the mountains and could not sleep. Things howled at me. Sometimes I felt plenty good and sometimes I was plenty puzzled, but I knew a lot all the time when I was doing it, but it might have been bad for my powers, I don't know."

"I've had the same feeling," I said.

"We will talk about it," said Loquito. "If you have took LSD you must have thoughts about it. Which do you like the best?"

"I prefer organic mescaline from the cactus," I said. "Or opium."

"I have never took opium or mescaline," said the *brujo*. "I think it is wrong to cook the cactus down to mescaline. The spirit in the cactus may not like the cooking. They grow opium poppies in a village to the north of here, but I'm happy with what I have."

"Dope talk is boring," Carlos said.

"You dope fiends tell each other stories some other day," said Erwin. "I want to get done with our business and hit the road."

Nunio drew a map on a piece of brown paper. It showed a road that led out of Zihautanejo northeast into the mountains for twelve kilometers. At the end of the road was an X.

"Bring the stuff closer to town," Erwin said.

"Our truck has broken," said Loquito.

351

"I warn you, we're going to shoot holes in people if there's a trick," Erwin said.

"We're honest men," said Carlos. "If there is cheating, it will be by you, and you won't see the sunset."

It was about five o'clock in the afternoon when we left the café. Erwin took the .44 out of the glove compartment and kept it in his lap while he drove the camper behind the three Mexicans, who were in a yellow Volkswagen with Carlos at the wheel. The VW turned off the main highway into what appeared to be a grove of palms and found a narrow climbing track. Fronds and branches squeaked against the sides of the camper. The road leveled off along a bare ridge from which we could look back down at the bay and the jumble of buildings that made up the town. To the west the rim of the sea was turning pink.

"Did you mean it about shooting?" asked Dorothy.

"You got to talk in terms they understand," Erwin said. "If a Meskin says you're making him unhappy, next thing he'll do is shoot or stab you. I wanted them to know we're serious."

Dorothy was chewing her lip and seemed to be getting scared. I felt only a mild and pleasant tension, smoothed by the tequila I drank in the café. This movie had caught my interest. I could detect no menace in Loquito or Nunio, and I wasn't afraid of Carlos or of guns as long as one gun was mine.

"Honey, it won't come to shooting," Erwin said. He tried to pat her thigh but had to grab the wheel again as the camper whanged into a rut and bounced off a rock. We had come onto a plateau covered with scrub brush. The road was very difficult to see in the dust. The VW had gotten so far ahead that we followed it by its cloud. We passed a couple of shacks and a corral with two cows in it but saw no people. We went down a steep gully in first gear, across a shallow running stream, and back up on the other side, honking several pigs out of the path. Now the ground was flat again, strewn with boulders and marked with an ancient lava flow that made a black line down the side of a mountain that rose into clouds. Where the mountain began, a quarter of a mile away, we could see a cluster of buildings that

352

appeared to be a village, or perhaps a hacienda. The road turned westward from the village, rounded a tall rock, and there was the VW parked in a field of rocks and cactus with the three Mexicans standing beside a mound of gunny sacks.

Erwin stopped the camper a hundred yards from the VW. We got out and looked around. To the left the field was clear for nearly a mile before it dropped off, and beyond was the ocean. To the right, fifty yards from the VW, and was a cliff of brown rock thirty feet high. Past the VW the field continued unbroken until it reached a brown hill.

"If they're going to ambush us here, it would be from that cliff to the right," said Erwin. "Why don't you take a look up there?"

"Why don't you take a look up there?" I said.

"John Lee, was you ever in combat in the Army?"

"No," I said.

"Well, I wasn't smart enough to register in college, so to keep out of the war I joined the National Guard up in Oklahoma where my real daddy moved to, and they shipped my butt straight to Korea," Erwin said, studying the rim of the cliff.

"How about that USMC on your arm?" I said.

"Aw, I got that done when we was in high school when ever'body thought it was glamorous to be a Marine. Anyway, one thing I learned in Korea was dumb guys got killed more often than guys who was smart and careful. If you was too lazy or stupid to check out a place like that cliff, your chances of staying alive was a lot worse."

"I know that, Erwin. So check it out," I said.

"I'm the leader," said Erwin.

"You're not my leader."

"I can still whip you, TV star," he said angrily, turning the reflecting sunglasses on me.

"I've got a gun," I said.

In the distance Carlos was waving his arms, and we heard him yelling at us.

"Some goddamn partner," said Erwin.

"You haven't changed from when you were a little kid," I said.

"All right, we'll both be bull-headed," said Erwin. "We'll drive over there and get burnt and there goes our movie back to the mountains."

I took another look at the cliff and could see a hawk low above it. Smoke rose from another ridge, but it was miles off, in the purple. Erwin got into the camper and slammed the door. I came around on the opposite side and through my open door saw him squeeze Dorothy's thigh at the crotch. I heard him say, "Back in Acapulco I'll show you a good time, honey." I waited a moment for her answer, but she offered only a frightened smile. I got in and slammed my door, and we approached the VW and the mound of gunny sacks with the three Mexicans watching us.

"Do you see Indians up there on the cliff?" Carlos said, laughing.

Erwin turned the camper around and backed up to the gunny sacks. Without a word he climbed down, looked at the sacks of unpressed weed and unlocked the rear door of the camper.

"Let's get this stuff unloaded," he said.

He pushed the .44 pistol into the waistband of his trousers and crawled into the rear of the camper. Carlos wore a .45 automatic in an old leather holster with US stamped on it. Erwin shoved the crates out, and Carlos and I lifted them to the ground beside the marijuana bags. Nunio and Loquito stood and watched. Dorothy joined them. I glanced at her, an elegant-looking girl in tight yellow slacks, nervously smoking a cigarette beside a male witch and a dope farmer far out in the Mexican mountains, and I couldn't help but smile at the situation.

"What's the joke?" said Carlos.

Up close he smelled like a goat. Sweat shone on the muscles of his chest and arms. I shook my head, and we put down the final crate. Erwin sat in the camper door.

"Let's rest a minute," Erwin said.

Carlos patted a crate and grinned.

"When I was a student for a year at the University of Mexico, I read some books and listened to much intellectual bullshit talk," he said. "All those words never did one thing to help the people so much as one gun can do."

354

"That's not many guns," I said, gesturing toward the crates.

"For forty men to have guns is many," said Carlos. "They can kill crooked politicians, kill the wicked *caciques,* kill the soldiers, steal food, medical supplies and money. When the revolution starts in the U.S.A., you'll see what I mean."

"What revolution?" Erwin said.

"There must be a revolution now the Fascists have killed Kennedy," said Carlos. "The people will rise."

"I'll tell you the fact of the matter," said Erwin, sliding down from the truck and dusting his palms. "If I wasn't in a good-time business like this, or in the movie business like I soon will be, I'd be working on some goddamn assembly line paying high taxes and high interest and trying to keep a nigger from getting my job. I'd be leading the revolution. It wouldn't be fucking college kids and deep thinkers who don't have nothing better to do than make up something to worry about. It would be me. But I've got off the assembly line, and as far as I care the U.S.A is all right."

Erwin produced a pocket knife and dug into one of the sacks.

"Smell that," he said.

The handful he had gouged out had a delicate aroma something like old dung.

"It's good," said Loquito.

Erwin's reflecting sunglasses aimed at me.

"It's dry. It smells fine," I said.

"Can you tell for sure?" said Erwin.

"Not unless I smoke it."

"Is that too much to ask of a partner?" Erwin said.

"I don't have any cigarette papers," I said.

"Use this," said Dorothy. She began pinching the tobacco out of a Winston. I picked out seeds and stems from the handful and crushed a small amount of leaf and flowers. Carlos returned from the VW carrying a short crowbar and looked at us with disgust. I sucked up enough of the leaf into the Winston shell that I could twist the end and then I licked the paper very carefully, so as not to tear it but to make it burn slower. Carlos jabbed the crowbar into a crate and began

355

to pry off a board. Erwin was looking at me.

After two long drags off the Winston I felt a jarring and a sort of whizzing in my ears and saw everything in sharp detail, and then as I breathed the sensations lessened but I could tell that in a few moments I would be modestly high. I started to stop then and pronounce the weed as acceptable, but without really noticing I had stuck the joint back into my mouth and was puffing again when Carlos raised up and screamed, "Goddamn you white son of a bitch these guns are rusted!" and yanked the .45 automatic from his holster and shot the startled Erwin full in the face from a distance of two feet. Without a conscious thought, for I had done this hundreds of times before, I very quickly drew the .32 nickel-plated revolver out of my hip pocket, flicked off the safety and shot Carlos twice in the stomach. It sounded like firecrackers. The two holes popped and puffed. He sat down on the crate and looked up at me with dark eyes rimmed with red and tried to lift the heavy automatic, so I shot him in the chest and saw blood and bits of flesh spatter on the wooden crate behind him, and Carlos flopped back on the crate moaning.

Dorothy's face and T-shirt were splashed with blood and pieces of Erwin's teeth. She was looking at all of us as if about to demand to know what we were up to. I realized that the wetness I felt on my face and the shower that had flown before my eyes had come from Erwin. The explosion had knocked him five feet. He lay on his back with his knees drawn up and his arms outflung and dark spreading in his crotch.

With their eyes on me, Nunio and Loquito were edging away, their hands in the air. I aimed the revolver at them.

"Please, don't shoot, don't shoot," said Loquito.

"John Lee, don't shoot those men," Dorothy said in a scolding tone.

As I lowered the revolver in the smell of gunpowder smoke, Loquito and Nunio began running away across the field, crashing through cactus and stumbling over rocks.

"I told you I didn't like guns. Goddamn," Dorothy said. She started crying and sat in the dirt. A blistering pain struck my chin. I peeled off the broken Winston and threw it down.

30

There was a large red bubbling hole in Erwin's face. His upper lip, gum, front teeth and the lower part of his nose were a mess. Blood oozed out of the hole and fizzled with mucus when he breathed. His reflecting glasses had blown loose and twisted around his right ear. Erwin's eyes stared into the sky, but as I bent over him the eyes moved slightly and blinked in blood. With the rag that had helped to conceal the pistol that was still in my hand, I wiped blood out of his eyes.

"There's not much I can do but try to get you to a doctor," I said. "It won't be quick."

I walked off from the staring eyes. Dorothy sat down in the dirt.

"Get up and help me," I said, but she didn't stir.

Carlos gargled and coughed. The two red holes close together in his stomach and the hole a few inches higher in his left breast looked like boils that had burst. There were red-gray powder burns around the holes but not much blood. The blood that soaked the crate came from what would be much more ragged holes in his back.

Carlos looked at me and spoke, a frothy mumble I could not comprehend. His eyes swung wildly around, and suddenly he tried to sit up. Instead he tumbled off the crate. A flood of squashy yellow shit flowed down his legs in a hideous stink. On his back on the ground, his mouth open like a boated fish's, he ceased to gargle.

"You better take care of this one, Jesus," I said, looking at the sky. I had seen people die close up from wounds and injuries when I was a police reporter, and had watched an old man die on a New York sidewalk after he had fallen and bashed open his head against a streetlight post, and it never had seemed genuine, no wraith floating out of the body, no speeches to remember. All the old man in New York had said was, "Did I hurt myself?" One moment Carlos was

357

gargling and trying to rise, and the next he was gone, leaving behind an embarrassing odor and a slop for the great outdoors. I stuck the pistol back into my hip pocket, this little nickel-plated machine that seemed almost to have acted on its own. I nudged Carlos with my toe.

"Good-bye, Carlos. Say hello up yonder," I said.

Idly I picked up the M-1 rifle that had caused Carlos's rage. There were bits of rust around the trigger housing and breech and flecks on the barrel. Termites and spiders crept over the other rifles inside the crate. The crates must have been stored for a short while in a wet place. But the crates still smelled of cosmoline inside, and the M-1 barrel in my hands was slick with oil. There was nothing wrong with these rifles that a few hours of cleaning would not cure.

I tossed the rifle and Carlos's .45 into the crate. I looked at the crates of guns and ammunition, and at the mound of marijuana sacks and then at Erwin. How long would it take to load up the sacks? The guns could stay. They were too heavy and of no use to us.

I squatted beside Erwin.

"I'm going to take this weed out with us," I said. "Another hour might make a lot of difference to you, but the weed is what we came for. I know you wouldn't want me to leave it."

Erwin bubbled and snorted.

"See, Erwin, I can handle real-life adventure. I'm doing better at it than you are," I said.

I poked Dorothy with a finger.

"Get up," I said.

When she continued to blubber, I rose and kicked her in the ribs.

"Get up! If you've got the guts to give away a baby, you can get up and help us out of here."

"You bastard, those men are dead," she wailed.

I kicked her again. Once you start kicking somebody, it's hard to stop. Dorothy stood up, weeping, snot on her lip and blood and bone on her face and T-shirt. Her voice whined in hatred.

"I know why I never could love you, you're a devil, you're a sorry evil shit!" she said.

I placed my fingers against her back and pushed her into the pile

358

of burlap bags. I enjoyed doing it. Working hard, sweating as colors built up in the sky over the ocean around a cherry sun, we diminished the pile of bags. I put Dorothy inside the camper to stack them up as I carried them from the pile. I was becoming giddy from the pollen dust and fumes. With still about ten of the fifty-pound bags on the ground, the truck was full. Had the bags been carefully stacked, the truck would have held them all, but Dorothy was snuffling and cursing and being sloppy. While she tried to straighten the sacks at one point, I paused a few minutes to plunge a piece of rag through the bore of an M-1 rifle with a cleaning rod that was in the crate. I wiped out the breech and worked it a few times, slipping my thumb out neatly in the remembered way, and then cracked open a can of ammunition and loaded a clip and stuck the clip into the M-1. I was half expecting Nunio and Loquito or other bandits. With the pistol I couldn't do much, but the M-1 would reach the top of the cliff or the tall rock and hit with power.

When we had loaded all the bags that would fit into the camper, I realized there was no room in back for Erwin to lie down. He had removed the beds himself, and I had forgotten him as we worked, perhaps assuming he would have died in any case before we could have found a doctor. But he was alive and moving his hands and squinting as the flesh around his eyes became swollen and turned purple and he began feeling pain. I helped him to sit up. He kept pointing at the hole in his face. I sensed what he wanted and stuck a forefinger into the hole and probed upward through the destroyed palate and touched the bullet. It was wedged in the sinus cavity beneath his left eye. I had decided that the old powder in Carlos's ammunition must have lost much of its force, and the two-foot range must have somehow kept the bullet from building velocity, otherwise the .45 slug would have blasted out the back of Erwin's head. But the bullet was firmly planted in bone now. When I attempted to pry it out, I thought I saw his left eyeball sink. I removed my hand from his mouth and wiped my finger on my pants.

"You'll have to keep that bullet, Erwin," I said.

I dragged and carried Erwin to the camper and heaved him into the seat. My heart was banging like a fist on a door. I tasted bile, but there was nothing to throw up. Summoning what felt like the last of my spit, I swallowed two more Dexedrine tablets and a spansule. If the heart held out, that much Dexedrine should ram me down that road to town if I had to pull the camper with a rope.

"You sit in the middle and prop up Erwin," I told Dorothy. "I don't want him flopping all over me while I drive."

"I've never seen anybody become so mean so fast," she said.

"You said the devil was always inside," I said. "This is what you've been wanting to see."

I put a double handful of .30-caliber ammunition in the glove compartment, placed the .32 pistol and Erwin's .44 on the dashboard, propping them there with his magnetic drink holder, and stuck the M-1 between Dorothy's legs. I laughed at myself and wished I had two belts of bullets to hang in a cross across my chest to dress up the appearance. A dirty, shaggy-haired outlaw with a drooping mustache and three guns, rambling through the Sierra Madre of Mexico with a beautiful girl, a wounded comrade and nearly a ton of dope. I wished Buster could film this with the Bolex. And Franklin, would he say this was far-fetched? I let out an amphetamine howl as the motor started, but I kept cracking my hand against the M-1 as I shifted gears, and before we reached the tall rock I had to stop and put the rifle between Erwin's legs. His head lay on Dorothy's shoulder, juices dribbling onto her breasts. I thought he was unconscious, but he grasped the M-1 stock and squinted at me.

Past the tall rock, scraping through greasewood and cactus, the camper roared and bounded, springs twanging under the load. Clearly, Erwin had reinforced the suspension to hide hidden weight from Customs inspectors. Off to the left I saw the buildings of the village or hacienda and the black line of the lava flow disappearing into the shadow of the mountain. Driving fast but with concern for the road, with perhaps almost an hour before real darkness, I came to the edge of the gully. If they were going to get me, the bottom of the gully should be the place. There was no use trying to hide. They could have been watching the camper's dust for two miles. I jumped down from the truck, grabbed the M-1 and ran to the rim of the gully. Kneeling, I fired two rounds down into the brush on the right of the path through the stream and two more rounds to the left. On the first round the M-1 kicked my thumb against my cheek, so I tightened the butt into my shoulder and felt a pleasurable bucking jolt for the next three shots, and then fired one more across the gully along the road. I expected to hear threshing in the brush but heard only the echoing shots.

Dorothy's eyes reminded me of bubbles, and she smiled at me, as though she had given up her senses. With the camper in first gear I let it creep down the slope of the gully, Erwin pitching forward against the dashboard, and then gunned it in the dark at the bottom and heard water showering from the wheels, and climbed the other side onto level ground and ran into a cow that was lying in the road.

I honked and the cow did not respond. It occurred to me that my last rifle shot might have killed the cow. There was no way around it through cactus, rocks and brush. Taking Erwin's .44, I got out and saw that the cow did for a fact have a bullet wound in its neck. But as I started trying to drag the cow out of the road, I saw something else. One front leg and one hind leg were tied with ropes to trees on either side of the road.

"They will shoot you dead if you don't put down that pistol," said Loquito's voice from the brush.

"Tell them we surrender," I said and lobbed the pistol into the road.

Loquito rose up from the left side of the road with Nunio and another man. They had hidden on that one side so they could shoot the driver of the camper without shooting themselves. Had I fired the M-1 six feet further to the left, I would have hit at least one of them and maybe scared the others off. It was stupid of me to shoot in the road rather than to the sides of it, but I had thought they would block it with a vehicle, not with a cow. Nunio had a new automatic rifle, of the type being used by the U.S. Army, aimed steadily at me. The other man, who was fat and dark and was wearing a billed khaki cap with a badge on it, thrust the muzzle of an old .38 pistol at Erwin and then stepped back scowling and looking away from the bloody hole. Loquito also wore a cap with a badge on it.

"Is Carlos dead?" he said.

I nodded.

"That is too bad," he said. "You will have to come with us."

"I see you're a cop."

"Oh yes. Now you come along. Nunio will drive the truck. Ciro will walk behind you with his gun in your back."

"Walk to Zihautanejo?" I said.

"I told you our truck is broken," said Loquito. "But we don't go to Zihautanejo. We go to our little jail out here. It is not far."

"What's the name of the town this jail is in?" I asked.

"It is not really a town," said Loquito, smiling and rolling his green-grape eyes. "It is really more like my house."

31

Loquito's place was made up of two shacks we had seen from the road, but there was only one cow in the corral now. The fat, dark man, Ciro, made me put my hands against the plaster wall of one shack and searched me while Loquito chased pigs and chickens out of the building. Ciro took my wallet that had five hundred pesos and all my credit cards in it. They sat Erwin against the wall and went through his pockets. He had three hundred pesos and about five hundred American dollars, not enough to have paid me the promised thousand. Ciro grinned and felt Dorothy's breasts with both hands through her bloody T-shirt and reached down and felt between her legs. She looked at me. I shrugged. Ciro unbuttoned his pants, pulled out a short thick pecker and placed one of Dorothy's hands on it, closing her fingers around it. She stood for a moment holding him by the pecker and then, realizing what she was doing, jerked her hand away. Ciro laughed.

"I guess he's going to rape her," Loquito said.

"You can keep the money if you let us go," I said.

"We already have the money," said Loquito.

"This girl just had a baby," I said.

"Ciro don't care. His wife has had nine children."

"John Lee, make him stop!" Dorothy said as Ciro tried to lift her T-shirt.

"Try to picture something romantic," I said.

Nunio drove off in the camper, back in the direction of the field where Carlos lay.

"He's taking his mari-hwana home," said Loquito. "He will get his sons and hide the guns before some thieves find them. Too bad the guns are no good, but we will keep them."

"Those guns are all right. Carlos was foolish," I said.

"He won't be foolish any more, eh?"

"In the morning you'll take us to town to the judge?" I said.

"When I was put in jail in San Antonio for one year for being a wetback, I couldn't speak no English and did not even know what I had did wrong."

"That's not my fault, I'm not a cop," I said.

"Look here then," said Loquito. He took off his cap with the badge on it and smiled. "Now I'm not no cop either. But Ciro is."

"Tell him I'm only twenty years old," Dorothy said.

Ciro had squeezed her against the wall and raised her T-shirt and was laughing and mashing her breasts and saying, *"Melón, melón."*

"His wife is an old woman of twenty-five. He would like you to be much younger than you are," said Loquito. I looked at Erwin's pistol, which Loquito had cocked and was pointing at me. "I will shoot you. I don't want to shoot you, but I don't want you to hurt me."

Loquito spoke in Spanish to Ciro. The fat man laughed and gave Dorothy a hearty nipple-pinch that made her screech, "Goddamn greaser shitball!" So she was clinging to her mind still. The fat dark

363

cop left Dorothy peering at her bruised breasts. He grabbed Erwin under the armpits and dragged him into the shed. Dorothy pulled down her T-shirt and glared at me.

Loquito waved me into the shed. As I ducked inside the door I looked back at Dorothy, who was slumping in the shadow of the building and clutching her elbows and watching Ciro coming toward her with his cap pushed back and his thick arms out to his sides in preparation for an embrace. She looked at me for an instant, understanding finally that there was nothing I could do, and once again I got a flash from another's mind, as Dorothy assembled herself to survive. Loquito shut the door behind me. I heard a padlock click. It was very dark inside the shed, ripe with the sweetly sour smell of pigs and chicken crap. I could hear Erwin's breath bubbling. I groped over and sat beside him on the earth floor.

"I don't know if you're conscious," I said. "I can imagine how bad your pain must be, but I can't feel it for you. I'm sorry, Erwin. We do it better on TV."

I sat in the dark, listening to Erwin. He had added a whistling noise to his boiling-water sound.

"Erwin, you must be pretending. You couldn't suffer like that and live. Act it out. In a little while, your mama will call you home to dinner. Pork and beans, white bread, sliced baloney, a glass of milk with a layer of cream on top. How's that sound? You've played too late and already missed Jack Armstrong, Don Winslow, Hop Harrigan and the Green Hornet, but this is the night for Fibber McGee and *I Love a Mystery*. Jack, Doc and Reggie are in the big old house where every time you hear the "Brahms Lullaby" you know somebody will die. Wouldn't want to miss it tonight, Erwin."

His head thumped against the wall.

"Were you aware that you knocked out most of my baby teeth? Do you remember that you broke my nose with the top of your head playing 'Red Rover Come Over' in elementary school? Do you know that I knew you were the one who terrified that idiot girl so bad in the third grade that they put her in a state hospital? Do you have any idea how miserable you used to make me? Do you know that when

364

I tried to kill you with a knife I felt so good about it and got so scared of myself that I never let myself reach that point again until today? I almost got there when Kennedy was murdered, but I guess it takes you to show me what I'm capable of."

I could hear Erwin's fingers scratching in the dirt.

"I even got jealous of you trying to make out with Dorothy because you were making me look bad, Erwin. But I don't hold a grudge against you for any of those things. There's no sense in it. But I like it inside my own head better than I like it inside yours. I'm not going to play with you any more. My mama warned me about that a long time ago. It's hard enough to tend my garden without guys like you walking in it."

"Uhhhhhhhhhhhh," said Erwin.

"You don't think I mean it? If I killed you right now, nobody would ever know it but you and me. They'd think you died of a bullet in the teeth. I've felt worse about killing possums than I did about killing that fellow Carlos. You made me find that out."

It sounded as if Erwin blew his nose.

"I'm taking back the handshake. If I ever do make a movie, you might be in it but you won't be producing it."

My God, I heard myself say that in my Clive Riordan voice, and I had to start chuckling. Poor Erwin, he was dying anyhow, he didn't need a lecture.

"Listen, Erwin, it's hard to tell what part is me talking and what part is amphetamine. The chemicals are all mixed up and all part of the same thing. I remember one night we'd eaten some hash brownies, and a friend of mine named Buster asked how they were working. I'd had two codeine tablets, a tab of mescaline, a Dexamyl spansule, six or seven joints, three or four pipes of hash, five or six martinis and about half a gallon of white wine on top of the brownie, so I tried to sort out which part of the total sensation represented the brownie, and I decided the brownie section was sort of weak. We called it The Slice of the High Pie Test. Do you think that's funny?"

"Uhhhhhh," he said.

"The whole trick is not to seem confused."

I heard the padlock clack against the door. Yellow lines appeared in the cracks in the door and then a yellow burst and Loquito came in with a kerosene lantern. In his other hand was a clay dish. An old GI entrenching tool was clasped under an arm. The door closed again and locked. Loquito sat on his haunches in the lantern light.

"Nunio is outside with his gun," said Loquito.

"Where's the girl?"

"Behind the corral with Ciro. I think he didn't have to beat her. Hold this lantern so I can see."

Loquito stuck a funnel into Erwin's hole and poured a bottle of brown liquid down his throat.

"This comes from a plant the Indians throw in the river to stun fish," said Loquito. "In a few minutes your friend will not have no pain for twelve hours."

"What's the name of the plant?"

"What's the difference?" Loquito shrugged. "The Indians call it the plant that stuns fish. It don't have no name. It is just a part of nature. There are many plants with no names that do strange things."

With his fingers Loquito dipped into the bowl and began to plaster Erwin's hole with green mud that smelled like cough medicine.

"He has to breathe," I said.

"Do you think I never heard of breathing?" Loquito said.

By now the flesh around Erwin's eyes was so swollen he could barely see out, but he was watching me as I held the lantern. Loquito finished with the plastering, and I took the lantern away. Loquito handed me a joint rolled in a cornhusk. It looked like a tamale.

"Maybe I'll smoke it later," I said.

"I have brought a gourd of water. I will leave it inside."

He kept sitting on his haunches, the light shining up weirdly on his gray stubble and gray hair and grape eyes, with deep shadow creases on either side of his nose and mouth, as if he was introducing a midnight horror film.

"How did you learn to be a *brujo?*" I said.

"I listened and watched the things around me. It takes a long time. You have to be alone very much, and very quiet. It's hard to do that

366

in your country. Out here I can pass for weeks with no people."

"You like this kind of life then."

"Carlos talked all the time about political victory," said the old man. "My victory is in my spirit."

"How long since you've been in the States?"

"I got out of jail the last time in 1939 and never have go back again."

"So you never have been tempted with our Cadillacs and television. How can you believe you're wise by staying out here if you haven't had a real chance at another kind of life?"

"Money and privilege and comfort don't bring wisdom, even you must know that," he said. "To have power over people and things can make you feel important but also awkward and afraid. In my visions I do everything and see everything. Wisdom is all that matters."

"There's a lot to be said for lying out here in the mountains stoned on mushrooms, but there's no need to justify it by trying to make your stoned dreams into wise, important visions. You're just high is all, you've taken in some chemicals. Mushrooms make your living conditions enjoyable for you and give your life a structure and a sense of power you couldn't have otherwise. But don't pretend to be profound. Opium smokers don't pretend it."

"Then I wouldn't like to smoke no opium," grinned Loquito. "What are you talking about, this being profound? I didn't use that word. You sound like you have taken LSD again. How could you think of such a problem? There are many things I don't know about. I know there are many worlds I can't visit but many that I can, and I know the difference when I put my foot in the dirt of this floor or when my mind is in some other place. They exist at the same time but are not the same. When I took LSD I sometimes was informed about things that do not exist for me, and I was part of the time what is called crazy. But I know the difference."

"Being a witch, can you turn into a wolf or a bird?"

"Yes, of course, in the way that a child can."

"Don't you ever think you've dreamed this whole strange life?"

"No, I am a thing that grows in nature, like the mushroom, and nothing in nature can be strange. If your way doesn't understand a thing in nature and says it is strange, that is of less interest to me than sweat on my balls," he said. He cocked his head as if having a pleasing thought, and scratched his crotch.

"You hear that, Erwin?" I said. "This man is not a bit confused. He's built his own box around oblivion."

"I don't know oblivion," said Loquito.

"Being forgotten. Being nothing."

"I don't understand that," he said.

"You build a box around it and many intricate passages through it, and windows into it, but you always know the difference."

"You should smoke that mari-hwana and not talk so much," he said. "You should stay outside alone in the wilderness for many days and be quiet. Then you wouldn't have to ask no questions."

"But you can't explain it."

"I have explained it," he said. "If you are trying to annoy me, stop it. I don't get annoyed. My life is better than yours. Too bad for you if you don't learn that."

We heard the padlock rattle again.

"I will leave now," Loquito said. He tossed the entrenching tool into the darkness of a corner of the shed. "Later you might try to dig out if you want to."

"Why dig out?"

"So many questions, it makes me laugh," said Loquito, standing up with the lantern. "Ciro will get very drunk all night. By daylight he will probably decide to shoot you. Carlos was Ciro's cousin. You made a bad insult on him."

Stooping, Dorothy entered the shed as Loquito, holding the lantern, waited until she walked across to me. Her slacks were smeared with dirt, and she was carrying her panties crumpled in her hand. Her eyes were set and calm, and her lower lip was bruised.

"Nothing is forgotten just because you don't think of it," Loquito said.

When he had gone it was black again. Dorothy sat beside me. We heard Erwin gently bubbling, as though he might be asleep.

368

"How was it?" I said.

"I've had worse."

"He did have a certain charm."

"There's something attractive about being wanted, can't deny that," she said.

We sat and listened to Erwin.

"Oh shit, John Lee, what if I'm pregnant again?" she said.

Dorothy settled back against me, and I put my arm around her.

"That feels good," she said. "Goddamn, I'm tired."

In a few minutes she was asleep. My chemical energy was fading, and I was descending fast into a delicious blackness so desirable that my bones ached for it. I heard Ciro somewhere outside singing in a drunken voice, but holding Dorothy against me, feeling her breath, I felt too exhausted and peaceful to care about Ciro, and I slowly slid away.

32

But I awoke to hear Ciro singing again, or still, and the perverse nature of our situation became real to me. Though I could not quite bring myself to believe Ciro would walk in and shoot me in cold blood, it didn't appear to be an act that was out of character for him. In the morning light that now soaked through cracks in the roof and doors and chinks in the walls, I saw the entrenching tool and considered that maybe I should have used it to dig out. But if Ciro had heard me or Loquito's scrawny dog had barked an alarm, I would without question be full of bullets. This way, I had the chance of depending on Ciro's humanity, either not to commit murder or else to get passing-out drunk. Too, I could ask Dorothy to be raped some more and distract him, but that was an unworthy idea and besides did not account for Nunio and his automatic rifle.

Dorothy mumbled and snuggled her face into my shoulder. Dirt clods clung to her hair. Being careful not to wake her, I stretched my legs and breathed deeply, feeling heavy and weary as much from the speed hangover as from illness or exertion. I glanced at Erwin and saw that he was peeping at me through slits in purple flesh above the green mud crusted over his hole.

"Uhhhhhhh," Erwin said, holding out a hand toward me.

I tried to imagine what he wanted. Not to be helped to his feet, surely, or to shake hands. I pointed at the entrenching tool. "Uhhhhh," he said, lifting a finger to his head and snapping his thumb like the hammer of a pistol. What then? He seemed to be reaching toward Dorothy. I followed the direction of his fingers and realized he was reaching for her silk panties. They had fallen from her hand and were lying on my knee.

I picked up the panties and looked at Erwin.

"Uhhhhh," he said, gesturing for me to throw the panties to him.

So I did. If fondling panties would ease his mind, I wouldn't be the one to deny him. Dorothy's head edged down from my shoulder across my chest and into my lap and she shifted around in her sleep, drawing her heels up to her butt and hugging my thigh as if she was adjusting a pillow. She sighed and smiled, dreaming. The snap at the back of her pants was torn, and the zipper undone, and I could see a bit of cleft. I looked at Erwin, who had pulled up his knees and was doing something with the panties that I could not see. I heard a rooster crowing and the mooing of Loquito's remaining cow. The dog barked. After a moment of silence, Ciro took up another song. He was getting hoarse. I thought about dying and couldn't force myself to make sense out of it. Unless Nunio and sons had buried him last night, vultures had gone to work on Carlos by now. Well, it hadn't been words that had stopped him, but in my mind it didn't seem to have been me, either, any more than it was Clive Riordan who rubbed out all those rustlers. My own death was incomprehensible. A common insight on acid is that one is a unit of the cosmos and death only a

370

phase of existence, and of course there was the time I had realized I could kill myself easily and with some amount of curiosity and so did not need to fear death so much as horrible madness. But sitting against the wall of that shack with Dorothy's head in my lap I could not force those ideas to emerge again convincingly. Hearing Ciro out there, I wondered why the old dread did not take me. Surely, if I could sink into a fit of terror at the sight of myself on television after swallowing a chemical, and could be unraveled by the conjured presence of lunacy, murder and disorder, then now that I could hear the real thing out there staggering drunk with a gun and his own reason for using it, I should begin to tremble. But the only thing that was happening was that I could feel myself getting a hard on against Dorothy's face.

I couldn't help it any more than a hanged man can help it. Buster always said if he was in a plane that was crashing he would make a terrible effort to get it in the stewardess before he died. If my head seemed to think it could be the boss over Ciro by refusing to accept death, another part of me also was definitely choosing to continue. I raised my right knee to conceal myself somewhat from Erwin, though I don't know why I should have bothered. Then with a savory sense of abandonment, grinning like an ass, I delicately moved Dorothy's head a few inches and unzipped my fly. She was sleeping with her mouth open.

Dorothy opened her eyes.

"I thought I was dreaming!" she said.

"In a few minutes Ciro is going to come in and shoot me," I said.

"Goddamn, I'll yell for him if you don't get your thing out of my face!"

"I mean it, Dorothy."

"Do you really mean it?" she said.

"Loquito told me."

"John Lee, please let me up."

She sat up and rubbed her eyes and looked at me very solemnly.

"I don't want you to be shot," she said.

"He's going to."

"What would I do without you?" she said.

Tears began to appear as she thought about our final separation.

"Oh John Lee, I don't want to lose you," she said. "Please stay alive."

She kissed me on the lips and then lowered her head, cuddling into my lap.

I heard Erwin puffing and looked around at him. He wadded the panties and threw them to me. Dorothy sat up again. She was not even surprised any more to see that Erwin had been playing with her panties. She laid her head against my shoulder and I dropped the panties.

"Uhhhhhhhhhhhh," said Erwin, motioning for me to pick them up.

Reluctantly I did, wondering what he wished me to find.

Written on the panties in ballpoint pen was:

I killed Carlos in self defense

Erwin Englethorpe

Erwin nodded.

"Thanks, Erwin, but Loquito and Nunio know you didn't do it," I said.

He waved a hand as if to say I ought to show it to them anyhow.

"What can you lose?" said Dorothy.

"I don't even know if Loquito can read," I said.

We had not heard Ciro singing lately, but suddenly his voice was outside the door, sounding thick and angry. There was another voice that I took to be Nunio's, for I hadn't yet heard him speak, and someone rattled the padlock.

I kissed Dorothy, stood up and stuffed the panties into my right hip pocket.

"Dorothy, tell them I was dead game to the end," I said.

"What are you doing?" she said.

Feeling light-headed and breathless, feeling my blood rushing but yet nowhere near angry, as though I knew I was superior to this, I hefted the entrenching tool and took a place beside the door where I could bash Ciro when he walked in.

"Don't be stupid, show them the panties," said Dorothy.

I motioned for her to be quiet. Erwin was watching me. He looked as if he had fallen into a buckwheat cake from a great distance. The padlock clattered. I raised the entrenching tool. The leather hinges creaked, and the shadow of a man lay in the rectangle of sunlight on the dirt floor.

"No!" Dorothy screamed.

"*Señorita, dónde están los hombres?*" said the strange voice.

I saw Dorothy's face changing from fear into astonishment and then into perplexity.

"John Lee, they look like soldiers," she said.

"First one through the door gets it," I said.

"There's six soldiers out here," called Loquito.

Gradually I peeked around the door frame into the brown, sweating face of an officer in khakis and soft cap. Behind him in the white light of the yard I saw several young soldiers with M-1 rifles. They appeared to be very curious about what was going on inside this shack.

"What is it, a firing squad?" I said.

The officer spoke in Spanish.

"The soldiers have come to take you to town," said Loquito.

I stepped outside. One of the soldiers aimed his rifle. Ciro wobbled around scowling and cursing. The officer stared at me.

"It was reported you were in Zihautanejo yesterday," said Loquito. "The Army wants your friend on a charge of smuggling guns. They have been searching for you all night. They found Carlos."

I pulled out the panties and gave them to the officer. He looked puzzled and angry. The soldiers laughed. I told Loquito what the message was on the panties. He told the officer, who began laughing and holding up the panties and shouting at the soldiers.

"They're glad Carlos is dead," Loquito said. "He made them very much trouble. It's a good thing for your friend to have killed him."

"*Dónde están los canones?*" said the officer.

"I don't know anything about any guns," I said. "I'm a tourist."

"*Dónde está el camión?*"

I looked at Loquito. His round green eyes did not flicker.

"Tell him somebody stole our truck while we were walking in the woods," I said.

Loquito smiled and repeated what I had said. The officer shrugged and said he was sleepy and in a hurry. He growled at the soldiers. Four of them went into the shack and carried Erwin out. They dropped the tailgate of an olive drab two-and-a-half-ton truck with a canvas top and flung Erwin inside. We heard him hit and skid.

"They're going to take him to the capital in Chilpancingo," said Loquito.

I looked inside the truck, where Erwin lay amid a heap of canteens, web belts and field packs.

"I won't forget you," I said to Erwin.

He tapped his forehead. I'm not sure what he meant.

The officer ordered Dorothy and me to climb into his jeep.

"What about our money?" I said to Loquito.

"Yes, take your money," he said.

He gave me two hundred pesos and my billfold with the credit cards.

"Where's the other five hundred dollars?"

"Somebody shot my cow," said Loquito.

"Five hundred dollars will buy a herd of cows."

"But you must stand trial for the death of my cow. This is your bond. If you don't come back for the trial, you don't get your money."

The officer spoke to the driver, who jammed the jeep into reverse, snapping our heads. The driver turned the wheels and shoved the jeep into forward, and we grabbed the sides as we bounced beside the pole corral going away from Loquito's house. Ciro gave us the finger and yelled at Dorothy, and I saw Loquito looking small in the dust. Driving into town with the truck roaring behind us, Dorothy and I clung to the seats. The officer kept looking at the panties and glancing back at us and grinning.

They drove us straight to the bus station. An old Greyhound, painted red and blue, was preparing to leave for Acapulco. The officer made it clear we had to be on it. I bought our tickets with the money I'd gotten from Loquito, and we made our way along the aisle inside the bus. Babies were crying, children screaming, the driver shouting, the engine idling, the inside of the bus hot and full of fumes. We squeezed past a man who was holding a pair of squawking chickens upside down by the feet. At the rear of the bus was an empty seat. Dorothy sat by the window. I mashed one knee against the back of the seat in front of me, and stuck the other leg into the aisle beside the chickens.

"I want to go home," Dorothy said.

"Show me where you think it is," I said.

"It's wherever you're going," said Dorothy.

"When we get there," I said, "we're going to hock your pearl ring. Then I'm coming back down here to see Loquito, and I'm going to take enough dope to Texas to pay Buster's lawyer and finish our movie."

"They'll put you in jail," Dorothy said, touching my thigh with her fingers.

"They'd better stay out of my way. The only respectable thing I can do is be an outlaw, and I know how."

Brown knuckles rapped on the outside of our window. The army officer was out there holding up the panties and grinning in the midst of a laughing crowd of tourists, fishermen, soldiers, hustlers and children. The officer tapped again and motioned for me to raise the window.

"Don't open it," said Dorothy.

"I've got to breathe," I said.

I mashed the releases and pulled up the window. The officer's thin, damp face split open with joy as he looked at me and waved the panties like a flag.

"Tore-zan!" he cried.

375

72 73 74 75 10 9 8 7 6 5 4 3 2 1